DOG NANNY

by

Ann Whitaker

Dedication

To my husband, Bill Whitaker,
for his enduring faith in me and my writing;
and to my mother, Ava Howard,
for giving me a passion for reading
and the gift of laughter.
Their unconditional love and support
can't be matched.

Acknowledgements

A Texas-sized thank you to the following: my first reader, Terry Spear; my wonderful Elements of RWA critique partners for their encouragement, insightful comments, eye for detail, and enthusiasm for my writing; authors Lynn Reynolds and Cara Marsi, for their friendship, wealth of knowledge, and understanding; pilot, teacher, and fellow writer Sarah McNary and her husband, flight instructor Lt. Dave McNary of the San Diego County Sheriff's Department, who taught me how to "talk pilot"; Lisa Oatman, for answering my early questions on airport protocol; Marilyn Patterson, for offering yet another set of eyes; Lynn Reynolds, who proofed the second edition; Gwen Kane, for her long-term support and whose love of animals has always inspired me.

SPECIAL DOGGY TREATS to...
our love child, Jolie Blon, and Mardi Gras, our Tiny Tim, who taught me adopted animals have a special knack for working their way into our hearts. Extra treats to all the special companion-animals who await our reunion on Rainbow Bridge.

"Angel" Mardi Gras Whitaker
October 1998-July 3, 2011
Rest in Peace, Mr. Mardi

Chapter One

"I want my dog de-loused," said the Pekingese-faced woman with the Welsh corgi body. "My husband says we got crab lice from sleeping with her."

I looked at the floor so she couldn't see me grimace. Her husband might have gotten crabs from sleeping with someone, but he didn't get them from the frightened Chihuahua the woman dangled at arm's length over the examining table. Her perfume alone was strong enough to make a louse gasp for fresh air.

My nostrils burned, and I felt a headache coming on. A dog in the waiting room yapped incessantly.

Dr. Arthur was unusually patient. For the third time, he tried to explain. "Ma'am, lice aren't transmitted by dogs. Lice can't survive on domestic animals."

"Well," the woman huffed, "I want a second opinion." She waddled to the door on her short corgi legs and thumped the door shut.

"People," I grumbled. "There ought to be a test before they can own a dog."

Normally, Dr. Arthur would agree, but today he just laughed. "Lighten up, Julie. It's a beautiful day. The sun is shining—"

"It's *summer*. This is *Texas*. The sun is always shining." Why was he so cheery? The waiting room was packed, it was ten o'clock on Friday morning, and I was already starving.

After the corgi woman, we treated a butt-scooting dog, a car-sick cat, and a gerbil with separation anxiety. By noon I was dog-tired. Of people. The corgi woman's

1

problems had been a painful reminder of my last boy-friend's infidelities.

When we locked the doors for lunch, Dr. Arthur motioned me into his office. A broad smile creased his face. "Good news."

A raise? That would be good news.

He sank into his leather chair. "I'm closing the clinic for a month."

Had I heard him right? "You're closing the clinic?"

Though Dr. A was pushing sixty, his smooth round face and pink cheeks reminded me of a cherub. "I'm not getting any younger, you know. It's something I've always wanted to do. Climb the Alps."

"The *Swiss* Alps?"

He spread his arms wide. "The chance of a lifetime. Switzerland beckons."

"Like *The Sound of Music*?"

He laughed and leaned back. "You and your old movies. You need a real life. Don't worry. Your job will be here when I get back."

If he *comes* back.

He was going to Switzerland. In the meantime, I would be jobless for a month. So much for a raise.

I plopped down on a chair in front of his desk. "But this means no paycheck for a month. I really need that money."

Dr. Arthur's eyebrows shot up. "Since when have you needed money?"

Like everyone else in Abilene, Dr. A knew my father amassed a fortune during the oil boom.

"My mother has money, not me."

He leaned forward and patted my hand. "Didn't your father leave you anything?"

I sighed. "A house so big I can barely afford the upkeep. I've put it on the market, but who knows when it will sell?" I reached back to massage the tension from my neck. "That's not the problem. It's the new animal adoption center. Building is set to begin, and we still

2

need money. I'm donating every extra penny I earn." I was too embarrassed to mention the trust fund I couldn't claim until I married.

"Your mother hasn't helped?"

"You kidding? The only donations she makes are to the country club."

Dr. A rubbed his chin. "I might have a solution." He turned toward his computer and punched a few keys. The laser printer hummed, and a sheet of paper slid out. Dr. A plucked it up and thrust it at me. "Friend of mine in Waco sent me this email yesterday. Some woman he knows needs help."

My marriage is on big rocks. I squinted at the words and read them a second time. She must mean "on the rocks." I read the next part out loud. "*My husband says I have one month to get control of my two poodles or he's leaving me.*"

When I looked up, Dr. Arthur was smiling. "The timing is perfect. I understand she also has money."

"So why doesn't she call a real professional, like the Dog Whisperer?"

"She did. His 'people' said he was too busy to spend a month in Waco."

I leaned forward and pounded my forehead on his desk. "I'm a vet tech, not a dog trainer."

"Didn't you take some classes for certification?"

"Years ago."

"But you do know dogs. Remember how wild your little poodle acted after you rescued him? That ugly face he made? Last I heard, he'd won some awards in obedience."

I blinked. "But Waco is almost two hundred miles from here." An admittedly weak argument for a man about to travel halfway around the globe.

He looked at me over his little reading glasses, his eyebrows raised. "That's not so far."

"You want me to play dog nanny to two delinquent poodles?"

3

He bestowed a beatific smile upon me. "Did you see how much she's offering? More than you'd make here. With room and board. Besides, Waco's not so bad. They call it the 'Heart of Texas.'"

I know a placebo when I hear one.

"I'll think about it." Klaus Kinski's line from *Venom* was my favorite stalling technique, but this time, I did need to think about it.

Before he'd let me leave, Dr. Arthur insisted I look at the photograph attached to the email. Two beautiful standard poodles: one black, one white. I could have sworn they were smiling at me.

* * *

After leaving his office, I grabbed my lunch sack from the refrigerator and headed for an empty examining room for some alone time. I bit into my peanut butter sandwich and chewed over the proposal's possibilities. Maybe a break would do me good. But Waco? I'd never even been to Waco. I didn't *know* anyone who'd ever been to Waco. A whole month. In Waco. Training two *big* poodles.

Poodles. My heart warmed at the thought. Who knew what their fate might be without a proper education? They could end up in foster care or become mangy street dogs not knowing where their next bone was coming from. Just call me a doggy do-gooder, but the idea of those poor poodles growing up in a broken home really hurt my heart. Dogs were so helpless. So faithful.

Not only that, I'd be saving a marriage. Though I'd yet to experience the holy state firsthand, I did believe in the sanctity of the institution. Happy marriages did exist. Maybe new surroundings would help me find myself a husband before the battery in my biological clock ran out of juice. Next time, I'd find a man I didn't have to fix.

A month in the "heart" of Texas? Could that be a sign?

On my own home front, I did have Philip, my live-in partner, to think about. Though he could deal with my absence, he wouldn't be happy about my being gone that long. To tell the truth, leaving him wouldn't be easy for me either. We'd been together three years now, and I'd gotten used to his head on the pillow next to mine each morning and snuggling against his warmth. I loved him unconditionally, but it was time to face facts—Philip simply wasn't husband material. He was, after all, a ten-pound toy poodle.

I gulped the last bite of my sandwich, dropped the wadded paper bag into the wastebasket, and marched into Dr. Arthur's office. Shelves along one wall held an array of medical books; his wife and children smiled up at me from their framed photograph atop his wooden desk.

I gritted my teeth. "I'll do it."

He slapped his thighs. "I knew you couldn't say no. I've already made arrangements." Then he smiled kindly. "You know, we all need a little adventure now and then."

For him, that meant climbing mountains. My adventures, unfortunately, often involved a man. The wrong man. After my last regrettable experience, I'd sworn to stay away from the kind of men I'd been unlucky with in the past—darkly handsome, distant, and deceitful.

Dr. A handed me a sheet of paper. "Here are the details. The lady's sending her private pilot to pick you up."

My tongue dried up like a strip of beef jerky, and I could barely speak. "Pilot? As in flying?" Had Dr. Arthur forgotten my father, the crash?

He swiveled his chair toward the computer and peered at the screen. "His name is...let me see here...Nick Worthington. Meet him at the airport Monday afternoon at one."

With little time to prepare, I shifted into high gear. My sister agreed to take care of Philip, keep an eye on my house, and pick up my mail. Since I was low-maintenance, I packed one large suitcase and was ready to go. Maybe this assignment would be easier than I'd thought.

That was before I saw the pilot.

* * *

No sooner were my feet off the Abilene tarmac than I was in triple trouble.

I judged the pilot to be a few years older than me, maybe mid-thirties. Devilishly handsome, with dark hair and eyes blue as denim, like the ones that always broke my heart—exactly the kind of man I'd vowed to avoid. Something told me that before I could even get a couple of dogs to *sit*, I'd have to vanquish this black knight sent to fetch me.

Too, I hadn't flown in a small plane since my father's crash two years ago. So instead of looking at the man next to me in the cockpit, I gazed silently at the checkerboard fields thousands of feet below, my hands clenched together in my lap, my pulse racing.

His soft voice startled me. "Are you always this quiet?"

"Only when someone holds my life in his hands."

When I worked up the nerve to look at him, he gave me a slow, smoldering grin that made me think he'd like to hold more than my life in his hands.

"Afraid of flying?"

"Nope. Just don't like small planes." When I did have to fly, I preferred jets, big ones. The propeller outside my window looked fragile, spinning like a tiny windmill in a West Texas sandstorm.

He scanned the gauges. "Safer than driving. In a pinch you can land this Seneca V easier than a 747. Look, two engines." In case I'd missed them, he pointed at each. "We'll be there in less than an hour." He reached over and patted my arm.

Since this was my year for making resolutions, a few months ago, I'd declared myself a born-again virgin until the right man came along. I'd read somewhere you could do that. Despite my inner warnings, an involuntary wave of desire surged through my newly virgined parts.

I shrugged off his hand, trying to hide my reaction. "Shouldn't you keep your hands on the wheel or stick or whatever you call it?" I tucked a lock of hair behind one ear in an effort to appear casual, but my hand trembled.

He chuckled. "You know, you aren't at all what I expected."

Bristling at his arrogance, I glared at him. His eyes held mine for a moment, then wandered lower. My back stiffened. I was glad I'd worn my best jeans and had my top tucked in. My stomach was still flat and my waist small, but when it came to breasts, he might have to use his imagination.

"And what did you expect? For me to be covered in dog hair, with slobber running down the front of my shirt?"

He laughed, revealing straight white teeth. I looked for fillings. He couldn't be perfect.

"No, I just expected someone more...someone older and more rugged, I guess. Instead..." His voice trailed off.

When I didn't respond, he looked at me again, this time with curiosity. I smiled to myself and swelled up a little, proud of my willpower. Then he winked, and I cursed myself for flushing. This man was way too sure of himself and his effect on women. But if I could handle dogs, surely I could handle one Lone Star Lothario. Besides, as soon as we got to Waco, I'd be rid of him.

Though the sky was as clear as Nick Worthington's intentions, suddenly the plane began to bump, first little dips, then hard jolts. I clutched the seat and squeezed my eyes shut, but I sensed him watching me.

"Don't worry," he said. "A little turbulence in summer is normal."

But it wasn't merely the turbulence shaking me up. A combination of his masculine presence and my testosterone receptors confined in the small plane's cockpit was breaking down barriers I'd erected.

I fought back the best way I knew how. "Sorry I'm not great company. Missing Philip, I guess." He'd never know his competition was a dog.

His smile faded.

"How much farther to Waco?" I finally asked.

"Almost there." His voice had turned distant.

A few minutes later, we began our slow descent into unknown territory.

* * *

When the landing gear locked into place with a thump, I lowered my head and closed my eyes. I swallowed hard to get rid of the sour taste in my mouth. Though I'd braced myself, I barely felt the wheels touch down. We taxied off the runway to a private hangar.

He cut the engines, then reached out and lightly touched my upper arm. A pleasant quiver coursed through my body. "You can wait here in the air-conditioned office," he said. "I'll get the car."

"I can walk."

"Too hot. You'd melt."

Oh no, the old cliché about my being so sweet.

He strode off without me, and when I stepped out into the sunshine, I understood what he meant. This heat wasn't oven-dry like Abilene's. Steam rose from the pavement, my T-shirt stuck to my chest like cling wrap, and sweat beaded on my upper lip and forehead.

I tried to conceal my relief when I spotted Nick wheeling a black BMW convertible to the front of the hangar. Thank goodness the top was up.

He alighted from the driver's seat and lifted my bag with ease. Though I'd brought only one, it was heavy. As he tossed it into the trunk, I watched his face for signs of exertion, but if he felt anything, he kept it well hidden. Smiling, he opened the door for me. Evidently, chivalry was still alive in Waco, and for the moment I was grateful. I sank into the leather seat with a moan of contentment.

He grinned and held my gaze until my face turned warm. Evidently my comment about Philip hadn't deterred him. I should have known. Men like Nick Worthington thrived on competition.

As we left the airport, I surveyed my new surroundings. So much *green*—trees, shrubs, grass. All so alive. In Abilene by this time of year, most vegetation had turned brown, except for the trees.

He drove without speaking. I stole glances at him from time to time, telling myself there was no harm in looking. The drive turned out to be a short one.

After rounding a corner, Nick slowed, pulled onto the side of the road, and braked. My body drew as taut as a steel guitar string.

"Why are we stopping?" For some reason Ted Bundy flashed through my mind. "People know where I am!"

Nick raised an eyebrow, then leaned over and pointed out my window. "Look up." I suppose he had an excuse for moving so close, but that didn't mean my reaction was any less visceral. He'd been right. I *was* melting, though the air-conditioner was up full blast.

I looked up to where he pointed. In the distance, perched atop a nearby hill, sat a Mission Revival style mansion. "So?"

"Welcome to Casa del Lago."

He pulled back onto the road, and we cruised to the top of the hill and up the circular driveway in front of the house. I opened my door and got out before he could do the honors. I'd expected rich. I hadn't expected ostentatious. From the red-tiled roof to the white stucco exterior and rounded archways, the house was a masterpiece of design and landscaping. Live oaks and tall tropical plants graced the façade, while red and yellow hibiscus in huge pots added color.

I'd be spending the next few weeks here? *Bless you, Dr. Arthur.* Climbing Swiss mountains might be his idea of fun, but I appreciated certain amenities—like indoor plumbing—though I could live without fancy gold fixtures.

Nick's voice shook me out of my musings. "Wait till you see the view of the lake."

He lounged against the side of the BMW, watching me with an amused grin. My heart lurched. I was painfully aware of how well he filled out his jeans and the bulge of well-defined biceps under the sleeves of his T-shirt. As a defensive measure, I tried to imagine him bald. It didn't work.

"Waco has a lake?" I asked. Being from West Texas, I did like looking at water. In fact, water was a bona fide collector's item in my hometown of Abilene, though you couldn't exactly buy it on eBay.

"Let's get inside and find something cool to drink." He hefted my suitcase from the trunk and pulled out the handle. "Have you talked with the lady of the house?"

"Just email. This trip was pretty sudden."

"She's a firecracker, but you'll like her."

A firecracker? She'd sounded pleasant enough in her messages.

Effortlessly rolling my suitcase behind him on its squeaky little wheels, he guided me by the elbow through one of the archways. Though his touch was gentle, my pulse raced. As we entered a large courtyard, a man in his fifties greeted us. He wore loose-fitting linen trousers and a white Mexican wedding shirt. I caught a breath of Old Mexico.

"Julie, meet Ramón. He's the one who keeps this place running, from plants to pool."

Nick rolled the *r* in Ramón. I was impressed.

I shook Ramón's hand. "Beautiful job."

He rewarded me with a warm smile. "*Gracias.*"

Nick handed him my suitcase, and Ramón gave me a quick bow. "I will take good care of it." Then he disappeared around the side of the house. Nick opened one of the massive double doors and waited for me to pass through. Beside each door, vertical panes of stained glass depicted Saint Francis of Assisi, one with a dog at his side, the other with birds. I took it as a good omen.

We made our way across floors of Saltillo tile through a foyer, which led into a large living area. Muted Mexican tapestries and crosses with silver milagros adorned the walls, and an art niche held an original hand-made Talavera vase from Central Mexico worth hundreds of American dollars. More hibiscus and greenery added an air of tranquility.

"Welcome to Casa del Lago." The honeyed voice bore a trace of a Spanish accent. I turned toward the sound. A petite woman dressed in a white sleeveless blouse, khaki shorts, and leather sandals strolled toward us. Her face was bare of makeup—she didn't need any. She looked to be in her early forties, younger than I'd expected. What Carmen Esposito lacked in height, she made up for in presence and a smile that filled the room with light.

Nick introduced us. "Carmen Esposito, Julie Shields."

"I'm so thankful you've come," she said. The Spanish cadence of her speech was soothing, but I felt awkward around her poise and self-assurance. Dogs I could handle. Warming up to people sometimes took longer.

Carmen stood on tip-toe and pecked Nick on the cheek. Her long dark hair, caught behind her neck with a silver clasp, was as glossy as a shampoo ad. "And did this wicked one behave himself?" She eyed him seductively, her long lashes fluttering slightly. The only time I'd ever tried that with a man, he'd asked if I had something in my eye.

"He's a skillful pilot." I refused to say he'd "behaved."

"Come, sit, and let me get you something cool to drink," Carmen said. "Would you like wine, beer, lemonade, tea?"

Nick didn't hesitate. "I'll take a Dos Equis."

"Same for me," I said, wanting to keep it simple.

He scanned my face. "You like Mexican beer?" It sounded like a challenge.

"Sure." Although my drink of choice was wine, I wasn't fussy about brands, just so it came in a bottle and not a box. Preferably with a cork. I did have my standards.

Nick made himself at home on a sumptuous loveseat, patting the cushion next to him for me to sit. Instead, I sank into a big chair across from him, shooting him a brief look of victory.

He stretched out his long legs. "What do you think?"

"About the house?"

"That will do." He flashed a smile I tried to ignore.

"Must be like living in a shrine." The house was an impressive piece of work, but not enough to make me swoon into his arms if that's what he was thinking. Besides, it wasn't even his.

Carmen reappeared with a tray containing three bottles of beer and frosted mugs. Nick jumped up and took the tray from her, placing it on a square, rustic table large enough for a flamenco dancer's performance. She sat beside Nick and waited while he poured her beer.

"*Gracias*," she said. "Always the gentleman."

Laughing, he glanced toward me as he poured my beer. "Well, not always."

When he stood and handed me the mug, our hands brushed. I tried to suppress a tingle of pleasure. Then I caught him eyeing my bare ring finger.

"Too bad Berto's not here," he said.

Carmen's eyes dimmed. "As usual, his business in Mexico took longer than expected." She turned to me. "My Berto is gone much of the time, and I miss him so. But you know what they say: Absence makes the heart grow fonder." She smiled and sipped her beer. I did the same, trying to drink as gracefully as Carmen while wielding the heavy mug.

Nick set his beer on the table. "Or out of sight, out of mind." He flashed his white smile at me. No doubt he was referring to my comment about missing Philip.

Carmen gave Nick a little kick. "Oh, you know better than that. When Berto is here, it's like our honeymoon all over again."

Nick held up his arms in mock surrender. "I know. Just kidding. You're lucky. Not everyone has a happy marriage like you two."

"We work at it," Carmen said. "It doesn't just happen. But enough of that—I want Julie to meet my two *niños.* I'll be right back."

No one had said anything about *children.*

Nick jumped to his feet as two huge fur balls bounded into the room—one white, one black, just like the photo. These dogs were obviously well fed and probably weighed fifty pounds each, but with the abundant fur, they seemed much larger. No sissy clips for these two. They looked more like giant bichons. Real Texas big hair.

Their behavior made it seem as if ten poodles, not two, had been let loose. They ran around the room, barking joyfully, vaulting over furniture and jumping onto chairs and sofas as if the furnishings were doggy trampolines. One swipe of a wiggling butt almost knocked the tray of bottles off the coffee table. Even in their wildness, they made me smile. These were happy dogs, still pups in many ways.

Without warning, the black one leaped onto my lap. "Whoa, there," I said, but not before he'd sloshed beer all over my T-shirt.

"Meet Noche and Blanco, the other loves of my life," Carmen said.

Nick grinned at my surprise, but his smile disappeared when Blanco ran behind him and poked him in the rear with her snout. I burst out laughing. Nick didn't look so cocky now. Served him right.

"That's Noche on your lap," Carmen said, as if allowing a fifty-pound dog to jump into a chair on top of a guest was nothing unusual. "I almost named him Nick because the ladies love him. And Blanco"—Carmen paused, kissing the huge fur ball who'd run to her and was licking her face—"is my white beauty. She's a sweetheart, too."

The top half of Blanco's body was in Carmen's lap, and the dog's back legs were scrambling to reach higher. The comment about Nick wasn't lost on me, but I had my own dog to deal with. Lowering my voice, I gave Noche an *off* command, but he ignored me and began licking spilled beer from the vicinity of my right boob.

I jumped to my feet. "No!" I said, my voice firm. Nick had been watching intently, probably getting his own ideas, so I looked straight at him when I gave the command. Noche leaped off, ran to Carmen, and began humping her leg. I looked away. Tonight wasn't the best time to talk to her about doggy etiquette. No wonder she'd almost named him Nick, though so far the human Nick had better manners.

Dr. Arthur had warned me the dogs would be a handful, but I hadn't expected pandemonium.

"They'll settle down in a minute," Carmen said. "They get excited around company. They're just babies. They celebrate their first birthday this month."

That meant teenagers in dog years, but these two showed no evidence of any schooling. I looked at Noche and at Blanco and then at Nick. He simply raised his hands in a helpless gesture.

Carmen disappeared with both dogs in tow, leaving Nick and me alone again.

"So you're a dog trainer." He made *dog trainer* sound like a dirty word.

Who did this guy think *he* was? Top Gun? Just because he was a hot-shot private pilot was no cause for him to adopt a condescending attitude.

"Yes, and no. I *have* trained dogs before. But I'm really a veterinary technician."

I might be ill prepared for this job, but I wasn't about to let him know it. "In case you're interested, I have a bachelor's degree in biology, which means I could be making a lot more money doing something else. Instead, I *choose* to be a vet tech because I love animals and feel people need to be educated about their welfare. Do you know how many dogs are put down every year because people don't care enough to train them? Right now, thousands of dogs—"

"Hey, hey. Just a minute." He put up his hand in a gesture a trained dog would recognize as *wait*. "I think what you're doing is great. If anyone needs help, it's Berto and Carmen."

I rubbed my temples. "That's obvious."

"You're the last chance to save their marriage. Berto says it's either him or the dogs."

"So I'll be responsible for the breakup of their marriage if I fail?"

He looked as if I'd hurt him. I knew better. His kind didn't hurt.

"Look, I'm on your side," he said. "But Carmen is desperate. She's tried other trainers, but they didn't work out."

"She fired them?"

"Let's just say you're her last hope. She and Berto have been married twenty-five years. They grew up in Mexico, and now they're living the American dream. They can't lose it all over a couple of dogs."

"Those two are more than dogs to Carmen. Didn't you hear her? Calling them her children?"

"But Berto is her husband."

I rolled my eyes. "I'm sure she's aware of that. But the dogs are with her every day. Her husband isn't. He could cut her some slack."

"He has. You saw how they acted."

Nick just wasn't getting it. I changed the subject. "What's your connection, other than their pilot? Why all the concern over the fate of the Esposito marriage?"

"I've known Berto a long time. And I've flown for them for years. We're also friends."

"You a dog person?"

He hesitated. "Sure, dogs are okay."

"You have a dog?"

"Not with my job. I'm gone too much of the time."

I detected something more behind the words, something he wasn't telling me. I remembered how he'd stood up and kept his distance from Noche and Blanco.

But what did I care? I'd decided early on I wasn't getting involved with him, even if he turned out to be president of the ASPCA.

"So why were the last trainers fired? Poodles are the gifted and talented of the dog world. They usually make their owners look smart. Only a few repetitions, and—"

Carmen's reappearance stopped me. She motioned us to follow her. "Let's take our drinks out onto the patio."

We picked up our drinks and trailed behind her. The sun was setting, the sky streaked with shades of orange and pink, contrasting with the cool blue of the water. I gazed at the lake, and for the first time in a long while, a sense of serenity swept over me.

"This is nothing like West Texas."

"Doesn't Abilene have a lake?" Carmen asked.

"Not like this," I said. "This one has *blue* water, not brown."

Carmen laughed. "It's not very deep, and it's polluted from the dairy farms upriver."

Like some men. Shallow and polluted. "Still beautiful," I said, refusing to let her ruin it for me.

Her next words snapped me out of my peaceful trance. "Okay, let's talk business."

I'd hoped Nick would leave before we got to that point, but he was hanging around us like a sheepdog. I wanted to tell him he'd done his rounding up for the day, now get along home.

"You've met my Blanco and Noche," Carmen said. "What do you think? Can you train them?" Though she smiled, I detected tension in her voice.

"They're beautiful, but as you said in your email, a little out of control." A *lot* out of control. "Did you try puppy kindergarten or obedience classes when they were younger?"

"I did." Her dark eyes turned fiery. "But the trainer was cruel, so we quit."

I looked at Nick. He raised his eyebrows but said nothing. The dull ache in my temples increased to a throb. "Cruel?"

"Yes, the walking was fine, though the last trainer lady wasn't happy because they walked ahead of me. And she wanted me to pull on the chains and force them down on the floor and make them stay there. I told her it would break their spirit, but she wouldn't listen. She even called my *hija*, Blanco, a bitch. *Mis pobres perros.*"

Ho boy. I took a gulp of beer to cover my smile and almost choked. Now I understood why the professional trainers were fired.

Nick merely grinned. I frowned at him, irritated he seemed to be enjoying himself. I pulled a notepad from my purse and clicked my pen open, hoping to look efficient.

"So can you help?" Carmen asked.

"I'll try. But I'll need your assistance. First, and most important, you must establish yourself as pack leader and not think of them as your children."

"But *mis perros* are my children," Carmen protested. She reminded me of a pouty child herself. "My two *niños*. I suffer from empty-neck syndrome."

I looked toward Nick, baffled.

"She means empty nest," he explained. "One of her children lives in California, the other in New York. She doesn't see them as often as she'd like."

"Yes," Carmen said. "I've always loved the big family. Then one day, poof, they're gone."

I scribbled on the pad, pretending to take notes. "Did you discipline your children?"

"Of course. Berto was very strict. They said *yes ma'am* and *no ma'am* from the day they could talk."

I made another fake note. "How do the dogs behave when Berto is here?"

"That's part of the problem. Berto stays away more and more. He says the dogs are my responsibility. He's even accused me of loving them more than him. He says when the dogs behave better he'll spend more time at home. I don't care if they can walk beside me or if they can *sit* and *stay*. But Berto..." She let out a heavy sigh and pooched out her lips. "He says they're ruining our sex life. That's where I need help."

I cleared my throat and kept my eyes averted, while Nick sat there calmly exuding testosterone till the air felt thick with it.

Carmen fluttered her hands. "That's enough. Let's leave the rest for tomorrow."

Relieved, I put away my non-notes.

"You must be tired and hungry. I've had Rosa prepare a light supper for us. You probably want to freshen up. Then we'll eat, and I'll show you to your living quarters out back."

Living quarters? Out back? I'd assumed I'd be staying in a bedroom here in the big house.

* * *

The "light" supper included enchiladas, guacamole, taquitos, and chiles rellenos, washed down with red wine, followed by a delicious flan for dessert. Had I been flying again, the plane would never make it off the ground.

Carmen finally brought the meal to a close. "I sleep late, so you can relax by the pool in the morning, and we'll start work tomorrow afternoon. We have a little ballroom we can use."

A ballroom? And a private pilot, a gardener, and a cook? Even my mother wasn't that extravagant. Carmen was obviously a woman used to getting what she wanted. I, on the other hand, was beginning to wonder if I had a snowball's chance in Waco of delivering.

I swallowed my apprehension. "If they have choke chains and leashes, then we're all set."

Carmen leaped from her chair. "No! Not you, too! *Choke* chains?" She glared at me. "I fired the last trainers when I found out they were going to use those horrible things."

"But we need to get control. Used properly, they won't hurt the dogs." Some trainers advocated other methods, but I had only a month, and if we were to succeed, I had to depend on what I knew. "I promise I won't do anything that will hurt them."

She folded her arms across her chest. "*No.* I will not have them choked."

Nick surprised me by intervening. "Carmen, I'd listen to the lady if I were you. Berto said this is your last chance."

"*Berto*," she spat out. "What does he know? This is *all* about Berto."

"Have you told Julie what Noche did to him?"

Carmen's shoulders drooped.

Nick stared at her until she looked up at him. "She needs to know," he said.

Carmen glanced over at me and chewed the end of her thumb. "It was Berto's fault. He tried to take a bone away from Noche."

I waited, but she didn't finish. "And?"

"Noche growled and snapped at him. But it was Noche's bone, not Berto's."

So Noche might also be food-aggressive. What had I gotten myself into? "Back to the...um, training collars."

The shift in terminology didn't fool her. Her dark eyes burned into my blue ones. "I refuse to have my *niños* choked."

"You have to trust me. I've done this before." It was partly true, but I felt as if I'd just added liar to my list of many sins.

Carmen tossed her head and gave a small snort. "I'll let Nick show you to your rooms."

He motioned toward the door. "Come with me."

By now, I was as pooped as Philip after a day with the groomer and too tired to protest. Nick led me out back to a brick path trailing downward toward the lake. I wondered if I'd misjudged him. "Thanks for supporting me."

"No problem."

Gaslights illuminated the path, but the footing was uneven. When I stumbled, he reached for me. I leaned into him, and his warm body commanded me. *Julie. Stay. Good Julie.*

"Thank you again." My voice quavered, and I fought the urge to fold myself into his arms.

"You're very welcome." Even in the darkness, his teeth gleamed. "Are you okay?"

His smile looked mocking in the moonlight. I pulled myself up to my full five feet, four inches. "I tripped on a rock. I'm perfectly fine. Where are you taking me?"

He leaned close and lightly touched my back. "Where would you like me to take you?"

I squirmed away from him, though my body wanted to sit up and beg for more.

"How about heaven by the lake?" Nick asked.

"In your dreams," I said, an edge to my voice.

He laughed.

The man was impossible. He hadn't thought it so funny when Blanco poked him in the butt with her nose. My voice took on a shrill quality I didn't like. "Why do you keep laughing at me?"

"I'm laughing because that's the name."

"The name of *what*?"

"The name of where we're staying. *Cielo por el Lago*. It means 'heaven by the lake.' Carmen and Berto always name their houses, even the guesthouse."

That woke me up. "What do you mean, where *we're* staying?"

"You didn't think I was going to fly out of here at this time of night, did you? After all the food and drink? I'm a good boy. I don't drink and drive, *or* fly."

Bad enough I'd soon be training the poodles of the Baskervilles and their unruly mistress, but I'd assumed by day's end Mr. Oozing-Sex-Appeal would be well on his way to his next conquest. Did the Espositos expect me to spend the night with him?

At this rate, I'd have choke chains on all of them before the week was out.

Chapter Two

When Nick and I reached Cielo por el Lago, I was in for another surprise. Stretched out under a thicket of live oaks on a good-sized lot, the guesthouse was huge. I counted at least six sets of windows on the front side alone.

Nick opened the door and escorted me into a Texas-sized living area, but the lavish decor was anything but Texan. African, East Indian, Latin-American, Oriental— you name it. Either the Espositos were world travelers or they had a hefty account at an imported furniture store. I seriously doubted they'd bought any of these furnishings in Waco. From the carved wooden trunk to the lacquered and gilt frames, the room reeked of expensive artifacts, not cheap imports from Pier 1 or Hobby Lobby. Judging from the number of crystal chandeliers, they must be procreating.

"Look over there." Nick pointed to an entire wall of glass. "Wait till you see the view in the morning. It's the same in the bedroom. All glass."

This reminder of the sleeping situation snapped me back to reality. I waved toward a gold brocade sofa. "I'll sleep there."

He smiled. "Come on. Take a look at the rest of it."

Since my new motto was looking can't hurt, I agreed.

"Here's the kitchenette." He guided me with his hand at the small of my back. A disturbing yet pleasant sensation flowed through me. Since a kitchenette seemed like fairly safe territory, I didn't shrug him off this time.

"If you get hungry in the middle of the night, the fridge and cupboards are well stocked. For breakfast here's coffee, some rolls..." He continued opening cabinets and pointing out various foods and appliances.

The kitchen was galley style with a narrow passage between a wall of appliances on one side, sink and cabinets on the other. I'd walked in ahead of him, not realizing I was trapping myself in a dead end. In fact, Nick was so close I could feel the heat radiating from his body. Or maybe it was my own radiator. A scene from *Fatal Attraction* popped into my head. The one where Michael Douglas and Glenn Close have steamy sex in the kitchen. I began to pant like a poodle.

Nick glanced over at me. "You all right?"

"Fine," I gasped.

I opened the freezer on the pretext of looking for food and stuck my head in next to a bag of broccoli to cool off. I realized this was not such a good idea when the cold air made my nipples pop out like pencil erasers.

"Just need some air," I said. I pushed past Nick and moved into the living area where I could once again breathe like a human being. Picking up a loose sofa cushion, I hugged it to my chest to hide the nubs on my small but heaving bosom.

He gave me a puzzled look, obviously oblivious to my heaving. "Let's make sure Ramón put your suitcase in the bedroom before we turn in."

Hearing the words *bedroom* and *we* in the same sentence made my palms sweat. Nick opened the door to an adjacent room. This time I followed. Against the far wall was a king-sized bed of dark, burnished wood, covered with a tapestry quilt in jewel tones. Behind the tall headboard were blood-red decorative curtains that seemed to serve no purpose but to assail the senses with more color.

I imagined Nick swirling around, decked out in a matador's cape, wielding a sword of glinting steel, offering me a rose to clamp between my teeth.

"Bathroom's over there," he continued, like a tour guide on autopilot. "Ah, here's your bag." He pointed to the top of a low chest where Ramón had placed my suitcase. Nick was so solicitous that for a second I wondered if he was going to unpack for me.

"Look at this." He pushed a button next to the window, causing the drapes to slide back, revealing a wall of glass similar to the one in the living area. Moonlight reflected off the lake. The view was magical.

Nick walked over and stood beside me. "*Muy bonita.*"

"Yes, very pretty," I replied, managing a translation, thanks to my limited high school Spanish.

But when I looked at him, he was looking at me, not at the lake. If I'd been a thermometer, my mercury would have popped to the top. Somehow I managed to shake myself out of the spell brought on by the wine and the room and this man. I strode over to my suitcase, hoisted it off the trunk with a grunt, and began rolling it out of the bedroom.

"What are you doing?"

I didn't look in his direction. "I need sleep."

"But the bed's in here."

"I *told* you I'd sleep on the sofa," I said, as my suitcase bumped over the tile floor.

"Suit yourself. But it won't be as comfortable as the bed. Hope you get a good night's rest."

I straightened my back. "I'm sure I will." I pulled an afghan from the back of one of the chairs and sat on the sofa, waiting for him to shut the bedroom door.

Instead, he walked to the front door, opened it, and stepped outside. Then, before shutting the door, he stuck his head back inside. "Sweet dreams," he said, grinning.

If we'd been actors in a movie, I'd have smacked the devilish grin off his face, but it wasn't a movie, and I wasn't the violent type. Instead, I picked up a pillow and threw it at the door. By then he was gone.

I sat there wondering what he might do next. Surely he wouldn't walk away and leave me, not after all the attention he'd given me today. Had my overactive imagination misinterpreted his interest in me? Where was the instant replay when I needed it?

The only answer I got was silence.

I got up and switched off the lights, then peeked through the window blinds, half expecting him to jump out of the shadows. Craning my head, I tried to see where he'd gone. With the help of the moonlight, I could make out the pathway leading back to the house, but Nick had vanished, along with any evidence of his ever being here. Even my eraser nipples had disappeared.

* * *

The next morning when my feet hit the cold tile floor, I did a quick-step to the bathroom and sank my frozen toes into the thick island of bathmat to warm them up. After the heat I'd given off yesterday, the cold was a shock to my system. I turned the thermostat up a notch.

The room had been designed with a woman in mind. The windows, full-length mirror, and shower entry all had the same tiled archways as the main house. Potted plants and candles surrounded a raised garden tub. Bottles of shampoo, lotion, and thick cream-colored towels beckoned. Add to all that the matching terrycloth bathrobe hanging inside the door—it was enough to make Paris Hilton feel at home.

As I stood there taking it in, I heard water running through the pipes. Climbing to the edge of the tub, I stood on tiptoe and peered out the high window but could see only trees and lake. Then I heard the faint sounds of music. I climbed down from the tub and put my ear to the wall. A man was singing in Spanish, though I didn't recognize the tune or the words. Obviously, there was another apartment or room on the other side of the wall, and either the Espositos had another guest or Ramón was working inside.

Putting it from my mind, I made a quick call to my sister, who said Philip was fine and assured me I was missing nothing in Abilene. I should have known. Life there was like a soap opera. You could tune in once a month and nothing would have changed.

Relieved Nick was gone and no longer dogging my every move, I decided to go for a swim. As I pulled on my black bikini, the image in the mirror reflected a slim, *very* white woman in her early thirties with a firm bottom and shapely legs. The push-up bra allowed me to pretend I saw cleavage when I bent forward. The sight of my own bare flesh caused my thoughts to stray to Nick again, but I quickly banished them. It was a new day, and I had several hours to kill before my first lesson with the dogs. Even better, I was Nick-free.

I wrapped a black sarong over my suit, slipped into my flip-flops, and opened the front door. Carmen had thought of everything—a copy of the *Waco Tribune-Herald* lay on the porch. I picked it up and tossed it inside to read later. Might as well stay abreast of local goings-on while I was here.

The sky was bright blue, the sun blinding. I looked around for signs of life, saw none, and headed up the trail Nick and I had taken the night before. The swimming pool was about halfway between the guest quarters and the main house. Near the pool, a brass armadillo on a fake lily pad squirted water into a fish pond filled with Japanese koi.

I unwrapped the sarong, draped it over a lawn chair, and tested the water with my big toe. It was warm, so I stepped into the shallow end and swam to the other side. I'd forgotten how relaxing a swim could feel.

Leaning back to wet my hair, I let the sun bake my face. After a few laps, I lay back and floated, allowing the sun to caress my body, idly wondering if my vow of celibacy extended to self-gratification. No, it was men who got me into trouble, not sex.

Lucky for me, I didn't get past the thinking stage.

"Good morning," boomed a male voice, yanking me out of my hedonistic reverie.

I jerked in the water like that girl in *Jaws*, and my arms involuntarily crossed over my chest. "What are *you* doing here?" I'd assumed Nick would be miles away by now, and I didn't like being blindsided. "Why aren't you at work?"

The fact I was half-naked made me feel extra vulnerable. Nick was fully dressed in crisp khakis and a polo shirt, his hair still wet from a shower. For a moment, I could imagine what he must have looked like as a little boy. Then he grinned, and my pulse quickened.

Treading water and glowering at him, I used one hand to shade my eyes from the sunlight. Since Nick's grin was aimed at annihilating my defenses, I re-erected my mental barriers, poured burning oil from the parapets while he rammed the heavy castle doors. But my metaphors played against me.

"I am working," he said, unaware of all the burning and ramming taking place in my head.

"Ha. Sure you are."

"Would I lie to you?" He was still smiling.

"I don't know, would you? How can you call this working?" The sarcasm dripped from my tongue like a leaky faucet, a cold one.

"Carmen said to tell you lunch would be served on the patio in about an hour."

Why was Carmen using Nick as her lackey?

"You can go tell Carmen you've accomplished your mission."

He ignored me, settling into a lawn chair and leaning back, as if in no hurry to leave. His eyes never wavered from where I bobbed upright in the water, trying to keep as much of my body covered as possible.

"Go ahead. Don't let me interrupt," he said. "Swim, do whatever you were doing."

Thank God he couldn't read minds.

I bobbed to the other side of the pool, keeping my back to him. When I glanced over my shoulder, he smiled and waved. Since my fingers were beginning to shrivel, I'd have to let him win this hand. I bobbed back to his side.

"Do me a favor and hand me my cover-up, would you?" I tried to sound sweet.

Nick glanced toward the chair where my sarong lay. He reached over and plucked it off the chair, then slowly ran his hand down the length of silky fabric. "Feels nice."

A throb of excitement made me ache for more. *Stop it. This is as close as he's going to get to you.*

He walked toward the edge of the pool and knelt.

"You can leave it there." I nodded toward the ladder as I paddled like a dog to stay afloat.

He didn't budge.

"Just leave it, please," I repeated, but still he didn't move. "*Thank* you," I said curtly, trying to release him, but like a well-trained dog, he held his *stay. What nerve.*

I held onto the ladder with one hand and tugged at the bottom of my swimsuit with the other. I'd bought the suit a few years back while in the throes of passion over another charmer, thinking a tiny bikini would keep his eyes from wandering. It hadn't. When I caught him in my bed with a Hooters waitress, I figured it was time to call it quits.

I snatched the sarong from Nick's hands and draped it around me best I could while mounting the ladder. No makeup, wet hair—that alone should send him running.

He reached into his pocket. "I have something you need."

I raised an eyebrow.

He pulled out two slip chains. "I thought you might be able to use these. Carmen doesn't know. I found them in the garage."

I looked up, trying not to show the gratitude I felt. "Thanks," I mumbled. His hand brushed mine and I shivered, but I was far from cold. When our eyes met, I could tell he was fully aware of the effect he had on me. To get even, I moved toward him, deliberately dripping water, forcing him to step back or get wet. I was tempted to shake myself dry.

"Great view this morning," he said.

As a tart reply started to slip from my lips, I realized he was looking at the lake, not me. I stifled my smart-ass comeback just in time.

"Did you remember to look outside when you got up?" he asked. "From your bedroom window, the lake shimmers at dawn."

Mention of my bedroom felt way too personal, so I avoided the question. "You were up that early?" It was well after midnight when we'd finally reached the guesthouse. Did the man not need sleep?

He shrugged. "I like to take an early morning run over the dam."

I deliberately flicked a few droplets of water from my hair onto his face. He jumped back and said, "Hey!" and we both laughed.

"You should do that more often," he said. "Laugh, I mean. You're even more beautiful." His eyes, like blue flames, seared mine.

My laughter died, and I drew inward. Most women would feel flattered, but to me it was just more smooth talk. I clasped my arms over my chest and shivered again. "I need to get cleaned up for lunch." Not waiting for his response, I took off for the guesthouse at a fast clip.

The lake was a brilliant blue, and the sun's heat had opened blooms on the moss rose lining the pathway.

Like living in Paradise. Better watch out for snakes.

* * *

An hour later as I neared the patio, Carmen spotted me and waved. I saw no sign of my personal snake.

Someone had spread out quite a feast on a large wooden table. At this rate, I'd need a plus-size bikini by the end of the month. Multi-colored hand-painted plates sat atop woven placemats the color of straw. Neatly folded green and gold cloth napkins, sterling silver flatware, crystal goblets—I could hear my mother saying, "It's all about presentation." Personally, I didn't understand why people bothered with such time-wasting amenities. But then, I'd always been the dirty white sheep of my family.

I took a few seconds to study my new boss. Even in the bright sunlight, Carmen's light brown skin was smooth and clear except for a light dusting of freckles over her nose. "Did you sleep well?" she asked, her smile warm.

"Like *el vampiro* after a night on the town. Thank you for all the food and supplies."

"Oh, it's nothing." She waved dismissively. "We're used to company. But sit. I can't wait to see the lesson plans for *mis niños*." She held out her hand.

"Uh, you mean you want something in writing?"

Her dark brows drew together, and she pulled back her empty hand. "When my children were in school, their teachers always had the books with plans in them. You know, with objections and activities."

The muscles in the back of my neck tightened. I had a feeling she would be providing the "objections." I took a deep breath.

"I know they're like your children, but these are dogs, you know. I don't have a written plan, but I do have some commands we can work on."

"*Commands?*" She spat the word out, like soured milk.

"Okay, let's pretend it's school. We'll call it puppy kindergarten. But I hope you understand that at one year, Noche and Blanco are teenagers who haven't learned their basics."

Carmen pressed her lips together and looked straight into my eyes but didn't speak, so I continued my lesson.

"I thought we'd begin with a few simple commands and see how they respond. We'll go from there. Once

30

they get on lead, it'll be easier to control them." I cringed inwardly as I said the word *control*, fearing it might set her off, but considering the antics of her two hooligans last night, they needed some boundaries.

Carmen glanced past my shoulder and her face brightened. "Oh, here's Nick."

Still here? Did he just hang around the Espositos' house whenever he wasn't flying them somewhere? He surely didn't live here, and he obviously wasn't on vacation. Despite my curiosity, I had too much pride to ask.

"Hi there, beautiful women," Nick said, pulling out Carmen's chair, then looking toward me. I sat down before he could do the honors. Maybe Carmen's presence would keep him from sniffing around me for a while.

He took a seat between us, unfolded his napkin, and placed it in his lap. "So, this is the big day. Everyone ready for the first lesson? Thought I'd tag along and watch, if that's okay."

My eyes widened and met his denim blues. "It won't be very interesting for you," I snapped.

What was wrong with him? The worse I treated him, the harder he tried. Surely he didn't think I was playing hard to get. I was seriously un-gettable, and he wasn't getting it.

"You might be surprised what interests me," he said, his voice husky and low.

* * *

After lunch, my stomach full of enchiladas, I hoped someone would suggest a siesta, but no one did.

While Carmen went to get the dogs, Nick ushered me into the ballroom.

By now I should have been beyond surprise, but when we entered a room the size of a small gymnasium, I gaped. The four massive crystal chandeliers must have cost as much as my annual salary. Antique chairs and sofas lined the walls. Polished hardwood floors, stained glass windows, and a mural covering an entire wall completed the picture. Scarlett O'Hara would have fit right in. Such waste. I'd grown up with money, lots of money, but the Espositos' furnishings made my mother's lifestyle look downright frugal.

Echoes bounced off the walls when Nick shut the door. "You were quiet at lunch. Everything okay?"

"I'm fine. Just doing my job."

Actually, I had the jitters. I'd never trained someone else's dogs before, and a marriage was riding on my success, not to mention the fate of two dogs. Adding Nick Worthington to that equation made my cellulite quiver.

But I had little time to fret further. The door burst open and in ran Noche and Blanco, dragging a panting Carmen behind them. She was so tiny that together they probably weighed as much as she did.

"They're full of energy today," she gasped, as they pulled her toward me. Once they were close enough, both dogs rose up on their hind legs, determined to put their paws on my chest. If I hadn't backed up, and if Nick hadn't stepped in and taken hold of their leashes, they'd have knocked me flat on my butt. He held them off while I talked to Carmen.

"First lesson." I used a low, stern voice I hoped both Carmen and the dogs would respond to. "You must establish yourself as the alpha figure, the pack leader. That means you have to be firm and in control."

I reached out and took Blanco's leash from Nick. "Think of them as children if you like, but children who need discipline. I don't mean spanking. Just a firm hand."

Last night I'd observed that Blanco, like most bitches, was top dog of this poodle two-pack, so I'd start with her. My job was to out-bitch her *and* the humans.

"As long as you're here, you can help," I told Nick, trying not to let his spicy, fresh scent distract me. "You and Noche follow me. Carmen, you watch." For the first time since we'd met, Nick didn't seem so confident. In fact, he looked downright unnerved. I, however, was getting a control-freak rush now that I was in my element. I could do this.

I knelt beside Blanco and slipped the training collar over her head before Carmen realized what I was doing. "Think of it as the letter *P*. It's important you don't put it on backwards. That *could* hurt her."

Carmen reached out and grabbed the leash from my hand and pulled Blanco away from me. "When I said, no choke chains, I meant *no choke chains*."

Nick put his hand on Carmen's arm in an attempt to get her attention. "Carmen, won't you give Julie a chance?"

Carmen planted her feet firmly and drew Blanco closer. "I'm giving her a chance. She can use collars and leashes. No choke chains."

Nick turned to me. "Can you try it without the chains for now?"

I stretched my neck from side to side to relieve the tension and looked at Carmen. "Do I have any choice?"

Carmen slipped the chain off Blanco's neck and threw it against the wall. "No. Now let's get started."

I took a deep breath to calm the thumping in my chest and bit my lip to keep from saying something I'd regret. "Okay, follow me with Noche as I walk Blanco. Do what I do, but don't get too close."

I kept reminding myself to remain calm and think positive, knowing my emotions would travel right down the leash to the dogs. I held a treat over Blanco's head to get her attention and got her to sit, then gave the *heel* command, walking forward with my left foot first. "Every time they get out of heel position, say *watch*. Our goal is to teach them to walk by our side without pulling. And give lots of praise in a high voice when they do it right."

"A high voice?" Nick asked.

"Don't worry. I'm sure your masculinity will remain intact." I restrained a laugh.

I demonstrated with Blanco to help Nick get the hang of it, smiling inwardly when he used a high voice, remembering his natural husky tone.

"Then reward with a small treat, but not every time. Intermittent reinforcement works best when using food. But always reward with verbal praise."

We made a few laps around the ballroom. "Nick!" I barked at one point, "You have to take charge. He has to know you're boss."

Nick grimaced. "I'm trying. But it isn't working."

"It takes time. When you stop, he needs to stop and sit. Take your hand and push his butt down gently. Then tell him *good sit*. Remember, you're in control. Think of it as flying a plane. You have to be alert at all times."

Nick took a deep, shaky breath and let it out. "I don't think he likes this. He keeps giving me funny looks."

I glanced at Noche's big brown eyes, then narrowed my blue ones at Nick. "Your turn, Carmen."

She reluctantly took hold of the leash, but Noche knew an easy touch when he felt one. He rose up and knocked Carmen backwards with his front paws. If Nick hadn't managed to catch her, she'd have fallen hard.

I threw up my arms. "Listen up. This is proof. You've got to get control. If not, someone's going to get hurt."

Carmen looked miffed but took Noche's leash and circled the room, while I called out instructions. I demonstrated again with Blanco, parading around the room, growling at her when she tried to take control and praising profusely when she did it right. "Good girl, that's a good girl." At least Blanco realized I meant business.

"Remember to control them with your voice. Higher pitch when you're pleased, lower tones for correction. That's what the mother dog does. She growls if the pups get out of line. Now, you try it, and I'll watch. Nick, you take Blanco from me, and Carmen, you try it with Noche."

At first both dogs and people seemed to be catching on. Then, as Nick and Carmen rounded a corner too close to each other, Noche mounted Blanco.

"Pull him off, pull him off!" I yelled at Carmen. "Nick, help her!"

Carmen dropped the leash and put her hands on her hips. "He's just doing what comes naturally."

By now, I was hot and sweaty and *not* amused. "This is what he's going to do when you have guests. This is not good. This is bad." I sounded like a page from a *Dick and Jane* reader.

Maybe I was being too hard on them. After all, this was only the first lesson.

"One more time," I commanded, brushing a strand of hair out of my eyes.

"How much longer?" Carmen wailed.

"We need to work at least an hour a day. Two sessions would be best. But you also need to reinforce the same behavior when we aren't officially working."

Carmen sat cross-legged on the floor and let the two dogs lick her face and arms as if she were a big doggy treat.

"Stand up," I ordered. "If you get down on their level, they'll think you're a littermate and treat you like one."

She looked up at me and whined. "But I'm their mommy." She put her arms around them and kissed their faces. "Good babies."

"Up, get up! High voice is for praise. You don't want to praise inappropriate behavior."

She hugged them to her chest. "But I *like* them loving me. They're doing better, don't you think?"

I groaned inside. "It's a start." That's when the realization hit me hard. I had one month to perform a miracle. "Let's stop for now. I see some tired faces."

"Yes, *mis niños* are tired, aren't they?" Carmen continued kissing them.

"I meant you and Nick. The dogs don't seem tired at all."

We had to untangle the leashes from around her as she stood up, and by the time we finished, Nick was nowhere in sight.

"What's up with Nick?" I asked. "He just kind of disappeared."

Carmen rolled her eyes. "He's a man."

"So?"

"You may know a lot about dogs, but you don't seem to know much about men."

I lifted my chin. "I know enough about men like Nick Worthington."

"Then you should know men don't like women telling them what to do. Nick's mama was a bossy woman. And no man wants a woman like his mama."

Was she serious?

"Uh, this *is* the twenty-first century," I reminded her.

She tossed her head. "Men, not just men like Nick, *any* man wants to be in control. Or think he's in control."

I twisted my sweaty hair behind my neck, wishing I had a clip or rubber band. Training dogs was harder than it looked. "I don't play those kinds of games."

She eyed me in disbelief. "Men are like dogs. They need praise...and treats. You should be nicer. Has Nick done something he shouldn't?"

Her question caught me off guard. She was right. I'd been playing alpha-bitch to Nick. I thought back to how he'd insisted on getting the car and how he'd wanted to pull my chair out for me. Finding the choke chains. Defending me to Carmen.

I lowered my head. "No, he's been a perfect gentleman."

"Then what is the problem? Most women *want* to please him."

A corkscrew of jealousy twisted between my ribs. "I'm not *most women*. And I'm not submissive like a dog, ready to roll over and pee on myself simply because an attractive man like Nick looks my way."

Carmen tossed her head. "Nick could have any woman he wants. He's—what you call it?—the pick of the litter."

"I'm not looking for another dog." She was starting to sound like my mother.

Her brow furrowed. "You could do worse."

Oh, did I ever know that. I'd already done worse. That was the problem. Nick did seem too yummy to pass up, but I'd made a vow, and I was trying like hell to keep it. Even if it meant wearing a hair shirt and sleeping on a bed of nails.

Chapter Three

The next night, after a light supper, Carmen and I retired to the library. At one end soft leather chairs, grouped around a stone fireplace, took up an entire wall. Rich wood paneling and a beamed ceiling added ambiance.

Waving her hand for me to sit, Carmen picked up a heavy crystal decanter and poured dark red liquid into two Waterford wine glasses, then handed one to me. I recognized the Lismore pattern. It was the same as mine. My mother had thrown a fit when I'd sold all but two stems to help raise money for the new Lookin' For Love Animal Adoption center.

Carmen sat in a chair next to mine, kicked off her sandals, and tucked her bare feet beneath her. I took a sip of wine and leaned back. As the warmth flooded through me, I thought of Nick. He'd been gone for over a day. Though I should have felt relief, his absence had left me with an unexpected hollow feeling. With Nick around, the house seemed full of life, but without him it was cavernous and empty. I was beginning to understand Carmen's "empty neck" syndrome.

"When is your husband coming home? Is he still in Mexico?"

Her face lit up. "Business usually keeps him out of town except on weekends. But this week, he's coming back early..." She took a sip of wine. "...to meet you."

My stomach flip-flopped. I wasn't too keen on meeting the man of the house until I had his errant hounds under better control. Maybe I had daddy issues, but powerful men made me nervous, and I doubted Berto Esposito would be an exception.

"That's great." I smiled, attempting to mirror her joy. I hadn't felt comfortable enough to ask before, but now the timing seemed right. "What kind of business is he in?"

She pointed to the small, ornate wooden table between us. "Imports. Mainly furniture, but he also picks up decorative items. I shouldn't complain. He does very well. But I do get lonely with him traveling so much, especially now that my *niños*—our children—have grown up and moved away. That's why Berto let me get Noche and Blanco, but now..." As her thoughts trailed off, she puffed out her lips in an exaggerated pout. "Berto will ask you if we're making progress." The slight tremor in her voice reminded me her marriage hung in the balance.

"Don't worry. I'll make it sound good."

The hand holding her wine glass trembled slightly. "I think they're fine the way they are, but Berto..." She sighed and set the glass on the table. Her perfectly manicured nails matched the wine. With her money, she could have sent the dogs off to a posh doggy boarding school for training rather than risk breaking a fingernail. I had to admire her for wanting to do it herself.

"You like them?" she asked suddenly. "*Mis niños?*"

Her question took me by surprise. "Of course I like them. I love dogs."

Carmen chewed on her bottom lip. "The others didn't like them. They pushed on them and said *down* with a loud voice."

Uh-oh. We weren't ready for the *down* command yet, one of the most submissive positions for a dog to learn. For both our sakes, I hoped when the time came, subtler techniques than wrestling them to the floor would work.

I tried to reassure her. "We'll take it a little at a time. Now, if you had terriers, you'd probably have more of a problem, but poodles learn quickly."

"I hope so." She stared at the empty hearth, twirling a strand of her long dark hair around a finger. "Berto doesn't understand."

"Does Berto like the dogs?"

"Oh, he likes them." Her tone was defensive. "But he says I'm the one who's with them all day, and I'm the one who has time to train them."

"He does have a point. It's not something you can do in a weekend."

Her eyes filled with distress. "Or a month?"

"We're going to give it our best," I said, wishing I could promise more. The pressure of having only a month weighed on me too. As I took another sip of wine, the library door flew open and in stepped a tall, broad-shouldered man with a Van Dyke beard.

Carmen leaped from her chair. "Berto!" She ran to him and threw herself into his arms. He easily lifted her small frame off the floor with one arm, and they kissed passionately, which was pretty impressive after twenty-five years of marriage. I was still watching them, entranced, when Nick sauntered in, causing my breath to catch.

Carmen extracted herself from Berto's arms to introduce us. "Julie, my husband, Berto."

I stood, ready to meet my master. Berto's hand reached out and gripped mine, while his eyes assessed my worth.

I faked a confident smile. "Nice meeting you," I said, turning toward Nick. "And good to see you again." After Carmen's lecture about my treatment of him, I'd decided to be polite. Nick gave me a brief nod and greeted Carmen with a friendly hug but merely glanced at me and nodded.

Berto wasted no time getting to the point. "So, Miss Julie. You think you can tame these wild animals of hers?"

"They're not wild," Carmen said, sticking out her bottom lip and giving him a light punch on the arm. "Can't we just let them be dogs?"

A muscle in Berto's jaw tightened, and his dark brows drew together as he answered her. "Don't forget we made an agreement. Nick tells me you won't let Julie use the training collars. You've got to listen to her. That's what we're paying her for."

"But...I like *mis niños* as they are. Happy and having fun."

"Carmen, we've discussed this at length. These dogs are out of control. Noche snapped at me. What if he bites one of us, or someone else? We could be sued." He glared at her before adding, "I have spoken." With that declaration, he strode out of the room, his face grim. Carmen ducked her head.

Whoa. This *was* serious.

Nick reached over and gently lifted Carmen's chin, forcing her to look at him. "He means it, Carmen."

She slumped into a chair and gave Nick her pouty look. Frankly, I was tired of her pouty look. Feminine wiles had never been my strong suit.

"It's not fair," she said. "Making me choose between my *niños* and him."

Nick shook his head, his lips grim. "Sorry, can't help you. We've both known him long enough to know when he means business."

Carmen looked at me, her eyes challenging. "So. Y-you have to do it. You have to make them better."

My neck was getting stiffer by the minute. I reached back and grasped it with my hand and did a couple of neck rolls. "I'm doing the best I can, but we've just started. Poodles are smart, but training any dog takes time and consistency. You're going to have to be the pack leader all the time, not just when we're working them."

"*Working* them," she huffed. "You make them sound like slaves."

41

"What about the training collars?" I asked.

Carmen lifted her chin. "No."

I took a deep breath and looked at Nick. I needed an ally. But his eyes were stony and unreadable, and he still hadn't spoken one word to me.

Great. Now I had all of them put out with me. "Look, I'm trying, but I'm not a miracle worker. It took Annie Sullivan over a month to get through to Helen Keller."

Carmen looked baffled.

"It's a play," Nick explained. "About a woman who was deaf and blind."

Hands on hips, Carmen pushed her face up close to mine, invading my personal space. I wanted to lean back but held my ground. "This isn't a play," she hissed. "This is real." Then she played the money card. "I'm *paying* you to perform a miracle."

That's when I exploded. "It's not about the money!"

Carmen had just tapped into my personal prejudice— rich people. They thought because they had money they could lord it over everyone else. I should know. I'd spent my whole life around them.

After the burst of anger, tears welled in my eyes, and I turned away so Carmen and Nick couldn't see. But when the tears spilled over and ran down my cheeks, I headed for the nearest door without looking back.

Once outside, I drew a deep breath of night air to clear my head. That's when I realized how angry I really was. Angry with myself for losing control. Angry with the Espositos for expecting miracles and treating me like an inferior. And angry with Nick Worthington for...for being so damned desirable.

I took off for the guesthouse at a fast clip. Nothing was keeping me here. I could go back home to Abilene tomorrow. I didn't need any of them. But then I thought about the poor, undisciplined dogs. Who would take care of them if the Espositos split up? Too, there was a part of me that couldn't admit failure. Was I willing to give up so easily? If I stayed, even if I failed, I'd have done my best. There was also the issue of money, though I'd denied it.

Halfway to the guesthouse, I heard footsteps behind me. I walked faster.

"Julie, it's me, wait." Nick caught up, grabbed my arm and turned me to face him. The night was warm, his hand on my arm even warmer. "You know how to give a guy a run for his money."

Sweet fragrance of magnolia blossoms suffused the air. Moonlight softened all it touched, including Nick's face.

"Don't pay any attention to Carmen. I told you she was fiery. Stubborn, too. That's part of the problem with her and Berto. She doesn't listen to reason."

He reached up and lightly touched his thumb under my eye, still wet from where a tear had fallen. "Hey," he said softly. "Let's have none of that."

I was tongue-tied. He was simply delicious. *Delicioso.* When he pulled me to him, I was too weak to resist, and my body dissolved into the warmth of his embrace. A sense of comfort and safety gathered me up and transported me to Wonderland, Neverland, Disneyland. I could have stayed in his arms forever.

Then something happened. Whatever it was, I was keenly aware he felt it too. Maybe it was the moonlight. Maybe it was the scents engulfing us. Or maybe it was just biology, a man and a woman alone on a dark summer night. I quivered as a throb of longing swept over me.

We looked into each other's eyes for a long moment. Then Nick cupped my chin in his hand, tilting my face up to his. He slowly bent down and brushed his soft, warm lips against mine. Then, he moved closer, kissing me more intensely. By now we were both trembling.

I pulled my lips from his and with a shaky laugh broke the spell. So this is what happened when I tried to be nice. If I wasn't careful, I could end up in that king-sized bed with him, angry at myself for being such a pushover.

Nick continued looking at me, his heart thumping against my breast. Reluctantly, I drew back and repeated his last words, my tone light. "Hey, let's have none of that."

His laugh was husky. "You drive a hard bargain, lady. Follow me." He led me to a bench beside the pathway and pulled me down beside him. Any closer and we could have been Siamese twins, joined at the hip.

"I have an idea. Tomorrow, after the dogs' lesson, let me take you up in the plane...for fun. It'll be good for you."

Much as I wanted to say yes, the thought of facing my fear of small planes and being in the air under Nick's control made me hesitate.

"You can't stay here at Casa del Lago for a whole month and never leave the house."

I laughed. "But I've only been here a few days."

"You're halfway through your first week."

He was right. My time here was on fast-forward. I smiled. He touched his finger to my lips, and they parted slightly as he traced their outline. Then he reached up and brushed a strand of hair out of my face, ever so gently. Like a heroine in an old romantic movie, I wanted to grab his hand and pull it to my heart. But this was no movie, and my life hadn't exactly been filled with happy endings.

"I'll make you a better deal," he said. "You're afraid of flying, and you've probably noticed I'm...well...uneasy around dogs."

"You're afraid of dogs?"

He avoided my eyes and my question. "Fly with me, and I'll help you with Carmen and the dogs tomorrow." He paused. "That is, if you want me to." Twice now, he'd come to my defense. Though I hated the thought of being indebted to him, his offer was a godsend because Carmen did listen to him when she wouldn't listen to me.

"It's a deal. But no fancy stuff." I could imagine him getting me thousands of feet in the air and doing loop-de-loops to show off.

He chuckled. "I'm not an aerobatic pilot. I promise I'll take as good care of you as I would my own sister. Not that I see you as sisterly."

"Oh, you have a sister?"

"No."

We both laughed.

"Until tomorrow then." He turned and walked toward the main house. As I watched him, he stopped, spun around, and blew me a kiss. Though I was seated, my knees went weak. I stayed on the bench for several minutes after he left, luxuriating in the memory of his soft lips and the warmth of his strong, hard body. Like a conjurer, he'd cast a spell that lingered long after he was gone.

A rustling in the brush broke the spell. I squinted into the darkness and saw a man slipping from the trees and onto the pathway between me and the house. I recognized Berto from his build. Was he outside blowing off steam after his encounter with Carmen? Or had he followed us and hidden behind a tree, watching as we kissed? Whatever the reason, an uneasy feeling began churning in the pit of my stomach.

Chapter Four

The next morning as I brushed my hair, my hands trembled at the thought of flying again in such a small plane. Or maybe it was the memory of last night's kiss still fresh in my mind. I leaned into the mirror, reached up and lightly outlined my lips with a finger, as Nick had done, trying to replay that moment.

I walked to the bedroom window, pushed the button that automatically drew the drapes, and watched the first rays of sun embrace the lake. Nick was right. The view was spectacular—miles of green shoreline in the distance and blue water dotted with an occasional fishing boat or graceful sailboat, propelled across the surface by an unseen breeze.

Though she'd balked at the idea at first, claiming it was too early, I'd convinced Carmen to bring her poodle children and meet me outside at ten. She was probably hoping to stall any training at all, expecting me to create some sort of magic on my own. But since she didn't trust me, she insisted she be there at all times. I totally agreed. She had to learn to control them herself since I wouldn't always be around.

This time we would work outside. By ten a.m. the temperature would be inching into the 90s but bearable. Nick was right. I was getting slightly stir crazy from being inside so much, and Noche and Blanco could also use some fresh air.

To my surprise, Carmen was waiting with the dogs when I reached the main house. Neither of us mentioned last night's blowup. She looked as if she hadn't slept well, but then she'd admitted she wasn't a morning person. "Nick said he'd meet us as soon as he gets back," she said, handing me the leashes while she lifted her hair from the back of her neck and secured it with a wide tortoise-shell clasp. "He had an errand to run in town."

Or maybe he'd decided to skip out on his promise to help. Which meant I wouldn't have to fly with him after all. Now that it was daylight, I was embarrassed at my behavior the night before. Though it had been only a kiss—okay, two kisses—I was being paid to work here, not to carry on romantic trysts in the garden. Despite what Carmen said about Nick being the pick of the litter, I doubted the Espositos wanted me carrying on with their longtime friend. I was hired help, which put me several rungs below them all on the social ladder.

I put the dogs in a *sit-stay*, keeping them on a short lead to make sure they didn't budge. They looked at Carmen as if hoping she'd release them, but I shot her a warning look. "Before we start, I need to ask you some questions about Noche and Blanco. They're housebroken?"

"Oh, yes. The people we bought them from did that."

Bad sign. Good they were housebroken, but bad because she'd evidently done nothing with the dogs except indulge them.

"No hiking?"

"Ugh," she said. "I hate the outdoors, though sometimes we walk around the yard."

I kept my expression bland and pressed my lips together hard to keep from laughing. "I mean, does Noche hike his leg, inside...to pee."

"Oh no! Noche is a good boy, aren't you Noche?" She knelt down and hugged his neck, burying her face in his dark fur. Noche rewarded her by turning his head and flicking his pink tongue out in what amounted to a French kiss. Carmen didn't blench.

"See, he loves me. He also knows how to hug me. Watch." She stood up and pulled Noche onto his hind legs and wrapped his front legs around her waist. "You love to hug your mommy, don't you?" she said in baby talk. Noche's hips began to hunch forward and back.

Carmen turned around so Noche was facing her back, his front legs still holding on to her waist. "He can also line dance. Watch his feet."

I couldn't think about his feet. All I could see was a dark pink protuberance between his legs, growing longer with each swing of Carmen's hips. I'd heard of a dance from the 1960s called "the dirty dog." Now I knew where it got the name.

"Enough! Enough!" I cried in disbelief. "I think I understand a big part of your problem now. Tell him *off!* And push him down. Please!"

But she was ignoring me, and I couldn't wait. I grabbed the lead near Noche's neck and pulled hard, telling him *off* in a low, commanding voice. Once I had them uncoupled, it was time to be blunt. "Carmen, he's not hugging you, he's *humping* you!"

"What?"

"Humping. He thinks he's having sex with you."

Her eyes looked troubled, but she shook her head in denial. "You have a dirty mind. Noche's just a baby."

I clapped a hand to the top of my head. "He's almost a year old. That's a teenager in dog years, and he thinks you're his *woman!*"

Carmen gave me a fierce look. "That's ridiculous. I'm his mama."

I'd planned to add he also needed neutering but decided I'd already given Carmen more information than she could handle in one day.

"Come on, let's get to work." I walked toward an open, grassy area that would give us plenty of room. "I'll take Blanco," I said, giving Carmen no choice. "We'll work on the *down* command today." I prepared myself for some major resistance. "This isn't the same as *off*. Use *off* when they jump on you. *Down* means lying down. And, please, no more dancing."

Despite their lack of formal training, the poodles were already responding well to *heel*, *sit*, and *come* commands, so I thought we'd keep them challenged while their learning curve was on its way up.

"One thing you can do to reinforce what we learn here is to work it into your daily routine. For instance, when you see either of them lying down, praise them. Say, 'Good *down*.' Or anytime they're doing something you want them to learn. Like now. See, Blanco is sitting." I went over to Blanco and patted her fluffy white coat. "Good *sit*! Good *sit*!" Blanco wagged her tail and gave me a doggy smile, mouth open, tongue in lick position. "See, she knows she's doing something good."

I reached into my belt bag and broke off a piece of fat-free wiener and held it in front of Blanco's nose so she could get a good whiff. "Watch," I told Carmen. "I'm going to lower the treat as I pull down on her collar. And as I'm pulling down, I'll say *down* in a low voice and lower the treat so she'll have to lie down to get it."

Carmen put her hands on her hips. "I don't understand how this is going to help at all. It's in *bed* Berto is complaining about. I can't do this when we're in bed!"

I paused a moment to pray for patience, remembering I was training the owner as much as training the dogs. Somehow I had to make Carmen understand. Where her dogs were concerned, she had a blind spot as big as Texas.

"Once they know you're in control and acknowledge you're the alpha figure or the pack leader, they'll be more likely to obey you in other situations. Remember, even the mother dog sets boundaries for her pups."

"But they won't like me if I order them around and make them obey my every command," she wailed.

"I promise you they'll still like you. But right now, they think you're their littermate, not their mother. It's like trying to be a friend to your children instead of a parent."

"I'll try," she said reluctantly, pooching her bottom lip out like a spoiled brat.

As soon as Blanco lowered into a *down* position, I gushed. "Good girl! Okay!" I gave her a treat. She wagged her whole rear she was so happy. "She's a wiggle-butt!" I said in a high voice, causing Blanco to wag more excitedly.

"See, it makes her feel good to please you. They want to please you. And they like learning. Dogs get bored if they don't have some enrichment. You try it now with Noche."

I reached into my belt bag again, broke off a chunk of weenie, and handed it to Carmen. "After he obeys and you release him, reward him with just a tiny piece." If she could master this, then maybe there was hope.

She held the treat in front of Noche's nose, but before she could ease him down, he grabbed at the weenie and Carmen let him have it. "Good boy," she said. "He's *hungry!*"

"*No*, Carmen." I used the same tone with her I used with the dogs. She gave me a withering look, but I didn't blink. "Sorry, but you can't let him have the treat until he's done what you want. It sends him the wrong message. Let's try again."

I bent over at the waist to stretch out some tension, and when I looked between my legs, Nick was standing behind me getting an eyeful. I jerked upright and let out a loud "Eeeek!" My squeal set the poodles off on an ear-splitting rampage. "Quiet," I barked back, loud as I could, and silence descended.

Nick looked unperturbed. "Need some help? I know a thing or two about submission."

Carmen made a face at him. On her it looked cute. "I'm sure you do. And if I weren't happily married to Berto, I'd be one of your love slaves, like all the other women."

I felt totally unqualified as a love slave. My hair was plastered to my head, and I'm sure I'd sweated off all my makeup. But why did I even care? Nick and Carmen's repartee reinforced what I'd already decided about him. He wasn't the kind of man to stick around once he'd made his conquest.

I nodded to him and explained the *down* command, trying not to sound bossy this time. "Take Noche and watch me with Blanco."

When Nick took the leash from Carmen, Noche whined and looked up at her to rescue him. Frustrated at losing his sex partner, no doubt.

After I demonstrated with Blanco, Nick did the same with Noche, moving the treat in front of his nose, gently pulling Noche's collar until he was also down. "Good boy," Nick said, patting him gingerly on the head.

"Good job, Nick!" I said, thinking he might be of help after all.

"That's mean." Carmen whined like Noche. "Choking him like that."

"It's not mean, and he's not choking. If he does what Nick wants him to, then he'll get a reward. Does Berto get paid if he doesn't do his job? Or Ramón?" I added.

"Or you?" Carmen asked.

Her unfair remark caused me to draw back, but I didn't take the bait.

Nick, who'd been squatting next to Noche, stood up, towering over Carmen. "You're way out of line," he said, his words clipped. "Julie's doing everything she can to help you, and you've resisted her at every turn."

Carmen's face puckered at the reprimand, and she turned toward me, her dark eyes apologetic. "I'm sorry," she said softly.

"It's okay," I said.

Talk about an alpha. Nick had just assumed the position of leader in our little pack. Was it possible he might be a white knight after all?

I looked up to see Berto peering at us from behind a tree. Judging by the look on his face, he wasn't impressed with our little dog school. When he caught my eye, he stiffened, then tried to cover up his snooping by reaching up and grabbing a branch, pretending to examine the foliage.

Nick spotted him and called out. "Hey, Berto! Want to watch Julie in action?"

I cringed at the thought of one more man watching me "perform."

"Just checking for oak wilt," Berto replied.

He was lying. The tree was definitely a magnolia.

* * *

Since Nick had helped with the dogs, I now had to fulfill my deal with the devil and fly with him. That meant facing my dislike of small planes, plus once again having to fight the spell he was casting over me. I took a quick shower, and Nick whisked me away to the airport, telling Carmen he'd see to my lunch.

I hated takeoffs, but once we were in the air, I felt calmer. When I finally opened my eyes, I could tell Nick was really in his element from the euphoric look on his face.

"You love this, don't you?" I asked.

"Nothing like it. Soaring above the cares of the world. Feeling free."

"Don't start feeling too free. I wouldn't want you to forget to move an important flap or something."

He chuckled as if I'd said something funny. "So you're also a back-seat driver. You ever think you might have control issues? Maybe you'd feel better if *you* were the pilot." He looked over at me and grinned.

"Ha. No way I'd ever fly a plane."

"Take hold of the yoke." He pointed to the odd-shaped steering wheel on my side of the cockpit. "It's okay. I'm a flight instructor."

I thought of my father and the trips our family used to take, but I was always seated in the back. Then his accident...I closed my eyes...trying to forget.

"You can do it."

At first I hesitated, but the yoke looked like little arms reaching up, beckoning me to hold them. I reached out and grasped each one.

"I've got you covered over here," Nick said. "I've trimmed for straight and level. Relax your grip. Hold it loosely. Keep your wings level with the horizon."

I took a deep breath and let it out slowly.

"Good, now let's try a slow turn."

I followed his instructions, and the plane banked to the right.

"See, now you're making her do what you want."

"Her?" I asked. "The plane's a female?"

"Just a manner of speaking. You know, like ships."

"Yeah, sure."

So women were like planes. A mere touch of Nick Worthington's hands and they soar. I was more likely to go into a tailspin, crash, and burn. I needed to avoid another romantic nosedive. "That's enough. You take over," I said, though he'd never really given me full control at all.

We flew in a comfortable silence after that, Nick somewhere in the clouds, me in my own private hell. Wanting him, but knowing better. I stole a glance from time to time. His hands looked strong and competent, but they'd been gentle when he held me, kissed me. *Stop it!* I told myself. Once we landed, my side of the bargain would be fulfilled. Then maybe he'd go back wherever he came from. I was only human, after all.

I looked at my watch. We'd been gone over two hours, and we were still headed in the same direction best I could tell.

My reverie was broken when the plane began a bumpy descent. The terrain below looked flatter than that of central Texas, and in the distance I could see several large planes landing and taking off.

"Where are we?" I leaned over and looked down. "This doesn't look like the Waco airport."

"I told Carmen I was going to feed you before I brought you home."

"I'm not sure I'll have time. I've got another session with the dogs later this afternoon. Where are we?"

"Ever been to New Orleans?" He pronounced it *Nwah-lins*, like a native.

I bristled at his insinuation. "You think I've never been out of Big A, right?" When he didn't answer, I clarified for him. "You think I'm some vet tech who's never been out of Abilene?" His gigawatt smile could have powered runway lighting.

"Welcome to the Big Easy, lady."

* * *

Big Easy, Big Apple, Big D, Big A—you name it, I'd been there. Big, or not so big, they were just towns, and I saw no glamour attached to having been to any of them.

Soon we were on the ground and Nick was opening the door to a rental car and waving me in. I didn't try to disguise my irritation. The moment he seated himself behind the wheel, I began to lecture. "I don't like surprises. You of all people should know I don't have time for this. You were the one who kept telling me how important it was to get those dogs trained. And you never said anything about flying out of town."

He adjusted the rearview mirror and turned the key. "Fasten your seat belt. It's only for a few hours. I promise I'll have you back well before sundown."

He reached over to pat my hand, but I jerked it away. "Sundown comes at nine o'clock this time of year! I need to be back way before then."

Nick navigated the traffic around the airport with ease. "Relax. We're in one of the most romantic, laid-back cities in the world. We'll be back in plenty of time for you to work with the dogs."

I shot him a look of disapproval. "I'm not dressed for this." Then I looked down at my jeans and over at his jeans and realized I didn't have a boot-cut leg to stand on.

When he reached over and placed his hand on my thigh, I thought my jeans would surely ignite. "You look mighty fine to me."

I might as well have stuck my finger in a light socket considering the surge of electricity that shot through me. Inside I moaned, but my sense of self-preservation prevailed. It took all my willpower to pluck that hand off my thigh and return it to its owner.

"Better keep an eye on the road." I took a deep breath and held it till I was even dizzier. "Dangerous. Lots of traffic."

Nick merely smiled, turned on the radio, and hummed along with some song I'd never heard.

I fished in my purse for some lip gloss and smeared it on. "Will you tell me now why we're here?" The road signs indicated we were headed for the French Quarter.

"It's a surprise."

"I told you I don't like surprises."

"I thought women loved surprises."

"In case you haven't noticed, I'm not *like* most women."

This time he didn't look at me, just lifted a brow. "Oh, that I *have* noticed."

A few minutes later, he was pulling into the covered parking garage of a large hotel. When he killed the engine, I reached for the door handle, but Nick stopped me, saying, "Wait here. I'll be right back." Then he was gone.

Other than running after him, which I was not about to do, I had no choice but to wait. Though we were in covered parking, it quickly grew hot inside the car, so I opened the door for some air.

Where had he gone? Surely he wasn't renting a room. I looked at my watch. Five minutes had passed. I hated waiting, especially with nothing to do but stare at a concrete wall. I rummaged in my purse for the paperback I'd been reading, but it wasn't there. Then I re-membered leaving it on the bedside table.

I opened the glove compartment and poked around inside, hoping some previous renter had left something to read. Even a romance novel or a western would be better than nothing. No luck. All I found was the owner's manual, so I pulled it out and read the instructions for adjusting the clock and the recommended tire pressure. I'd worked my way up to the anti-lock brake system when I heard footsteps approaching. I checked my watch. Twenty minutes he'd been gone. I was steaming, and not just from the heat.

I turned around and stared at him as he popped open the trunk and placed a small cardboard box inside.

"Mission accomplished. We're good to go now. You look hot." He didn't mean it in a good way. "I'm sorry. I should have left the key so you could turn on the A/C. But then you might have run off and left me." He winked.

Since I'd promised to be nicer, I bit my tongue, but I tasted blood.

* * *

Considering the royal treatment I'd received from the Espositos, I was expecting a five-star restaurant. I was surprised when we ended up at The Coffee Pot, a hole-in-the-wall consisting of five tables covered with plastic red and white checked tablecloths. We must have hit at a slow time of day because we were the only people in the place. Nick led me to a table by the window.

A stoop-shouldered black man brought us menus. Nick ordered coffee and crawfish étouffée for both of us without bothering to look at the offerings.

"Wait," I said. "Crawfish? As in crawdads?"

"That's a specialty here." Nick handed the man his menu.

I opened mine and quickly glanced through it. "I'll have the beans and rice."

Nick looked to the waiter for help.

"Crawfish étouffée is very popular," the waiter said, nodding.

"They're really good," Nick said. "Like little lobsters."

"I know what they are. When I was twelve, I had one for a pet. His name was Charlie." Next thing I knew he'd be ordering frog legs.

Nick glanced at the waiter and shrugged. "For the lady, beans and rice it is." I'd half expected him to make fun of me, but he didn't.

We people-watched as we waited for our food, which was out in no time. I tried not to look as Nick ate the little Charlies.

Afterwards, he insisted we ride the trolley through a tree-lined area with old two-story homes, watch artists painting and selling their wares around Jackson Square, and walk down Bourbon Street, listening to the music that seeped out onto the street from the bars.

He was right about one thing. New Orleans was a romantic city with someone like him squiring me around. Even the devastation of Hurricane Katrina hadn't broken the city's spirit. I tried to forget about the dogs and what the Espositos would think about my extended absence, but the worry hunkered in the back of my mind.

* * *

By the time we got back to the airport, it was late afternoon. Nick left me in a waiting room of the FBO while he filed a flight plan for our return. FBO or *fixed base operator* provides ground support for private planes, and this one was particularly nice, but I had no desire to explore. All I could think about was getting back to Waco.

I plunked down on a seat and stared out the window. With Nick gone, my old fears returned. Too many times

I'd been taken in by men like him, only to regret it later. Attracted by good looks and sex appeal, I fell hard, but in the end was crushed. These affairs of the heart always followed the same flight pattern. The men I got involved with seemed to have eyes only for me, but when I wasn't around, some other woman took my place. I was always last to know and left feeling like a fool.

I checked my watch again, thinking I should have been back in Waco hours ago. Where was he anyway? Restless, I scouted around for something to do.

I found a row of vending machines and studied the options. All junk food. Besides, I was still full from my beans and rice. I went back to my seat and tried to read one of the complimentary newspapers but couldn't concentrate. No way could we make it back in time for another lesson. I checked my watch again. Nick had been gone over an hour. I nervously jiggled my leg as I chalked up another debit in my mental Nick-ledger.

That's when I saw the man in a business suit, homed in on me and walking swiftly. Our eyes met, his never wavering. I looked away, but when I glanced back, he was still staring straight at me. As he came closer, I noticed the shoulder holster under his jacket.

"You Julie Shields?" His voice was gruff.

"Yes," I gulped.

He flashed a badge. "Federal Marshal Solomon. Come with me."

Chapter Five

When Agent Solomon took me by the elbow and pro-pelled me to a hallway outside the waiting room, my head swiveled like a pole dancer as I looked for Nick, but he was nowhere in sight. "What is it? Has something happened to Nick?" The agent didn't answer, and I had to do some Texas two-stepping to keep up with his long stride. "Where are we going? What's going on? Has he been hurt?" Agent Solomon's face was immobile, and he said nothing.

He steered me through a narrow hallway to a door void of identification. He pulled a key from his pocket and inserted it into the lock. The tumblers clicked. He opened the door and gave me a nudge, but I drew back.

"Hold it. I'm not going one step further till you tell me what this is about. How do I know you're really a federal agent? You didn't exactly give me time to study your credentials."

He tried again to ease me through the open doorway, but I put my weight against the door jamb and planted my feet firmly. I'd seen enough crime shows to know about impersonating officers of the law for sinister purposes. What if Nick was dead? What if "Agent" Solomon was really one of the bad guys and thought I possessed some secret knowledge, which I didn't. At least I didn't think I did.

"Just go in," he said, shoving me through the door.

The windowless room was brightly lit with ceiling-mounted fluorescent bulbs. Except for a rectangular table and some cheap folding chairs, the room was bare.

A long-faced man right out of *X-Files* sat at the table, an open briefcase full of papers beside him.

Agent Solomon jerked his head toward the other man. "This is Agent Hopper."

Hopper wore a black suit with a skinny tie, and from where I stood, I could see black cowboy boots under the table, the toes so pointed they could kill a cockroach in a corner.

"Sit," Hopper said without preamble.

I snorted to clue them in I wasn't happy to be there but obediently walked to the table and sat. I looked around, planning my exit strategy in case they started torturing me, but the door we'd entered seemed to be the only way out.

"You must have me mistaken for someone else," I said, adopting my mother's haughty tone.

"You're Julie Shields, right?"

I raised my chin. "Yes, I am. But I haven't done any-thing wrong." As soon as the words were out of my mouth, I realized I sounded like a character in a TV show, the kind who always talks too much, then wishes she'd asked for a lawyer first.

Agent Solomon pulled a tape recorder from his pocket and clicked a button. "What's your business in New Orleans?"

I eyeballed the red light on the tape recorder and wondered if he had the right to record me. I'd always hated hearing my voice on tape, afraid I sounded like Lady Bird Johnson, pure Texan. Much as I wanted to say something flip—like I'd come early for Mardi Gras—I decided to tell the truth. "I flew in...with a pilot." I tried really hard not to say *pah-lit*. If my mother could have heard me, she'd have been proud she spent all that money on elocution lessons.

The look the two men exchanged made it pretty clear they thought I was an idiot.

"I mean, I flew in with a pilot who works for some people in Waco. I didn't even know where we were going."

"Are you saying you were taken against your will?" Hopper asked.

"Yes. I mean, no. What I mean is, I didn't know we were coming here, to New Orleans. I thought we were just going for a ride...a flight."

"Where did you go after you got here?" Solomon asked, his face blank. Good thing we weren't playing Texas Hold'em. He'd have the edge.

"I don't know...I mean, Nick, the pilot, rented a car, and we went to the French Quarter."

"Did you make any stops along the way?" Hopper asked. His stern look dared me not to lie.

The air in the room was stifling, thick with the nauseating, stale smell of cigarette smoke. My beans and rice rumbled. "Only one. Would you tell me what this is all about?"

Solomon's eyes looked like they could shoot bullets. "Where did you stop?"

"I don't know. Some hotel. I didn't notice the name. What difference does it make? I sat in the car the parking garage." I could tell from their sad-sack faces they didn't believe me. Hopper picked up a ballpoint pen and rolled it between his palms. Late for his smoke break, judging from his yellowed fingernails.

"And what did you do while you waited in the parking garage?" Hopper stretched out his long legs under the table, catching me in the shin with a pointy toe.

"Ouch," I yelled and jumped up. Solomon's hand started for his gun.

My hands shot up in surrender and I froze, while a rivulet of sweat began a slow journey down my side.

"Sorry," Hopper said, glancing at Solomon and pulling his legs back.

I lowered my arms and sat back down, turning my legs away from Hopper's lethal footwear. "What was the question again?"

"What did you do in the parking garage?" Hopper repeated.

"Nothing. I, uh...I read the owner's manual."

Solomon jerked his head toward me like a turkey gobbler. "Excuse me?"

"To the car. You know, the owner's manual. When Nick left, I didn't have anything else to do."

"And what was Mr. *Worthington* doing while you were 'reading the owner's manual'?" Solomon asked.

An uneasy feeling washed over me. I hadn't told them Nick's last name. I reached back to rub the tension out of my neck, moving slowly this time, so as not to set off Agent Solomon's trigger-happy hand. "Mr. *Worthington* didn't tell me, and I didn't ask."

Agent Solomon took a deep breath, blew it out, and rolled his eyes toward Hopper. "I find that hard to believe, Ms. Shields."

I shrugged in an attempt to look nonchalant. "Believe what you want. It's true."

"How well do you know Nick Worthington?" Hopper asked.

Why were they asking about Nick? And where was he anyway? "I met him a few days ago when he flew me to Waco. Why all the questions? What's going on?"

Hopper peered up at me under dark brows in dire need of a trim. "Let us ask the questions."

That did it. I refused to be treated like a criminal, badge or no badge. "Excuse me, but don't I have some rights, like Miranda or *habeas corpus* or something?"

Hopper looked at Solomon, who nodded. Hopper spoke. "I work out of the Dallas office for ICE, that's U.S. Immigration and Customs Enforcement. We're the largest investigative branch of the Homeland Security Department. We protect the borders by targeting people, money, and materiel that support terrorist and criminal activities."

I wondered if I should be taking notes for a test later on.

Hopper continued. "We got a lead on a plane, like the one you flew in on."

I frowned. "What kind of lead?"

All at once the metaphorical light bulb over my head flashed on. Nick must be involved in some kind of criminal activity. Drugs? Illegal aliens? Or was it possible Nick was a terrorist? My instincts told me he was dangerous, but not *that* kind of dangerous. But what about the package he'd picked up at the hotel? Could it be drugs? Maybe he'd taken me along to make it look innocent, a couple taking in the sights of New Orleans. Could the Espositos be using him without his knowledge? Or maybe he was using the Espositos.

"We've got people searching the plane. So if there's anything you want to tell us, now is the time," Hopper said. He tugged his tie in a vain attempt to loosen it. I wanted to grab it, pull it tight, and growl in his face I was innocent.

Instead I leaned forward and tapped my finger on the table in time to my words. "*I. Don't. Do. Drugs.*"

I plopped my purse in front of Hopper with a loud clunk. "Here. Search it." When he just sat there staring at me, I reached over and turned it upside down, dumping the contents on the table. A box of breath mints flew out and landed in Hopper's lap, causing him to jerk upright as he grabbed at them. Loose change rolled onto the floor, and dog biscuit crumbs spilled onto the table. Hopper eyed them suspiciously. I half expected him to lick his finger, touch it to the crumbs, and do a taste test for cocaine.

I stood up and pulled out the pockets of my jeans. "See, nothing here." More crumbs fell to the floor.

"Take it easy, lady," Hopper said.

"Take it easy? You bring me in here and threaten me and then tell me to take it easy? I demand...I demand a lawyer!"

If it worked on TV, maybe it would work here. Demand a lawyer and they had to arrest you or let you go.

"We haven't threatened you, Ms. Shields. You don't need a lawyer. Yet. Now calm down, would you?" Hopper pulled out a handkerchief and blew his nose with a loud honk. Then he stood up, towering over me. I took it as an attempt at intimidation, so I stood up too. Since I barely came to his shoulders, I felt empowered when he sat back down and sighed. I gathered the contents of my purse and crammed everything back in. Then I sat down, my back straight. "You can't hold me here. I want to make a phone call."

"You sit tight, Ms. Shields," Solomon said. "We aren't accusing you of anything."

Just then, the door burst open, and a younger man, minus the scowl, poked his head into the room, rubbed his eyes, and motioned the men over.

Solomon and Hopper stood. I jumped to my feet, grabbed my purse, and backed away from them. They weren't going to take me without a fight. I waited while the two older men conferred with the younger man outside. Finally, Solomon walked back to where I stood. I held my purse in front of me for protection.

"You're free to go," he said.

"What do you mean, I'm free to go?"

"Just what I said. You're free to go."

"Don't I get an explanation?"

"Nothing to explain. You wanted to go. Now go."

He looked at Hopper. "Some days, you know..." Then he turned back to me and hitched up his pants. "Ms. Shields, did anyone ever tell you that you have a vivid imagination?"

"Mr. Solomon, did anyone ever tell you that you have a big gun and a badge? That's kind of frightening to a person who's never even had a parking ticket!"

He rolled his eyes at Hopper, opened the door, and motioned me through.

"You wait till my father hears about this," I said, trying to sound important.

He didn't have to know my father had been dead for two years.

* * *

At the end of the narrow hallway, Nick leaned against the wall. When he saw me, he straightened his runner's body and gave me a small wave, his eyes apologetic. I walked past him without saying a word, leaving him to trail along behind.

"Julie, wait a minute. I'm so sorry. This is all a mistake."

"Some mistake." I kept walking, though I had no idea where I was headed. "I'm interrogated about what I'm doing in New Orleans and told they've got a *lead* on your illegal activities, and you call it a mistake?"

He reached for my arm, but I jerked away and picked up my pace. I was so angry, all I could think of was getting away from him, but I knew better than to break into a sprint. After my encounter with the feds, I wasn't eager to have them after me again.

"Julie, please," Nick pleaded, as he fell back and I plunged forward. A feeling of power and freedom surged through me, a vindication for his making me wait at the hotel, for having the kind of eyes that always hurt me, and for his role in the Solomon and Hopper charade. My instincts had been right from the start. The Nick Worthingtons of the world were bad news.

Give me Noche and Blanco any day. They might be unruly, but they weren't going to get me in trouble or break my heart. I'd been wrong to let Nick charm me. I should have stayed in Waco where I belonged. It was late now and past time for the dogs' next training session. I had only limited time to teach them, and here I was in New Orleans wasting precious hours. I had a job to do, a marriage to save. But more important, the future of Noche and Blanco was at stake.

As I turned a corner, I saw a women's restroom, ducked inside, and took my time. After fifteen minutes or so, I peeked out. Nick was nowhere in sight. I crept down another hallway, found an unlocked conference room, and eased inside. I stood in the darkness a few moments to calm my racing heart before feeling my way further into the room. When my eyes grew accustomed to the dark, I spotted a padded swivel chair and rolled it next to the plate glass window at the end of the room. I eased into the chair, then leaned over and pressed my cheek against the cool, damp glass.

That's when I saw it. While I'd been in the windowless room with Hopper and Solomon, fog had enveloped the airport, suffocating all activity. The entire airport was grounded.

I stared into the grayness as if it held the answer to my dilemma. My choices were limited. I could go back to the waiting room where Nick had left me earlier, hope the fog would lift, and swallow my pride by letting him fly me back to Waco. That is, if he was even waiting for me. Or I could rent a car and drive back, but Waco was over four hundred miles away. Either way I looked at it, I was screwed.

Then, as if sent by the god of Java, the comforting aroma of coffee wafted through the air, summoning me like one of the Pied Piper's rats. I lifted my face. My nose twitched. I followed. I soon found myself in the refreshment commissary.

A kindly-looking, cocoa-colored man standing next to the counter welcomed me with a smile, providing a stark contrast to the pasty-faced men I'd just escaped.

"Coffee?" he asked.

"Please."

"You look like you could use a cup. *Nwahlins* not treatin' you good?"

"New Orleans is treating me fine." I rolled my aching shoulders. "It's everything else that's treating me bad."

"Go on now. You too pretty a lady to let the bad stuff get you low feelin'. I know we all got our crosses to bear. Yes, ma'am. Bet you got a loved one waiting for you at home and can't get back to him."

His words hit me hard. I'd given scant thought to little Philip in the past few days. And here I was, even farther away, with a man suspected of who knows what, and me not even knowing how I was going to get out of New Orleans.

The man filled a Styrofoam cup with steaming coffee and handed it to me.

"Thank you," I said, plucking a handful of creamer containers from a bowl of ice and heading for a dark corner table. I bent my head over the coffee and inhaled the rich aroma, an elixir for my sinking spirits. Then I poured in three containers of Coffee-mate, watching the creamy liquid swirl into the coffee's darkness, turning the contents a rich, soothing mocha. I took a sip of the strong brew, leaned back, closed my eyes, and drew a breath of relief.

The respite was short lived.

"Julie! What the hell do you think you're doing?"

I didn't have to open my eyes. I recognized the voice.

* * *

Nick was on his second cup before either of us spoke again. We'd sat drinking and staring at each other, a duel to see who would break the silence first.

Finally, I could stand it no longer. "Okay, tell me your story."

"There's no story to tell." A muscle pulsed in his clenched jaw.

I had to admit I took pleasure in knowing I could provoke him.

"Oh, come on. You really think I believe the federal government is going to haul me in and question me because of a *lead*? They must have had a better reason than that. What aren't you telling me?"

He took a deep breath and slowly let it out though his nostrils, his lips pressed together.

I took a sip of my third cup of coffee, keeping my eyes riveted to his.

"Like I said. It was a mistake. Wrong plane. Wrong guy. They got a lead on a Seneca V carrying drug money, but it wasn't mine. Do you think they'd have let me go if I was guilty?"

"Why did you stop at that hotel? What was so important you left me sitting in a hot car for twenty minutes?"

"You were counting?"

I said nothing but looked daggers at him.

He broke eye contact and stared into his cup. "Sorry about that. I didn't expect it to take so long. Something I needed to pick up. It's personal."

"Ah...personal," I said, my voice laced with sarcasm.

"What is this, the third degree? Fine. You don't have to believe me. Let's get out of here and find a place to stay. First thing tomorrow, I'll take you back to Waco, and you won't have to worry about associating with a *drug* dealer again." He reached for my arm, then changed his mind. "Come on. There won't be any available rooms near the airport in this weather, but I know a hotel not too far from here where we can spend the night."

Did the man think I was that naïve? "I'm not going anywhere." I folded my arms across my chest.

His eyes turned steely gray like the fog. "Don't be an idiot. You think you're going to stay in this airport all night?"

I tilted my head down and looked up at him with lifted brows. "That's exactly what I plan to do. You go on." I fluttered my fingers at him dismissively. "When the weather clears up, I'll be in the waiting room."

He gave a wry laugh. "The weather isn't going to clear up tonight. There's no way we'll get out of here before tomorrow morning. So we might as well get a good night's rest...in a bed."

The mention of the word *bed* renewed my resolve to stay put. "No thanks. You go ahead."

I picked up my purse and strode off, not looking back. This time Nick didn't try to stop me or follow. I found my way back to the empty conference room.

I wondered what the Espositos were thinking. Surely Nick had called them. Then I realized I couldn't trust Nick to do anything. Times like these I almost wished I had a cell phone. Almost. So far I'd resisted my mother's and sister's attempts to get me connected to the new century. Let my mother call my sister five times a day, not me.

I fumbled around in the darkness, found a phone, and managed to punch enough buttons to get an outside operator so I could charge a call to my home number. I was relieved when the Espositos' answering machine picked up. I left a short message explaining our situation and hoped they'd understand this fiasco was all Nick's doing.

By now, the view outside the window had faded into nothingness. No runway or tower lights were visible in the heavy darkness that had settled over us. I found a spot in the corner, half concealed by a potted palm. Curling into a fetal position, I imagined I was home in my own bed with Philip next to me. Using my purse for a pillow, I closed my eyes and tried to sleep, but adrenaline from the encounter with Solomon and Hopper and the caffeine from the coffee had me wired. At some point I finally drifted off into an exhausted, dream-filled state of unconsciousness.

The next thing I knew, someone was shining a light in my eyes. I squeezed them tighter and pulled the blanket over my head, thinking how warm Philip felt behind me. Spooning. I rolled over and wrapped my arms around him, snuggling into his familiar warmth. Arms enfolded me and pulled me closer. The lips nuzzling my neck felt as if they belonged there, and the scent of shampoo and bristly skin against my face reminded me the sea, white capped and salty.

But I wasn't home. And the body against mine certainly wasn't Philip's. It took a few seconds for me to wake up and remember where I was, namely, on the floor in a conference room of an FBO at the Louis Armstrong New Orleans International Airport. Someone had covered me with a blanket in the night, and the light was a streak of sunlight from the window announcing a new dawn. The someone I was pressed against was Nick. A surge of longing made me want to nestle closer to his hard male body.

Being a born-again virgin wasn't as easy as I'd thought when I made the vow. I'd like to have a talk with whoever thought up that idea. I summoned all my strength and twisted away, trying to sit up, but my back was kinked. I rubbed my gritty eyes and tried to swallow. My mouth was as dry as a West Texas drought.

Nick gave me a slow, lazy grin and tried to pull me back against him. The man was incorrigible. Any other man, a *normal* man, would have given up by now.

"Good morning, Sunshine," he said.

Even with a day's worth of stubble, he looked good. I fought the urge to reach up and touch his face. Then I remembered yesterday's events, and the old rage returned. I sat upright, holding my head in my hands and groaned with regret. Finally, I managed to stand, slowly and stiffly, and brushed off my clothes, attempting to regain my composure.

"Have you been here all night?" I croaked through dry lips. "I thought you were going to a hotel?"

"I said *we* would go to a hotel, but you shot down that idea."

"You could have gone by yourself."

"And leave you here alone? Not hardly."

"I can take care of myself."

"I wasn't going to take that chance. Besides, you needed a blanket, so I got one from the plane."

My body was still throbbing from Nick's sleepy embrace, and I needed a distraction. I reached down, picked up the blanket, and began folding it. "I suppose I should thank you."

His eyes glinted with amusement. "Oh, I think you already have."

My face on fire, I shoved the blanket at him. "What did the Espositos say when you told them we were fogged in?"

"Berto wasn't there, so I talked to Carmen. She was *not* happy the dogs missed their afternoon session. I tried to explain it was my fault."

So he *had* called. "Tried?"

"She wasn't in the mood to listen. She just kept going on about Berto's ultimatum."

"Great. Now I'm on her bad side again. If we're going to get those dogs trained, she's got to trust me, and this isn't going to help."

* * *

In the air once more, I flipped through the newspaper I'd picked up the day before and tried to read but couldn't focus. "What's the real story on those federal guys?"

A muscle in Nick's jaw twitched. "I *told* you. Wrong plane. With all the drug trafficking in and out of Mexico, these guys have to follow up on any information they get. A case of mistaken identity. These things happen."

I thought again about the package he'd picked up at the hotel in New Orleans. He'd taken it out of the trunk when we got back to the airport. And he'd taken it with him when he left me to ready the plane for our return flight. Where was it now? What was in it?

"What about the package?" I asked. If he was really innocent, he shouldn't mind telling me.

He let out a tired laugh. "Julie, give me a break. You've been watching too many crime shows. You think it was drugs? Sorry to disappoint you. Just something Carmen asked me to pick up." He gave me a pointed look and frowned. "What kind of guys are you used to hanging around with anyway?"

"Not the kind who get themselves interrogated by federal marshals and drug enforcement agents." I felt grubby and grouchy. I ran my hands through my flattened hair trying to fluff it up.

"Let me as *you* some questions. What about Philip?"

Philip? Then I remembered he thought Philip was my boyfriend. "What *about* Philip? You mean does Philip use drugs? No, he does not."

"No, I mean what does your perfect Philip do?"

Was that a hint of jealousy in his voice? Okay, he'd asked for it, so I laid it on thick. "For one thing, he doesn't have run-ins with the law. He's...well he's very sweet...and handsome. Blond hair, brown eyes. He's intelligent, educated, and he loves me."

Nick laughed. "I mean, what does he do for a living?"

"Oh, he's...he's got a private income." I knew I was making Philip sound like a milquetoast, but I wasn't going to lie.

"You mean he's out of work."

"He doesn't have to work."

"Ah, one of the indolent rich."

"Think what you want. He's good for me, and he loves me for myself, not—" I broke off before I said too much. The less of my background Nick knew the better.

We didn't talk much after that. At my insistence we hadn't taken time to eat before we left New Orleans, and both our stomachs were growling so loud you could hear them over the roar of the plane's engines. That and sleep deprivation had us both on edge.

By the time Nick pulled the BMW into the circular driveway at Casa del Lago, his brown shirt could have served as body double for a shar-pei, and I still had a crease in my face from using my purse as a pillow. The overpriced toothbrush kit I'd bought from a vending machine and my efforts at cleaning up in the FBO bathroom left a lot to be desired. All I could think about was food, shower, and sleep.

Nick left the engine running. "I'm going to drop you off here. I've got some business I need to take care of in town."

"You're going to dump me out and leave me to face Carmen alone?" I made no move to get out. "You *will* be back to explain to her what happened, won't you?"

"I've already explained it all on the phone. Besides, you told me you could take care of yourself, remember?" He gave me a mock salute.

I shot him a searing look, grabbed my purse, and yanked open the door. "Fine. Thanks for everything."

He drove off without looking back. I stood in the driveway, watching the BMW fade into the distance. The fragrant morning air was filled with the scent of roses and freshly mown grass. I breathed deeply. Lucky for me, it was too early for Carmen to be up, so I headed for my apartment, thankful I didn't have to face her just yet.

I was almost to the pool when I heard someone running behind me, breathing heavily. The feds! The feds had followed us to Waco and were after me again. I spun around, ready to declare my innocence one more time. To point the finger at Nick.

"Julie! Wait!" I wasn't sure whether to be relieved or not when I saw Berto. But this was not the debonair Berto I'd met before. This Berto's hair stuck out in all directions, and his clothes were rumpled like mine, as if he'd slept in them. And he claimed the *dogs* were ruining his sex life?

"We have a problem," he said.

My mouth grew drier, and a dull ache began to pulse in the top of my head.

"Come with me," he commanded.

Chapter Six

Carmen stood on the patio, her hair loose, a few dark wisps clinging to her tear-stained face. Her long white cotton nightgown was streaked with dirt. Her tiny feet, bare.

"Noche! Come, Noche!" she cried, her eyes frantic.

"Get inside," Berto said, teeth clenched.

Instead, Carmen grabbed his arm, her face contorted with grief. He brushed her off, opened the back door, and herded us inside. Without the scowl, he would have made a great border collie.

Carmen turned to me. "Julie, you've got to help."

Berto snorted. "She was supposed to be helping you yesterday. You expect her to help you *now*?" He shot me a look that made me want to hunker down and whimper.

"I'm sorry," I said. "Nick can explain."

"Never mind that," Carmen wailed. "Noche is gone!"

"What do you mean, *gone*?" I searched their faces for some explanation.

Carmen slumped to the floor. "Berto put him out. And now he's gone."

Berto reached down and pulled her to her feet. "Come on, Carmen. Enough of the drama queen routine." She hung over his arm like a drunk on a dance floor.

"Is it true?" I asked him.

He ran a hand through his hair, while trying to extricate himself from Carmen. "I've put him out before, and he never goes far. The property is partially fenced. But it's a big area."

Carmen moaned. "He's been gone over an hour, and this time is different. You didn't just put him out. You yelled, *Out! Out!"* She pushed away from Berto, grabbed my arm, and pointed a quivering finger at him. "He talked to Noche like he was...like he was...a *dog*!" She leaned against me and began to sob.

I could see I would have to be the voice of reason. I silently cursed Nick for not being here to help me deal with this crisis. Berto had a point. If I'd been here where I was supposed to be, maybe none of this would have happened. Though Nick couldn't have controlled the fog, it was his fault we'd ended up stranded in New Orleans. But right now, more important issues were at stake.

I hugged Carmen and frowned at Berto. "Look, let's find Noche, and then you can fire me if you want. The longer he's gone, the less likely our chances of finding him." I almost added *alive.* "You say he's been gone an hour?"

Berto and Carmen exchanged glances; Berto checked his watch. "Maybe a little longer."

"The first twenty-four hours are crucial." I'd picked up this bit of trivia from a TV program about missing persons.

Carmen pulled away from me. "Twenty-four hours? We have to find him *now*!" She squinched her eyes and wrinkled her nose as if in pain. Then, suddenly, she straightened her back and opened her eyes wide. "I know! We can let Blanco out. *She* can find him."

"Not a good idea. Then you might end up with two missing dogs. Unless you put her on a leash." I looked up at Berto. "Where does Noche usually go when you let him out?"

"Just around here. Close to the house. Or out there by the trees." Berto swept his arm out toward the lake. "He's never out for long. And never out of my sight."

"Well, he's out of your sight now!" Carmen shouted. "And all because you...you..."

"I'm going to start looking," I said. "Let's hope he knows me well enough by now he'll come if I call." I knew this was expecting a lot, since we had yet to master the recall command, but Noche did come to Carmen most of the time. I grabbed her arms, forcing her to look at me. "Tell Ramón to start looking. Get everyone else in the house to search. Call the neighbors if you know them. Call animal control, give them a description, and ask if they've picked him up." I unclipped the shoulder strap from my purse. "I can use this as a leash if I find him." I dropped my purse to the ground. "If we don't find him in the next hour, we'll call the Humane Society, all the vets in town, post signs, and run an ad in the newspaper offering a reward. Don't worry. We *will* find him."

With that, I trotted off toward the area where we'd trained the day before. I tried to think like a dog. What would I do if my master yelled at me and told me to get out? Where would I go? How long would I even remember I'd been yelled at? Dogs lived in the present. They usually ran if someone or something chased them or they found something to chase. They sniffed, they peed, they rooted around looking for something nasty smelling to roll in. But in the course of all the peeing and rooting, they wandered. I just hoped Noche hadn't run.

"Noche!" I called, then stopped to listen. After being around Carmen, I halfway expected him to answer back. She anthropomorphized her dogs more than I did Philip. I slowed to a fast walk, keeping my eyes on the ground in case Noche was trapped or unconscious. In the distance, I could hear Carmen and Berto calling his name.

At one point, I crossed paths with Ramón. He shook his head when he saw me and said, "No find." We moved on in separate directions.

Maybe Noche had headed for the swimming pool or the lake. Poodles were originally hunting dogs, bred to retrieve waterfowl, not foo-foo French dogs with weird hairdos and shaved body parts. Poodle was actually a derivative of the German word for puddle, *pudel*. I crossed my fingers, hoping if Noche headed for water, he'd remember his German roots and stay afloat.

"Noche!" I called. "Come, Noche!" I stopped to listen, but all I heard were birds twittering. A squirrel clung to the side of a tree, swishing his bushy tail and eyeing me suspiciously.

I made a large arc and headed toward the lake to check the shoreline, just in case. As I neared the guest-house from the lake side, I realized it was even larger than I'd initially thought. Because of the dense foliage and trees, most of what I'd seen had been confined to the area near my front door. But there was more. Much more. In fact, the guesthouse was like an L-shaped duplex grandioso—the other half, an entire wing, a mirror image of my own. I walked the length of it, won-dering why the Espositos had built two large adjoining houses by the lake when they already had a palatial mansion on top of the hill. I mentally doubled the square footage of my portion and calculated the entire guest-house must consist of almost six thousand square feet of living space. Just call me Peeping Julie, because I crept toward a window on the other side and peered through a gap in the drapes, but it was too dark inside to see anything. I began walking the perimeter, looking for Noche.

"Noche," I called, then waited. The lake was gray and still as death. I shuddered, thinking about Noche trapped beneath the surface, tangled in debris. Though all dogs, with the exception of basset hounds, were natural swimmers, they *could* drown. What if Noche had been bitten by a water moccasin!

As I rounded the end of the building, I noticed a dark shape resembling a lawn and leaf bag on my front porch. Inching closer, I realized it was Noche, and he was very still. I imagined him hurt, crawling onto my porch for shelter. Dying alone. Tears pricked my eyes at the thought of it.

"Noche?" I said tentatively. His head popped up, his dark eyes met mine, and he began to wag a very wet tail. I rushed to him and wrapped my arms around him and squeezed, not caring about the mud or wet leaves that clung to his fur. "Noche! *Good* boy! *Good* boy! You don't know how happy I am to see you!"

Judging from his coat, he'd taken an early morning swim in the lake. His paws were caked with mud, and his coat curled in tiny corkscrews. Unfluffed, he closely resembled a giant Chihuahua.

"*Good* boy," I told him over and over, wanting him to know if he ever got loose again he could come to my door. He stood up and shook himself, spraying water and mud and muck and leaves. I didn't care. "*Good* boy." Because I was praising him, he looked expectantly at my right hand, which in Noche's mind was his personal treat dispenser.

"Sorry, boy. I left my purse with the treats back at the big house."

Not willing to take the chance he might opt for another swim, I hooked my purse strap to his collar and led him inside, too relieved to care about the mess he'd make. I rewarded him with half a fat-free wiener. He gulped it down whole, then licked my hand.

After drying him off the best I could with one of Carmen's designer towels, I mustered my courage to face the Espositos again. Even though I'd found their dog—or he'd found me—I doubted my next encounter with them would be pleasant. I felt stuck in the middle of *The War of the Roses*.

* * *

"I've got him! I found him!" I called as I neared the back of the big house, Noche trotting beside me.

The door burst open and Carmen ran out and fell to the ground, wrapping her arms around Noche's neck. She covered his wet face with kisses as if they were two reunited lovers, while Berto stood on the back patio and watched, his eyes expressionless.

"He's back. Crisis over," he said in a cavalier tone.

Carmen stiffened, and her dark eyes turned fiery. "How can you be so calm about it? Noche could have died, and all you can say is *crisis over*?"

Berto's lips tightened. "It's more proof the dogs are out of control. And *you*"—he pointed at me—"were supposed to train them."

His use of past tense and the pointing put me on the defensive. I took a deep breath, trying to hold back my anger but not succeeding. "I *am* training them, but it doesn't happen overnight. How could I have known Nick was taking me to New Orleans? He told me it would be a short flight. Then those federal agents cornered me, and then the fog rolled in. Talk to Nick. He can explain everything."

Berto blanched at the mention of federal agents. "I think you're right. It sounds as if I do need to talk to Nick."

I thought about the package Nick had picked up at the hotel. Was it really for Carmen? Could it be for Berto? But if it had been drugs, wouldn't the ICE men have found it?

"Tell Julie what happened this morning," she told Berto. "Maybe she can help."

She turned to me, her eyes imploring. "Tell Berto you can help, please."

"I'm already doing everything I can. But I need more time. It's barely been a week."

Berto's dark brows drew together. "That means you have a little more than three weeks left."

I looked at him, my face impassive, my tone business-like. "What happened this morning? Why did you yell at Noche and put him outside?"

Minutes before, he'd been angry with me. Now he looked embarrassed. He fidgeted, shifting from one foot to the other.

"Tell her, Berto," Carmen said flatly.

He looked at Carmen, then at me. Without warning, he deflated like a blow-up toy, his swagger gone. "The dogs were in the bedroom with us *as usual.* Carmen read somewhere that the pack stays together at night, so the dogs sleep on the bed with us. I'm a big guy, and believe me, it gets pretty crowded with a wife and two poodles, even in a king-sized bed. Anyway, this morning..." He hesitated, pulled on his ear, and looked at Carmen as if asking permission to stop.

"Tell her," she said. "It wasn't as bad as you made it seem."

Berto took a deep breath and avoided eye contact. "Carmen and I were...we were...we were *trying* to make love when Noche...he tried—"

"I think I get the picture," I said. I hadn't forgotten Noche *hugging* Carmen. This morning, Noche evidently had a *ménage* in mind, but not a *ménage à trois.*

"He *growled* at me," Berto said, color rising to his cheeks.

Uh-oh. Noche wanted Carmen all for himself.

I held up a hand for Berto to stop. "Let me try to explain it from Noche's point of view. As I've told Carmen, Noche is now a teenager, with the same urges as most teenage boys."

"Yes, Berto, try to think back," Carmen said.

I gave her a sharp glance, hoping she'd take the hint and hush. If she wasn't careful, Berto would storm out, and I'd be in the doghouse for sure. I began again. "I've tried to explain this to Carmen. You see, in Noche's eyes—I don't know a delicate way to put this—but...well, in *his* eyes, Carmen is his woman."

Berto's face turned a lighter shade of tan. "His *woman?*"

"I know it sounds a little perverse, but Noche doesn't know he's a dog. He has run of the house; he's sleeping in your bed. In Noche's eyes, *you're* the usurper. His competition. Think about it. You're gone most of the time. When you *are* here, Noche thinks *you're* the one moving in on *his* territory."

I had a feeling if it had been another man in the picture, Berto would have known how to deal with it. Instead, he'd almost been cuckolded by a dog.

Berto slumped into one of the patio chairs and put his head in his hands, trying to digest the information. Finally, he raised his head, a look of amazement on his face. "My honor has been compromised."

He looked serious. I hoped he didn't have a gun.

"May I make a suggestion?" Maybe I could head him off at the pass.

Berto's eyes filled with hope. "Yes, we need to get rid of him. Both of them. You agree with me now, don't you?"

"Both of us!" Carmen screeched. "Get rid of *both* of us!"

"Not *you*," he said to Carmen. "I meant both *dogs*."

"Noooooooo!" Carmen howled.

I closed my eyes and rubbed my forehead, stalling, because I doubted they'd accept my recommendations willingly. "There's a better solution."

Berto looked doubtful. "What could be better?"

I looked him directly in the eye, and my voice didn't waver. "First of all, you need to keep the dogs off the bed and out of the bedroom. Allowing them to sleep with you makes them think they're your equals. It won't hurt them to spend the night in another room. They have each other for company. Or you can crate them in the bedroom."

Carmen switched to her whiny voice. "But they've always slept with us."

How could I make her understand? I took a deep breath and massaged the back of my neck. I needed sleep. I needed food. I needed a shower. "Sleeping with them is a big part of your problem." I paused, wondering how they'd take my next suggestion. I lowered my voice a notch. "There's something else you should seriously consider."

Carmen and Berto tilted their heads.

"Neutering," I said.

Carmen, who still sat on the floor consoling Noche, or vice versa, looked up, her eyes wary. "Noooo," she cried. "You mean cut off his...cut off his *bobbit?*"

I suppressed a smile. "No, no," I said. "That stays intact. It's only the testicles that are removed."

"His testicles!" Berto boomed with such force I jumped back. "No way!"

I'm working for crazy people. One minute he's ready to get rid of Noche, and now he's outraged at the thought of neutering him? Men.

A vein on Berto's temple throbbed. "Take away his manhood?"

Berto acted downright bi-polar when it came to the dogs.

"But...he's a *dog*," I said meekly. "It's done all the time. He'd be given anesthesia, and he wouldn't feel a thing. He'll forget he even had them."

Berto looked at me with skepticism and squirmed. Unconsciously, he put a hand in his pocket and checked his own boys to make sure they hadn't strayed.

I leaned forward and spoke intensely. "Neutering should keep him from getting...so excited. There's also less chance of cancer. And if you don't have him neutered, you're going to end up with little parti-poodles on your hands."

"Party poodles?" Carmen asked.

"*Parti*, as in parti-colored, black and white puppies. If Noche and Blanco mate, their offspring could be of mixed colors. Some might be black, some white, some even silver, but some could be like Oreos, black and white."

"Oreos? Like the cookie?" Carmen asked.

"Blanco's skin is pink and some of her toenails are white and others black. That's a sign she may carry the parti gene. That would disqualify the pups from ever showing. You'd have to sell them as pet quality. But I'm digressing."

Berto removed his hand from his pocket and adjusted his pants, obviously still fixated on the concept of neutering. "You mean castrate him, right?"

"It would solve part of your problem. It should have been done sooner, when he was younger. Do it early enough, and it reduces their tendency to hike."

"Hike?" Berto asked.

"His leg. Most dogs who are neutered early, squat instead of hike their leg to pee."

Berto's eyes grew large. "Squat! Like a girl?"

I was making things worse.

Berto winced. "You're a woman. You don't understand men."

He was right about that. I chewed on a ragged fingernail. How could I get through to him? "You do have another option...a kind of reconstruction, I guess you'd call it."

Carmen looked interested, but the neutering discussion seemed to have drained Berto of his strength. "What do you mean?" she asked.

"Neuticles."

Noche cocked one ear. Carmen and Berto furrowed their brows. "Neuticles?" they said in unison.

"Neuticles," I repeated.

Behind me, a deep voice echoed. "Neuticles?"

I turned to face Nick, determined not to lose my professional demeanor, but my eyes surely gave me away. I softened when I looked into his comforting, smiling face, but I willed myself to concentrate on Neuticles instead. "Neuticles are...well, they're artificial testes for dogs. Implants. You can't even tell the difference. They have the same weight and feel and shape—everything."

Berto scowled. "I'll bet *Noche* could tell the difference."

I continued my mini-lecture. "They come in different sizes, from petite to large. They're made out of silicone or polypropylene. And you can get them in different shapes. You can even have them custom made if your dog has an extra-proportional testicle size." I glanced over at Noche. "He'd probably take a medium or large."

"Artificial plastic balls for dogs?" Nick was bent double with laughter. Carmen and Berto looked totally perplexed.

"Laugh all you want," I said. "They've been around since the early '90s. They're great for pet owners who are neuter-hesitant. And they're relatively inexpensive. Anywhere from seventy-five to four hundred dollars, depending on what kind you buy. Cats, horses, even bulls can be implanted with them."

"Wait, wait...I have an idea," Carmen said. "Couldn't he just have one of those things Berto had instead?"

Oops. I had the feeling Berto wasn't going to like what was coming.

I was right. Berto glared at her and snarled, "*Carmen.*" He'd have slapped a muzzle on her if he'd had one.

Carmen ignored him. "They didn't have to remove Berto's." She smiled innocently. "You know, a bastectomy."

Berto crossed his legs awkwardly, a pained look contorting his face.

I sucked in my cheeks to keep from laughing. "Dogs *can* have vasectomies, but it's not normally done. For one thing, it doesn't prevent aggressive behavior. So if you want Noche to calm down and be less likely to mount, then neutering is the best solution. According to research, after thirty days or so, the testosterone will leave his system, and he'll quit marking his territory and be less likely to roam, like he did today." *Unless Berto chases him out of the house again.*

Nick gulped between guffaws. "How long does it take...to attach them?"

Difficult as it was, I kept a straight face. "It takes only two to three minutes. Neuticles will help his self-esteem," I said, looking directly at Berto.

Noche, missing the attention, chose that moment to bark, startling all of us. When we turned to look at him, he whined and buried his head in Carmen's lap. It didn't help my case.

Carmen squeezed Noche to her, trying to soothe him with a sing-songy voice. "*Mijo.* My poor Noche. My *pobre* lost Noche."

When Nick saw the look of despair on my face, he quit laughing, and his voice took on a serious tone. "You look tired."

"No kidding. Sleeping on the floor at an airport isn't exactly the same as Hotel ZaZa in Dallas."

"You did have a choice."

"Huh," I muttered. But I could have licked his hand for what he said next.

"Hey, everybody, why don't we call it a morning? Noche is safe, Julie and I are back, so let's all get some rest. This afternoon, Julie can get on with the training. Berto, how about a cup of coffee? I'll tell you all about New Orleans."

No one protested. We were too exhausted.

With that, the men moved into the house, unless you counted Noche, who'd be less "man" before long if I had any say in the matter. I gave Carmen a weak goodbye wave and headed back to my rooms, but as I started down the path, I had second thoughts. I was curious about the other apartment. What was it for? Though it was none of my business, I turned back. Carmen's dark head still rested against Noche's dirty black one. "Say, Carmen. Can I ask you a question?"

She looked up, her eyes weary. That's when I realized how much was at stake—her marriage, these dogs' lives, and life as Carmen knew it. "Okay," she responded listlessly.

"The guesthouse. I didn't know until this morning how big it really is. I've heard water running on the other side. Is Ramón working there?"

She looked puzzled and shook her head. "No, what made you think that?"

"The singing. Someone was singing in Spanish on the other side of my bathroom wall."

Her lips curved up in the hint of a smile. "That would be Nick," she said, her eyes twinkling. "I thought you knew."

"Knew what?"

"Nick has been staying on the other side."

"Ah." I tried to sound nonchalant. "Does he live there?"

Her laugh was clear and girlish. "Oh, no. Nick has his own place. But he asked if he could stay there the night he flew you in." Her eyes looked amused. "We built it several years ago in hopes our children would be more likely to visit if they had their own place, but..." her voice trailed off and her eyes grew distant. "The apartments were built as reflections of each other. Like our children...twins...a boy and a girl."

Like Noche and Blanco. Now I understood her fierce attachment to the dogs—surrogate children.

Carmen's eyes narrowed in thought. "And now they live far away. From me and from each other."

"I'm sorry."

She smiled sadly. "But I have my Noche and my Blanco."

"Yes, you do." *And you're going to keep them. Somehow I'm going to see to that.*

* * *

Back in my apartment, I stood in the shower under a blast of hot water, ridding myself of the grime left over from New Orleans and Noche. No matter how tired I was, I had a training session this afternoon I couldn't miss. In the meantime, Nick had better set things straight with Berto and Carmen. I told myself she needed me too much to fire me. She'd said herself I was her last hope. And we *had* been making progress.

I collapsed on the bed, pulling a blanket over my head to create my own little womb. But my sleep was fitful. I kept thinking about Nick. Now I understood his comment that first night—"Where *we're* staying." But why was he staying here instead of his own place? And why did I care? I'd taken my vow of celibacy, and I intended to uphold it.

Mirror images. That means...ohhh. That means Nick's bed and mine share the same wall. We're sleeping mere feet from each other.

That was my last thought before I conked out for the next few hours.

The phone woke me. Groggy, I struggled to say hello, but Carmen's voice was distinct and loud. "I need to talk to you about a matter of great importance."

Something told me I was in serious trouble.

Chapter Seven

Carmen met me on the patio and motioned me to sit. "What would you like? Tea, diet soda, Corona?"

I loved the way she rolled her *r*'s. But I could also hear her saying, "You're fired," using two rolled *r*'s. I considered the Corona, since I might need fortification but opted for a diet Dr Pepper instead. If a Dr Pepper museum was good enough for Waco, then the drink was good enough for me.

"Did you know that Dr Pepper was originally called a *Waco*?" she asked.

Why was she prolonging the agony?

"It's the world's oldest major soft drink," she added.

She left to get our drinks, and I stretched my neck, bracing myself for termination. When she got back, she placed a paper napkin in front of me and set a frosted mug on top of it. Then she settled herself across from me, her eyes sparkling with excitement. She must get off on these "Trump" firing moments. She looked up at me over the rim of her glass as she took a sip, while I nervously poked a hole in my wet napkin.

"You ready?" she asked, not pausing for me to answer. "I have an idea. When the month is up, we'll have a graduation ceremony."

She waited, but no sound issued from my lips.

"Are you okay?" she asked, leaning over and touching my arm with her fingertips.

I hugged myself and swallowed hard.

"We can decorate the ballroom, invite everyone, and show how much *mis niños* have learned."

I took a big gulp of Dr Pepper and began choking.

Carmen jumped up and pounded my back, but that only made it worse. "Julie! Are you okay? Do I need to *hindlick* you?"

I waved her away before she could grab me around the chest and break my ribs in her enthusiasm. "I'm okay. It just went down the wrong pipe." I coughed a few more times and took a slow sip of my Dr Pepper to ease my throat.

So I wasn't getting fired after all. Much worse. She wanted me to attend a party. A dog party. "Don't you think that's a little much?"

"No, I do not." She leaned back and crossed her arms over her chest.

I grimaced. "To tell you the truth, I'm not much into parties." I was thinking of all the fancy events my mother had dragged me to over the years. She'd never understood I hated large functions, especially the kind requiring me to dress up.

"Oh, don't be a pooper," Carmen said. "I *love* big parties. It will be fun. We'll invite Nick and our friends in San Antonio and our parents in Mexico." She continued, mentally checking off what sounded like a few hundred people. "Of course, you'll want to invite Philip. You can ask anyone you want." She clapped her hands and bounced up and down in her chair like a little kid.

My hand flew to my heart, but Carmen mistook the gesture. "Oh, you miss him, don't you?" Her voice was full of sympathy.

I drew a deep breath. "How do you know about Philip?"

Carmen laughed and rubbed her hands together. "Wouldn't you like to know?"

I sat frozen, staring at her. Did she know? And did that mean Nick knew?

When I didn't speak, she relented and smiled. "I can't keep a secret. It was Nick."

My heart thumped. "Uh, what exactly did Nick say?"

Carmen pooched her lips out and drew her arched brows together as she tried to remember. "That you have a boyfriend back in Abilene, and his name is Philip. And he lives with you. Nick said it sounded serious."

Relief flooded through me. Whenever I'd talked about Philip, I'd been careful to call him my little boy or my little poodle, so Carmen was none the wiser. Though I was curious why I'd been the topic of conversation, I didn't want to appear interested, so I didn't ask. She'd just said she couldn't keep a secret, so I decided to continue my subterfuge. "Well, I care about him, but he's not the marrying kind."

"Then you need to find someone who is." She reached up and tucked a wayward strand of hair behind her ear. "You're too pretty to go to waste. I'm surprised you aren't married already."

"You sound like my mother."

"Mothers often know best."

"Well, I'm looking. Just not having much luck. There's also this matter of a trust fund. My father set it up so I couldn't touch any of the money unless I got married."

"He sounds like a wise man. Husbands are good. Money is good. I know. I've been without both."

I didn't tell her about my born-again virgin status. Somehow, I didn't think she'd understand. "It's not just the money. I'm also tired of the dating rat race."

"I understand. My daughter feels the same way, so I've been helping her."

"How are you doing that?"

"Easy. Like everyone else. Mr. Gore man's invention."

What was she talking about? "Mr. *Gore*man?"

Carmen laughed. "The Interweb, silly."

* * *

A few days later, Carmen called me again, saying to come quickly, she had important news. I raced up the hill, hoping Berto had agreed to neuter Noche. She was waiting on the patio and without preamble took my arm, guided me into the library, and shut the door. The dark wood paneling, stone fireplace, and built-in bookcases filled with leather-bound books made me feel as if I were walking into Sherlock Holmes' study.

I pointed to the fireplace. "Does it ever get cold enough here to use it?"

The corner of her mouth turned up, and she snickered. "It's not for heat. I told the man who put in the gas logs I like the atmosphere of a fireplace. You know what he said?"

I waited for enlightenment.

"He said—" She lowered her voice an octave, pretending to be the fireplace man. "'Like I told my ex-wife. You want atmosphere? Hang a picture. It's cheaper.'"

She giggled, and I couldn't help joining in. In the past few days, I'd discovered Carmen had a sense of humor. Not only that, she was much smarter than people gave her credit for. She might get words mixed up, but that was part of her charm. She'd read several of the books that lined the walls, and they weren't all romance novels.

She propelled me to a corner and stopped in front of a large armoire. Though we were alone in the room, she whispered. "Don't tell Berto. He's afraid I'll do something wrong and someone will steal our identity."

Instead of Casa del Lago, they should have named their house *Casa de Secretos*. Carmen opened the doors of the armoire, revealing a desktop computer and enough state-of-the-art electronic devices to keep Bill Gates in business another year.

"You say you want a husband. Okay, José, we're going to find you one."

"I don't think my prospective husband is in this cabinet," I said. But I knew what she had in mind.

She commandeered a chair from the game table, pulled it up to the computer, and pointed at it. "Sit there." Then she plunked her butt in the pneumatic desk chair. "Just wait. I've watched Berto, so I know all about how to surf the Interweb. When he's gone, I come in here and look up stuff."

I glanced toward the door, expecting to see Berto walk in any minute.

"Don't worry," Carmen said. "He's out of town."

I felt uneasy with the whole situation and tried to rise, but she grabbed my arm and pulled me back down.

"Look, Carmen. I'm not sure we should be doing this. Berto might have confidential information in there he doesn't want me to see. Like financial records. You said he doesn't like you messing with his equipment."

Carmen giggled again, then turned to me and winked. "I mess with his *equipment* whenever I want, and he never complains."

"I'm talking about his personal stuff."

She gave me a sly grin. "So am I."

I stood up again.

"Sit," she ordered, rising from her seat and bumping her hip into mine till I sat. "We're doing this together." Carmen adjusted her chair a few inches higher and gave me a thumbs up. "See, I'm getting better at commands."

"That you are," I said, though she'd never had a problem with people. "You know, that's the attitude I want you to take with the dogs."

She smiled and punched a button to boot up the computer. "And here's your treat."

We both sat there waiting, staring at the screen like pilgrims waiting for the manifestation of a miracle. Carmen tapped her foot impatiently while the computer went through its machinations. "We're going to find you a man. *Husband* material."

"On the computer?" I raised a brow.

She flipped her long hair behind her. "You've heard of computer dating, haven't you?"

"I know it's gotten people in a lot of trouble. Like my mother's friend. Met a guy and got involved in some steamy online sex talk. When her husband found out, he left her. Called it cyberspace betrayal."

Carmen ignored me, grabbing the mouse and aiming the cursor at the search engine address bar. "You don't have to worry about that. You aren't married."

I squirmed in my chair and eyed her with suspicion. "Have you really done this before?" The idea of finding a man through an online dating site made me uncomfortable.

"I told you. A couple of times...with my daughter. Here's the sign-in screen for muchas-dates.com. First, we need to create an online name for you.

"Great way to start a relationship. Using a fake name," I said, but she ignored me.

"Hmmm. How about *dog woman*?"

"Makes me sound like a circus attraction. 'Step right up, ladies and gentlemen and see The Amazing Dog Woman.' Couldn't I just give my real name?"

Carmen's eyes widened. "No way, José! You want them to think you're not with it? This is the way it's done. Give me a minute to think." Carmen wrinkled her brow as she tried to come up with a name for my husband-hunting alter ego. She thought out loud. "Dog, woman, poodle woman, poodle lover..." Carmen snapped her fingers. "I've got it! *Dog Nanny*. You know, like that TV show, *Nanny 911*."

"It makes me sound ancient."

"Then you think of something better," she demanded, her face inches from mine, but my mind went blank. "So how old *are* you?"

"Thirty-two."

"Thirty-two! I'd been married fourteen years when I was thirty-two. And had two teenagers!" She looked at me as if I were an aberration of nature, like the dog-faced woman.

I tried to defend myself. "Women wait longer these days. They get educated, establish careers..." I didn't add I'd graduated from college ten years ago and still wasn't really established *or* married.

"Well, you have to start somewhere," she said, obviously undeterred by my advanced age. Her fingers moved deftly over the keyboard until a screen with fill-in blanks popped up.

"Zip code," she said, typing in hers. She bent close to the screen as she typed, *DogNanny*. Her fingers flashed over the keys. "Your password is *Abilene*," she said.

I leaned in closer, peering at the monitor while she clicked on the tiny boxes. "Are you sure this is safe?"

"Of course. This is the way people—what do they call it?— 'hook up' these days. You can find anything on the Interweb. Shopping for a man is no different from shopping for a...for a *dog*! That's how I found Noche and Blanco. Hmm, age range. What age you want? Let's see, you look young for thirty-two. You want to go younger? You can have from eighteen up. That's legal." She gave me an appraising look. "You could handle eighteen."

"*Carmen*." I shot her a warning look, but she just laughed, clearly having a better time than I was. I might want a husband, but finding one online seemed beyond desperate.

When she typed in eighteen, I reached out and grabbed her arm. "If we're going to do this, let's be realistic. Thirty-two is young enough."

She looked at me, her eyes amused. "Whatever you say, *dog* woman." She laughed again and typed in thirty-two. "But if I were you, I'd go younger. Get a fresh one."

I thought back to my first year in high school, when senior boys seemed like men. Now eighteen seemed totally infantile. "I've already had my share of fresh ones. One my age is fine. Or a little older."

"How old you want to go?" she asked, typing in fifty-two before I could stop her.

"Wait, not that old. I don't want some guy I'm going to have to take care of in his dotage. When he's seventy-two, I'll be only...yikes—" In twenty years, I'd be fifty-two. "Put thirty-five. That's three years. Old enough."

"Okay, but you're limiting your choices." She punched in thirty-five. "And you're a *woman*," she spoke as she typed, "looking for a *man*."

"What else would a woman be looking for?"

"Other *women*," she said, giving me a knowing look. "And men can look for men. Abilene must really be behind the times."

I didn't bother to answer. The computer had Carmen in its electronic clutches. "Now, we'll go to advanced search options. Are you looking for casual dating, a serious relationship, friendship, or activity partners?"

"Activity partners?"

She clicked on a blue line of text and read aloud to me: "Someone to play card games, someone for your softball team, book club, etc."

"Oh. What's that last one, the one called *play*?"

Carmen clicked the mouse, and a pop-up box appeared. I leaned over and read the explanation: *If you're up for purely lascivious liaisons, check this box.*

"Not hardly," I muttered. "Check serious relationship." Carmen stuck out her pinky, hit the enter key, and a list of about twenty guys appeared, some with photos so small and dark they must have been shot in a bar.

One look at the names and I had serious doubts about Carmen's idea. "You can eliminate Boobhound."

As she slowly scrolled through the list, police lineups crossed my mind. "Uh, oh. Look at that one!" A fiftyish, bare-chested man stared back at us. "His breasts are larger than mine!" Granted I was no Pamela Anderson, but what was this guy thinking? First lying about his age, then posting a photo like that.

"Wait, this one doesn't look so bad," Carmen said.

"Uh, he's got a pile of dirty laundry behind him. I don't think so. Scratch him, too."

She scrolled past a guy with his head thrown back, swigging a beer. "Hmmm, not this one, but don't get discouraged. We'll find one for you."

The optimism of these men was nothing short of fascinating. "Keep going." I watched with awe as she scrolled past Wolfman, Dimwit, Red-Hot Fireman, and Slutlover.

"Do these guys seriously think a woman is going to respond to a name like that?" I asked.

Carmen peered intently at the screen. "You have to be patient. What's the line in the Bible about separating the wheat from the chaff?"

"Show me some wheat."

"Okay, okay. Here's one. He says he's an Iraq war veteran and he's stationed close by at Fort Hood. That means he has a steady income and can follow orders."

"No thanks. I have nothing against the military, but I want a man who's going to stay home, take out the trash, and help raise our future children."

"What about this one. Single Italian Stallion. Woo hoo!" She gave me a wide grin.

I gave *her* a withering look. "Carmen, he has on a bow tie and no shirt."

"Maybe he's one of those bear dancers."

"If you mean *La Bare*, that strip club for women, forget it."

"Okay, we've got more."

I had to admit the woman was determined.

"How about this one? He says he's looking for Miss Perfect."

"He's covered with *tattoos*! And I'm *not* Miss Perfect."

"*He* doesn't have to know that."

"Moving along," I said.

"Okay, okay, moving."

"Wait! That's him!" I said, catching her off guard.

"Where? Which one?" Carmen's eyes widened with excitement.

"That one." I pointed to a guy seated behind the wheel of a Mack truck. "The one that says, 'picture of me when I was younger and thinner.'"

We laughed so hard we gasped for breath. When the spasm passed, Carmen resumed her crusade and pointed the cursor to another part of the screen. "Maybe we need a silver or gold account. It says here you can watch videos, read their blogs, and send instant messages for a fifty-dollar upgrade."

"It's the men who need to upgrade," I said.

"You can pay someone to do that. It's called a profile makeover."

"These guys need more than a profile makeover. They need total body-personality makeovers. I think I've seen enough for one afternoon."

Her shoulders drooped. "Promise me you'll try again tomorrow? If forty million other people are using computers to get dates, it has to work."

I felt sorry for her. She was trying to help, after all. "I'll think about it," I said, though I had absolutely no intention of following through.

* * *

Though she'd failed as matchmaker, Carmen continued to improve as a dog trainer. As a result, the poodles were showing marked improvement. She took my advice more seriously now. Like not slipping them treats for no reason.

Without fail, we worked the dogs consistently twice a day. Between times, Carmen and I added supervised playtime and mini-sessions to reinforce what they'd already learned. Occasionally, Nick dropped by between flying Berto one place or another, but usually Carmen and I were so engrossed in the training Nick and I had little time to talk, a fact that made my life easier. Too, best I could tell, he hadn't stayed in the other half of the guesthouse since we'd returned from New Orleans.

One day, as we worked outside, Carmen managed to keep Noche in a *sit-stay* for three minutes. "Good *boy!*"

she told him in a high voice when the time was up, then looked to me for approval.

I gave her a thumbs up and smiled. "Looking good." I praised Carmen right along with the dogs and could tell it pleased her. Noche rewarded me with a doggy grin. Against his black coat, his teeth gleamed like Chiclets. When Carmen squatted to pet him, his pink tongue reached out and gave her a wet kiss.

"Good kiss!" I called.

Carmen laughed and wiped her mouth on her sleeve. "*Very* good kiss." She walked over to where I stood with Blanco and handed me Noche's leash. "Trade dogs with me and watch this."

She unclipped Blanco's lead. Then, holding a wiener poised over Blanco's head to get her attention, Carmen walked in figure-eights around some trees with Blanco strutting beside her in heel position like a champion show dog.

"Blanco's turning into a dream dog," I called to Carmen. "And you're getting really good!"

When they stopped, Carmen praised her profusely. Blanco gulped a piece of wiener and leaped into the air.

"See how smart they are?" I beamed. "Didn't I tell you?"

"Yes," she agreed, a big grin spreading across her face. Her smiles appeared more frequently, and she seemed increasingly relaxed. I still had reservations about how the dogs would perform in front of a crowd, but Carmen was more determined than ever. She was having a graduation party for them, and nothing was going to stop her.

She'd also managed to get Noche and Blanco in the *down* position, though Noche sometimes thought it was a game and rolled onto his back. I couldn't help thinking about Neuticles when he unashamedly exposed his real *cojones*.

Noche's escape had scared Carmen so much she'd given the dogs their own bedroom across the hall from hers and Berto's. Carmen was calling it "the nursery" and had begun redecorating the room in a doggy motif. She spent hours poring over catalogs, constantly asking my opinion on wallpaper and draperies. She even ordered special dog beds and comforters—Noche's in blue, Blanco's pink.

One day, after a training session, as we sat on the grass under a tree and watched the dogs play chase with each other, she began to talk about her life as a young girl in Mexico.

"My family was large, and we were very close. But very poor. I met Berto at a dance, and we got married a few months later. I was eighteen. Most of my friends married much younger."

"How did you end up here?"

"It was Berto's dream. And he knew English. I didn't. It was easier then to get permission from the government. Berto got his citizenship and taught me English so I could get mine. So we're legal."

I shook my head. "I never thought—"

"Sometimes people say things. Hurtful things. That's why I wanted my children to get an education."

"Did you ever think of going back to school yourself when the children left home?"

Carmen looked off into the distance. "Women in my country—in Mexico I mean—they don't go to school and have careers like they do here. Not where I grew up, anyway."

"It's never too late to start."

"What would I do? Berto makes all the money we need. Besides, I like being here with my niños."

She had a point. But I knew her well enough by now to think she might be happier with something besides the dogs to keep her busy. She seemed so lonely when Berto was gone, and I wouldn't be here forever.

"Berto is really going to be proud of you when he sees all you've accomplished."

"Yes, isn't he? He'll see what a good dog mama I am."

"We still have lots of work to do, and when Blanco comes in heat, you'll have bigger problems."

"In heat?"

"I mean if Blanco..." *How to put it?* "At some point Blanco will reach a time when Noche can get her pregnant. I'm surprised it hasn't already happened. That's why it's important to have him neutered and her spayed. Otherwise—"

"I remember," she said. "Party time."

I laughed. "Yes, little poodles that will grow up to be big poodles. People need to be responsible pet owners. There are too many homeless dogs as it is."

Abilene's new animal adoption center would be a small step, but it was only a step. The problem couldn't be solved overnight.

Carmen lay back on the grass and propped her head on her arm. "Convincing Berto won't be easy. When he got neutraled...I mean got his bas...vasectomy...he didn't want anyone to know. But the doctor said it would be dangerous for me to have more children—I wanted more, many more. In my country we have big, big families. Anyway, Berto had the operation because it was easier for him and best for me, but I could tell it bothered him."

Carmen was right about one thing, Berto would be a tough nut to crack.

* * *

The next afternoon, Carmen went to the beauty shop, so I worked the dogs alone. When we finished, I brought them inside, removed their leashes, and helped myself to a diet Dr Pepper from the kitchen fridge. The house was quiet except for the dogs' slurping spring water from their His and Hers dishes. Berto and Nick were out of town again on business.

As I walked past the library, something caught my eye. The armoire doors were wide open, and the screen saver on Berto's computer beckoned like a porch light to a June bug. Though I had no intention of going back to muchas-dates, I did want to check out the Lookin' for Love website to see if anyone had posted an update on the new building.

I lowered myself into Berto's chair, jiggled the mouse to shut off the screen saver, and typed in the Web address. The home page popped up. The shelter appeared to be doing fine without me. The roof on the kennel's main wing was going up in a couple of weeks.

For some reason, I clicked on the "bookmarks" tab. There, right in front of me, was the muchas-dates link.

What would it hurt to take a peek? Maybe Carmen was right. Maybe this was the modern way to meet men. It beat going to smoke-filled bars and waiting for some single guy to fall off a stool and declare his undying love.

Positioning the cursor, I clicked on the sign-in space, typed in *DogNanny* and the password, and hit enter. I ignored the pictures I'd seen last time and skimmed for new entries.

A park ranger looked promising until I read his list of hobbies—dancing, golf, and outdoor activities. I'd never been coordinated enough for dancing or sports. Though he was kind of cute, I eliminated him and moved the little elevator at the side of the screen further down. I craned my neck forward, trying to make out details from the postage-stamp photos.

Suddenly the word "dog" leaped out at me. I moved closer. A guy in a gimme cap leered back. "Most guys are dogs," he'd written. "My cat has to like you, and he's not particular." Sheesh.

Then, as I moved my chair back, about to give up, there he was. He'd listed his *dog* as his number-one hobby; movies, number two. He was even a blood donor. "Needs little maintenance," he'd written. Though he wasn't dark and hunky like Nick, he looked nice in an average-Joe sort of way. In fact, his name *was* Joe, Joe Griffon, computer analyst. The name had a nice Irish-American ring to it. I detected a slightly receding hairline, but that made him even better suited for me. I'd had my share of perfect-looking men, men like Nick. I was on a quest for a husband now. My standards were lower. And Joe's smile was wide and cheerful, not sullen or smoldering. Definitely not the kind of guy I usually dated. It could be a match made in, well, in cyberspace.

I composed a short introductory message I hoped would pique Joe's interest. "Hi, I'm a fellow dog lover looking for a committed relationship." No need playing coy. I didn't want him to think I was the kind of girl who'd go out with someone called Slutlover.

After some thought, I added: "I'm new to Waco and would like to meet for lunch if you're interested." I figured lunch was safer than dinner or drinks. That way he'd have to go back to his computer job, and I wouldn't be stuck with him more than an hour or so. I signed it *Julie* and hit send. No need to give my last name.

Yes, Joe Griffon, a thirty-two-year-old computer analyst, might one day be the father of my children, though I wasn't sure I'd tell them where we'd met. I'd probably say he spotted me from across the room in a restaurant, came over and told me I was the woman he'd been looking for all his life.

Much as I tried to imagine myself with Internet Joe, my thoughts kept straying back to Nick. I leaned back in the chair, remembering the touch of his lips. That's when I saw it, wedged in a cubbyhole of the armoire—the cardboard box from New Orleans Nick had picked up for Carmen. I looked around to make sure I was alone, reached over, and pulled out the box, which was heavier than I'd expected. The flaps on top were loose. What could it hurt to peek? Peeling back one of the flaps, I peered inside, almost dropping the box when I saw the contents. Lying on some tissue paper was a gun, black and ominous, like Berto's BMW. My hands trembled as I quickly crammed the box back in the cubbyhole and sank into the chair.

"Doing a little Web surfing, I see."

I screamed so loud my eardrums rang. As I screamed, I leaped from the chair, lost my balance, and toppled onto the floor.

"Whoa, are you all right?" Nick laughed nervously as he leaned over to help me up. "You scared me."

"I scared *you*! What are you doing sneaking up behind me like that? Don't you know better? How would you like it? How long have you been there, lurking behind me?" My face grew hot. Had he seen me trolling for a mate? Or worse, seen me looking inside the box? As he helped me to my feet, his hands felt warm, his face close enough to kiss.

"Sorry," he said. "I didn't realize you spooked so easily."

I squirmed out of his arms and scrabbled for the cordless mouse so I could close the muchas-dates window, but the little bugger had fallen to the floor and slid under a nearby table. I could tell from the gleam in Nick's eyes, he'd already seen plenty.

"I was just browsing," I said, pretending to smooth my shorts while I regained my composure. My heart pounded so hard I wondered if he could hear it.

"Umm, I noticed," Nick murmured, the corners of his mouth curving upward. "What would Philip think of your...browsing?"

"None of your business," I sputtered, relieved he hadn't seen me looking at the gun.

Home from the hairdresser, Carmen picked that moment to walk in. "Julie, hey. I see you went back to muchas-dates after all."

I clenched my teeth. "I was just looking."

"Julie is trying to find a husband," Carmen said. She might as well have held a blowtorch to my face from the way it started to burn. I could only hope she wouldn't tell Nick about the trust fund. No need making him think I was desperate. Besides, it sounded mercenary.

Nick cocked his head, unwilling to let the moment pass. "I thought Philip was your main man." His eyes glittered with amusement. "So it *is* out of sight, out of—"

"Philip isn't the marrying kind," I said curtly. I wanted to escape to my rooms, but Nick and Carmen stood in my way.

Nick had moved to the door and leaned against the jamb. From the grin on his face, he seemed to be enjoying every minute of my discomfort. "So it's marriage you're after? The ring. The white dress. The church wedding. That's typical."

"What do you mean?" I didn't like being called *typical.*

Nick shrugged. "It's what most women want, isn't it?"

"I don't know about most women. But I know this woman doesn't like to be spied on."

As I tried to get past him, he said with a laugh, "Hey, where are you going?" and grabbed my arm, pulling me close, which sent a current of electricity surging through me. "I wasn't spying," he said. "Berto sent me in here to get some papers."

Nick let go of me and walked to the armoire where muchas-dates Joe watched us from the screen. "See, I'm getting them out of this drawer right now. You go ahead and continue your browsing."

"I'm done," I snapped, as Nick left the room, humming. Good riddance.

But the feel of his hand on my arm lingered, and the pleasurable tingling didn't subside until I was back in my apartment and I thought about the gun.

Chapter Eight

Carmen handed me the keys to her Lexus. "It's time for *mis niños'* checkup with Dr. Julie, and it's tomorrow at nine...in the *morning*." She shuddered. "I'll write down directions."

Another "Julie," I thought, ready to identify with this vet-woman because we had names and dogs in common. Though I knew Carmen didn't do mornings, I also suspected she didn't want to see the poodles' nether regions poked and prodded, needles injected, and blood drawn.

Carmen checked off instructions from a hand-written list. "Rosa will have them ready at the back door at eight-fifteen. Be sure they go *big time* and *little time* before you leave. And drive carefully. Don't speed. Berto says traffic is heavy in the morning. Don't forget to fasten their seat belts. And give them treats when they leave the doctor's office. Can you remember all that?"

"Yes, ma'am," I said. "I'll take care of them as if they were my own."

The next morning, as soon as the dogs pooped and peed, we were off.

"Don't worry, guys," I said, as we pulled out of the garage. "You'll get a treat when we're done." I turned around to make sure they were securely strapped into their doggy seat-belt harnesses. Blanco quivered with excitement. Noche looked at me and gave a low bark, no doubt remembering our discussion of Neuticles and wondering if his bark would soon be higher pitched.

"Just a little checkup," I said, hoping the sound of my voice would pacify them. "Think of it as a grand smelling adventure. You don't get to go bye-bye in the car all that often."

Neither did I. For once, I'd have a chance to see something of the town. Other than my trip to New Orleans with Nick, I'd hardly left the lake house.

Carmen's white Lexus glided easily down the hill. I looped around, and soon we were cruising down Lakeshore Drive, aptly named because it wound around Lake Waco before turning into Valley Mills, one of the busiest streets in town. Eight lanes in places. They should have named it *Death* Valley Mills considering its fatality rate.

Traffic in and around Waco was twice as heavy as that in Abilene. Drivers wove in and out of traffic at high speeds, jockeying for positions, ignoring red lights and stop signs. They reminded me of taxi drivers in Mexico and Moscow. From fender-benders to major smash-ups, Waco had them. If you really had a death wish, you could always get on I-35 and head for Austin to the south or Dallas-Fort Worth to the north, each only ninety miles away.

Though Waco and Abilene both had populations over a hundred thousand, Waco seemed twice as big, thanks to all the contiguous communities. One was called Beverly Hills, but it was short on the Beverly, long on hillbillies.

When we reached the top of a rise just past the water treatment plant, even *my* excitement mounted. Just ahead of us was supposedly one of the most magnificent views in Waco. I slowed, ready to take in the splendor I'd only read about, anticipating that precise moment when the lake became visible. Suddenly, it appeared in bright blue brilliance. I gulped and my stomach lurched with the sensation we were about to plunge headfirst into the water. Then, the road surprised me, taking a sweeping curve to the left.

"Hang on, guys." As we rounded the bend, I peered into the rearview mirror to see how the dogs were doing.

Noche leaned sideways and whined. "It's okay," I said, using my high-pitched voice. "Almost there."

At thirty miles per hour, the thrill was brief, but for those few seconds, all seemed right with the world. I felt free.

A few minutes later, we pulled into a parking spot in front of the vet's office. I grabbed both leashes, unbuckled their seat belts, and held on tight. No way were they going to get loose.

When we entered the waiting room, heads turned to watch the two beauties trot in, sporting fresh puppy clips from the mobile groomer. When Noche heard the "oohs" and "ahhs" and "beautiful dogs," he preened as if he'd been awarded Best in Show at Westminster.

I gave the receptionist their names and took a seat. Noche and Blanco sat on either side of me, politely ignoring the yapping of a five-pound Yorkie, who seemed intent on ridding the room of any competition.

About fifteen minutes later, a pretty young woman in scrubs opened a door and popped her head out. "Esposito?" I jumped up, the dogs shook themselves, and she led us into the examining room. Her navy top bore illustrations of various dog breeds. I looked for poodles and finally found one under her arm.

"Good morning, I'm Dr. Julie." I started at the deep voice and hoped the surprise wasn't apparent on my face—Carmen had failed to mention Dr. Julie was male.

"Julie Shields," I said, reaching out to give his hand a firm shake.

That's when I heard my biological clock ticking. I performed a quick examination of Dr. Julie, checking him out as husband material. No wedding ring, though that was no sure sign of availability. Yes, the thought did cross my mind that if we married, my name would be "Julie Julie," but I could live with that. I added him to my list of possibilities.

The list now had one entry. I wasn't counting on Internet Joe just yet.

Dr. Julie didn't have Nick's dark good looks, but he was attractive. Clean cut. No outstanding features, but no outstanding flaws. Another average guy. Certainly not my usual type, but I had to keep reminding myself I wasn't looking for my usual type. I envisioned our off-spring as healthy, outdoorsy kids who would make good grades and not get into too much mischief. Dr. Julie and I would live outside Waco on a ten-acre ranch with some horses and chickens. I'd make fresh omelets for the crew every morning before sending them off to work and school, and then I'd...what would I do? Well, I could worry about that part later.

First, I had to win him over using my feminine wiles. Since my range was limited, I'd have to rely on my observations of Carmen. She was a pro. When Dr. Julie looked my way, I licked my lips, just as I'd seen Carmen do.

Dr. Julie took one look and said, "Don't be nervous."

It dawned on me too late that lip licking was not a good technique to use on someone familiar with dogs. It signaled anxiety.

"Oh, I'm not nervous," I said, batting my eyes at him instead. He looked away, probably thinking I had a nervous tic. This stuff worked for other women. Why didn't it work for me? What was I doing wrong? I needed training, that's what. Someone should open a flirt school for people like me.

I shifted to Bill-Clinton eyes, the kind that glinted with amusement and said, *You're the sexiest creature alive.* Bill had used those eyes on me several times. Not that I knew him personally, but whenever I saw him on TV, he had those eyes, even during his State of the Union addresses. Those eyes, with that look, even lurked behind the seriousness when he said he did *not* have sex with that woman. Those eyes could make women salivate like Pavlov's dog. But even my Bill-Clinton eyes didn't help me. Dr. Julie was avoiding all eye contact.

After hoisting Blanco onto the examining table, Dr. Julie had no qualms about looking into *her* eyes, her ears, or feeling her up for lumps. I tried to imagine it was me on the table, but I felt nary a tingle.

"Do you plan to breed these dogs?" Dr. Julie finally asked.

Nick asking me that question would have brought on a hot flash. Dr. Julie might as well have asked me what brand of dog food they ate.

"Oh, they aren't mine. I'm just helping the owner train them." Then I added, "I'm a vet tech...from Abilene." Maybe I could impress him with my credentials.

If he was impressed, he hid it well.

"Okay, I remember these two now," he said. "The owner...kind of high-strung and overly protective?"

"She loves these dogs and wants the best care available," I said. I swear I saw a beach in Tahiti reflected in his eyes. With routine testing, X-rays, shots, dental care, sundry illnesses—these dogs were a gold mine.

Dr. Julie sucked on one of his incisors. "She needs to spay and neuter them. And have their teeth cleaned."

"We brush their teeth every day. With their favorite toothpaste, the poultry-flavored."

"I'm seeing some tartar build-up here," he said, lifting Blanco's lip.

"I'll pass that along," I said, tired of trying to look cute for someone as oblivious as Dr. Julie.

"Hand me a cover," he said to the assistant.

Did Dr. Julie think I didn't know that this so-called cloth "cover" was really a muzzle? "Is that necessary? My boss never uses them."

A haughty look crossed Dr. Julie's face. "He'll wish he had if he ever gets slapped with a lawsuit. Doesn't matter who they bite. Even if they bite the owner, I can get sued."

As she handed him the "cover," his assistant looked me straight in the eye and said to him, "Here you are, hon."

Something sparkly caught my eye, and I glanced toward its source. When the assistant saw me eyeing her big engagement ring, she gave me a smug smile. I scratched Dr. Julie's name off my lottery ticket of prospective husbands.

* * *

Back in the car, I gave the dogs a drink from their travel bottles. Before I could strap them in, Blanco pushed Noche out of his original seat and took over his side of the car. I waited for them to get settled, then fastened their seat belt-harnesses and looped the car's seat belt through the strap. Then I split a Pup-Peroni between them, which they gulped down.

When we stopped at a red light, I felt vibrations from a boom box on wheels. The car beside us had its windows down, and the teenage driver was slapping the door in time to the music, a misnomer if I ever heard one. Noche and Blanco whined, so I turned up the volume on the Lexus's CD player, hoping the Mexican music would drown out the racket beside us. The light changed and I goosed it, wanting to put as much distance as possible between us and the rap-mobile.

Finally, I was out of heavy traffic and back on Lakeshore Drive, almost home. We slowly wended our way up the busy street, driving defensively. According to the newspaper, city officials had recently discovered a weakness in the earth under a hill that sloped down toward the lake. At some future time that no one could predict, the ground underneath would give way to a landslide, which would manifest itself as a large wall of earth rising up in the middle of the road. As I got closer to the spot, I felt a surge of excitement tinged with fear, wondering if today would be the day.

When I saw the police car in my rearview mirror, I didn't think much of it. According to a local magazine, Waco had no traffic patrol. The police department was too busy fighting crime to worry about minor issues like speeding and running stop signs. Drive-by shooters, burglars, and all kinds of molesters and abusers made the daily news. In the short time I'd been here, police had pulled two bodies from the Brazos River—one still behind the wheel of his car. And just yesterday, police had arrested a seventy-year-old constable for indecent exposure in a grocery store parking lot. He claimed the witness who reported him was mistaken, that he was merely sitting in his car shaking a bottle of Pepto-Bismol. I was grateful the Espositos lived high on a hill in an isolated area.

I looked in my rearview mirror again. The police car was still behind me. I checked my speedometer. It read thirty, and I was in a forty mile-per-hour zone. I slowed down anyway, feeling guilty for nothing. Soon as I did, I heard the short yelp of a siren and saw the flashing lights.

I drove until I came to a side street and turned in, rather than stop on the Waco autobahn. Better the policeman think I wasn't going to stop at all than for me to get smeared all over the street like grackle guano.

I quickly rolled down my window, shut off the ignition, and dug my license out of my purse. Knowing he would ask, I reached into the glove box for proof of insurance but found only gummy bears, a makeup bag, and a package of dog treats. That's when I panicked. I rummaged in the side panel, pulling out maps and magazines, but found nothing. Carmen surely had insurance. It was state law, and she couldn't get license plates without it. I hoped like hell she had plates. I hadn't thought to look.

Blanco and Noche heard the officer approach before I did and strained against their seat belts, barking feverishly.

Heavy footsteps grew louder as I continued my search. A male voice bellowed out. "Hands on the wheel!"

Did he think I was reaching for a gun?

"I don't—"

"On the *wheel!* Now."

Two run-ins with the law in less than two weeks. Did I look like a criminal?

I grasped the wheel as he instructed and stared straight ahead. No need letting some overly zealous rookie snuff me out right here on a quiet, residential street. If I was going to get killed, I wanted it to be a video moment. Jimmy Cagney always made a run for it.

The officer's voice rang out again like a shot. "Your license, please."

Blanco's and Noche's barking grew louder and more ferocious.

"Ma'am, your license and—"

"May I take my hands off the wheel?" I sat stiffly, still facing straight ahead.

"Do it slowly."

Very, very slowly, I removed my hands from the wheel, leaving a wet impression. I wanted to wipe the sweat off my forehead but was too afraid. I reached over and gingerly retrieved my license from the pile of maps and magazines I'd thrown onto the seat beside me. Without looking at the patrolman, I handed it through the window, then slowly placed my hands back on the steering wheel, hoping he'd forget about the insurance.

"Ms. Shields, do you still reside at 33 Peasant, uh, Pleasant Place in Abilene?"

"*Pheasant* Place." I tried not to grimace. "Like the bird."

"Do you still reside there?" Blanco and Noche were snarling and barking so loud I could barely hear him.

"Yes. Well, not right now. I'm living here in—" Blanco interrupted with a snarl the Wolf Man would have envied. I tried to swallow and couldn't, wondering if the cop's gun was pointed at my head. "I'm living here in Waco at Casa del Lago. Just for the month," I managed to squeak.

When Blanco and Noche launched another round of barking, I decided this had gone far enough. "I'm getting out of the car so I can hear you!" If he'd had any sense, he'd have already said, "Step from the car please."

"Okay, but do it slowly." His notebook quivered slightly when I reached for the door handle, and I wondered if I should put my hands in the air for safety's sake. I turned my head toward the window. As I opened the door, he shouted. "Don't let those dogs out!"

So that was his problem. "Don't worry." The last thing I needed was for him to take potshots at Noche and Blanco. I deepened my voice. "Noche! Blanco! Quiet!" Noche whined, but the barking stopped. "Good dogs."

After exiting the car, I inspected the policeman. He was kind of cute. Another all-American looking guy. Sandy blond hair, stocky build. Probably played football in high school, barely graduated, then joined the police force.

"Ma'am, did you realize you were going under the speed limit back there?" he said in a Joe-Friday voice.

When I noted his gun was still holstered, I regained my normal smart-ass attitude and came close to telling him this wasn't *Dragnet* but doubted he'd get the reference. "*Under* the speed limit? You're telling me you stopped me for going *under* the speed limit?"

"Yes, ma'am. It's dangerous to drive too slow on Lakeshore Drive."

"You're kidding me, right? Why aren't you out there saving this town from some really scary people?" I waved my arm toward a row of houses. "Like the criminals who get their pictures in the paper every day. Some of their mug shots appear so often they're beginning to feel like family. Do *I* look like a threat to the community?" I raised the pitch of my voice just enough to make him wonder if he was dealing with a sane person. When Noche and Blanco heard me, they resumed their barking. "Look in the backseat. Will you take a look?"

He scratched his head and hesitated. "What do you mean, ma'am? What have you got in the backseat?"

I saw myself mirrored in his sunglasses. My hair had looked better. "I'm talking about the dogs."

"The dogs need to stay *in* the car, ma'am."

"That's. My. Point. These dogs are also law-abiding citizens."

He scratched his head again. Irritating habit. Someone should tell him.

"*Seat* belts. They're wearing *seat* belts," I said.

He ventured a quick look in the backseat and gave me a lopsided grin. It was the first thing he'd done that looked human. Seeing the dogs safely buckled in brought about an instant change in his demeanor.

"I'm going to let you off with just a warning this time," he said, lifting his hat back, pulling out a handkerchief, and wiping beads of sweat off his brow.

To my relief he didn't ask for proof of insurance—he didn't even check my license against the database. In fact, his grin turned into a full-fledged flirty smile. "So you live at Casa del Lago?"

I held a hand to my eyes to block the sunlight. "Just for a few more weeks."

"So what do you do, I mean, what are you doing for fun...here in Waco?"

His question caught me off guard. "Uh, I'm not really here for fun."

"Driving a Lexus and not here for fun? Just driving a Lexus must be fun."

How old was this guy, anyway, sixteen?

"I can think of other things that are more fun," I said matter-of-factly.

His grin widened.

"I mean like...watching movies, going out to dinner..." It had been so long since I'd done anything just for fun, I wasn't sure what to say.

He looked down at my license. "So, Ms. Shields, why don't I show you a little southern hospitality tonight? Dinner on me. My name's Butch, Butch Justice."

He paused a moment, as if expecting me to make some crack about his name, and when I didn't he smiled sheepishly.

"Is that legal? Asking out someone you've stopped?"

He grinned again. "I won't tell if you won't."

Five minutes ago I'd have said absolutely no way. But the vow I'd made was beginning to nag at me. I was looking for a man who wasn't my type, and Butch Justice was just the kind of guy my mother would abhor. She'd call him middle-class poor for one thing. He also wasn't tall, dark, or my kind of hunky. He was looking better all the time.

"Why not?" I said, though I could think of one big reason. Butch might be cute, but he couldn't hold a candle to Nick, whose flame burned as blue as his eyes.

Back in the car I took a big swig from one of the dogs' water bottles, wondering what I'd just agreed to.

* * *

Butch was picking me up at eight under a tree near the circular drive. The arrangement seemed all right with him, though he did specify "no dogs," as if I might bring them along as chaperones. "Macho Cop" must have a fear of anything with more than two legs.

No need for Carmen to know I was slipping out at night with an officer of the law. I remembered how Berto looked when Nick mentioned the feds. And then there was the gun. Lots of people keep guns for protection, but why would Nick have brought one all the way from New Orleans?

When I saw the old pickup making its way up the road to the house, I hoped someone had made a wrong turn or one of Ramón's friends was paying a call. No such luck. The truck with splotched primer that looked straight off the set of *The Grapes of Wrath* belonged to my date for the evening.

It didn't take me long to discover Butch's boots had more polish than his manners. He hopped out of the truck, but when he saw me heading toward him, he hopped back in. The truck sat high off the ground and didn't have a side step. I lifted one leg and stretched it inside, then looked around for something to hold onto so I could heave my one-hundred-ten pounds up and in. Butch finally reached his arm out for me to grab.

I could tell he'd tried to spiff up the inside when the smell of Armor All and piña colada hit my nasal passages. I looked him over while he drove. His face was sunburned, his hair bleached out by the sun. He wore a white, short-sleeved polo shirt, and his arms were red, like his face. Every now and then he'd look over at me and smile, but it was wasted on me. I reminded myself I'd asked for this, a guy guaranteed not to break my heart. I tried to be more optimistic. Dogs could be trained, after all.

After fifteen minutes of bumping up and down on bad shocks, we pulled into what looked like an old warehouse complex someone had developed into shops and restaurants. "This is River Square," Butch said, "on account of the Brazos River being right over there." He pointed toward some buildings and a clump of trees about a block away.

He got out of the truck, and when it was obvious he wasn't coming around to open my door, I shoved it open myself and slid out. The buildings were lit up with neon signs of restaurants offering cuisine from steaks to seafood to Italian. My mouth began to water at the thought of a thick, juicy steak, medium rare, but Butch didn't bother to ask what I had a hungering for. He led me straight to the Mexican food place. I'd wanted a different kind of guy and now I had one, so best not complain. He probably didn't make much money protecting the citizens of Waco from themselves, and Mexican food was cheap. I should count my blessings. He could have taken me to McDonald's.

"I been to Abilene," he said, after we were seated. "Nothing but tumbleweeds, dirt devils, and yellow grass."

I'd cut him slack on the Mexican food, but I wasn't about to let him badmouth my hometown. "What's wrong with tumbleweeds? Better dirt devils than the kind you have here—child molesters, drunk drivers, murderers. In Abilene no one even locks their doors at night." I looked out a window to see if a lightning bolt was about to strike me dead for lying and thought I heard a distant rumble.

"That so," he said.

"Yes, that's so." I was glad I hadn't shaved my legs or put on any makeup, save some lip gloss and a touch of mascara. Maybe I'd scare him off before he proposed.

But if he was trying to woo me, he was pushing all the wrong buttons. "Must be nice having money."

Surely this yahoo couldn't read my financial worth in my face, and I certainly wasn't dressed like someone rich. "What makes you think I have money?"

"You kidding? Driving around in a Lexus. Living in a mansion."

"It's not my Lexus or my mansion."

"Yeah, but I can tell you're one of them women of privilege."

"And how can you tell that?"

"Something about you. I've known rich girls. Not that I'm holding it against you. I like women with money."

This time his cute lopsided grin didn't look so cute.

I was relieved when we finally got our food and I could stuff my face and not feel forced to make conversation. When we were almost finished with our enchiladas, Butch resumed his interrogation.

"So, Miss Julie, what's it like living at Casa del Lago?" I could tell he thought he was being sexy when he reached over and slowly ran a finger down my cheek. I narrowed my eyes at him and drew back, cringing inside.

If Nick touched me like that, I'd be tempted to roll over and let him rub my belly.

Butch's calling me "Miss Julie" made me feel old, though the lines around his eyes said he wasn't any pup.

"Just Julie," I said, looking at my watch.

"I like your Rolex." His accent seemed to get more country as the night wore on. "Your" came out as "yore."

I gave him a look meant to wither his acorns. "It's like living in any large house. Nice. Big." I didn't tell him I had my own place out back. No need giving him ideas he didn't already have.

"What about those Espositos? They're not from around here. Got a private pilot and make lots of trips to Mexico. Kind of suspicious, if you ask me. You might want to be careful. I've heard rumors."

"What kinds of rumors?"

"Drugs, illegal aliens, you name it. They're Mexicans, you know."

Anger shot up from my feet to the top of my head. I didn't bother keeping my voice down. "I beg to differ. They're Americans, just like you and me!" Heads turned at a nearby table.

Why had Butch really stopped me? Had he asked me out because he thought I was rich? Did he think I had inside information on the Espositos that would get him a promotion?

Just then, a large clap of thunder shook the restaurant. I shoveled in my last bite of chicken enchilada and stood up. Butch got the hint I was ready to leave.

Outside, as we walked out onto the covered porch in front of the restaurant, drops of rain started pelting the ground. I hoped he'd offer to run out and get the pickup, then drive around and get me. Instead, he grabbed my hand and shouted, "Let's make a run for it!" and pulled me out onto the parking lot. About halfway to the truck, all hell broke loose. Old-timers would call it a frog-strangling gulley washer. By the time we got to the truck, we were both soaked. This time, I was glad Butch didn't help me in. The last thing I wanted was his hands near my butt. I took another vow right then. If I got back to my rooms in one piece, I'd never go out on another date.

Butch yanked an old rag from behind the driver's seat and toweled off his hair. Then he dried his face and arms. As an afterthought he offered the rag to me. "No thanks," I said. No telling where it had been. I leaned forward and wrung my hair out on the floorboard. Butch gave me one of his lopsided grins. "Wet T-shirt. I like that. How about us going dancing?"

I gave him a you-gotta-be-shittin'-me look and snorted. Was he as obtuse as a triangle, or what? Just in case he was one of those crazy psychopathic cops I'd seen on TV, I decided to lie my way out of this one.

"That's very nice of you, but I told the Espositos I'd be home early so I could help them with some...some dog business."

"They *do* need to do something about them dogs. They're vicious. *Attack* dogs."

"*Attack* dogs? They're *poodles!*" Why had I subjected myself to his prolonged stupidity? "They're pets."

"Well, you could've fooled me. The way they was snarling, if I hadn't had a gun, I bet they'd have ripped my arm clean off."

"They had on seat belts, remember? And they didn't know you had a gun. They were just protecting their territory."

By now we were bumping down Martin Luther King Jr. Boulevard, and the rain was pouring down so hard the visibility was about one foot.

"Are you sure you can see well enough to drive?" Much as I wanted to hurry my homecoming, I also didn't want to end up getting my name in the paper days or months from now when they pulled Butch and me out of the river.

"Oh, sure. Grew up here. Know it like the back of my hand."

I hoped we were headed home. For all I knew, he was driving me out in the country so he could rape and kill me. Now I wished I'd told Carmen where I was going. I tried to think of a movie where the heroine thwarted the bad cop and came out alive, but none came to mind.

"Sure I can't interest you in a drink?" Butch asked. I half expected him to pull a flask from under the seat and offer me a swig. "I got some Jack back at my place."

"Jack?"

"Daniels. You know, whiskey."

"No thanks," I said, then added quickly, "but that's very nice of you. The Espositos will worry if I'm not back by ten." I kept waiting for that lightning bolt to strike. I'd done more lying since I'd come to Waco than I had in all my years in Abilene. Maybe it was something in the nasty-tasting water. The phosphates or the algae.

As we rounded a curve, the rain let up enough to make out the road leading to Casa del Lago up ahead. I'd been saved. It was almost enough to make me reach over and hug Butch's thick red neck. But not quite.

My heart was singing in the rain as the pickup chugged up the slope to the house. I mentally segued into the "Hallelujah Chorus" when we reached the top and Butch swung into the circular driveway.

As soon as he rolled to a stop, I gave him a quick "thank-you-for-the-dinner" and jumped out. Before I closed the door, he asked, "Can I call you?" I pretended not to hear and took off in a fast jog down the path to my rooms without looking back.

On the way, I said a prayer of thanks for being spared the mortification of Nick's seeing me with such a bigoted, ignorant boor.

By now, the rain had slowed to a steady drizzle. As I neared my front porch, I saw something move. I jerked to a stop, thinking Butch had somehow transported himself ahead of me. I jumped when the beam of a spotlight struck me in the face, blinding me. I darted behind a nearby tree, wondering if I should make a run for the big house, hoping Butch's clunky cowboy boots would slow him down.

Before I could decide, a voice from the darkness wrapped around me like a warm, dry blanket. "Julie! I've been looking all over for you! Where in hell have you been?"

Nick. Call me melodramatic, but I wanted to throw myself into his arms and tell him how close I'd come to death at the hands of a stranger.

Chapter Nine

My heartbeat slowed when I realized it was Nick, not Butch Justice, standing on my porch. I moved toward the sound of his voice until I could make out his features. His wet hair formed dark tendrils on his forehead, and his denim shirt was soaked. At that moment, I could easily have given up my vow of celibacy, but Nick's thoughts were elsewhere. Tight lips replaced his usual grin. "Where have you been?"

I started to tell him he wasn't my father but stopped myself. I was too relieved to see him to snap back. "Out," I said, as if that explained all. I must have looked quite the prize with my hair and clothes sopping wet and my eyes raccoon-ringed with mascara.

"Out?" His eyes flashed with anger. "We've been looking for you since before dark. For all we knew, you'd fallen in the lake or gotten yourself kidnapped!"

For once Nick's imagination matched my own. In the distance, Berto and Carmen called my name. Nick spun around and shouted in the direction of their voices. "Down here! By the guesthouse!" Then he turned back to me. "We were about to call the police!"

The irony of his remark struck me as amusing, and I spoke before I thought. "Huh. I was *with* the police."

His lip twitched slightly and he frowned. "What do you mean you were '*with* the police'?"

Could there be any truth to Butch's accusations? Could Nick and the Espositos be involved in something unlawful? Drugs? Illegal aliens? Sex slaves? Nick had flown Berto to Mexico more than once since I'd been in Waco. What if Noche and Blanco were mules, like little

122

Heroina, the pup found with cocaine sewed into her belly? I quickly discounted that theory. None of these people could be that cruel.

Nick grabbed my shoulders, his eyes scanning my face. "What police? Out *where*?"

"What difference does it make? But if you have to know, dinner. I was at dinner."

Carmen and Berto, speaking in rapid Spanish, their voices tense, broke through the bushes. Her dark hair was plastered to her head, Berto's shirt was stuck to his chest, and both were out of breath. Berto was holding the black revolver I'd seen in the box, but at least it wasn't pointed at me.

Relief flooded Carmen's face when she saw me. "Julie, thank God, you're here. We were so worried."

I lowered my head, almost wishing I *had* been kidnapped, rather than admit I'd been inconsiderate. "I'm so sorry. I had no idea anyone would even miss me."

Berto glowered at me under dark brows. "We were about to call the police."

"I told her. She says she was *with* the police." Nick's tone was sharp.

Carmen wiped her forehead with the back of her hand, her eyes questioning. Berto was breathing through his nose in short huffs, like a racehorse.

I lifted my chin, and shot back at Nick. "I had a date." Though none too proud of my voluntary brush with the local law, I wasn't about to admit what a fiasco it had been. "With a policeman."

The three of them stared at me, waiting for more.

Nick finally broke the silence. "A date?"

Carmen looked first at Berto, then at Nick, her dark eyes full of concern. Berto ran a hand through his short, wet hair. "A *Waco* policeman?"

I winced, remembering Butch's accusations and his disdain for the Espositos. "It was just dinner. I don't even know him. He stopped me this morning on my way back from the vet. For driving too slow." I was digging myself in even deeper. "I'm really sorry. I didn't think I needed to tell you I was going out."

Berto eyed me suspiciously. "You went to dinner with someone you didn't even know? This *policeman* you'd never met before?"

I looked up at him and nodded. His dark eyes bored into mine. "What was his name?"

I hesitated, afraid speaking his name might conjure him up, but Berto's commanding presence finally forced me to speak. Unlike Nick, Berto did seem like my father. "Butch," I muttered. "Butch Justice."

The three of them exchanged knowing glances. Nick's lip curled up in distaste. Mine quivered.

Berto's eyes were hooded, like Don Corleone's, and I half expected him to send me on my final ride. "Did this policeman say anything about us?"

My voice cracked. "About you?" No way could I tell him Butch intimated he might be involved in drug trafficking or illegal aliens, but I wondered why Berto asked. "No, not a word."

When Berto continued to stare at me, my eyes welled up and two fat tears spilled out. Nick surprised me by coming to my rescue. "That's enough for tonight. Let's all get dried off and go to bed."

His words dissolved the tension. Berto exhaled heavily and his shoulders slumped. Carmen took hold of her husband's arm and buried her head in his side. "Nick is right. Let's go in, Berto."

I did my best to look repentant. How was I to know they'd miss me, send out a search party? But I had to admit, it was a good feeling, being missed.

Nick took me by the arms and pivoted me toward my door. "I'll make sure she gets inside." When Butch touched me, I'd cringed. With Nick, I had no desire to pull away. He opened my door and guided me inside. "Lock the door behind me. And don't think of going out again tonight."

Before I could protest, he shut the door. When I didn't hear him walk away, my hopes momentarily soared, thinking he would surely burst in and ravish me on the spot. I pressed my cheek to the door but heard nothing except the sound of his footsteps fading away. I sighed and turned the deadbolt until it clicked into place.

So much for any hope of comfort. I dragged myself into the bathroom, stripped out of my sodden clothes and towel dried my hair. Then I pulled on an old, extra-large T-shirt, and slid my frozen feet into my old bunny slippers. I imagined myself with Nick in some faraway place, like standing atop the Eiffel Tower in Paris, having dinner in a small café in Italy, or even on a deserted beach somewhere.

As I was turning down the bed covers, I heard a light tapping on the front door. I turned out the bedroom light and crept into the living room, hoping whoever it was hadn't noticed the light go out. Had Butch come back to wreak vengeance for my hasty exit? Was he standing outside this very minute with a chainsaw dripping blood from the massacre of the Espositos? I tiptoed to the window, quietly lifted a slat in the blinds, and peeked through. With the help of the gaslight, I saw the dim outline of a figure standing on the porch.

I grew weak, and my whole body began to tremble. I heard a metallic sound, and when I looked down, the doorknob jiggled. I sucked in air and held my breath, certain I'd locked it. Then, it began to turn, ever so slightly. Could Butch have found a key?

The deadbolt held. I began to breathe again. I couldn't just stand there and let someone break in. I had to take action. Pretending I was Angelina Jolie in an action movie, I called out, "Stand back! I've got a gun!"

If Butch *had* come back, I hoped his weapon of choice *was* a chainsaw, not a shotgun. I didn't want to be blasted into a million tiny pieces. I moved to the side, just in case.

"Wait! It's me! Don't shoot!"

Nick?

I turned the deadbolt and yanked open the door, but no one was there. Then I saw him, hiding behind a potted hibiscus. Even in the dim light, his face looked pale.

Once again I'd made a fool of myself. "Why didn't you tell me it was you?" I grabbed his shirt, pulled him inside, shut the door and locked it. I didn't ask him to sit down. "Why were you trying to break in?"

He caught his breath. "I wasn't trying to break in. I was checking to make sure your door was locked and you were safe. What are you doing with a gun?"

"I don't have a gun. I hate guns. I was bluffing." I used the dimmer switch by the door to turn a table lamp on low.

Nick held his hand to his chest and exhaled. "Well, it worked! You sent me diving for cover."

I covered my mouth and stifled a laugh. "If I'd *had* a gun, I doubt that hibiscus would have helped."

Nick wasn't smiling. "I came back for another reason. I want you to stay away from him."

I feigned ignorance. "Stay away from whom?"

"From that policeman."

"Is that an order?" Though I had no intention of ever going out with Butch again, I didn't like Nick telling me what to do, or not to do.

"I'm serious, Julie. He's not for you."

"So now you're an expert on the kind of man for me?"

Nick moved closer, put a hand on my shoulder and rubbed his thumb up the side of my neck. A quiver of desire made my ears buzz. "Maybe. Why can't you trust me?"

Oh, let me count the reasons. For starters, his blue eyes and the way my legs got weak when he was within twenty feet of me. I'd resisted him for two weeks now, probably setting some kind of record. In another two weeks, I'd be home free. If I could resist Nick Worthington, I could set my sights on someone who *was* husband material. It might not be Dr. Julie, Butch Justice, or Internet Joe, but I would eventually find the right man. This was, after all, the Chinese Year of the Dog.

I backed away from him, crossed my arms, and raised an eyebrow. "How do you expect me to trust you when you keep secrets from me?"

Nick tilted his head. "What secrets?"

"Oh, don't give me that look! You know exactly what secrets. The package in New Orleans, the feds who almost hauled us in, the—"

"They didn't almost haul us in. I explained all that—"

"No, you didn't explain it. You give me half answers or you say you can't tell me. There was a gun in that package."

"How do you know?"

"I saw it. Near the computer. In the same cardboard box."

Nick sighed. "Berto wanted a gun. He's gone so much he thought Carmen needed protection. She found one advertised, wanted to surprise him, and I agreed to pick it up. That's all."

"So why didn't you just tell me?" I didn't wait for his reply. "All right, answer this one, Mr. Honest. If you have nothing to hide, what's so bad about my going out with a policeman?"

Could he be jealous?

"You'll just have to trust me."

I looked up at him without blinking. "Trust works both ways."

The old Julie would have given him the benefit of the doubt and fallen into his arms without another word. But much as I wanted to, I knew if I did, I'd be letting someone down. Someone who needed more, someone who deserved better. Me.

He turned, released the deadbolt, and shut the door behind him.

I locked the door and grasped the arm of a nearby chair to stop myself from rushing after him, begging him to come back. After a few minutes I looked outside, but he'd gone for good. I shivered.

Nick and I were like those Scottie-dog magnets that repel, attract, or chase each other depending on which way they're turned. Tonight we'd gone in opposite directions. But I could feel his magnetic field drawing me in. And each time, the pull grew stronger.

Later, I lay in bed thinking about Nick just feet away from me, alone in his own king-sized bed. I turned sideways in the bed, pressing myself against the headboard, hoping some heat from Nick's body would penetrate the wall. But all I felt was cold, hard wood pressing into my soft, naked flesh. Long after midnight, I finally fell asleep.

* * *

The next afternoon when no one was around, I slipped into the library to see if Internet Joe had answered my email. He had. I shot an email back arranging to meet him for lunch.

I couldn't wait to tell Carmen, but first I needed to apologize. She was sitting under an umbrella by the pool, reading. As I approached, she looked up from her book and smiled. I pulled up a chair and sat beside her, thankful for the shade. "Sorry I worried you last night. I didn't think anyone would notice I was gone." I felt like a teenager who'd been caught sneaking out of the house.

"Of course, we noticed," she said, puckering her lips.

I wanted to remind her I was thirty-two and not accustomed to accounting to anyone, but the fact was, I'd worried them. "I won't do it again. Next time I leave, I'll let you know."

"Water or Dr Pepper?" she asked, reaching into the ice chest beside her.

"Water's fine."

She handed me a cold bottle of spring water. Her fingernails and toenails were a freshly polished burgundy. I looked down at my own nails, ragged and unpainted. No wonder I couldn't keep a man. But now I had a prospect.

I waved a copy of the email in Carmen's face. "I did it. I found one."

Carmen looked surprised. "One what?"

"A man. On muchas-dates.com. His name is Joe, and we're meeting for lunch tomorrow. Guess I'll have to start calling you my personal matchmaker."

She broke into a big smile and laughed. "I charge ten percent." She reached over and hugged me. "See, I told you. What's he like?"

"All I know is he likes dogs and movies."

Carmen's eyes danced. "What does he look like?"

"From his photos, he looks okay." I snickered. "He's got a round smiley-face, kind of like the emoticon. I'm not looking for Brad Pitt, you know. Husbands don't have to be handsome. I'm looking for someone who's affectionate, friendly, devoted to me..."

Carmen closed her eyes and sighed. "You've already got a *dog*." She placed her book on the table and leaned forward. "Are you excited?"

I took a swig of water. "Ask me again after our date."

"Where's he taking you?"

"We're *meeting*. At the Cotton Patch."

Carmen drew back. "The Cotton Patch? That's not a very romantic place to meet your future husband for the first time."

"I'm not looking for romance. I'm looking for marriage."

"Well, it could be worse," she said.

"What do you mean?"

"Beats Burger King."

* * *

I ran through the woods trying to elude chainsaw-wielding lunatics. My house in Abilene materialized before me, and I raced inside, slammed the door and twisted the knob on the deadbolt. Then I ducked behind a potted plant and closed my eyes. Outside, the crazies chanted: "Brains, brains." They pounded on my door, calling my name. "Julie, Julie. Wake up, Julie."

I opened my eyes, thinking I was in my bed back home in Abilene. The clock on the bedside table said nine a.m. I jerked up. The banging on my door was real. Carmen was calling my name. Something was wrong. She never got up this early.

"Just a minute," I called, trying to clear the fuzz from my brain. Grabbing a pair of shorts I'd draped over a chair, I pulled them on under my baggy T-shirt. "I'm coming!"

Carmen's face was swollen with sleep, her hair pulled into a messy ponytail. Her robe was wet at the hem where it had dragged on the ground. She staggered in, but before I could shut the door behind her, Nick appeared, wearing nothing but a pair of jersey pajama bottoms. His chest was muscular and tanned from his morning runs.

"What's going on?" he asked. "Why all the pounding." My eyes were drawn to a fine line of soft brown hair extending from his navel to the drawstring of his pants at which point my imagination took over. When I looked up and found him watching me, my face turned hot as a jalapeño and all my senses shifted into overdrive.

Carmen seemed unaware of the electrical current crackling the air between Nick and me. "The thunderstorm the other night must have knocked your phone out," she said. "Your sister just called. It's Philip."

"Philip!" I grabbed Carmen's arms, my knees buckled, and I would have fallen, taking her down with me, if Nick hadn't moved quickly and caught me around the waist.

He swept me up into his arms as if I were weightless, gently laying me on the sofa, and placing a pillow under my head. Then he knelt beside me and smoothed the hair back from my face. He smelled fresh, like cucumbers and alfalfa.

Carmen lowered herself to the floor beside him. "Your sister said he had an accident, but he's okay. He's having surgery this morning. Not an emergency, but the doctor said he needed to do it as soon as possible because," she hesitated, "he *is* in some pain."

Fear stabbed my heart, but when I tried to sit up, Nick moved from the floor to edge the couch, his warm thigh pressed against me.

"What happened?" I asked, dreading the answer.

Carmen clasped her hands. "It's his DSL, but they can fix it."

Mrs. Malaprop had nothing on Carmen when it came to getting words mixed up. My voice sounded high and panicky, and I struggled to sit upright. "His DSL? Is it his liver? His kidneys? What did she say?"

"Your sister said you'd know what it meant."

"Was he hit by a car?"

"No. She said he was running. Just running. No car."

Nick interrupted. "Did she say ACL by any chance?" He shifted his body and put an arm around me. I leaned into him, as if closer contact would allow me to draw from his strength.

Carmen anxiously rocked back and forth. "That's what I said. His ASL. She said it broke. But don't worry. She said he would be fine. The surgery will take a couple of hours. She'll call back when it's over to let you know how he's doing, but I told her you needed to be there when he wakes up."

I tried to think straight. *No cars. Just running. Suddenly changing direction, his knee wrenched sideways, the ligament popping.* An ACL injury was not a dire emergency, though I would like to be there for the little guy. On the other hand, time was running out for Carmen, and we still had work to do if Noche and Blanco were going to "graduate."

Nick's hand was now rubbing my back, and I could barely concentrate. "If it's his ACL, I really don't have to be there. I promised you a month. Noche and Blanco need more practice." I leaned into Nick's hand, my eyes half-shut.

Carmen stood up and stomped her foot, jolting me wide awake. "No way, José! Your place is with Philip. He will need you by his side."

She was right. I did need to be with him. I wanted to be with him. This separation had been harder than I'd thought. "Okay, I should probably go, but I'll be back tomorrow. As soon as I know for sure he's all right. Let me get dressed, and I'll come up to the house and call Sarah from there and order a rental car."

Carmen wagged her finger at me. "No car. Nick will be happy to fly you back. Won't you, Nick?" A big smile creased her face when she looked at us. I suddenly realized I was plastered against him like a heat patch. I moved away from him and straightened my T-shirt.

Nick smiled. "Don't mind at all."

I had to give the guy credit. No matter how much I discouraged him, he kept coming back for more. When I looked into his blue denim eyes, my heart pounded and all the warning signs went up. Still, I couldn't exactly pass up his offer.

Carmen got to her feet and steepled her hands in prayer. "Then it's all settled."

Nick grinned. "At last, I get to meet Philip."

* * *

When I talked to Sarah, she assured me Philip was in good hands and said she'd pick me up at the airport. I showered and threw a few things in a tote bag. Carmen offered to email Internet Joe to let him know I'd been called out of town unexpectedly. An hour later, Nick and I were in the air. I insulted him shortly after takeoff by saying I didn't need a babysitter when I got to Abilene, so we talked little except for some cursory comments on the weather. No way was he going to "meet Philip."

Two more weeks. Half my mission accomplished. No-che and Blanco were becoming model students, and if Carmen continued the way she was going, the Espositos could share another twenty-five years of wedded bliss. Once I got back to Waco, I'd ratchet up my husband search. Nick had been an interesting diversion. Eye candy. Guys like Nick were like temporary spare tires, good enough to make it to the next station, but unrelia-ble for the long haul.

After Nick dropped me off at the airport in Abilene, I'd make sure Philip was okay, then drive my own car back to Waco the next day.

"Here we are," he said, as we began our final ap-proach. I looked out the window at the flat, dry terrain below. People wondered how anyone could love a place with hard-packed clay soil and the horizon visible from almost any vantage point. Abilene might be as hard and dry as an old rancher, but it was home.

When we landed, I realized the flight hadn't caused the usual quivers, not even during takeoff. As the wheels touched down, I got the same feeling I always did when returning from a long trip. Safe.

Nick helped me out of the plane. "Thanks," I said. "I appreciate the lift. See you back in Waco."

He tilted his head and gave me that slow, smoldering grin, just like the first day we'd met. "You aren't getting rid of me that easy. Besides, what would you think of me if I just left you here?" His eyes were warm with sympa-thy.

"That's nice of you, but I can handle this. My sister's picking me up. I have my own house, my own car. And I'm sure you have better things to do."

"Sorry. Carmen's orders."

I didn't know whether to believe him or not, but I couldn't stand around debating it. I turned and stalked from the hangar to the lower deck of the terminal at a quick clip, hoping he'd get the idea he wasn't needed.

When I caught sight of Sarah's short blond hair, I felt a burst of gratitude and love that immediately dissipated my irritation with Nick.

"Julie!" she squealed as we hugged. "I've missed you! Now don't worry. Philip just got out of surgery, and he's doing fine. He'll be able to come home late this afternoon, as soon as he's fully awake."

"Thank you. For everything."

She elbowed me lightly. "No problem at all. Your house is clean. Your fish are fed. Your yard mowed."

That was Sarah. Always the efficient one. "And how's Mother?"

"Oh, you know Mother. She wants to take us to the club for dinner tonight. I told her you might want to stay with Philip, but she insisted. She—holy moley, would you look at that!" Her big blue eyes opened wide as she stared at something over my shoulder. "And he's headed this way."

I knew who it was without having to look. Two worlds were about to collide, and I couldn't do a thing to stop it.

Chapter Ten

When Nick wasn't looking, Sarah mouthed, "He's gorgeous."

I made a face at her and crossed my eyes. Around my big sister, I always felt about ten years old—and managed to act accordingly. Nick introduced himself, and before I could stop her, Sarah invited him to join us. Next thing I knew, the three of us were in her SUV headed toward town, Nick in back, me riding bitch.

Where my interests ran to dogs and their welfare, my sister had inherited the business acumen of our father. She had a law degree and her own business: The One-Stop Shop. She could plan your estate, set up investments, and figure your income tax. Needless to say, I was proud of my big sister, though we were nothing alike. Sarah was at ease with everyone.

While she drove, she and Nick chatted like old friends about the price of fuel and its effect on the airline business. I kept mum, not wanting to cause a scene—Sarah hated it when I did that—but I managed to give Nick a few hostile looks.

When their conversation turned to politics, I interrupted, turning around in my seat and giving him a fakey sweet smile. "Which motel are you staying in?" My intentions were to drop him off as soon as we could and let him fend for himself in Big A.

Sarah twisted toward me, raised her sunglasses to the top of her head, and narrowed her eyes. "*Ju*-lie. We can't let him stay in some motel." She glanced back toward Nick and gave him one of her bright and perky trademark smiles. "Don't mind her. We've got lots of room. Julie doesn't always mind her manners."

"Really? I hadn't noticed," he said.

He *did* notice when I unloaded a couple of eye-bullets into him.

At the next red light, Sarah looked back at Nick. "Tell you what. I've got an appointment, and we can't pick Philip up till four. I'll just drop the two of you off at Julie's house, since it's on the way. After my appointment, I'll swing by, pick up Philip, and bring him home."

That was Sarah, always trying to organize everyone's life. The light turned green, and soon we were passing a strip of motels. Somehow, I had to get Nick into one of them.

He'd seen them, too. His eyes met Sarah's in the rearview mirror. "Julie's right. I should stay in a motel. I don't want to put anyone out. I doubt Philip wants me underfoot."

Sarah laughed. "Philip won't mind. He loves company."

"But in his condition, I'd think—"

Sarah waved her hand toward the backseat and said, "Trust me. He'll like you."

I cleared my throat loudly, but she ignored me.

Nick shrugged. "If you say so, but I don't want to be in the way. Actually, I figured Julie would want to stop by the hospital first thing, to see Philip."

Sarah frowned. "The hos—?"

I stopped her by picking up some papers lying between us and poking her with them as hard as I could. Instead of taking my hint, she leaned toward her door and grimaced. "Ouch! What?"

I lowered my voice. "Philip will sleep for several hours, and he needs his rest. Let's not bother him now."

Sarah opened her mouth to speak then thought better of it, giving me a sidelong glance full question marks.

I was trapped. Sarah did not stop at a motel. Nick did not protest further. I did not think of a way to get rid of him.

When she pulled up in front of my two-story Tudor in Pheasant Place Estates, I braced myself for Nick's reaction. I'd kept the Shields' family jewels a secret, even from the Espositos. As far as Carmen knew, the trust fund was a pittance. Though the big money belonged to my mother, people assumed I was rich because I'd been brought up that way. Finding a man who loved me for myself was a hurdle I'd yet to clear. Though Nick wasn't on the prospective husband list, if he thought I had money, he'd probably turn up the charm, and I was feeling needy. Lately, my celibacy vow had begun to encroach on my nocturnal dreams as well as my daytime fantasies, with Nick playing the starring role.

As we got out of the SUV, Sarah called out, "See you around four!" and with a quick wave, she was off.

She'd done a good job making sure the lawn got watered and mowed. Though I'd been gone only two weeks, grass turned yellow from the heat this time of year without constant watering. Normally, I tried to conserve, but if I was going to sell the property, it had to look well-cared for. I'd opted out of a For Sale sign in the front yard until I returned for good. No need signaling the house might be empty.

"Nice place," Nick said, looking up at the ivy-decked walls. "Balcony over the sunroom—I like that."

"Thanks." I kept walking. Nick stayed where he was, shading his eyes with his hand as he examined the house and landscaping. "Philip's private income must be substantial."

Of course. It hadn't occurred to me Nick would think the house was Philip's. "He does okay," I said. Now all I had to do was figure out some way to get rid of Nick before Sarah got back with the little guy.

I opened the front door and breathed in the comforting smell of home, but I wasn't able to enjoy it. I needed a plan, so as soon as I got Nick situated in the guest room downstairs, I told him I was going upstairs to rest.

Even if I called Sarah's now and told her to take Philip to her house, what would I tell Nick? I had to get Nick out of the house somehow and into a motel. Sarah had already said Philip wouldn't mind if Nick stayed with us, so I couldn't use that as an excuse. Everything had happened so quickly. If I'd known Nick would tag along, I could have warned Sarah, but now...

I looked at my watch. Two o'clock. I had a little over two hours to come up with a solution. I paced. I sat. I paced some more. I flopped on the bed and tried to think. Three o'clock came and went. Time was running out.

Then it hit me. I'd simply tell Nick I wanted to be alone with Philip. Why hadn't I thought of it sooner? My car was in the garage. All I had to do was load Nick into it and haul his good-looking butt off to the nearest Holiday Inn.

As I started downstairs to tell him, the doorbell rang. Great. The last thing I needed was more company. I glanced at the clock. Three-thirty. I offered up a silent prayer it wouldn't be my mother. It wasn't. It was worse.

"Yoo hoo! Julie! I'm back!"

My heart gave a thump. *Sarah.*

By the time I got to the bottom of the stairs, she'd already let herself in with her key. Philip was cradled in her arms, his injured leg shaved several inches above and below his knee with only bloody, jagged stitches holding the skin together. I'd seen it countless times on other dogs, but this was my own little Philip. Tears stung my eyes. His tiny leg trembled from the trauma, and when he saw me, he emitted a soft, high-pitched whine.

Sarah's face was flushed from the heat and the effort of holding Philip without hurting him further. "I hope you don't mind. My appointment fell through, so I picked Philip up early. The vet said he's doing fine, and I knew you'd be eager to see him."

A rush of love filled my heart as I looked into Philip's tiny brown eyes. For a moment, I forgot all about Nick. When Sarah gently handed over my little blond fur ball, I buried my face in his neck and kissed him. "My poor baby. I'm so sorry you had to go through this. Mommy's going to take good care of you now."

I looked up to see Nick staring at the three of us, his eyes wide. "*Philip* is a *dog*?"

* * *

One look at Nick's face alerted Sarah she needed to hit the road, and I followed her out to her car, putting off the inevitable.

"He didn't know Philip was a dog?" She shook her head in disbelief. "Julie, what on earth have you told this man?"

"Nothing," I muttered. "He just assumed."

"It's too hot to stand out here and talk," she said, unlocking the car doors and motioning me in.

I got in and sat immobile while she walked around, slipped behind the wheel, and started the engine to get some cool air flowing. "What kinds of games have you been playing in Waco? Who did he think Philip was?"

I leaned forward and put my face against one of the vents. "I sort of let him think he was my live-in lover."

Sarah leaned her head back against the seat. "Why, for heaven's sake?"

"You know why. Because he's the kind of man who's always meant trouble. How many times have I let the Nick Worthingtons of the world trample on my heart, then kick it a few more times? I vowed never to let that happen again. So, yeah. I let him think I was attached."

"Julie, *Julie*," she moaned. "You're my sister and I love you, but I've got to tell you, when it comes to men, you have a lot to learn. Can't you see it?"

"See what?"

"How he feels about you?"

"I *know* he's attracted to me, if that's what you mean. And yes, I *know* he's tall, dark, and hunky. Otherwise, there wouldn't be a problem."

"Listen to your big sister for a minute. That's *not* what I mean."

"You mean he's *not* attracted to me?"

Sarah beat her hands against the steering wheel a couple of times. "Of course he's attracted to you. But any fool could tell it's more than that by the way he looks at you. My dear little sister, that incredibly tall, dark, and hunky man in there is crazy about you."

"You *think*?"

"More than *think*. I *know*."

I moved away from vent, put my hands over my face, and let out a deep breath. "I don't know. You could be wrong."

"Wasn't I the one who told you Brett was after your money when you thought you'd finally found the perfect man?"

I sat up straighter. "Yes, but—"

"Remember Dave? You thought he was madly in love with you till you found out he was screwing around with his secretary? I knew right off he was a loser, something about his eyes."

"But—"

She continued, counting them off on her fingers. All the times I'd been wrong and she'd been right about men. "No *buts* about it. I know these things. Now get in there and apologize and try to be nice to the guy." She glanced at her watch. "Time for me to go. Don't forget. Mother expects us for dinner at the club tonight. Just the three of us. John's out of town on business."

Sarah had met and married John in law school and had since provided my parents with two grandchildren. When I failed to do the same, Daddy stipulated I wasn't to receive a penny of my trust fund until I married. In my family, marriage was up there with finding the Holy Grail.

140

"Mother said six and don't be late. She expects Nick, too."

"*Please*," I moaned. "Not the club. Nick doesn't know."

"*Now* what doesn't he know?" Sarah asked.

"Anything. He thinks I'm a vet tech."

"You *are* a vet tech."

"He doesn't know about the family money, and I don't *want* him to know. Try to talk Mother into eating at Texas Roadhouse or Luby's, would you? For *meeee*?"

Sarah burst out laughing. "You've got to be kidding. *Mother*? Eating at Texas Roadhouse? Or *Luby's*? Besides, he's already seen where you live. How are you going to explain that?"

"He thinks it belongs to Philip...uh-oh."

"Yeah, uh-oh. What are you going to tell him? That Philip made his money acting in TV commercials?"

"That might work," I said, considering it for a moment.

I drummed my fingers on the console between the seats. What was I going to say to Nick? Crow was not my favorite dish.

* * *

That incredibly tall, dark, and hunky man in there is crazy about you.

Was Sarah right? If so, why couldn't I see it? I'd automatically written him off from day one because he *was* incredibly tall, dark, and hunky. But if Nick really cared about me, it changed everything. I thought about how I trembled at his slightest touch, the kiss in the moonlight, and that morning at the New Orleans airport. I couldn't deny the way my body responded when he merely looked at me. But how did I really feel? I'd tried to block my own feelings under that born-again virgin business, but deep down...

I eased open my front door and peeked in, trying to assess the damage. Nick sat in a blue Queen Anne chair, his back to me. Philip snoozed contentedly on the sofa where I'd left him. When he saw me, he opened his eyes and wagged his tail. Poor little guy.

I walked past Nick, afraid to meet his eyes. Lowering myself to the floor next to Philip, I reached out and gently stroked his head.

The silence dragged by slower than a funeral procession until Nick finally spoke. "So. This is Philip. He's not quite like I pictured him."

I finally forced myself to look up at Nick. His eyes were steely gray and hard like his voice. "The intelligent, handsome, educated Philip with a private income is a dog. A *poodle*." Nick's lips tightened to a thin line. "You must think I'm really stupid—"

"No, Nick. I don't think—"

"Then why did you lie to me? Why did you make a fool out of me? All this time I thought you were in love with some guy named Philip." He laughed, the sound low and mirthless. "I thought I was doing you a favor, flying you to Abilene to be with the man you love, while all the time you were laughing at me. I guess Carmen thinks it's funny, too."

"No, she doesn't know. Like you, she assumed. I didn't lie. I never said Philip was a man."

Nick stood up and walked to the fireplace, turning his back to me. Philip whimpered in his sleep, and I patted him gently until he stopped.

When I could stand it no longer, I eased up off the floor and inched my way over till I stood behind Nick, wishing he'd turn around, say something, anything. Yelling at me would be better than this silence, but he didn't move or speak. I reached out and gingerly touched his back. He jerked away as if I'd burned him, then turned around and grabbed my arms. "*You*. You accused me of telling half-truths. Well what the hell do you think you've been doing? What was it you said? Trust works both ways? Lot of room you have to talk."

"I'm sorry, Nick. I had...reasons."

142

"What kinds of reasons could you have for making me feel like an idiot?" He threw his arms over his head, then let them fall limply to his sides.

"I never intended for you to find out. I didn't think I'd ever see you again when the job in Waco ended. I'd been hurt—"

"Oh, and *that's* supposed to make me feel better? You think you're the only person who's ever been hurt?"

"I'm sorry." A sob caught in my throat, and I turned away.

"What about this house? Philip must be one hell of a show dog to make this kind of money."

I hung my head. "No, the house is mine. I inherited it. It made sense to live here."

"So what else have you lied about? I suppose you aren't really a vet tech. Let me guess. You're an internationally famous movie star, and you've changed your appearance to come and mix with the mortals of Waco. You've been doing research for your next role. You're playing the part of a woman who gets back at all the men who've wronged her by making fools of one who...who—"

"I'm sorry. I really am." When I reached up and hugged him, his body went rigid. "Can you forgive me?"

I waited, but he didn't answer. Finally, I could bear it no longer. "Please, say *something*."

His face was expressionless. "I don't know." He left me standing there and retreated to his room.

I sat on the floor next to Philip and stroked his soft little body, hoping it would make us both feel better. My stomach let out a long, low growl, reminding me I'd had nothing to eat all day except a piece of toast on the run. I hadn't forgotten my mother's summons. Might as well kill two birds. I called a dog sitter I'd used before, who said she'd be glad to stay with Philip a few hours. I didn't want him left alone so soon after surgery.

Nick finally returned to the room, and before he could speak, I seized the moment. "My mother's expecting us for dinner tonight."

"So?"

"Well, you've got to eat. You don't have to sit by me."

He sat down, picked up a book, and began to thumb through it. "Not a problem."

"You won't need a tie. The slacks you're wearing will be fine."

I got up and straightened some magazines on a nearby table. Did this mean he wasn't *too* mad at me? "I'd better warn you. My mother is...well, she's rather eccentric."

"Like her daughter?"

I gave a wry laugh. "We're nothing alike."

If I was lucky, Sarah would play peacemaker tonight, as she always did. Not only had Sarah inherited Daddy's business smarts and his disposition, she knew how to humor Mother. I, on the other hand, was not the humoring kind. When the two of us got together, sparks usually flew. Even if Nick was—or had been—as crazy about me as Sarah said, one evening with my mother could put an end to that.

* * *

I slipped into some black pants and a black top with a gold beaded pattern on the front. The black suited my mood, and I didn't want Nick to think I was trying to impress him by getting too fancy. I also didn't want to give my mother any ideas about mine and Nick's nonexistent relationship.

At the Abilene Country Club, a dozen staff members "Miss Julied" me into the main dining room where Mother and Sarah waited. So much for trying to hide my past. Nick eyed me appreciatively. "You're pretty well-known around here."

I tried to downplay it all. "Yeah, well...my mother hangs out here a lot. She plays gin once or twice a week." And drinks her share of it, too, I almost added.

"And your father?"

"Dead." I hesitated, then added, "Airplane crash. *Small* airplane."

"Oh, sorry." Nick's smile didn't fade. It vanished. "I guess that explains why flying makes you nervous."

"I know it's silly considering the statistics. I'd never been afraid before, but after that..."

"Not silly at all." He gave me a brief hug, filling me with a warm glow that didn't last long enough.

Time to feed Nick to the lioness. As we neared my mother's table, I saw her red hat and knew my fears were well-founded. Ever since she'd taken up with some group calling itself the Red Hat Hot Tamales, she wore a red hat whether she was with them or not. Mother thought it was a hoot. I found it pretentious. Sarah took it in stride. Tonight's chapeau bore a striking resemblance to a giant male cardinal with ruffled feathers perched atop a nest.

As soon as Mother spotted me, she arose, reaching out her arms dramatically. "Julie! I'm so glad you're back." But her eyes never left Nick.

Heat rose to my face. I'd always hated her displays, her flamboyance. "I've only been gone a couple of weeks."

For a woman in her mid-fifties, she was attractive in a high-maintenance sort of way. Her hair was blond, like Sarah's, though Mother's had a lot of help from her friends at Hair Today, where she had a standing appointment every Thursday. Her bright red acrylic nails matched her hat and blouse. Her black skirt was short, revealing well-muscled, shapely legs. Though she rarely dated, I sometimes wondered if she was on the lookout for another husband. Something about her struck me as vaguely predatory.

"Mother, Nick Worthington. Nick, my mother, Elizabeth Shields." *And please don't call her Liz.*

Nick took her hand. "Good evening, Mrs. Shields. It's a pleasure to make your acquaintance. Very kind of you to ask me to join you." Then he nodded toward my sister. "Good to see you again, Sarah."

Mother's eyebrows shot up. She was impressed, no doubt about it, and obviously sizing him up. None of my former boyfriends had possessed Nick's dignified manners. He pulled my chair out for me and took the empty place next to mine across from Mother. How would he ever keep a straight face with the bird hat across from him? I slid my eyes to the side, trying to catch his expression. He was giving my mother one of his dazzling full-frontal Chiclet smiles, like Noche. I could hear the ka-*ching* as she racked up points in his orthodontic ledger.

After the waiter served our drinks, I pretended to study the menu, steeling myself for the fusillade of questions my mother was about to unload. I didn't have to wait long. "Sarah tells me you're a pilot. Is that your occupation or just a hobby?"

The question might have sounded innocent to Nick, but I knew the subtext. She was fishing for some sign of Nick's monetary worth.

"A little of both." Nick lifted a glass of water to his lips, so I couldn't tell if he was smiling or grimacing.

"You mean you fly by choice?"

"I guess you could say that. I've wanted to fly since I was a kid. At one point, we lived close to an Air Force base, so I decided when I grew up, I wanted to be a pilot. For me it's freeing to transcend the world below." He paused. "I'm sorry. Julie told me about your husband's accident."

My mother mumbled a *thank you* and changed the subject. "So you're from Waco. I used to know some people from Waco. Do you know the Hudsons? They lived in Castle Heights."

Castle Heights was one of the oldest, most elite parts of town, home to many of Waco's movers and shakers, the ones with "old" money. I loathed my mother's practice of dropping names, trying to impress people, and she was on a roll. "I think I attended UT with a boy named Worthington. He was studying to be a doctor."

Then, before I could stop her, she zeroed in with *the* question people in Abilene over fifty always ask a person they've just met. It usually came right before: "Have you found a church home yet?"

"And what does your father do, Nick?"

"Which one?"

My mother drew back in surprise. "How many do you have?"

"There's my adoptive father, a retired alcoholic proctologist. And then my birth father, a carpenter in Mexico."

My mother's painted-on brows drew together. "I love New Mexico. What part?"

Nick chuckled. "*Old* Mexico."

Sarah held her menu in front of her face. "What are you going to have, Julie? The chicken-fried lobster looks pretty good to me."

Mother was not deterred. "My heavens. Why would anyone choose to live in Mexico? I've read about people retiring there because the cost of living is so low, but think of all the amenities one would have to relinquish."

Nick smiled. "My father was born in Mexico. So was my mother. The Worthingtons adopted me."

Mother's head bobbled, and I wondered if the bird hat was about to take flight.

I sucked in my cheeks to keep from bursting with laughter at the look on her face. A hush fell over the four of us, and for a moment I thought Mother might choke. Instead, she surprised all of us by throwing her head back and braying like a donkey, after which she used her napkin to wipe a tear from the corner of her eye. "Oh, that's priceless. Born in Mexico, indeed. Which would make you Mexican?"

"No, ma'am. Born here in Texas. I'm afraid I'm an ugly American, just like a lot of other people."

I stole a quick glance at Nick and saw a shadow pass across his face. Was it possible he was telling the truth? It hit me I knew nothing of Nick's background except for Carmen's comment about his mother being a bossy woman. Now he was getting a shit-pot load of *my* mother. If her antics didn't make him cut and run, nothing would.

I gave silent thanks when the waiter served our food. My mother continued to hold court, wrapped up in her own small world. She soon got around to one of her favorite topics—my life choices. "We wanted Julie to be a doctor. She took all the required courses for medical school, then decided she wanted to be a veterinary technician. Can you believe that? Why would a young woman with her looks and intelligence want to work with dirty animals all day when she could be treating *people*?"

My mother needed one of those T-shirts that said, "I'm talking, and I can't shut up." I concentrated on chewing my steak, letting her ramble on. Fighting her was useless.

She took a sip of wine and pointed a red fingernail at Nick. "Can you believe Julie refused to attend her coming-out parties?"

Nick looked baffled. "Coming out? They give parties for that?"

At first Mother appeared confused. Then she caught on and brayed again. "You are so funny. Julie, wherever did you find him?"

I'd like to say my mother had a few under her belt by this time, but her wine glass was only half empty. Mother's drug of choice tonight was serving as Queen de la Dinner Table.

"Coming out. *You* know. Here we call it the Cotillion. In Waco it's the Cotton Palace. Cotillion Belles, princesses. When a girl reaches a certain age—it varies by region—her family and friends host coming-out parties to mark her entrance into society. When Sarah came out, there were parties every weekend, and teas…why, it lasts months. The newspaper runs their pictures. And on the final night, they're presented to family and friends at a ball in their honor. They wear designer gowns and long white gloves. Such a lovely affair…*very* elite. Of course, not just any girl can be a deb. She has to be sponsored by someone who's a former belle or debutante."

I suppressed a yawn as Mother shifted from Cotillion Belles to Sarah's pledging the "right" sorority in college and her involvement with the Junior League. Sarah had the decency to look embarrassed, but we both knew it was useless to try to change the subject. Poor Nick. He'd be sorry he ever set foot in Abilene.

My mind drifted off, but I was jerked back to reality when something warm touched my thigh. It was Nick's hand, and it was on the move. A slow burn crept upward to my face, while lower, a throb of pleasure pulsed. I ceased to breathe as I slowly turned to face him.

Eyes as unfathomable and as blue as Lake Waco met mine. I think that's when I made my decision.

Chapter Eleven

I took the long way home, hoping to engage Nick in conversation, but once we left the country club, he spoke little. Probably shell-shocked from two hours with my mother, not to mention my own offenses regarding Philip. I'd deluded him and made him feel like a fool. Still, he'd piqued my curiosity with the mention of his parents, and I'd never been one to let questions rest unanswered for long.

I glanced toward him, but all I could make out in the darkness was his profile, silhouetted against the window. "Were you serious? About your parents being from Mexico?"

He gave a wry chuckle. "Do you think I'd make up something like that?"

"Maybe."

"All true. The blue eyes throw people off."

I drove slowly. "And your real name?"

"Short version—I was christened Nicolás Tomás Solano-Perez. Born in America. When I was two, my parents had to return to Mexico, but they wanted a better life for me. My mother cleaned house for a couple who couldn't have children—the Worthingtons. She was the controlling type and wanted children; he didn't like kids. She convinced him they should adopt me. I was twenty-eight before I knew any of this. Sorry, I guess that's not the shortest version."

An incredible sadness filled me. Sorrow for the parents who'd lost a child, and for Nick, who grew up not knowing the truth about his past. "Did you ever see them again? Your real parents?"

He paused for so long I wondered if he was going to answer. "Only my father," he said, as we pulled into my garage.

Maybe Sarah was right. Maybe he was more sensitive than I'd given him credit for. Sure, he had the dark good looks I always fell for, but had I judged him too harshly, writing him off as just another handsome hunk with an airplane?

Once inside, I told Nick to make himself at home while I paid Philip's sitter and sent her on her way. Then I checked on Philip, who'd settled under a table. I lowered myself to the floor and crawled over beside him, putting my face close to his and petting him gently while I crooned. "My poor baby. Poor little leg."

I was still crouched down with my butt in the air when I heard a noise and looked up to see Nick standing in the doorway watching me. I jumped up quickly, bumping my head on the table.

"You okay?" Nick asked.

I reached up and rubbed the top of my head. "Yeah. I'm hardheaded."

"What about him?" His eyes darted in Philip's direction.

"He's doing okay. Just needs time and some TLC." I leaned down again and kissed Philip's furry head, making sure my butt wasn't facing Nick this time. "Don't you, sweetie? You know your mama loves you."

"You sound like Carmen," Nick muttered.

I laughed. "Guess so. You jealous?"

"Of a dog?"

I grinned. "Wouldn't be the first time."

Nick moved to the sofa, and I curled up in a chair opposite him.

"So your mother—"

"Enough about me," he said. "What about you?"

"Me?" He was interested in me?

"Why take a job as a dog trainer when you evidently have plenty of money?" He held his palms up and looked around the room.

"My mother inherited the money. I got this house." I didn't mention the sizable trust fund a marriage would yield. Getting caught husband hunting on the Internet had been embarrassing enough.

Nick looked at me expectantly. This was the part where most guys I dated tuned out. "For a long time now, I've had the dream of opening an animal adoption center, where throwaway animals have hope of finding a forever home. I've raised enough money to start building, but we need a whole lot more. When this house sells, the proceeds will go toward the new Lookin' for Love Animal Adoption Center, but until then, I need money. And Carmen needed me. That simple."

Nick crossed his legs, leaned back, and stared at me as if seeing me for the first time. Finally, he spoke. "Quite an ambitious venture. And selfless."

"Hey, don't get me wrong. I'm no saint."

He chuckled. "Don't I know *that*. But who is? I think it's a great idea. I'm all for giving back to the community."

Enough talk. It was time. I'd made a decision and needed to set the stage.

Nick's hand on my thigh under the table at the country club had roused my libido from hibernation. Maybe a few months wasn't all that long, but I wasn't a bear either. At dinner, each time I'd looked into his blue denim eyes, a green light signaled "GO!" Add it all up, and it was enough to make me to renounce my decision to remain a born-again virgin.

I poured us each a glass of wine and sent Nick out onto the deck with his, telling him I needed to freshen up. I'd made a decision and needed to set the stage. Nick was right about one thing, I did have control issues. I wanted everything perfect. Maybe I was more like my big sister than I wanted to admit.

My imagination had always pictured us someplace exotic—like Hawaii, Rome, or Paris. Instead, here we were at my house in Abilene, Texas, USA. I'd have to make the best of it.

First, I pulled out my unopened set of *One Hundred Fifty Romantic Country Hits*, guaranteed to steam up the room or your money back. I popped the seal with a fingernail and placed all ten discs in the player. Since batteries wouldn't be involved, I might need some extra time. Then I lit about twenty candles. Soon, the scent of jasmine filled the air. I hoped some of it was making its way out onto the deck. Nick was in for one big surprise. Till now, I'd put up roadblocks. Tonight, I planned to take him cruising down the freeway.

I hurried into the bedroom and ripped off my black pants and white cotton granny panties and pulled on a pair of bikinis and a skirt. He'd just have to accept the fact the only thongs I'd ever wear would be on my feet. I slipped off my bra, then changed my mind. First of all, without my padded, push-up bra, all I really had up-stairs were my two pencil erasers that might not pop up unless I got cold. And it *was* summer in West Texas. Reason two—Nick needed something of mine to remove. Men liked doing that. Working at it seemed to raise the value of the goods. Not that my goods were bargain basement, but they were slightly used.

Then I practiced twisting my hips so my flippy little skirt would draw attention to my legs, but when I looked outside, I noticed the sun had set. I raced downstairs. Since it was too dark for Nick to see my legs, I grabbed up one of the jasmine-scented candles and carried it outside with me, hoping to create an aura of beauty and sensuality.

He was sitting on the glider. Good. Room for two.

I imagined I was Kathleen Turner in *Body Heat*. No wind chimes, but I had plenty of heat.

I moved slowly, like a snake. Some woman on *Oprah* teaching pole dancing said slow movement was the key, so I concentrated on changing my default from fast forward to slow motion. It was a stretch for me. Normally, I raced around like a greyhound.

"You all right?" Nick asked, tilting his head.

"I'mmm wonderrrfulll," I answered, my speech slow as a Texas drawl. I continued my sinuous walk across the deck until I stood mere inches from where he sat.

His eyes grazed my lower half. *Yes*, I thought. But when he spoke, his voice was full of concern. "Did you hurt your leg? You're walking funny."

"*No, I'm fine.*" I answered more sharply than I intended. Instead of sitting across from him as I usually did, I eased myself onto the glider, close as a tick on a dog, and held the candle up to my face, trying to look dreamy-eyed.

Nick's face seemed to brighten. He'd never seen this Julie before. My subtle change must be working. Men were supposedly intrigued by mysterious women.

"Nice house," he said. "Where'd you get the art?"

Another point for his side. He'd noticed it wasn't paint-by-number. "Oh, here and there," I said, trying to maintain an enigmatic air. "Why do you ask?"

"Not everyone owns a Georgia O'Keeffe." He sounded impressed.

I shrugged. "I don't know about that. I just liked the colors." I couldn't tell if he believed me or not. No need making him feel bad by reminding him my family had money, even if none of it was mine.

"All the trees in this area came as a surprise. And a fish pond. Very nice."

"Well, yeah. Abilene does have trees. And water. Not quite the same as Waco, but we have pecans, red oaks, mesquites...and the fish pond uses well water."

Then he hit me with a sneak play. "Let's talk about your sin." The expression on his face had turned serious.

"My sin?" I knew he didn't mean the perfume.

"The sin of omission. Why didn't you tell me Philip was a dog? All this time—"

"You never asked."

"But you led me to think he was the love of your life."

"Well, he is. I didn't lie. Everything I said was true. He's sweet, handsome, loving…"

Nick sniffed. "What else haven't you told me?"

"Are you mad at me?" I leaned toward him, pooching out my lips and wrinkling my brow as I'd seen Carmen do.

"I'll get over it." He draped his arm around my shoulders and gave me a playful shake. "But I don't understand why you couldn't tell me."

When I didn't answer, he turned to face me, moving his arm away. I wanted to grab it back and wrap it around me like a boa constrictor. Instead, I held up my candle so I could see his face.

He grinned in a way I'd come to love. "My little mystery girl."

Though my fake aura had attained success, I wished he'd said, "my *sexy* girl" or "my *beautiful* girl," but the thought of being his any-kind-of-girl sent one of those warm chills coursing through me.

"Julie," he whispered, leaning closer, his deep voice huskier than usual.

The way he said *Julie* made me feel like a James Bond martini, except I was shaken *and* stirred.

"Let me have it," he said.

Almost breathless now, I whispered, "Yes." If I'd been hooked up to a pulse monitor, the little electronic heart would have been flashing double-time.

He held out his hand. "The *candle*."

"Oh." I was too excited by now to be embarrassed.

He took the candle, blew it out, and pulled me to my feet. I wobbled slightly, but not from the wine. My whole body was crying out for him to decant me here and now.

"Look up," he said, turning me around so my back pressed against the front of his body. He pointed to the sky. "A falling star."

Moonstruck, I made a wish.

He seemed content to stand there, letting me lean against him. He bent down and inhaled the scent of my hair, and when he exhaled, his breath warmed my neck. I thought back to our first kiss. This time there would be no pulling back, no reluctance on my part.

I pointed up to a break in the trees. "Look. A full moon." Why was it taking him so long to kiss me?

He laughed.

"What?" I asked, angry with him for spoiling the mood.

"That's not the moon. That's your neighbor's floodlight."

"Well, it looks like the moon from here."

"That's what I love about you, Julie. You're so refreshingly honest—except for misleading me about Philip. You're different from anyone I've ever known."

I didn't want to be "refreshingly honest." I wanted to be sexy and desirable. Then it hit me, what he'd just said. He'd used "love" and "you" in the same sentence. It wasn't the same as "I love you," but it would do. I leaned back and twisted my head around so my face was against his neck. Inhaling deeply, I imagined microscopic atoms of his essence filling my lungs, circulating through my blood.

Nick put his hands on my shoulders, turned me to face him, and wrapped his arms around me. Then he placed his lips to the side of my neck right below my ear. Suddenly, I was Frankenstein's creature, a bolt of lightning surging through me. I half expected Nick to cry out, "It's alive!"

Instead, he nibbled lightly on my ear, his breath quickening.

A shiver of longing ran through me, and he held me tighter. "Cold?" he asked.

Considering the temperature, it was unlikely I'd be shivering from the cold, but instead of my usual smart-ass comeback, I tried to stay in character—the new, nicer Julie.

"Let's go inside," I said.

As we entered the living room, I checked out the CD player. "Disc 2" glowed in green digital numbers. I had plenty of time.

Nick glanced around the room. "You must really like candles."

Some were placed strategically, others clumped together on a side table next to picture of me and a toy poodle. Like Philip, whose full name was Philippe Guillaume, my last dog's name was also French—Joseph Robert—Joe Bob for short. Though I hadn't intended it, the table resembled a small shrine.

"Oh, I'm not Catholic," I said quickly, not sure why it mattered, unless birth control became an issue. No way could I tell him the candles were part of my grand seduction plan. He smiled, led me to the sofa, and pulled me down beside him.

We looked into each other's eyes, and slowly our bodies connected like two life-sized magnets. Even if I'd wanted to, I couldn't have pulled away. My arms reached up to his shoulders, and his hands clasped my waist.

"So tiny," he said.

"But unbreakable." Now I *was* lying. Though I'd thought my heart so tough it would take a gallon of meat tenderizer to soften it up, I realized a prime cut had Nick Worthington's name on it, a slice as tender as a filet at Texas Roadhouse.

Philip, who'd been sleeping in his little doggy bed, raised his head and eyed us suspiciously. Contrary to what Sarah had said, he wasn't used to male company.

Nick's lips brushed mine lightly, tentatively. I leaned into him, pressing as much of myself against him as I could, running my hands down his back and over his hips. His muscles were taut and sinewy. He shuddered at my touch, and his hands slid up and cupped my breasts, causing me to tremble. None of my fantasies could compete with Nick in the flesh. Something told me this man was special. Different from the others. In his arms, I felt safe. I hoped it wasn't merely wishful thinking.

His voice turned husky again. "Do you know how difficult it's been, knowing you were there, every night, in bed, with only a few feet of wall between us?" He bent forward and placed his lips on one of my breasts. His breath warmed the cotton fabric of my knit top, the heat radiating outward and down, burning my already parched body. My nipples hardened, and he flicked out his tongue and licked me through the layer of fabric, sending me past redemption. I had imagined this scene countless times, and now that it had arrived, I wanted to remember it forever.

I clutched the back of his head and pulled his face toward mine, while my hips automatically arched into him.

"Every night I've dreamed of touching you like this," he said.

Scrapping my plans to let him undress me, I leaned back, and moving slowly, inch by inch, lifted my top over my head. In the flickering candlelight, Nick watched my every move, his eyes hot with need, burning me with his desire.

As I watched him watch me, I grew less inhibited, performing for my audience of one. I pulled the straps of my bra off my shoulders and caressed my breasts with my eyes locked on Nick's, his on me. I reached behind me, undid the clasp of my bra, and let it fall. Then I reached upward in a gesture of surrender.

At first, he just stared, and I wondered if he was looking for my breasts. Then he reached out and touched my face and gazed into my eyes. "They're perfect. I've pictured them like this from the day we met." Warmth suffused my body. He was talking about my breasts, *my* breasts.

He cupped one in his hand, bent down, and took a nipple in his mouth. He held my other breast firmly, as if he didn't want to lose it. I pressed myself even closer, quivered, and a low moan escaped my lips.

Philip sneezed, jumped out of his little bed, and hobbled out of the room on his three good legs.

I leaned back against the sofa cushions, pulling Nick down with me. My flippy skirt flipped up past my waist. I felt delightfully exposed.

Below decks, Virgin Mary was resurrected. I'd named her Mary back when she was still a virgin and we'd first met. I was twenty at the time and a late bloomer. Though Mary could be contrary, before this night was over, Proud Mary would be rolling on the river.

Nick and I kissed again, this time with more fervor. Our tongues rolled around each other like two oil wrestlers.

Stretched out full length, Nick's body was lean and hard, his breath hot against my neck. He pressed his hips into mine, and we moved rhythmically against each other.

"Oh, God, I want you, Julie."

As I reached down and fumbled with his zipper, a wave of desire made me gasp for air. The room ceased to exist. The whole world ceased to exist. New Orleans or Abilene, at this one moment in time, it didn't matter which big-ass city we were in or even what planet we were on.

Though I tried to hold him back, Nick sat up and moved to the end of the sofa near my feet. I groaned but didn't budge, unless panting counted. He took my feet in his hands and rubbed them firmly from heel to toe. Toe to heel. He was punching all my autopilot buttons, and Proud Mary was revving up her engines, preparing for launch.

His tongue touched the inside of my calf, and slowly, *so* slowly, he began to lick his way home, over my calf, past my knee, then tracing a path inside my thigh. My legs were weak and trembly under his touch. When he got close enough, I held his head in my hands, wanting to guide him higher, but he moved back down toward my feet and tongued his way up my other leg, stopping way too soon. I wasn't sure what he was feeling, but to me *he* felt wonderful.

He gently rubbed his hands up and down the inside of my thighs. "Did you know this is the softest spot on a woman's body?"

All I knew was this man was starving me. Like little Oliver Twist holding up his porridge bowl, I wanted to plead, "More?"

Nick cupped his warm hand over Mary and began to run his finger under the elastic edge of my panties. I was immobile, like The Blob under house arrest. When he leaned over and placed his mouth between my legs and exhaled warmth breath, I arched my back and lifted my hips. That's when I finally saw that star Nick was talking about, but this one was shooting, not falling.

My breath came in short gasps, and my heart thumped like the woofer on my stereo when Waylon Jennings sang "Waltz Across Texas."

"Bedroom," I think Nick said, followed by "comfortable." By this time I was practically blind and deaf.

We got up and stumbled down the hall in the dark till we reached Nick's bedroom and fell onto the bed.

A low growl, followed by a snarling yip ripped me out of my libidinous stupor.

"Holy shit! He *bit* me!" Nick leaped from the bed, almost tossing me onto the floor.

"What? Philip?" I fumbled in the dark for the bedside lamp and flipped the switch. The bright light momentarily blinded me. I blinked. Nick stood at the foot of the bed, a look of astonishment on his face.

"Philip *bit* you?"

"That would be my guess, unless you've set a rat trap in the bed to ward off unwanted guests."

I looked around. Philip had retreated to the far side of the bed where he hunkered on top of a pillow, eyeing Nick warily. Nick's body language was remarkably similar. He headed for the door, his eyes locked on Philip.

"Oh, Nick, I'm so sorry. It's because he's hurt, and we were in his room."

"*His* room?"

"This is his territory. I mean, it's not really *his* room, but he *thinks* it's his room. He often sleeps down here when he's not sleeping with me upstairs. And tonight, after the surgery and all, it would have hurt him too much to climb the stairs."

"That doesn't mean he had to *bite* me!"

"We scared him. An injured and frightened animal will strike back. The only reason he bit you instead of me was because you were...closer." I started to say on bottom but decided against it. "Are you okay?"

"I think I'll survive, but it hurts like hell. You never told me your dog was a man-eater." Nick's normally husky voice was now a grumble. He twisted his head around, attempting to look at his backside. A circle of blood was spreading outward on the seat of his khaki pants.

"You're bleeding. Let's go in the bathroom so I can see how bad it is. I've got antibiotic ointment and alcohol."

"Oh, no. The only alcohol I'm getting close to is the kind you drink."

"Just let me look at it." He followed reluctantly as I pulled him into the adjoining bathroom. I grabbed my robe from the hook on the back of the door and slipped it on. "Dog bites can get infected, but don't worry. Philip had his teeth cleaned a few weeks ago. Now, take your pants off."

"No way!"

You were ready to strip them off a few minutes ago, I wanted to say.

"Then pull them down a little so I can see. I *am* trained in these areas you know."

"You're a vet tech, not a doctor. You decided against med school, remember?"

"It's not that different. At least let me put some anti-septic on it."

"Uh-uh. This was a bad idea. Let's get out of here."

As we passed through the bedroom on our way to the living room, Nick kept his eyes on Philip, as if fearing the little injured dog might suddenly morph into a werewolf.

I gave Nick a quick hug, hoping to placate him. "He's just scared. He's not going to hurt you."

"He just did!"

"Only because you startled him."

Nick grabbed my arm, pulled me into the hall, and shut the door to the bedroom behind us.

Then he strode down the hallway with me running behind him, trying to make things right. "I'm really sorry. He's never bitten anyone before."

Nick gave a rueful laugh. "That makes me feel a lot better."

"Philip loves everybody."

"He has an odd way of showing it."

"You're taking this too personally."

"My butt *is* pretty personal, if you want to know the truth."

"He's just a little dog," I whimpered.

"He's *your* dog, Julie. And he bit me."

Nick was right. And Philip was standing by his woman. That was my fault. I didn't tell Nick I often slept downstairs, too. I'd told Carmen that letting Noche sleep with her was a mistake, but I was just as guilty. Even though Philip had been neutered, he still viewed a strange man in my bed as an interloper. Especially when that man collapsed on top of him.

I stood watching, unable to speak while Nick searched the phone directory and punched in the number of a local cab company. "It's for the best. I'll sleep better in a motel."

"But I don't want you to sleep in a motel. I'm *so* sorry. What can I do to make it up to you? Please don't be angry with me."

Nick's tight lips softened a little. "I'm not angry, just disappointed. Maybe this was all a mistake."

Nooo, I cried inside, but I doubted it would do any good for me to get down on all fours, wiggle my tail, and lick his feet so he'd stay. The spell we'd woven was broken, my dream world crumbled.

For the next ten minutes, I sat silent on the sofa while Nick paced, waiting for the taxi that would take him away. At the beep of its horn, a pang of grief shot through my heart, shattering any leftover visions of Nick and me snuggled against each other when the sun came up.

He opened the door and looked over his shoulder. "I'm sorry, Julie. I'll meet you at the airport tomorrow at ten."

I hung my head, about to cry, then remembered something. "Wait!" I ran to the door and forced a tube of antibiotic ointment and some bandages into his hand.

Why had I been so foolish to think Nick and I could have a relationship? If Nick couldn't love my dog, we were doomed. I barely slept the rest of the night.

Philip, meanwhile, snored contentedly on the pillow next to mine.

Chapter Twelve

Around nine the next morning, I called Carmen, knowing I'd awaken her, but better she find out about Philip from me than from Nick.

Her voice was fuzzy with sleep. "Ju-leeee. How are you? How's Philip?"

"That's why I'm calling. About Philip...uh, he's fine. He's going to be okay. But there's something I need to tell you."

"Is this going to be bad?" Carmen suddenly sounded wide awake.

"Sort of. You see, Philip...he's...well, he's a dog."

Carmen's laugh tinkled over the phone line. "Of course," she said, lowering her voice conspiratorially. "They're all dogs. When Berto gets the slightest—"

"No, no. You don't understand. I mean, he really *is* a dog. Like Noche and Blanco. Philip is a poodle. A toy poodle." My confession was met with silence on the other end. "Carmen? Are you there?"

When Carmen began to giggle, I let out the breath I'd been holding. "A dog? Your live-in love is a dog? A *real* animal-type dog?"

"I'm sorry. It's just that, Nick...I mean, he thought..."

"Does Nick know?" Her voice had a hint of alarm.

"Yeah, I'm afraid he does now." I didn't tell her about Philip biting Nick, hoping Nick might be able to preserve some of his dignity.

"That's so exciting! Nick must be happy, too," Carmen squealed. "I can't wait to meet your little Philip. You can't leave him in Abilene. Not after surgery. He'll need his mama. Bring him back with you."

"What?"

"Bring Philip back to Waco with you today."

"But—"

"No *buts*. He'll be happier. He needs you. I insist."

"But he'll have to start aqua therapy soon. To make sure he'll use the leg. My sister has agreed to do it for me till I get back. She has a pool."

"So do we. You can use ours."

She *was* my boss for the month. And Philip *would* be happier with me. But I had a strong suspicion Nick wasn't going to like the idea at all.

* * *

As I dressed for the flight back to Waco, all I could think about was how Philip, my longtime love, had come between me and the man of my dreams. Like Nick, I was upset about our *sexus interruptus*. But getting bit on the butt—painful and embarrassing though it might be—was no reason to rush out into the night and head for the nearest motel. I should have followed my original instincts instead of letting passion rule my brain. I'd committed the one sin I'd vowed never to commit again. I'd fallen in lust, offered my newly chaste treasure to Nick, and what had it gotten me? Humiliation and abandonment.

Before I put my little fur ball in his travel crate, I hugged him to me, hoping some doggy therapy would make me feel better, but it wasn't the same as holding Nick in my arms.

How would Nick react when he found out his nemesis would be flying the unfriendly skies with us? I was soon to find out.

I walked into the hangar where the plane was housed, tote bag in one hand, Philip's crate in the other. Nick was already there, talking with a couple of men in mechanics' overalls. When he spotted me, he stopped mid-sentence and started toward me, a smile on his face.

One thing I'd discovered about Nick—he regained his composure quickly. But then he looked down at the crate. When he saw Philip's nose pressed against the wire-frame door, Nick came to a dead stop.

I pasted on my best smile, set the crate down, and walked toward him. It took some effort, but I could be magnanimous when the occasion called for it. I reached up and put my arms around him, but Nick stood immobile, making no effort to return my hug. In an instant, he'd turned frosty. Though the temperature was already in the upper 80s, I shivered.

Releasing him, I backed up a step. "So how are you today?" My voice was flat, my smile frozen like his.

"Fine," he muttered, but his eyes darted toward the crate, and his pitch rose a couple of steps on the scale. "You're taking *him*?"

"Yes, I'm taking *him*. He's hurt and he needs me. As soon as his stitches are out, he'll have to start physical therapy."

As if on cue, Philip whined. I turned my back on Nick, walked over to Philip's crate, and knelt beside it. "It's okay, baby. You're going to be fine. Mama's going to take care of you now."

When I glanced up at Nick, he was still eyeballing the crate with distrust. "Don't worry. He can't get out," I said, sarcasm oozing from my lips like dog drool. As soon as the words were out of my mouth, I regretted them. Philip had, after all, bitten Nick till he bled. "I'm sorry. That was uncalled for. How are you today? Is your—?" I looked around to make sure the men were out of hearing range. "How's your...bite?" I'd almost said *butt*.

I took hold of the handle on the crate and stood up carefully, hoping the movement wouldn't hurt Philip. "You should probably let a doctor look at it. Even though he bit you through your clothes, it could get infected. I'll pay for it."

Nick's body grew rigid at the mention of the dog bite. "I said I'm fine." Eyes averted, he grabbed my tote bag and climbed inside the plane. Behind him, I hoisted Philip's crate without assistance and maneuvered us both up the small steps leading to the rear door. Nick seated himself gingerly in the pilot's seat, wincing as his right buttock touched down.

Neither of us spoke during preparation for takeoff, except for some reassuring words from me to Philip when he whined. Soon we were airborne and headed back to Waco.

Nick kept his eyes straight ahead, though there was nothing to see but blue sky. "Does Carmen know?"

"She's the one who insisted I bring him."

Nick's jaw tightened. "So she knew Philip was a dog."

"Not until this morning when I told her on the phone. You found out first."

His laugh was grim. "Yeah, the hard way. I guess you also told her about him biting me."

"It's nothing to be ashamed of. I'm the one who should be embarrassed, not you. But no, I didn't tell her." I tried to lighten the mood. "You could always say *I* bit you."

I waited, and when the smiled I'd hoped for didn't appear, I made another attempt at summoning the old Nick. "Look, I've tried everything I can think of to make this up to you. I'm sorry you got bit. I'm sorry you're in pain. I'm sorry if you're embarrassed. But I'd like to get past this. Philip isn't Cujo. He's just a little guy who's been through a painful surgery, whose mama has been gone for two weeks, and who struck out defensively when he felt threatened. Can't you understand where Philip was coming from?"

"Can't you see where *I'm* coming from? You treat that dog nicer than you do me."

"Now you sound like Berto. Except *you're* jealous of a tiny, ten-pound poodle?"

"Don't be ridiculous."

"Then what is it?"

He shifted in his seat. I couldn't tell if the dog bite or the conversation was causing his discomfort. He didn't answer at first, and his cheek twitched when he finally spoke. "I helped you with Noche and Blanco, right? But this is different. This is your dog, and you obviously care a lot about him."

"So?"

"It's just that—"

"You *are* jealous."

"No, I'm *not* jealous," he said defiantly. "How could I be jealous of a dog?"

"Then what?"

His hands gripped the yoke, and his voice grew hard. "I don't want to talk about it. Let's change the subject."

"What do you mean? Don't you think you owe me some kind of explanation? What's the problem? Why can't you just—"

He turned toward me, wincing. "Julie!" he snapped, "I *said* I don't want to talk about it."

I defiantly held his gaze a moment then turned away from him and stared straight ahead, my face a blank. Inwardly, I seethed.

We arrived at the Espositos' house shortly before noon. I'd hoped to avoid seeing either of them until I'd had time to sort out my feelings, but Carmen was standing in the driveway as we pulled up in the Lexus.

When I got out, she rushed over and hugged me. "I'm so glad you're back. Berto is in San Antonio on business, and it's been lonely here without you." As I lifted Philip's crate from the backseat, she let out a squeal. "Ohhh, let me see the little one. I want to meet Philip."

"Better watch out," Nick growled, pulling his suitcase from the trunk. "His bite is worse than his bark." With that, he strode off toward the house.

Carmen's eyes grew large. "What's up with him?"

"He's suffering from IMS."

She looked puzzled. "What's that?"

"Incomprehensible Male Syndrome."

Carmen smiled. "They all have that." She squeezed my arm. "Did you two have a fight? I thought maybe in a new setting you might—"

"Uh-uh. You're too much the romantic. I told you Nick isn't the kind of man I'm looking for."

"Julie, I've known Nick a long time. I notice things—"

"Ha. And I thought *I* had a vivid imagination. Meet Philip. He's a good boy, but he's had a rough time the past few days."

She stooped down and peered into Philip's crate. "He's so little!"

"Ten pounds. But he's all poodle." And at only ten pounds, he was enough poodle to exert thirty pounds of pressure into a bite.

I could tell Carmen was itching for me to take him out of the crate so she could hold him, but now was not the time. "He's still pretty upset from the surgery and the trip. He's not used to flying. Once we get settled, you can come see him. He really loves people." That part was true. He was a friendly little guy. Nick just didn't understand. And I didn't understand anyone who didn't love dogs.

"That reminds me." Carmen sounded perturbed. "I told Berto you were bringing him and about the therapy." Color rose to her face, and her eyes blazed with anger. "He said he didn't want a dog in his pool. I argued with him, but he wouldn't listen. But don't worry. We'll work something out."

"It's okay," I said, though it really wasn't. I wouldn't have brought Philip except for her promise of the pool.

She stomped her tiny foot. "Berto's just so stubborn. Once when Noche and Blanco got loose and jumped into the pool, he made Ramón drain it. Said he didn't want to swim in water where a dog had peed."

"People are more likely to pee in it than a dog. Dogs have their standards, you know."

Carmen looked as if she might cry. "It hurts me Berto doesn't understand how I feel about them. He's jealous.

Hard to believe, isn't it? Macho man Berto, threatened by a couple of poodles."

She might be right about Berto, but Nick's reluctance to confide in me and his reaction to Philip was something more.

I was relieved when Nick left for San Antonio, more so when he said he'd spending a few days there before bringing Berto home. At the same time, I felt empty, which led to my imagination working overtime. Part of it, I blamed on Butch. He'd planted a seed of doubt with his hints about the shady nature of Berto's business transactions. Was Berto really importing more than furniture? And what about New Orleans? Could Nick be involved in something illegal? Were they partners in crime?

With only a couple of weeks left before the dogs' "coming out" party, Carmen and I stepped up our training to three sessions a day. Noche and Blanco seemed to relish the enrichment. We all seemed more relaxed and confident without the men around. Not only had the dogs mastered *sit* and *stay*, they could also perform a *down-stay* for three minutes. Even when we added distractions—like bouncing a ball—they remained in place, except to swivel their heads toward the ball.

"It's amazing," Carmen told me one afternoon when we'd finished a particularly successful session. "They're like two different dogs!"

"Yes, and you haven't broken their spirit. They're still as playful and loving as they ever were, but they know who's in command now."

"I can't wait for Berto to see them perform. And I have another big surprise planned for him the night of their graduation."

Knowing Carmen, I was afraid to ask what that might be.

* * *

Later that week, I noticed Carmen seemed unusually animated during our morning session with the dogs, but when I asked her what was up, she just looked at me from under her fall of dark hair and smiled mysteriously.

That afternoon, as I sat reading under an umbrella by the pool, I caught a glimpse of Nick coming out the back door of the big house. My heart lurched. His white shirt provided a stark contrast to his golden skin and dark hair. When he moved his arms, his muscular back strained against the fabric.

I tossed my book aside and sat up straighter to get a better view. Philip looked up from my lap where he'd been sleeping and sneezed. I waited, brazenly hoping to catch Nick's eye. Maybe by now he would have forgotten the biting incident, though I'd forgotten very little of that evening. In fact, as I rewound that night and replayed it over and over, it had taken on the proportions of an epic. Images of us in each other's arms, the feel of his body against mine, the warmth of his touch—I was Scarlett O'Hara, swept off my feet by his Rhett, while the Civil War raged in the background.

Why was Nick now lingering in the doorway with his back to me? Then I saw a woman—all long black hair and light brown skin. Her tinkling laughter wafted through the air in my direction. Each note tugged at my heart. Nick leaned forward, whispering in her ear. She laughed again and hit him playfully on the arm. Inwardly, I curled into a fetal position.

The resemblance was striking. She had to be Carmen's daughter, the one who lived in California and didn't come home often enough to suit her mother. I'd never seen Nick so animated. But what man wouldn't be—she was beautiful.

The physical ache in my chest grew stronger until I pulled my eyes away and gathered Philip into my arms, preparing to head for my apartment to nurse my wounds in private. Too late. Like Lot's wife, I looked back just as Carmen appeared behind the laughing couple. She caught my eye and motioned me toward them. I had no choice but to comply. She knew I'd seen her.

I set Philip on the ground and held onto his leash as he valiantly scampered on three legs toward the trio. Except for the fact his shaved appendage looked like a raw chicken leg and he held it aloft, no one would ever guess he'd had surgery a few days before. His energy and friendly personality had returned, and he'd already won Carmen's heart. When he saw her, he gave a yip of joy and tried to stand upright on his one good back leg.

"*Mi pequeño*," Carmen squealed, running toward him and scooping him up in her arms. "Just look at this little sweetie. He's going to be using his leg again in no time."

She didn't see the shadow that passed over Nick's face. "Nick, now that you're back, maybe you can help Julie with his therapy."

I still hadn't told Carmen about the biting incident and didn't intend to. Whenever she brought up our trip to Abilene, I was deliberately vague.

After she accepted numerous wet kisses from Philip, she set him down gently and ruffled the fur on his back. "That's more kisses than I've gotten from Berto in a year. Oh, Julie, seeing your little one makes me want another one of my own."

"Oh, no, Mamá. He *is* a cutie, but you've had a hard enough time getting Papá to accept Noche and Blanco."

Carmen smiled proudly and turned toward the gorgeous young woman who resembled her. "Julie, meet my daughter, Barbi."

My guess had been right. But *Barbi*? I'd expected Carmen's daughter to be named "Ángel" or "Catalina" or "Esperanza"—a beautiful Hispanic name to match her looks. But *Barbi*? Bewilderment must have shown on my face.

Carmen laughed. "Yes, I wanted her to have an *American* name."

Was she named after the doll or Hugh Hefner's former girlfriend?

Barbi smiled graciously and extended her hand, while I stood there pondering her name. "Please. Everyone but Mamá calls me Babe."

I stole a glance at Nick. The thought of him calling her Babe made me feel worse. She *was* one. Nick had grown quiet as soon as Philip and I appeared. I couldn't read his expression, but when I looked into his eyes and then at his mouth, my face turned warm. All I could think about was how his tongue had traced its way up my leg, the softness of his lips, and his hands and mouth on my breasts. My nipples grew hard and the tingle between my legs made me weak.

I tried to conceal my reaction by focusing on *Babe*. I even tried thinking of Paul Bunyan's blue ox of the same name to uglify her, but it didn't work. This Babe was stunning. My only option was to act sickeningly sweet. "I understand you live in California. How could you leave that wonderful climate and come to Texas during the hottest month of the year?"

She smiled and looked up at Nick in adoration. "For one thing, Nicky finally found time to come get me." She pooched out her full lips and grabbed his arm and shook it, as if scolding him.

Nicky? I expected Nick to cringe, but to my chagrin, he gave her a quick hug. I tried to tell myself it was brotherly. After all, he'd known the family for years and must be ten years older than Barbi, if not more.

Barbi's full, dark eyelashes fluttered against her cheeks. "I try to get home between shoots." For some reason I heard "chutes" and thought of bull riding.

Before my imagination had her biting the dust at the mercy of a wild bull, Carmen elaborated. "Barbi is an actress."

"Mamá has a bad habit of embellishing. So far only some television walk-ons and a small role in a soap opera."

Carmen stood up straighter. "I do not embellish. She is so good she's landed an important new agent who says she's going to be a star."

Barbi flashed me an award-winning smile. "See what I mean?"

Nick put his hands on Barbi's shoulders and gave her a friendly shake. Too friendly for my liking. "Don't be so modest," he said. "I've seen you and you're good!" I wondered how much of her he'd seen. By now the green-eyed monster had me fully in its clutches.

Barbi turned the conversation to me. "I hear you're doing great things with Mamá's wild *perros*."

It was my turn to be modest. "Your mother has done a great job." I meant every word of it. Surprisingly, Carmen was showing a natural talent for handling the two dogs now that she'd overcome her fear of breaking their spirit and gained the confidence to assert herself.

Carmen shook her head vehemently. "Julie is the one who deserves credit. Noche and Blanco *love* her."

Nick intervened. "Enough of the mutual admiration society. If we're going to make it to town before the mall closes, we'd better get going." His words were directed at Barbi. I was still having a hard time thinking of her as *Babe*. Since when was Nick also the designated driver? Did Barbi—*Babe*—not drive? Wasn't that a requirement for anyone living in LA?

Carmen smiled, opened the back door, and pushed them through. "You two get out of here. I'll see you at dinner. Julie, you're coming, too, of course."

I muttered a lame excuse about having to tend to Philip, but Carmen wouldn't take no for an answer. That meant I'd be stuck watching Nick and Babe make goo-goo eyes at each other. I resolved to come down with the *epizootis* or some other made-up disease.

As it turned out, my epizootis claim didn't work, but dinner was tolerable. Berto was back from another business trip, Carmen raved to him about the great strides we'd made with the dogs, and Babe told some

funny behind-the-scenes stories about the crazy characters on the soap opera set. If I hadn't been so jealous of
her, we probably could have been friends. She had a
great sense of humor, and I could have tolerated the
beautiful part if Nick hadn't been in the picture.

Nick said little that evening, even to Babe, which suited me just fine. Whatever he had on his mind, he was
keeping it to himself.

* * *

It was time to rededicate myself. I was back in Waco,
my not-so-happy husband hunting grounds, and I still
needed a husband. Butch had been a bad choice. But I'd
never let a bad choice stop me before. Carmen seemed to
think muchas-dates.com was the way to go, so maybe
she knew something I didn't. I'd tried every other way of
meeting men from smoke-filled bars to grocery stores,
and where had that gotten me?

I could kick myself. I *should* kick myself over the Nick
fiasco. I might as well admit he'd lost interest in me.
First Philip biting him, now Babe probably doing some
nibbling of her own. The odds were stacked against me,
and I didn't stand a chance.

Average Internet Joe could be my man. The more I
thought about it, the more I thought how perfectly suited
for me he might be. Low-maintenance Joe with his little
dog.

I emailed him to reschedule our date. Computer guru
Joe must have been at work, because a few seconds after
I'd shot my message off into cyberspace, I heard a beep
telling me I had mail. Joe had agreed to meet me for
lunch the next day. Something told me this was it—Waco
had finally produced a winner.

I hadn't asked for a description, since I figured I'd recognize him from his picture. I'd told him I was medium
height with brown hair and would be wearing jeans and
a pink T-shirt.

"Jeans!" Carmen said, as I was leaving.

I laughed and wiggled my hips. "He might as well know what kind of wife he's getting. If he doesn't like jeans, then we'll have a problem."

Arriving early, I pulled the Lexus into the Cotton Patch parking lot, looking around for smiley-face Joe. My hands were cold and clammy though the temperature must have been inching upwards toward 100 as I checked my lipstick in the rearview mirror one last time. We'd agreed to meet inside at eleven, as soon as they opened, because Joe wanted to beat the crowd. I checked my watch. Ten thirty-five. I didn't want to appear overly eager, but it was too hot to sit in the car. Employees were carrying boxes in and out one of the front entrances, so I asked if I could wait inside. They pointed to some wooden benches near the hostess stand, and I sat down to wait. I rummaged in my purse and pulled out the book I'd been reading. *Know Thy Dog* contained short chapters explaining certain doggy behaviors, like why they eat poop and love to roll in dead stuff.

I got so engrossed I forgot the time. When I looked up and saw people being seated, I checked my watch. Ten fifty-five.

Just then, the door opened. The man coming through the door couldn't be Future-Husband Joe, even if he *was* five minutes early. His hairline wasn't merely receding. He had a serious comb-over and was a good fifty pounds overweight.

If he was only thirty-two as he claimed, he'd had a really tough life. His teeth were as yellow as his hair, what there was of it. I'd told Carmen looks didn't matter. Maybe Joe had a great personality. It was only lunch. It wasn't like I knew anyone in Waco who might see me with him. He could be my boss for all anyone knew. Nevertheless, I looked around to see if anyone was watching. The hostess didn't even look up. At thirty-two, I was well on my way to becoming invisible. Before long, *men* would be looking straight through me, according to my mother. Maybe that's why she wore those crazy red hats.

"You must be Julie." The smiley face grew rounder, and he thrust out his hand.

"And you must be Joe." I forced myself to smile back, wanting to slip him some Crest Whitestrips.

Before I knew what was happening, Joe's outstretched hand pulled me to him in a hug. The smell of cigarette smoke was so strong I had to hold my breath. I stiffened and pressed my arms to my sides until Joe released me.

I nodded reluctantly when the hostess asked if we were a party of two and followed as she seated us in a booth. I told myself not to rule him out based on the first five minutes. Joe might be an uncut diamond. *Beauty and the Beast* immediately came to mind. But the Beast had been cuter, more like a fuzzy dog.

"Good to finally meet you," he said. "You won't believe this, but I've been on muchas-dates for three whole months now, and you're my first bite." He laughed so loud heads bobbed up from the other booths like prairie dogs popping out of their burrows. "Bite, byte, get it? It's a computer term."

I smiled lamely.

"Julie Shields," Joe crooned. "Such a pretty name for a pretty girl. And not married yet."

I especially hated the "yet." I gave Joe what I hoped was a withering look. "Definitely *not* married."

"How long have you been divorced?"

"And *not* divorced."

"You mean you've *never* been married?" Joe looked at me as if I were an anomaly.

"What about you?" I took my time as I unwrapped the silverware and placed the napkin in my lap. Anything to avoid looking at him.

"Couple of times. But I've been a swinging bachelor again for the past three months." He grinned.

I reassured myself it was only lunch and I would be free of him in an hour. I sneaked a peak at my watch, whose second hand seemed to be moving more slowly than usual. "How's single life this go-round?"

"Not bad, but I miss being married. My wife, my last wife, she found someone else. She wanted to go out all the time and didn't understand we couldn't afford it. Child support was killing me."

Joe kept talking, but I'd quit listening when I heard *child support*. For some reason, I hadn't thought about kids, only his dog. I couldn't help thinking about all the baggage Father Joe must be lugging around.

A perky waitress appeared and handed us menus. "My name is Amy. I'll be your server today. Can I get you anything to drink?"

Nothing they served would be strong enough.

"Hi, Amy," said Joe, waggling his eyebrows like Groucho. "My name is Joe, and this is..."

I swear he hesitated, as if he didn't know my name. I really hated it when guys flirted or got cutesy with the waitress.

"Just call me Ishmael," I told Amy, unable to meet her eyes. "A glass of Waco water for me, with some lemon, please." Waco water was an acquired taste I had yet to acquire. Lemon helped dull part of the nasty tang, which had been attributed to everything from excessive nutrients, such as nitrogen or phosphorus, to something called *geosmin* given off by dead algae.

"Sure you don't want something stronger?" Joe asked, as if he'd been reading my mind.

"No thanks."

"Bring me a Bud," Joe said. An image of Archie Bunker flashed through my brain. I held the menu close to my face to disguise the fact I didn't want to look at Joe. I studied it as long as possible, hoping if I was slow enough, Joe would have to go back to work.

"Take your time," he said. "I've got the afternoon off."

What? Was Irish-American Joe expecting to get lucky?

Amy the waitress reappeared. "Have you made a decision yet?" she chirped.

Oh, yes.

Joe was studying the menu as if it were a computer manual. "Give us a few more minutes." He looked up at me. "Don't order the meatloaf. It gave me diarrhea a few weeks ago."

My lip curled involuntarily. "Too much information. But don't worry. I never eat beef." It wasn't true. Joe was bringing out my perverse side.

He drew back and looked at me in disbelief. "You're kidding. You aren't from around here, are you?"

"No, but I *am* a Texan if that's what you mean."

"I can't imagine a Texan who doesn't eat beef. Wait a minute." He pointed a finger at me. "I'll bet you're from Austin. They've got lots of those veggie...vegan types there."

I gave him a slight grin. "Nope, Abilene. Born there. Lived most of my life there. Smack dab in the middle of cattle country."

Amy reappeared just in time and asked again if we'd made a choice. Joe evidently didn't know he was supposed to ask the lady, a.k.a. *me*, before he ordered for himself. "I'll have a double-meat double-cheeseburger and curly fries," he said.

Looming over us on the wall behind Joe was a large mural of cows grazing in a meadow. The cows seemed to be looking straight at me. The thought of ordering a hamburger made me queasy. Besides, I'd made my veggie bed, and now I had to order it.

Amy turned to me.

"I'll take the Wabbit Platter. Broccoli, green beans, black-eyed peas, and salad with vinaigrette on the side."

"Hey, you weren't kidding," Joe said. "You ever *tried* beef?"

"Only once." I fabricated the story as I spoke. "When I found out I was eating Dolly, my favorite cow, I got sick and could never eat the stuff again."

"You serious? So you had a *cow*?" He began to laugh at his own weak attempt at humor.

"It was my *pet* cow!" I'd begun to believe the story so much that tears welled up in my eyes. Maybe *I* should go to Hollywood.

I excused myself to powder my nose and considered slipping out through a side door, but I'd been taught better manners. I took my time, and when I returned to the table, *I* asked the questions.

"You said you're a computer analyst. Where do you work?"

Amy arrived with our food, and Joe wasted no time wrapping his tobacco-stained teeth around his burger, but he managed to talk with his mouth full and chew at the same time.

"Self-employed." Joe's beefy chest puffed out.

"Do you have your own shop, or do you work for someone else?"

"For now, I'm living with my grandmother and work out of my bedroom, but I hope to own my own shop someday."

Divorced twice, maybe more? At least two kids. Lives with his *grandmother*? More proof I was hopeless at choosing men. It wasn't his fault—it was mine. Therefore, I would maintain my poise, despite Joe's shortcomings, until I could make a dignified exit. That meant trying to carry on a conversation. I would tell myself he was a cousin I hadn't seen in years. That way I could disassociate myself from the reality of his being my date.

"Sorry to sound ignorant, but what exactly does a computer analyst do?" I knew how to use a computer, but beyond that I was technologically challenged and planned to stay that way. Cell phones, BlackBerries, iPods—people toys. I'd rather play with a dog.

Joe took another bite of his double-double burger. "Mainly, I do small repairs. Like, say someone gets a virus or has a configuration problem. I fix it for them. Most people I deal with don't know jack. Take the other day. This woman brings me her computer and says she can't get the little boxes off her desktop. All she has to do is click on the 'x' in the corner, but instead she keeps clicking on the browser icon, which creates more little boxes. People like that shouldn't be allowed to own a computer." Joe shoved the last of his curly fries into his mouth.

"But if it weren't for people like that, I wouldn't have a job. I can make fifty bucks in five minutes because she'll never know what I've done."

"So, you're like a computer doctor."

"Yeah, that's it." His face brightened. "I deal with emergencies lots of times. Or sometimes people need more RAM installed or they want to set up a wireless router. I also make house calls." He gave me a lascivious yellow grin.

"So tell me about your dog. What's his name?"

Joe sat up straighter at the mention of his dog. "His name's Kisser."

"Kisser. That's a sweet name." I thought of little Philip, who loved to kiss.

"Yeah, I say, 'Come here, Kisser,' and he plants a big one on me."

When I pointed to his mouth, Joe raised his napkin and wiped at the burger juice running down his chin. Maybe I *would* give up beef. "I'll bet Kisser is happy having you at home all day. My little guy just goes crazy when I come home from work."

"Yeah, he's always glad to see me, especially in the summer when it's hot outside and I let him in the house."

"You mean he's an *outside* dog?" From Joe's online profile, I'd assumed he and Kisser were close.

"I let him in sometimes, but he likes it better outside."
Probably avoiding all the second-hand smoke.

"You said he's your hobby. Is he a show dog? Or agility? Obedience?"

"Kisser? Nah, Kisser's full blood pit bull."

Dogs like pit bulls often got a bad rap, but they could make sweet companions with the right owner and proper training. I was just about to say as much when Joe continued.

"He's obedient *and* agile. I guess you could say he's in the sporting class." Joe laughed so loud this time my Waco water rippled. "Kisser's a fighter. Say, maybe you'd like to come watch him fight this weekend. He's going to be defending his title against Bloody Rex, this dog from East Texas."

I almost spit out my black-eyed peas.

When I'd read "computer analyst" on Joe's online profile, I'd thought Michael Dell, not Michael Vick. Now, in addition to being unethical in his business dealings, he was also involved in illegal and inhumane treatment of dogs.

I took a big swig of water, and as I lowered the glass, I thought I saw Nick walk in. My heart began to thump against my breastbone. I squinted. It *was* Nick. And Babe was beside him. The Cotton Patch was the last place I'd have expected to see either one of them.

I started to duck my head, hoping they wouldn't see me, but was too late. They were headed straight for our booth. Babe waved to me. My cheeks were on fire. I wiped the condensation from the side of my water glass and patted it on my face.

Babe looked gorgeous in a slinky purple skirt and tiny tank top. Now I wished I'd listened to Carmen and worn something dressier than jeans. Compared to Babe, I looked downright dowdy.

"Julie!" Nick called out. His white teeth could have starred in a toothpaste commercial. I hoped Joe would keep his mouth shut. "What a coincidence. Care if we join you?"

My worst nightmare was happening shortly after high noon in Waco, Texas. I began digging in my purse for my billfold. "We were just finishing up."

Nick stood at my end of the bench seat, blocking me in. "You can stay a little longer, can't you? At least do us the honor of introducing us to your friend."

Babe might not know it, and Joe didn't know it, but I knew it—Nick was making me squirm and enjoying every minute of it. Before I could protest, he'd wedged himself in beside me, and Babe had sat down opposite us, next to Joe.

Nick reached across the table to shake Joe's hand. "Nick Worthington. And the lovely lady next to you is Babe Esposito." Babe smiled sweetly, though she must have noticed Joe eyeballing her cleavage.

The warmth of Nick's thigh against mine unnerved me so much my knees began to quiver. I took a gulp of water. I think Joe told them his name, but I was too rattled to notice. Nick's proximity had transported me to the realms of heightened unreality.

"So, Joe," Nick asked, "how is it you and Julie know each other? Are you from Abilene?"

"You kidding?" Joe took a long pull on his third Bud. "Nope, we met on muchas-dates.com. Seems we have a lot in common. We're both dog people."

Nick's eyes sparkled with amusement. "Then I guess Julie told you she's here training a couple of poodles? Doing a great job, too."

"Poodles?" Joe gave a short bark of laughter. "What good are they? Fancy wuss dogs. Okay for women, I guess, but a real man needs a real dog." Joe glanced at Babe for approval, but she was looking at Nick.

"What kind of dog do you have?" Nick asked.

Joe reached into his shirt pocket, pulled out a cigarette, and tapped it on the table. "Pit bull."

One thing I loved about Waco. The city had an ordinance that prohibited smoking in restaurants. If I was lucky, Smokeless Joe would decide he could take it no longer and go outside, which would be my cue to say adios to all three of my lunch companions.

183

Amy appeared with menus for Nick and Babe, and as she took their drink orders, I planned my escape. Looking at my watch, I feigned a look of absolute horror. "Oh, no. Look at the time! I was having so much fun I totally forgot Carmen is waiting for me to give the dogs their next lesson." I pushed Nick's butt with mine as hard as I could, forcing him to stand up and let me out.

Nick grinned and stretched his arms out, his muscles rippling. "Just when we were all getting to know one another."

Aiming eye daggers at him, I used my sweetest voice. "Oh, you guys stay here and enjoy yourselves. On me," I said, slapping a couple of Alexander Hamiltons on the table. "Joe, great meeting you. Babe, good to see you again. We all need to do this again sometime."

To his credit, Joe tried to stand up, but Babe was blocking him in and I was faster.

"I'll call you," he said, but I'd already turned away. "Wait! I don't know your number!" he called out as I strode toward the door.

The next thing I knew, I was in the Lexus, speeding down Lakeshore Drive with the rest of the village idiots. "Free! I'm free!" I shouted out loud. Now I knew how the dogs felt when I released them from a *stay*.

Then Nick's last words hit me. I was pretty sure I'd heard him tell Joe, "I'll give you her number."

* * *

I saw little of Nick or Babe for the next few days. Carmen said Babe was visiting old high school friends and shopping. I still wondered why she needed Nick to drive her.

When Philip's knee had healed enough, I removed the stitches from his little Franken-dog leg and filled the tub for our first session of aqua therapy.

I stripped to my underwear and held him close to my chest as I eased into the big tub. Poodles might have been water dogs centuries ago, but Philip had never liked getting wet. The second his back feet touched the water, he began climbing higher until he was perched on my shoulder with his front paws scrambling to climb onto my head, his claws digging into my bare skin.

"Ouch, come on, Philip. Be a good boy." I pulled him off me, his little legs flailing, and lowered him into the water, holding him upright. "Bounce, bounce, bounce," I sang, as I pushed him up and down. The objective was to bounce him up and down on his back legs to build up strength in the muscles around his newly repaired knee and encourage use of the leg. Though the tub was wide, it wasn't deep enough, but it was all I had. I considered sneaking into the swimming pool in the dark of night, but with Berto's penchant for lurking around at all hours, I couldn't chance it.

After a few minutes, my arms and back were aching. "Break time." I held Philip close to me for a few seconds so we could catch our breath. I wasn't sure about Philip's leg, but my arm and shoulder muscles were definitely getting a workout. I was about to start the next set of bounces when the phone rang.

"Okay, long break, Philip. Gotta get the phone. Might be important." I'd always talked to Philip as if he were an equal, except for the times I used baby talk.

I stepped out of the tub, holding him in front of me. Setting him on the bath mat, I reached for a towel and wrapped it around him, but not before he shook water in my face and hair. I quickly grabbed another towel for myself and raced to the phone.

Let it be Nick. Let it be Nick. He would tell me how bored he was squiring Babe all over town and how he wanted me instead.

The voice on the other end was male all right, but it wasn't Nick.

"Julie? Butch Justice here. I need you to meet me. *Now.* It's an emergency!"

Chapter Thirteen

Butch's voice sounded raspy. "I said I need you *now*!"

Shocked he had the nerve to call me, much less make demands, I stood there dripping water with my mouth open and no sound coming out. The date from hell with him was still burned into my memory like a bad DVD. I set Philip down, held the phone away from my ear, and stared at it as if it had taken on a life of its own.

Water continued to drip onto the bedroom carpet from my sopping underwear, and I was about to lose the towel I'd hurriedly wrapped around myself. At that inopportune moment, Philip succumbed to a case of the doggy crazies. He began tearing through the apartment in a tuck-butt-run, like he always did after a bath. I tried to grab him as he headed toward the bed and missed. Using his good back leg, he sprang onto the pillows and shook furiously, leaving a dark circle of water on the bedspread before leaping down and taking off for the living room.

"Julie? You there?" Butch's voice twanged like an out-of-tune guitar. I was tempted to hang up the phone or pretend I was the maid, but the urgency in his voice aroused my curiosity.

"Yeah, I'm here. What do you want?" I growled into the mouthpiece. Reaching out, I managed to block Philip as he made another three-legged lap through the room.

"Hey, you don't have to sound so happy to hear from me. I'm calling about an important matter. I need you to meet me at Lovers Leap."

"*Lover's Leap*? You've got to be kidding."

Since I'd been in Waco, I'd heard plenty about Lovers Leap in Cameron Park. Every week the *Trib* ran a new story about someone who'd ignored the warning signs and ventured over the retaining wall onto the chalky incline where only a few scraggly cedars survived. Several people had fallen to their death in that area when the limestone gave way and sent them plunging down the rock face.

Undeterred, Butch turned on his cop voice. "I'm serious, Julie. I've got a critical emergency situation here, and I need you."

I let out a loud sigh so he'd be sure to hear it.

"It's this here injured dog, and it needs your help."

So did his grammar, but he'd said the magic word, *dog*. "What do you mean? What's happened?"

"Don't ask me. I was just driving through the park and heard him. I can't see him, but he sounds like he's hurting pretty bad."

"Doesn't Waco have an emergency vet service?"

"No. I've tried to get hold of several vets, but they're all at a convention in Dallas." The line crackled. "You're breaking up. There he goes again. You hear that wail?"

Butch didn't speak for a few seconds, and I heard what sounded like a dog crying in the background. That really got my attention. "Butch, I wish I could help, but I don't even have a car."

"Borrow one. Your friends have plenty. But don't say what it's for. The Espositos don't like me much."

I wanted to ask why, but this was not the time. "Do you know what kind of dog it is? Can you see it?"

"No, but I can hear it, and it sounds big. You need to get here fast."

He began issuing directions, but I cut him off. "I know where Lovers Leap is. What about the fire department? Have you called them?"

"Can't hear you, Julie. The connection's breaking up again." More crackling. "Uh-oh, I think my battery—"

"Butch? Butch!"

The line had gone dead.

My mind flashed back to the night I'd gone out with him, his insinuations about the Espositos and how Carmen and Berto reacted when they heard his name. And later, Nick ordering me to not to see Butch again.

As usual, when I faced a tense situation, my sister's voice echoed in my head. *Don't be so impulsive, Julie. Think before you act. You're like the girl in one of those bad horror films, the one who always checks the basement though she knows the killer is probably waiting down there with an ax.*

Someone had even come up with a name for these characters: "Too Dumb to Live."

But this wasn't a movie. Butch was a *policeman.* And though he might act like a hick, I hadn't given him much of a chance on our date, not to mention my tendency to let my imagination run away with me. Anyway, the thought of an animal in pain was more than I could bear—I had no choice but to try to help.

I replaced the phone, then tore through the apartment as Philip had done a few minutes earlier. I towel dried my hair, not bothering to comb it, and threw on some jeans and a T-shirt. Then I grabbed a roll of gauze for a makeshift muzzle and some Betadine solution from Philip's travel kit and stuffed them in my purse. After a quick hug and kiss for Philip, I was out the door and running up the pathway to the big house.

Carmen and Berto, along with Babe and Nick, were sitting outside on the patio under the ceiling fans, sipping beers and watching the sunset. *Cozy.* Two beautiful couples. Nick looked up and frowned when he saw me. Babe smiled sweetly. Berto scowled, and Carmen seemed puzzled.

Out of breath from running uphill and the adrenaline rush brought on by Butch's call for help, I blurted out my request. "I need a car. Carmen, can I borrow yours? Just for a quick trip into town? I hate to ask, but it's really important." Butch needn't have worried about my mentioning him. The last thing I wanted was for the Espositos and Nick to know I was seeing Butch Justice again, even if it was for a good cause.

Berto eyed me suspiciously, so I kept my eyes fixed on Carmen. "Please? I won't be gone more than a couple of hours."

She didn't hesitate. "Of course. Anything we can help you with? Philip's okay, I hope." Carmen's soft eyes reflected her concern.

"He's fine. There's just this...errand I need to run."

Berto's dark brows knit together. "It's almost dark."

I contorted my face in my best desperate look, pretending I was Ingrid Bergman. "I promise I'll be careful."

Carmen went inside without another word, and when she emerged a few seconds later she held out her hand. "Here, take my keys."

I raced off toward the garage without looking back.

* * *

The tires on Carmen's Lexus squealed as I pulled out onto Lakeshore Drive. For once I was happy the street served as the local autobahn. I headed northeast and drove well above the speed limit for about three miles, then hooked a right onto Martin Luther King Jr. Boulevard. Another mile or so, and I'd be in Cameron Park.

Berto had been right about darkness descending. Though Carmen and I had taken the dogs to the park a couple of times during the day, by the time I got there, it was almost dark. The winding, tree-covered roads confused me, and I took several wrong turns before I spied the sign pointing to Lovers Leap. The road led to a paved area, a dead end.

When I spotted Butch's pickup, I skidded to a stop, grabbed my purse, and leaped out, using the electronic remote to lock Carmen's car. Cameron Park after dark was not the place to leave a purse or a Lexus unattended.

But where was Butch? I walked to the other side of his pickup and found him leaning against the door. He stretched and looked at his watch. "Took you long enough."

I wasted no time on pleasantries. "Where is he? The dog. Where's the dog?"

Butch jerked his head to the side. "This way."

Beyond the pavement was a low stone curb. Past that, a few feet of level ground ended at a retaining wall about four feet high. Triangular-shaped signs warning DANGER DO NOT GO BEYOND THIS WALL left no room for doubt that danger did, indeed, lie in the darkness on the other side.

At the foot of the rocky cliff lay the Brazos River. Butch swung his leg over the wall and held out his hands to me. "You got to climb over."

"Are you sure it's safe? The sign says—"

"You want to help the dog or not?"

I swallowed hard and gingerly lifted myself onto the ledge.

"Come on," Butch said. "We don't got all night."

I slid over the wall and lowered myself to the other side, unable to see in the darkness. While seeking solid ground, my foot dislodged a small stone, causing it to ping off the rock hillside, then vanish quietly into the empty space beyond. My heart gave a heavy thump.

When Butch let go of my hands, I caught hold of a lone cedar and gripped its branches while tentatively feeling around with one leg, trying to find a foothold.

"I don't like this," I told him. "It's dangerous."

"Hell, *yeah*, it's dangerous."

"So let's find the dog and get out of here. Where is he?"

I didn't like the sound of his laugh. "Ain't no dog."

"What do you mean? You called me out here to help you with an injured dog." Standing beside me now, Butch yanked me around to face him and squeezed my upper arms. "Ouch! That hurts." I tried to pull away, but he held on. *Stay calm*, I told myself.

He maneuvered himself so he stood between me and the retaining wall. "Like I said, ain't no dog."

Though the temperature was still in the high 80s, goose bumps popped up on my arms. He pulled me closer. The smell of beer on his breath made me want to gag.

I gritted my teeth and spoke in the low tone I used with the dogs when I meant business. "Then why did you call me out here, have me borrow a car, and *tell* me there was a dog?"

Butch gave me a slight push backwards, then caught me before I fell. When I gasped, he laughed. "I knew it was the one thing that would get you out here. See, it's like this. I *know* Babe is in town. And I know she's seeing that pilot guy, that friend of her parents, but she's only seeing him because they want her to. I been following them, and I know she don't care nothing about him. It's me she really loves. She belongs to me. Me and her, we go way back."

My foot began to slip, and for the moment I was thankful Butch was holding onto me. A trickle of sweat ran down my side. This guy was definitely unhinged. "What do you mean she *belongs* to you?"

"Just what I said. If it hadn't been for them parents of hers, we'd be married by now."

"But what does that have to do with me?"

"Everything, Miss Julie. You're going to help me get my Babe back." He gave me another jerk, then caught me, but this time he didn't laugh.

Inside my head my sister said, *I told you so.* She was right. I should have listened to her. I was in deep doo-doo.

Think, Julie. Think fast. If Butch hadn't been holding my arms, I could reach inside my purse and push the panic button on Carmen's keychain. But even then, who would hear? Somehow I had to get back over the retaining wall and put a lot of distance between myself and this particular arm of the law by making a run for Carmen's car. For now, I'd have to pretend to go along with whatever he said. It wouldn't be wise to let him see my fear again.

I tilted my head and tried to look sympathetic, though it was so dark by now I doubted he could see my face that clearly. "I understand. That's terrible for them to treat you that way. Sounds like my parents. Always butting into my business, telling me what to do. What do you say we go back to the cars, and we can talk about this sitting down. I could sure use one of your beers about now."

He released one of my arms and scratched his head before answering. "Uh, I don't think so. Not till I talk to Babe."

"And how are we going to arrange that?"

"Well, the way I've got it figured, the Espositos trust you. So if you call and tell her to meet you someplace, she'll do it."

"Why can't you call her yourself?"

He pushed his face close to mine and looked at me as if I were the one without a brain. Right now I wished only for ruby slippers I could click together and return to Abilene. "Julie, Julie. Now think a minute. They see my number on their caller ID, and they ain't gonna pick up. Even if they did, they'd recognize my voice and that would be the end of that."

For an idiot, he had done some thinking. Surely I could outwit a halfwit.

"First we need to get back to the cars where it's safe," I said. "I don't want to end up a pile of broken bones at the bottom of this cliff or in the river." Of course, there was a bigger problem with his plan, but I wasn't about to mention it until I was on safer ground.

"Sorry. You got to call her *now*."

"Wait a minute. I thought you said they'd recognize your number. Can't you block the information so it won't show up on their caller ID?"

"Tried that. Any time they see *blocked call*, they know it's me. So you got to call her from *your* cell phone."

Oh, Houston, we do have a problem. I wasn't sure whether to laugh or cry. "That's not possible."

"Huh? You're probably going to tell me your battery is down."

"The fact is..." Butch was never going to believe me. "I don't own a cell phone."

His hold on my arms grew tighter causing me to wince. "Ouch, you're hurting me." I tried to squirm away, but he held on.

"Quit stalling. Get out your damned phone and call her. I want my Babe. I know you got a cell phone. Hell, even the poor SOBs I arrest have cell phones."

I closed my eyes, trying to convince myself I was merely a character in a one-star thriller. The story played out in my head, ending with Butch shoving me down the side of the cliff simply because I didn't have a cell phone.

Without warning, he yanked the purse from my shoulder and dumped the contents on the ground. I flinched as Carmen's keys went rolling down the incline. Butch, unconcerned, bent down on one knee and scrambled around in the dark for a phone that wasn't there, still holding onto me with one beefy hand.

"You don't *have* no damned phone!"

"I've been telling you—"

"What's wrong with you anyway? You're not normal, that's what." He picked up the bottle of Betadine solution and sniffed the lid, probably wondering if it was something to drink. I was tempted to tell him it was a margarita and be my guest.

Clearly, I was going to have to take some action in order to save myself. "Listen to me a minute," I said, hoping he wasn't too drunk to consider his options.

"We'll go to a pay phone, and I'll call Babe from there." I would be in Butch's pickup, still at his mercy, but I'd rather chance that than fall to my death below.

Butch, ignoring my logic, couldn't seem to get over the fact I didn't have a phone. "Are you sure it's not in the car?"

"If it was, we couldn't get to it now. The keys just went rolling down the cliff when you dumped my purse out!"

"Don't even have a damned cell phone," he kept muttering. Suddenly, he let go of me and slapped his hands to the sides of his head and began rocking forward and back, like one of those toy birds that peck at a glass of water. When he let go, one of my feet slipped, and I grabbed for the cedar but my hands flailed in empty air, and I had to hook a finger around a belt loop of his jeans for balance. Good thing I'd worn my running shoes instead of flip-flops.

"It's okay, Butch. I've got an idea." This time I grabbed *his* arm and tried to push him toward the wall, but as I pushed him, one of his cowboy boots slipped, and he began to slide away from me, reaching out and clutching the back pocket of my jeans, bringing me to my knees. As I slid further down, one of my legs dangled in space, while the other scrambled to secure a hold on something solid.

Then Butch lost his grip on my jeans. I took a gulp of air, caught hold of a rock, and managed to pull myself up to a small clump of cedar. I grasped it and held on.

Suddenly, Butch let out a scream that raised my hackles. Once I'd caught my breath, I called to him. "Are you okay?"

"No!" he wailed. "I think my damn leg is broke. Climb down here and help me back up. There's probably snakes down here too."

It was so dark by now I couldn't see him, but from the sound of his voice, I judged him to be several feet below me. I hoped he'd found a ledge and wasn't hanging onto a flimsy branch. Though I felt sorry for him, no way was

I going to try to climb down that incline. Even if I did, I'd never be able to get him back up without help. He had to weigh almost twice as much as me.

"Butch, can you hear me?"

"Help me!" Now he was sobbing. "My chest hurts. I think I'm having a heart attack."

"Can you reach your cell phone? Call 9-1-1. I'll stay here till they come. Try not to move."

"Hell, *no*," he moaned. "It's in my damn pickup."

That was the best news I'd heard all day. "As soon as I climb back to the top, I'll get it and call for help. Just hang on."

"Julie!"

"What?"

"The pickup is locked. You'll have to come down here to get the keys."

I didn't bother answering.

My first goal was to get up to the retaining wall and climb over without falling. I clutched a rock in one hand and the cedar in the other, still seeking a foothold for my dangling leg. My eyes had grown accustomed to the dark, and though there wasn't much of a moon, I could tell up from down. One slip and down I'd go. The cedar branches cut into my fingers but I held on. Finally, my foot found an indentation in the side of the cliff, and I pulled myself up until I could see the side of the barrier. Another few feet and I managed to brace my feet against another small bush and grab onto the top of the wall. With the little remaining strength in my arms, I pulled my upper body onto the ledge. I lay there a few minutes, breathing heavily, until I finally summoned the strength to swing my legs up. One leg. Rest. Then the other. Finally, I lay stretched out face down on the top of the retaining wall. Safe.

My feeling of salvation was short lived. I was alone, at night, in a very large park. Other dangers probably lay in wait behind every tree—wild animals, bad people. A moving shadow spooked me, and I rolled off the wall and onto the ground. I needed that cell phone.

Two vehicles and both of them locked. I looked around for a branch or a rock, anything heavy enough to break out a window on the pickup. The largest rock I could find was about the size of my fist and merely bounced off the window when I threw it, landing at my feet. I picked it up, climbed onto the hood of Butch's pickup, and banged the rock against the windshield as hard as I could, but it didn't even crack. Butch had probably installed bullet-proof glass, since he undoubtedly had enemies.

I slid off the hood and walked around back, where I lowered the tailgate and crawled into the bed of the pickup, hoping to find a crowbar, but all I found were dozens of empty beer cans. Cheap beer at that.

I had no choice. I'd have to hoof it and hope like hell the Cameron Park rapist was home watching *American Idol*.

* * *

Inky darkness surrounded me. At over four hundred acres, Cameron Park was one of the largest municipal parks in Texas. During the daytime, the park buzzed with activity, but tonight a shroud of silence had fallen over the twisting, tree-lined roads. Hikers, mountain bikers, horseback riders, families picnicking—all had gone. Many of the roads ended in cul-de-sacs with picnic areas or retaining walls that looked out over the Brazos or surrounding countryside. Even in the daytime it was easy to get turned around. Lovers Leap was just one of many dead ends.

I started off at a fast walk, looking around me as I did. Recently, a naked man had assaulted a woman jogger, commanding her to "get nekkid" with him, but she'd managed to escape and reached help on her cell phone. Until tonight, I'd thought of cell phones as public irritants, but if I survived, I vowed never to be without one, even if it meant admitting my mother was right.

I upped my pace from a brisk walk to a slow jog, hoping I'd hit one of the main roads that would take me back to civilization. As I trotted onto the road leading out of Lovers Leap, I had to make a decision. Left or right. The sky seemed slightly brighter to my left, so I struck off in that direction, hoping I was headed toward the park entrance and downtown.

As I passed a darkened picnic area, the brush rustled. I told myself it was probably an armadillo or a roadrunner. But when I turned my head and looked behind me, a man emerged from the darkness.

A low voice whispered. "Wait." A chill swept over me, and my heart began to pound. I whirled around and began to run as fast as I could, trying to remember all I'd read about escaping an attack. My Swiss Army knife was back at Lovers Leap in the purse Butch had dumped out, and I didn't even have keys to poke in someone's eye. Could Butch have recovered quickly enough to catch up with me, or was this some other predator? I wasn't sure which would be worse and didn't have time to decide. I twisted my head around and looked back. The man was gaining on me. I ran faster as I rounded a curve, but a sudden stitch in my side stabbed through me. I bent over and clutched my ribs, trying not to break stride. My chest heaved as I gulped more air. I headed for the trees. Maybe I could hide. My pursuer yelled something I couldn't hear over my labored breathing.

Then, arms suddenly reached out and grabbed me from behind. I squirmed as the man pulled me tight against his chest. I bent forward as far as I could and swung my right leg behind his, hooking my foot around his ankle to knock him off balance, the way I'd seen it done in a self-defense demonstration. When that didn't work, I went limp, hoping to throw him off balance. It worked. I clasped my hands together in a double fist and was primed to punch him in the crotch when he spoke again.

"Julie, stop! It's me, Nick."

I froze as he squeezed me so tightly I couldn't breathe. Or maybe it was the closeness of him that stopped my breath. My relief was quickly replaced with anger. "Why didn't you tell me it was you? You just scared the hell out of me!"

"I called your name, but you kept running. I was trying to be quiet so Butch wouldn't hear us. I know he's around here somewhere."

"Well, I didn't hear you!" As he continued to hold me, my body involuntarily molded itself to his.

He bent closer and whispered in my ear. "Julie, what's going on?" His warm breath sent a thrill of excitement through me, causing a familiar throb between my legs.

I yanked away in a feeble attempt to distance myself from the thrill of his touch. "Wait a minute. How do you know about Butch? How did you know where I was?"

Nick's mouth twisted, and a pained look crossed his face. "For one thing, Carmen's Lexus is parked back there at Lovers Leap next to his pickup. Didn't I warn you about him? Why did you meet him out here alone at night?"

He hadn't answered my questions. I stared at him, speechless. On the one hand, I was grateful he'd shown up, but on the other, he had a lot of nerve butting into my business while he was wrapped in the spell of Babe Esposito. Obviously, our Abilene encounter had meant nothing to him.

Before he could answer, a second figure loomed up behind him. I screamed. "Nick, look out!"

Nick spun around and was about to throw a punch.

"Whoa, Nick! It's me, Berto! You forget about me?"

Though I couldn't see him too clearly, Berto sounded mildly amused.

Nick dropped his arm to his side. "Sorry, man. When Julie took off running, I couldn't wait for you to catch up. Then when she screamed just now, I thought...well, you know what I thought. That you were someone else."

Berto pulled out a handkerchief and wiped his forehead. He was heftier than Nick, several years older, and evidently slower. But why was he here? Why were either of them here?

Chapter Fourteen

I took a step back and wiped my hands on my jeans. "Okay, you two. You owe me an explanation. What's going on? Why did you come looking for me, and how did you find me?" I tried to sound in control, but my voice squeaked.

Berto bent forward, trying to catch his breath. "How did we find you?" He gave a short laugh. "Carmen's car."

"What do you mean, her car?"

Berto straightened up, clutching Nick's arm to steady himself. "GPS tracking device. In case it gets stolen."

That explained how Nick knew I was at the Cotton Patch.

"But why did you follow me tonight?"

Berto ran his hands through his thick hair. "After you left, we got worried." He looked sheepish, as if admitting worrying about me was something to be ashamed of. "We knew it wasn't like you to ask for favors, and you seemed a little on edge. So we followed you. Don't blame Nick. It was my idea."

Though I was angry at the thought of Nick following me, I was disappointed it wasn't his idea.

I suddenly remembered Butch. Though I had little fondness for the weirdo, he needed help. "We can talk about this later. Right now, there's somebody on the other side of the wall at Lovers Leap with a broken leg or worse. And if he's not careful, he could end up falling farther and getting killed. One of you needs to call for help." I couldn't bring myself to utter Butch's name.

While Berto grudgingly pulled out his cell phone and made the call, Nick and I eyed each other warily. "I hope he's broken *both* legs," Berto said, pocketing his phone.

Nick took my arm. "Come on. Let's go back and get Berto's car. We parked it on a side road when we saw the Lexus and the pickup. We wanted to be careful till we knew you were safe. You can tell us what happened while we wait for an ambulance and the police. I'm sure they'll want to ask you some questions, and then we're going to get you out of here. This is crazy."

My eyes started to tear up and my nose began to run. I sniffed. "It's not what you think. He said there was a dog. And then he said these things about Babe."

The look Nick and Berto exchanged once more affirmed they knew something I didn't. "The police aren't the only ones who want to hear this story," Berto said.

As we walked to Berto's BMW and he drove us to the Lovers Leap cul-de-sac, I began filling them in on the night's events. Soon, the wail of sirens broke the silence of the still night air. The three of us got out and clustered together while the flashing lights and the shriek of ambulances, fire trucks, and police cars surrounded us.

A white squad car with POLICE emblazoned on the side in bold red letters pulled up a few feet from us. The face of the gray-haired police officer inside told me he'd already fulfilled his crap quota for the night.

"Wait here." Berto turned and stalked off toward the officer.

I started to follow, but Nick reached out and held me back. His hand on my arm was comforting, so I decided to put aside my curiosity and stay where I was. I couldn't hear what they were saying, but Berto gesticulated wildly toward me and then toward the area beyond the wall.

Then a younger policeman approached, his arms held wide over a heavy belt laden with an array of devices. I could identify only a revolver and what might be a stun gun. I moved closer to Nick.

The officer's steely eyes riveted first on me, then Nick. "Good evening, ma'am, sir. I'm Officer X."

The opening bars of the "The Twilight Zone" theme began playing in my head until a quick look at his badge revealed his last name was, in fact, "Ecks." He could have been a stand-in for Butch. I shivered, probably a delayed reaction to my close call with his look-alike.

If Butch had pushed me down the cliff, no doubt he'd have told everyone I jumped because he rejected me. Not only would I be dead, I'd be humiliated by his lies. When I shivered again, Nick put his arm around me and drew me to his chest. The resultant quivering in my loins had more to do with Nick's proximity than my brush with death. I wanted him to un-quiver me. Then I wanted to curl up in his arms and stay there forever.

Officer Ecks eyed Nick with suspicion. "You call this in?"

Before Nick could answer, I cut in. "I'm the one you want to talk to." I pointed toward Nick, then Berto. "They just got here."

"Sir, you wait out here." He tilted his head toward Nick. "Ma'am, get in the car."

Nick seemed reluctant to let me go until I looked up at him and nodded. Officer Ecks led me to his patrol car and opened the front passenger-side door. I hesitated, waiting for him to put his hand on top of my head and say "watch your head" like they do in the movies, but he didn't. Maybe he wasn't worried about my suing for brain damage, since I hadn't been arrested.

As he walked around the car, the radio squawked an unintelligible mix of codes and commands. Officer Ecks got in, listened for a moment, then frowned and contorted his mouth as if he hadn't understood any more than I had. He reached up and flicked on the overhead light.

"You got ID?"

"It's...it was in my purse."

"Where's your purse, ma'am?"

"Over there." I pointed to the wall. "On the other side."

He rubbed his tongue over his bottom lip, as if trying to decide which question came next on his list. I tried to make it easier for him. "I know my driver's license number if that helps." I called off the numbers I'd memorized years ago. Officer Ecks massaged his temples.

"Rough day?" I asked.

He glanced over at me. "That's an understatement. You wouldn't believe it."

Oh, little did he know.

We both looked up as another police officer stretched a long leg over the retaining wall. I saw something familiar looped over his arm.

"That's it! That's my purse!"

I reached for the door handle, but Officer Ecks leaned over and grabbed my arm. "Wait here. Don't move."

He got out and approached the officer carrying my purse, then pointed toward the car. I wondered if he'd found the contents or if they were lying at the bottom of the Brazos. Though the purse itself—a gift from my mother—was worth more than anything inside, I hated the idea of having to replace my license and credit cards.

Officer Ecks got back in and plunked the bag down between us. "Go ahead."

I pulled the purse toward me and looked inside. "Yuck. Everything's covered with dirt."

Officer Ecks grunted. "No kidding. You got ID in there?"

"I'm looking. Hold on." I reached into first one compartment, then another. Finally, I found my billfold, extracted it, and pulled out my license. When I did, dirt and dog biscuit crumbs fell out. "Here," I said, handing over the license and brushing my hands off on my pants.

Officer Ecks looked at my picture, then at me, then typed something into his computer. "Is Abilene still your legal residence?"

"Yes, sir. I'm just working here. For the month. Training dogs."

"Dogs?"

"Yes, sir. Poodles."

He yawned. Then he clicked his pen, retrieved a notebook from the dash, and scribbled something in it. "What happened out here tonight? You say there's an injured man on the other side of the wall?"

I wasn't sure where to start. "Yes, sir. He thinks his leg is broken and said he's having a heart attack."

"So you were on the other side with him?"

"Yes, but—"

"Didn't you see the warning signs?"

"Yes, but you don't understand—"

He held up his hand for me to stop, tapped the end of his pen on the pad to get the ink flowing again, and scribbled another note. "Do you realize you're endangering the lives of the men and women who have to go down there to get your boyfriend?"

"Yes, sir, I do. I mean, I know it's dangerous, and I'm sorry. But he's not my boyfriend. He's a policeman."

Officer Ecks snorted. "Sure he is. Like we don't have enough excitement just doing our jobs. Okay, so he's not your boyfriend. What were the two of you doing on the other side of the wall?"

"Butch—that's his name—said there was a dog on the other side that needed help. He called me because I'm a vet tech. But there wasn't a dog. He just made that up to get me out here so I could call Babe for him."

"Wait a minute. Slow down." I waited while he wrote. "You're saying this guy calls you about a dog that doesn't exist to get you to call another woman?" Officer Ecks looked up from his notepad. "You aren't making much sense."

"It didn't make sense to me either, but he'd been drinking."

"How many have *you* had?"

"Me? Drinks?"

"No, *dogs*, lady." He rolled his eyes. "Yes, *drinks*."

"I haven't had any. I was home in the bathtub with Philip when Butch called about this other dog."

The officer cleared his throat. "In the bathtub. With...who's Philip?" He squinted at me and smirked. I could feel myself growing a sweat mustache.

"Philip is my *dog*. The water is for rehab. He had surgery. On his knee."

"So this guy calls you about this other dog, the dog that didn't exist, while you're in the bathtub with your dog."

"Yes, sir."

Officer Ecks shook his head and jotted down some more notes. When I leaned over to see what he was writing, he drew his notebook closer to his chest.

Suddenly, screams penetrated the stuffy confines of the cop car. Officer Ecks rolled down his window and peered out. I leaned over, trying not to touch him, and looked over his shoulder.

Two guys in Emergency Medical Service uniforms were hoisting a stretcher over the retaining wall. From the obscenities piercing our ears, I assumed it was Butch. Officer Ecks and I watched transfixed as the EMTs passed by the patrol car with their cargo.

When Butch caught a glimpse of me, he screamed louder. "*She* did it! That's the bitch who pushed me down the cliff and broke my leg! Then she run off and left me out there to die like a *dog*."

It was an apt comparison. His rolling eyes and drooling mouth resembled a dog—one with rabies. Before Officer Ecks could roll up the window, I yelled back at Butch. "You should be so lucky!"

Butch had a lot of nerve, accusing *me*. I watched with satisfaction as they hauled his sorry carcass into the ambulance, revved up the siren, and sped off.

Meanwhile, Officer Ecks scribbled furiously. He finally stopped, holding his pen poised over his notebook. "Is that true? Did you push him?"

My voice rose several decibels. "No, I didn't *push* him. Like I said, he got me out here under false pretenses. Once we were on the other side of the wall, he grabbed my arms and acted as if he might push me off the cliff if I didn't do what he said."

"So he threatened you."

"Well, he didn't *say* he was going to kill me if that's what you mean, but it was pretty obvious if I didn't do what he said I'd be deep-sixed by now."

Officer Ecks tapped the side of his head with his pen a couple of times. "Deep-sixed? Lady, you've been watching too much TV."

"Movies," I corrected. "I also read the local newspaper every morning. You think I'm making all this up? Well, I'm not. He would've killed me. I could see it in his eyes. And when he grabbed my arms, I slipped."

"So you're saying you slipped, and he kept you from falling."

"No, I'm not saying that at all! If he hadn't gotten me out here in the first place and hadn't grabbed my arms, I wouldn't have slipped. He also dumped my purse out!"

Officer Ecks evidently didn't understand that messing with my purse ranked right up there with someone threatening to kill me. He sighed and shook out his hand, cramped from all the writing.

"Can I go now?" I asked.

Before he could answer, another policeman appeared at the window and knocked on the glass. Officer Ecks rolled down his window, and the other policeman whispered something I couldn't hear. When Officer Ecks whistled under his breath, I gathered the news wasn't good. He turned toward me and gave me a hard stare I couldn't decipher. "I've just been informed of the identity of the victim."

"The *victim*! *I'm* the victim here. He almost killed me!"

Officer Ecks took a breath and let it out slowly through rounded lips. "Are you aware that Officer Justice is a member of the Waco PD?"

"Yes, sir, I am fully aware of that fact. I *told* you he was a policeman. That's one reason I trusted him enough to come out here in the middle of nowhere in the middle of the night to help an injured dog!"

"Of course. The injured dog. How could I have forgotten?"

"You don't believe me?"

"It's not my place to believe or not believe. But Officer Justice claims you pushed him down the cliff. If that's true, you could be in big trouble. Assaulting an officer of the law."

"I did not push him."

"We're going to need you to take a breathalyzer test."

"Fine! You won't detect anything on my breath but the scent of fear with a hint of loathing. Your upstanding upholder of the law could have killed me. He's the one who should be taking a breathalyzer test."

"Well now, that's just your word against his, isn't it?"

* * *

After I proved I could touch my fingers to my nose with my eyes closed—a feat I found difficult even when sober—and passed the breathalyzer test, they said I could go. Nick whisked me into the Lexus, leaving Berto to drive the BMW, and we headed back to Casa del Lago, leaving Lovers Leap and its unpleasantness behind. As we neared the house, Nick reached over and patted my leg. "You okay?"

Even after the harrowing events of the evening, I still felt a surge of pleasure at his touch. With Nick, just a look could send me reeling, though I'd be the last to admit that to anyone, least of all to him.

"I'm okay. I feel like a fool, but I bounce back pretty fast. I still can't believe he said I pushed him. What a jerk. I was trying to *help* him."

"Worse than a jerk. He's also—"

I waited for him to finish, but he stopped.

"A *what?*" I asked.

But Nick had shut down. "Nothing," he said, his lips tight.

What did he know that I didn't? And why so reluctant to tell me?

"Surely they won't believe the ravings of a crazy person," I said quietly, pondering my fate, wondering if I would be arrested for attempted murder.

Nick gave a wry laugh. "Let's hope not, and no need to feel like a fool. You don't know him like we do."

"You know him? How? What is it I don't know?"

Nick didn't answer. Even more frustrating, he didn't say anything. My mother always said I had the tenacity of a bulldog, and I wasn't giving up this time. I'd try another tack, hoping to throw him off guard. "What's the connection between Butch and Babe?"

"Not my place to talk about that. And I don't advise asking Berto or Carmen. It's a sensitive subject."

"Don't I have a right to know? I mean, the guy almost shoved me down the side of a cliff because of her."

"Sorry, babe. Can't talk about it."

"My name's not *Babe!*" I sputtered. "Why all the secrecy? What could be so bad you can't tell me?"

"You're the one who's been dating him. You tell me."

"Ohhhh!" Now I was infuriated. "I have *not* been dating him. I went out with him once. The only reason I met him tonight was because he said a dog was injured, and I had no reason not to believe him. You could have warned me about him."

He clapped a hand to his forehead. "I tried. I told you to stay away from him."

"You could have told me he was crazy! And *dangerous.*"

"For all I knew, you two had hit it off great."

I gave Nick my best evil eye, but he didn't take his own eyes off the road. "You actually think Butch Justice is my type?"

Still not looking at me, Nick grinned. "You have a *type?*"

"Maybe." I turned away from him and faced the road ahead.

I was still in the dark in more ways than one. The Espositos and Nick had a secret I wasn't privy to, and no one wanted to clue me in. I was tired of the intrigue, tired of the secrecy, tired of Nick's hot and cold behavior. I tried to convince myself I didn't care but had little luck.

We drove the rest of the way in a silence so thick you couldn't have cut it with a Texas chainsaw.

* * *

The next morning, Nick sat under an umbrella by the pool, wearing a navy T-shirt and crisp khakis. I pretended not to see him as I walked past, headed for the big house to get the dogs for their morning lesson.

"Julie. Hold up."

When I kept walking, he reached out and grabbed my arm. "I know you heard me."

I lowered my sunglasses, peered over them, and looked him straight in the eye. Then I turned on my best fakey smile and sweetest voice. "Nick. So sorry. I didn't realize that was you."

"Yeah, sure you didn't. I thought you'd want to know. Berto called one of his connections at the hospital. Seems your friend Butch has a couple of broken ribs *and* a broken leg. And more good news. He's been suspended without pay, pending further investigation."

"He's *not* my friend."

"Then you'll press charges?"

"What? No! Believe it or not, I'd prefer to terminate any association with him *now*, if not sooner."

Nick's brows drew together, and he didn't smile. "After what he did to you?"

"He didn't exactly *do* anything. I'm okay. *He*'s the one in the hospital."

Nick banged a hand on the table so hard I jumped. "Dammit, Julie. Carmen and Berto are counting on you."

"This has nothing to do with Carmen and Berto. I was the one stupid enough to end up at Lovers Leap with a crazy policeman."

"It has a *lot* to do with Carmen and Berto."

"Care to explain?" I asked, knowing he wouldn't. "Look, I admire your loyalty, though I don't understand any of this. And I'd like to help, but Officer Ecks said it was Butch's word against mine. For all I know, he's going to file charges against *me*."

"Not very likely."

"What's this all about?"

Nick's face hardened. "Sorry, not at liberty to say."

I pulled away from him and took off for the big house, his words echoing in my mind. Nick said Berto had called one of his "connections." Berto, Hispanic Godfather of Waco. Don Esposito. I shuddered. Would I find a horse head on my bedpost in the morning? Would Berto himself call me in, make me an offer I couldn't refuse?

* * *

Back in my apartment after working with the dogs, I paced from room to room. Why was Butch such a sensitive topic? Philip, who'd been sleeping peacefully on the sofa when I came in, sat up and looked at me, his eyes questioning, his head pivoting each time I walked past. I finally gave up trying to figure out the situation with Butch. Maybe a nap would help. It seemed to work for dogs. I changed into some lightweight yoga pants and a T-shirt, plucked Philip off the sofa, and placed him on the bed. Then I plopped down, and he curled up next to me.

Just as I dozed off, I heard a light knock on the door. Philip's bark jolted me fully awake, and I grabbed him before he could jump off the bed and hurt his leg.

Stumbling into the living room, I looked out the window. Babe stood outside, nervously shifting from one foot to the other. She wore white cropped pants with a

Praise for Ann Whitaker's Books

Dog Nanny was a finalist in the 2008 Linda Howard Award of Excellence Contest.

"**A near perfect book**. If ever there was a story that made me glad that I am a Texan, this is it....a magnificent book that is witty in all the right places. There are some books that I wish would never end. *Dog Nanny* is one of them." **~Coffee Time Romance & More, 5 cups**

"...a charming and funny tale filled with the joys and problems loving dogs can bring into your life!...If you like humor, dogs, and really mixed up main characters, this is the book for you! I loved it!" **~The Romance Studio, 5 Hearts**

"...captivating from start to finish. It's a cute and charming love story. All of the characters of this book have a story of their own and I just love how Ms. Whitaker weaves them all together to make one incredible story." **~Long and Short of It, 4 1/2 Books**

"...two poodles who were hilarious throughout the book...[t]he chemistry between her and Nick was great too...her fear that he might be into drug trafficking added additional humor." **~Manic Reviews, 4 Stars**

"From comedy to a touch of mystery, to romantic interludes, to training tips, this would make a delightful movie." **~Books, Books, and More Books, 4 Stars**

"*Dog Nanny* is a sweet, steamy and often laugh-out-loud treat that will leave you wanting more." ~**You Gotta Read Reviews, You Need to Read**

"Just give this book a try and you will soon understand why *Dog Nanny* was a finalist in the 2008 Linda Howard Award of Excellence Contest." ~**CK2S Kwips and Kritiques, 4 Shamrocks**

"The dialogue is witty, the situations humorous, and the events move at an agreeable pace. A fun, hearty read!" ~**Mayra Calvani/Blog Critics**

"Carmen, the poodle owner, is my favorite and she provides a lot of comic relief when the main characters insist on being stubborn...It is sweet and interesting and made me smile." ~**Mistress Bella Reviews, 3 Smacks**

"**What a Treat!** I enjoyed the accurate reminder of feelings of new love and all the potential that comes with it. The sprinkles of Texas life were delightful...nailed the sexual tension of a new relationship!...got me remembering feelings from my teens and twenties." ~**Reader Review, 5 Stars**

"**Best of Show!** In *Dog Nanny*, Ann Whitaker shares a knowledge of dogs and their needs with a superb blending of romance, intrigue, mystery, excitement, and humor. This leads to one excellent read, appealing not only to the young, but also to those of us who are young at heart! *Dog Nanny* attracts pet lovers and romance lovers—what a beautiful combo!" ~**Reader Review, 5 Stars**

"**Laugh Out Loud!** Funny only begins to describe *Dog Nanny*. At points I was howling with laughter...It is truly hilarious. Can't wait for the movie!" **~Reader Review, 5 Stars**

"**More than a Romance.** Typical romance? *Dog Nanny* is much more than that: mystery and suspense, subtle lessons in dog training, a quiet plea for responsible dog ownership. Yet none of these elements overpowers the romantic plot delivered by a skillful writer who has a special gift for humor." **~Reader Review, 4 Stars**

"**A Tail-Wagging Romance.** This is a fun, lighthearted romance with a chick lit attitude. Julie's smart and good-natured, Nick's a heartthrob—and the two giant poodles just about steal the story. A fun romantic read, especially for dog lovers." **~Reader Review, 4 Stars**

"Every character made an impression and with a little bit of everything between the covers, romance, mystery, comedy, and plain good old-fashioned jealousy. This is definitely a must read—I had a load of fun with this book." **~E.H., On Books N' More, 4.5 Stars**

Woof! Woof! Loved, loved, this book
"Did I enjoy reading *Dog Nanny*? Hell, yeah!! This was a fabulous read and I just could not put it down...A movie from this book—I would love to see it. Who is hot enough to play Nick? Congratulations to the author also for the very, very few errors in this book. Such a change to see a well-edited book. I can certainly highly recommend this book, especially to anyone who loves dogs." **~Reader Review, 5 Stars**

sleeveless, crimson top that set off her tan skin. Around her neck on a silver chain hung a large silver cross. Her complexion, with no trace of makeup, was flawless.

As she lifted her hand to knock again, I opened the door and smiled weakly. Her expression was solemn.

"Come in." I swung open the door to the apartment built for her. "*Mi casa es su casa*," I muttered awkwardly. In this case, it was literally true.

Babe glanced warily behind her, but seeing no one, slipped inside.

I pointed to the sofa. "Have a seat. Want some iced tea? It's already made."

She nodded, her eyes darting around the apartment, taking it all in, then saying something I didn't quite catch about the colors.

"I'm sorry?"

"My colors," she repeated. "Mamá chose these colors because they were my favorites—ruby, gold, emerald. But this is the first time I've been inside in years."

I wasn't sure what to say so said nothing and went into the kitchen to pour the tea. When I returned she was still standing in the middle of the room, her eyes glistening with tears. I handed her the cold glass, and she took a gulp, looking up at me thankfully.

"Please. Sit." This time she did. "You don't stay here when you come back to visit?"

She hesitated, a pained look crossing her face. Her words came haltingly. "I stayed here for a short time right after it was built. But after what happened—"

She clutched at the cross around her neck, as if calling on a higher power.

"Mamá hoped I'd come back and stay here. I mean, I do come back, but never here. The memories are too upsetting." The hand holding her glass of tea trembled.

I carefully lowered myself onto the couch beside her, reached out and boosted Philip up, and watched him settle between us. Babe patted his head.

"You'd think I'd be over it by now, but I sometimes wonder if I'll ever get over it. Even in LA, when I'm feeling really good about myself and what I'm accomplishing, I think back to that night, and I feel so stupid, and so...ashamed. I really thought I was in love." Then she surprised me by changing the subject. "I just talked to Nick. He said you weren't going to press charges against...Butch." When she spoke his name, she grimaced as if she'd just tasted something bitter.

"You do know him then?"

She let out a rueful laugh. "Oh yes, I know him. Knew him. That's why I need to talk to you."

I gave a short, embarrassed laugh. "Pardon my French, but I never want to see his sorry-ass face again. Guess I'm not a very good judge of character."

"Don't blame yourself," she said, her eyes sympathetic. "He fools a lot of people at first. He's also gotten crazier over the years. He seemed like a pretty nice guy back when I met him."

I waited for her to go on, but she just stared into her glass of iced tea, as if reading her fortune in the stray leaves floating in the bottom. Or her past.

I finally broke the silence. "Well, like the policeman last night said, it would only be my word against his. So if that's what you're worried about. I mean, if he's your friend—"

"No, it's more complicated. About six years ago, at the end of my senior year of high school, we dated. My family hadn't lived here long and I didn't know anyone, so when he asked me out I said yes. I admit I was more than a little starry-eyed. He was older, a policeman. My parents thought I'd be safe with him." Her hand went once more to the cross around her neck. "I didn't have much experience and was naïve, to say the least. But I thought he really cared about me. And I believed him when he said he loved me and couldn't live without me."

"So he broke your heart. You know, I've dated my share of jackasses, but there are lots of men out there who'll treat you better than Butch Justice. I—"

"No, it wasn't like that." Her eyes pled with me to understand.

"I think I know where you're going with this. And to be honest, I just don't want to get involved."

I started to get up, but she reached over and put a hand on my arm. "Wait. You haven't heard the rest of the story. Not many people know everything. My parents. Nick. The police know some of it...but that came later. My brother and I had both been accepted to the University of Texas, and Mamá wanted us to have a place of our own to stay when we came back."

Babe seemed calmer now. She placed her glass on the coffee table. "One night after Butch and I had been to a movie, we came back here so I could show him the apartment. I'd just moved in and was excited about having my own place and was trying to play grown-up. Mamá didn't know—she would *not* have approved of my being here alone with him. She and Papá were always strict about those kinds of things." She gave a wry laugh. "Papá thinks I'm still a little girl. At twenty-*four*. Anyway, that night I was excited about showing Butch my *Cielo*.... As it turned out, it was far from heaven for me."

She sank deeper and deeper into the sofa, as if trying to lose herself among the cushions. "It was a moonlit night in the spring. You know the kind. When you're young and the air seems thick with romance. I'd just turned eighteen. He was twenty-five. We kissed. Things started heating up. I was ready to prove my love. And that's when it happened."

I interrupted, hoping to make her feel better. "It's like that for a lot of girls. I know the first time is supposed to be special, but if the guy turns out to be a loser, it makes it even worse." I did feel sorry for her. I reached over and placed my hand on her shoulder. "There *are* nice guys out there."

I couldn't believe I, of all people, was lecturing her on nice guys, when I'd given up ever finding one for myself. After all, she did have Nick. And much as I hated to admit it, she was drop-dead gorgeous, way out of my league. Her hair, dark and thick as kahlúa, tumbled over her shoulders as she continued her tale.

"I'd been protected by my parents...and my brother. I didn't know anything about men." Hesitantly, she continued. "Then Butch tried to get in my pants."

I was confused. Hadn't she just said she wanted to prove her love?

"Babe...he's a guy. Guys do that sometimes. It doesn't mean he didn't respect you...well, not necessarily." I fudged to make her feel better. Knowing Butch, I doubted he respected any woman.

"You don't understand. I mean he tried to *fit* into my panties. He's a big guy. I'm a size *four*."

Chapter Fifteen

Envisioning Butch in women's underwear was a bigger stretch than Spanx Power Panties on Oprah's butt. Of all the negative thoughts I'd had about him, macho Butch as a cross-dresser wasn't on my list.

My face must have shown my disbelief. Babe grasped the silver cross hanging around her neck and held it toward me. "I swear to you on this cross—"

I held up my hands in surrender. "I believe you. I'm just having a hard time wrapping my mind around that picture."

Babe averted her eyes as she continued. "I was probably the last eighteen-year-old virgin in Waco. Since I was leaving for school at the end of the summer, I'd decided it was time for me to become a woman. I went into the bathroom to slip into a nightgown, and when I came out, he was standing by the chest of drawers, his back to me, buck naked, bent over, with my panties wrapped around his ankles."

She leaned over and put her head in her hands, her shoulders shaking.

I tried to comfort her. "Don't feel bad. It wasn't your fault."

When she raised her head, tears ran down her face, but she wasn't crying from sadness, she was laughing. "It wasn't funny at the time."

I smiled, trying to relate. I'd dated some creeps but never a cross-dresser. I had, however, seen *Rocky Horror Picture Show* and had loved Johnny Depp in *Ed Wood* so much I'd bought the DVD. But I could cut Johnny a lot of slack. Butch was no Johnny Depp.

I reached over for my tea and took a big swig, not sure what to say. "I've read most cross-dressers are harmless."

Babe gave a wry laugh. "Try telling my father that. Besides, you know better now."

I turned sideways, tucked my feet under me, and leaned my head against the sofa cushions. "What did you do?"

"Screamed. Loud. So loud he fell over backwards trying to get his feet loose, but they were tangled in my panties." She giggled. "I was so shocked I just stood there, watching him squirm on the floor, trying to get out of them. They were my favorite pair, red...from Victoria's Secret. When I heard them rip, I yelled louder. Told him to get out and never come back."

"Wow."

She took a deep breath and sighed. "He claimed it was a mistake. That he'd accidentally twisted them around his feet and tripped."

"He's more creative than I thought."

"Nick and Papá think he's a pervert, but I've lived in LA for six years now, and he'd seem fairly normal there. But in Waco? And a policeman?"

"Who would have guessed?"

"It's all beside the point now. What came later was worse. That's why I'm telling you."

I lifted my brows and blinked. "Worse?"

"Oh, yes. When Mamá and Papá found out I'd broken up with him, they wanted to know why. Butch's manners were never great, but he'd always been on his best behavior around them. I thought Papá would kill him if he found out, and I didn't want either of them to know he'd been in my apartment."

"He began following me every time I left the house," she said, reaching up in a fluid motion and pulling her dark hair away from her face. Her bee-stung lips were full and seductive like her mother's. I wondered if Nick had ever kissed them and felt a twinge of jealousy.

"Sometimes he'd be in his squad car, other times in his pickup." She nervously picked at a thread in the fabric of the sofa. "Once, he even borrowed a car and wore a fake moustache, thinking I wouldn't recognize him. It was crazy. Another time, he saw my car parked at a friend's house and let the air out of my tires. Obviously it was him—he wrote *Butch Loves Babe* on the windows in white shoe polish. That's when I finally broke down and told Mamá the whole story. She told Papá. Then, a few nights later, Papá caught him on our property, looking in a window, and called the police."

"Did they arrest him?"

"You kidding? He convinced them he was conducting surveillance, though he never worked undercover. He said Papá's import business was a front for smuggling drugs and illegals from Mexico. He also said I was trying to get even for him breaking up with me. His buddies at the police department believed every lie, even though he had no proof."

Drugs and illegal immigrants. Butch had said the same to me. No wonder Berto blanched when I'd mentioned the feds. I flashed back to my encounter with the ICE men in New Orleans. Could there be some truth to Butch's story? Was it possible Berto and Nick *were* smuggling drugs into the country?

Babe broke into my reverie. "That's when I decided I couldn't go to school in Austin because it was too close to home. I was afraid Butch would come looking for me, so I moved to California to live with an aunt. I'd done a little acting in high school and thought I'd try my luck. It's taken six years, but I'm finally getting enough work to support myself."

Babe's whole body seemed to relax once her story was out. "When I do come back—which isn't often—Mamá and Papá don't let me go anywhere alone. The restraining order means nothing, so Nick takes me everywhere. I don't know what I'd do without him. He was my first love, you know."

No, I hadn't known. Evidently they were rekindling the old flame. It made sense. Even if she wasn't beautiful and young, she was Hispanic like Nick. I was a pale comparison. Besides that, you didn't have to use your imagination to tell she had boobs.

Babe looked up at me, her eyes pleading. "Now you know why it's so important for you to file assault charges. Butch is getting worse, and the police might believe *you*."

And have Butch after me? I didn't think so. I'd had more than my share of involvement with the law since I'd come to Waco. "I'll think about it," I said, trying to sound sincere.

Babe reached up and lightly touched my arm. "I know you don't owe me any favors. It's more for Mamá and Papá than for me. And please don't tell them I told you. It's been so hard on them, not knowing if they might be arrested for something they didn't do. Until he pulled this with you, Butch was just annoying. Now, I think he's getting dangerous."

I thought about how he'd claimed Babe "belonged" to him. But no need to tell her that. She seemed distressed enough.

She reached out again and touched my arm with her slender fingers. "Nick says you're a good person. If you won't do it for me or my family, then do it because it's the right thing."

I chewed on my not-so-plump bottom lip. "What makes you think the police would believe *me?* I went to Lovers Leap voluntarily."

Babe folded her hands in her lap and picked at a cuticle. "They'll believe you." She paused. "Because you're Anglo."

Thinking of myself as "Anglo" made me feel ashamed. Most of my life, I'd felt guilty about having been born into money. But Babe was proof money wasn't always enough.

She slipped out of the apartment, leaving me alone except for a loud voice inside my head I couldn't muzzle. And the germ of an idea taking form. Nothing to do with filing charges. My own Plan B.

So much for a nap. A glance at my watch announced it was time for Noche and Blanco's afternoon lesson, so I changed into shorts and sneakers and headed up the path toward the house. Carmen and I had decided earlier it was too hot to work the dogs outside, so we were meeting in the ballroom.

The thermometer near the fountain read 95 degrees, but the heat index made it feel more like 105. How did people here tolerate this humidity? I didn't mind sweating if I was working out, but sweat rolling down my forehead and burning my eyes while standing immobile in the shade made me even more eager to pack up and head back to the hot gusts and parched clime of Abilene.

Nick was back at the pool, sitting under an umbrella, a plastic bottle of water in his hand. This time I waved and kept walking. "Hey, Julie. Can I talk to you a minute?"

When he stood up, I stopped abruptly and faced him. My gaze drifted downward over his unbuttoned shirt, past his swim trunks to his legs, well-muscled and tanned, like the rest of him. I held my hand up to shade my eyes from the sun and deliberately looked at my watch. "Gotta hurry. Meeting Carmen. We have a training session."

Nick reached down and dusted off a nearby lawn chair with his bare hand. "I don't want you to think I was spying. I wasn't. But I just saw Babe leave your apartment." He pulled back the chair and beckoned me to sit. "She asked you to file charges?"

"Yes."

Nick waited for me to elaborate, and when I didn't, he held his palms up. "So?"

I paused a second. "I owe you an apology."

He laughed, his teeth bright against his dark skin. An ache in my chest made me look away. He moved closer, and the magnetic field around him began to pull me in, making it hard to breathe. If he was aware of my reaction, he didn't show it.

"Do I get to choose which transgression I'll have you apologize for?"

"Don't push your luck," I said, unable to keep my lips from arching upwards in a smile. But when my hips started arching toward his, I braced myself against the table and tried to keep my voice steady. "Look, Nick, I'm sorry I kept insisting you tell me about Babe and Butch. You were right. It wasn't any of my business."

"Babe told you?"

"Yes."

Nick sat down and pointed to the chair beside him. I sat on the edge, poised for flight.

He rested his elbows on his knees and leaned toward me. "Carmen and Berto felt humiliated and betrayed. It's a sore subject. But things have changed since then. I understand the new police chief is strict about ethics and discipline and has been trying to weed out the bad seeds. But if you don't press the matter, there's not much they can do. You're lucky you got away unhurt. If you'd fallen..." Concern filled his eyes. "Next time, it might be different."

"There won't be a next time for me."

"For someone else then."

I nodded grudgingly. "Babe said the police would believe me because I'm Anglo. To tell you the truth, that really offends me."

"So what if they do believe you because you're Anglo?"

"Because it isn't fair," I grumbled. "People could take a few lessons from dogs. A Chihuahua doesn't think he's better than a poodle. Dogs don't care whether another dog has a pedigree or is black, brown, or white."

Nick bent so close I could feel his breath on my face. "What have you got to lose? You might get a crazy cop off the streets."

"I'm not so sure. Cops also tend to protect their own."

"Maybe. But Carmen and Berto deserve better. And Babe *really* deserves it."

I closed my eyes and breathed in his scent, Coppertone laced with sex pheromones. "Officer Ecks said it's my word against Butch's." I glanced toward the big house. "The fact I work for the Espositos isn't going to help."

Nick sighed. "You may be right. But it will make Carmen and Berto feel better. And Babe, too. Don't you think it's worth a try?"

I hated myself for asking, but I couldn't stop myself. "And you care a lot about her."

"You kidding? Who wouldn't? She's beautiful, kind, talented. If I can help it, no one will ever hurt her again. I love Babe."

He'd finally answered a question.

I nodded slowly, then turned away and trudged up the hill to the big house wishing I could close my eyes and beam myself back to Abilene. Just as I'd thought, I was merely someone to fill the interludes when Babe wasn't around. That's what I got for not living up to my vow. Granted, technically I was still a born-again virgin, but I had Philip to thank for that.

Nick was probably right. What was the worst that could happen? Butch already blamed me for his injuries. For all I knew, I was just one step away from being locked up and made to wear one of those ugly jumpsuits—and orange was *not* my favorite color. I imagined myself being found guilty and dragged out of the courtroom protesting my innocence. But no matter how bleak a picture I envisioned for myself, it was Babe's face I saw. And her words that echoed through my mind: *It's the right thing to do.*

Though I wasn't a vengeful person, it was time to set Plan B into motion. Everyone else had a secret. Why not me? It would cost me big bucks, but if it worked it would be worth every dollar. All it would take was a couple of phone calls and some patience. Thank God for Master-Card.

Chapter Sixteen

Overcast skies met me when I left my apartment, and I saw no hope of the sun peeking through. The weather matched my mood. I longed for my Waco stint to end so I could return to my dull life in Abilene, but time crawled slower than a fully loaded eighteen-wheeler up I-20's Ranger Hill, and I was still no closer to finding a husband. So far, my only success had been with Carmen and the dogs.

My encounter with Butch had convinced me of one thing—I did need a cell phone. I waited till Nick and Berto were in town on business and borrowed Carmen's car. The last thing I wanted was Nick following me out of a sense of duty. Once more I ventured alone into the wilds of Waco, recently ranked sixth most dangerous town in Texas. Yee-haw!

I pulled the Lexus onto Lakeshore Drive and headed for the nearest Wal-Mart. This time, not even the vista of the lake rising up as I topped the hill boosted my flagging spirits. Like the sky, the lake was gray and lifeless, the humidity oppressive. I set the A/C on maximum and cranked the fan up to high. Then I leaned back against the leather seat and pretended I was back in the dry, open spaces of West Texas.

I parked at the far edge of the Wal-Mart parking lot, not wanting to chance a ding or dent. By the time I reached the front door, I was dripping with sweat. I pushed my hair back from my face, wondering if my melted mascara had left black rings under my eyes. Then I remembered I didn't know anyone in Waco, so what did it matter? It wasn't as if I would find a husband in Wal-Mart while shopping for a disposable cell phone.

The automatic doors opened, a welcome blast of cool air hit me, and a nondescript greeter offered me a basket. I smiled magnanimously, thinking I could brighten her day, and politely declined.

Weaving my way through the throngs of shoppers, mainly women with small children, I headed for electronics, where I perused a rack of prepaid phones, picked one off its hanger, and began reading the specs. They all seemed to have the same basic features, though they ranged in price from fifteen to fifty dollars or more.

All I needed was the ability to call and be called, but even the cheapest model had a calculator, a conversion table, and a calendar, plus some features I didn't even understand. I noted none of them had a husband-detector. Now that could make someone millions.

"Could I help you with a phone? Answer any questions?" The voice came in the vicinity of my left ear.

I jumped and let out a little "eek." Then I whirled around, embarrassed, and found myself looking into the soft, gray eyes of a very handsome young man. At least my built-in stud detector was still fully functioning.

"Sorry, didn't mean to scare you," he said.

I held a hand to my chest and gave a small laugh as I caught my breath. "My fault. I spook easily."

He was only slightly taller than me and close enough I could see the cleft in his chin and the promise of a dimple in one cheek. Judging from his smooth skin, he couldn't be more than twenty. I backed up a step for a better look.

"Our higher-end phones are in the display case. I'd be glad to show you those."

"Oh...no, but thank you. This one's probably all I need." I'd read that three kinds of people used disposables. Hookers, drug dealers, and terrorists.

I hoped he wouldn't think I was a hooker. "But I'm not sure how to...maybe you could explain."

"Sure. Activation is easy. You can do it by phone or online. But are you sure this one has all the features you'll need? Most of these have call-waiting, voice mail, and caller ID. We also have higher-end phones if you're looking to upgrade."

"I've...I've never owned a cell phone." It hit me I was probably the only cell-phone virgin in the whole store.

If he was surprised, he had the courtesy to hide it. Sliding a different model off its metal arm, he held it out for me to examine and began enumerating its features.

"If you're looking for a bargain, this one's your best bet. No camera, of course, but if you don't want bells and whistles, it should suit you fine. I sell a lot of these."

He was wrong about one thing. I did want bells and whistles. Just not the cell phone variety.

While he talked, I assessed his attributes. Sandy brown hair, slender build, neatly dressed. Not my usual type, but his youthful innocence was appealing. Maybe he could be trained.

He caught me looking and a dimple appeared. "Sorry if this sounds rude, but you don't look like a woman who's never had a cell phone."

I smiled. "And what exactly does a woman who's never had a cell phone look like?"

When he blushed, I wanted to reach up and pinch his cheek. It was the same feeling I got when I saw a puppy. In fact, he was so cute I wanted to pick him up and take him home without a second thought about how big he would get or how much trouble he'd be to housebreak.

"Sorry," he said. "It's none of my business. It's just that you look...well, you look...like you should have a cell phone. What if your car breaks down?"

"You sound like my sister."

He laughed. "Just so I don't look like her."

"Not hardly." I was enjoying the repartee. So what if he was a clerk in a discount store? I had no expectations, no hidden agendas.

"I'm surprised your husband hasn't insisted you carry a phone. I wouldn't let my wife out of the house without one."

"Oh," I said, slightly disappointed. "You're married?" He was just a kid.

"Not yet. I meant if I had a wife." He held up his bare ring finger, as if that proved it.

"Ah, I *thought* you looked too young to be married."

His eyes smiled. "Thanks, but I'm twenty-seven. Most of my friends are married with kids. I'm still looking for the right girl. Almost found her, but it didn't work out."

"Same here. Not girl...guy." I grinned and decided I should get back to business. I pointed to the phone in his hand. "I'll take that one."

"Great. Do you need me to show you how to program it?"

"I can probably figure it out. It does come with directions?"

"Yes, ma'am. I recommend you use scissors when you open the package. If you aren't careful, you can tear up your fingers on this hard plastic."

He'd called me *ma'am*. I knew it was just good manners, but as usual, *Miss* and *ma'am* made me feel ancient. He was only five years younger if he was telling the truth.

I swiped my credit card, punched *yes* I accepted the charge, and used the fake pen to squiggle a facsimile of my signature on the plastic screen.

"Thank you for shopping at Wal-Mart. I'm Marlon, by the way. Just call and ask for me if you have any problems."

"You're kidding?"

"No, seriously. I'd be glad to help you."

"I mean about the name. Marlon."

He reached down and turned his badge toward me. "Yep. Says Marlon right here. Everyone kids me about Marlon Brando, the old movie star."

I didn't need cute Marlon telling me who Marlon Brando was. "It's not that. Marlon was my father's name."

"Oh, cool."

An image flashed through my head. This Marlon—with a few more muscles—in a white T-shirt, on a motorcycle, with an unlit cigarette dangling from his lips. I glanced up at his lips. Full, soft, young. I shook my head to clear it, thanked him, gave a slight wave, and left the electronics counter with a smile pasted on my face.

I set off for the front doors, shaking my head every time the image of Marlon on a motorcycle appeared. What was wrong with me? I was not the kind of girl, okay, *woman*, who picked up guys at Wal-Mart. Correction, *fantasized* about guys she met at Wal-Mart, even if the fantasy was tame. My mother would be appalled.

Suddenly, a loud squawking assailed my ears and several heads turned in my direction. I'd just set off the anti-theft device when I walked through the exit doors. Or rather my twenty-dollar cell phone had set it off. I froze, expecting the long arm of the law to reach out and yank me back inside. Marlon's arm reached me first, as if he'd dematerialized in electronics and rematerialized at the door. If not for the fact he was out of breath, I'd have thought it the work of a transporter, à la *Star Trek.*

"I'm *so* sorry." He pulled me back inside and waved away the person on guard duty. "I forgot to deactivate the phone."

"Just so I don't go to jail." I'd come close enough to that with Butch and still wasn't sure how that story would end.

"No, no way. Here, let me go swipe this, and again, I apologize."

"Don't worry about it. These things happen."

He returned in seconds and handed me the plastic bag with my twenty-dollar phone. "Thank you for being so understanding." He lowered his voice and blinked at me with his puppy-dog eyes. "Let me make it up to you."

I smiled. "Really. It's not necessary."

"But I want to. I wanted to ask you earlier, but I didn't want you to get the wrong idea. I'd really like to see you again. Do you like steak?"

I almost laughed out loud. Marlon's question reminded me how I'd lied about being a vegetarian on my blind date with Internet Joe. What a slimeball. He'd had the gall to email afterwards, offering his services washing my back. I'd fired back a terse reply telling him I had a brush for that. I hoped I'd heard the last of him.

Was Marlon seriously asking me out? He was.

"Let me take you out to dinner. There's a new place called the Prime Rib. It's really good."

Something about Marlon was refreshing. Could it be his interest in *me?* I did a quick calculation. Five years wasn't so much. I was graduating from high school about the time he hit puberty. I was entering kindergarten when he was born.

I studied him more closely. Maybe I'd been conducting my husband search the wrong way. Men certainly didn't let five years deter them. Even Carmen suggested I go younger to increase my chances.

"Sure, why not," I said without further thought.

"You will? That's great. That's wonderful." For a minute, I thought he was going grab me and whirl me around. He fumbled in his pocket for a pen and something to write on. "Let me get your phone number and address. When would you like to go? I'm off the next three nights. You choose."

I was unaccustomed to such unabashed joy and beginning to wonder if I'd made a terrible mistake. "I live kind of far from here," I said. "Why don't we meet at the steak place?"

Marlon drew back. "No ma'am. If we're going out together, then I'm picking you up and taking you home. I know how to treat a lady."

Now of that, my mother would approve. Not a good sign. "Here," I said, taking the pen from his hand. "Let me write it down for you."

I wrote down the phone number of the apartment and the Casa address and handed it to him, expecting him to ask for directions, but he surprised me again. "I know where this is. Right off Lakeshore, right?"

"You must know Waco well."

"Lived here all my life. What time should I pick you up?"

I shrugged. "Whenever."

"Tomorrow night at seven then?"

"I'll be waiting out front in the circular drive. I'm only here for a few weeks, and I live in the back."

"It's kind of hot to stand outside and wait."

"I'll be fine. See you tomorrow at seven. Give me a call if you change your mind."

Marlon grinned as if he'd won the lottery. "No way!"

I walked off, wondering what I'd done. When I turned around, Marlon was standing where I'd left him. He gave me a little wave and a big smile.

If I was going to rob the cradle, at least I'd picked a cute baby.

I thought about Nick all the way home. I should have been thankful for his honesty regarding Babe. For some reason, I couldn't take much comfort in that fact. I told myself to think positive. Think about Marlon. But each time I tried to summon Marlon's face, Nick's image appeared.

The afternoon had grown even muggier by the time I got back to the house, which made me even grumpier than usual. I told myself I should be happy about having a date with a nice, normal guy, but I couldn't muster any excitement. Was that my problem? Was I doomed to want what I couldn't have?

When I reached the ballroom, Carmen was already walking the dogs in tandem heel position.

"Very impressive!" I called out. "Just think what they were like a few weeks ago." I spoke too soon. When Noche heard me, he barked and lunged forward to greet me.

When Carmen screamed, I thought at first she was trying to correct him. The next thing I knew, she'd let go of the leads and crumpled to the floor. Both dogs bounded toward me.

"*Stop,*" I ordered, grabbing the leads. "*Sit! Stay!*" As I gave the hand command for *stay*, their big brown eyes flashed from my hand to my face and back to my hand, no doubt anticipating a treat. I left them and walked toward Carmen, taking a quick backward glance to make sure they didn't budge.

Carmen was curled in a fetal position, moaning and holding her left hand. "My fingers, my fingers. I think they're broken." She began to sob. "They...got caught...in the leash. Ohhh, it hurts so bad! I feel sick." Her face was wet with perspiration, and she began gagging.

"Stay there and don't move. We need to get you to a doctor."

"Berto's not home. Call Nick," she said between gasps. "My phone...on the table. Call his cell."

I walked over and picked up her phone, but before I could ask her the number, Nick burst in the door with Babe close behind. "We heard someone scream."

He was out of breath, his face covered in a sheen of sweat. "What happened?" he asked, his eyes sweeping the room. Spotting Carmen on the floor, he rushed to her side, Babe at his heels. "Mamá!" she cried.

I quickly explained what had happened.

"Please...please don't tell...Berto," Carmen pleaded. "He'll blame Noche. And it...it wasn't Noche's fault. I...should have been...holding him more tightly."

"Don't blame yourself," I said. "He's a strong boy and packs a lot of pull. He leaped toward me, and you weren't expecting it."

"You've told me...I should always be in control... I don't want Berto...to know."

Would the secrets in this household never cease?

"Let's not worry about Berto now," Nick said. "We need to get your hand tended to. Julie, if you'll stay here and corral the dogs, I'll take Carmen to the doctor."

Then he leaned close to me and whispered in my ear. His breath smelled of mint. My body involuntarily leaned closer to his and a surge of electricity shot through me, but my power breaker kicked in when he tilted his head toward Babe and said, "Keep an eye on her. I know Butch is in the hospital, but we can't take any chances."

After they left, Babe promised she'd stay inside and went to her room. I worked with the dogs, hoping they'd keep my mind off Nick.

With everyone gone, Noche trotted around like the show dog he could have been, while Blanco maintained a *down-stay* and watched. When I reversed the roles, Noche stayed but barked as if applauding. We went through everything we'd learned—*come, down, stay, sit, heel.*

I suppose I couldn't fault the Espositos too much for their secrets. I now had two of my own, though one was more surprise than secret. For the past few weeks, I'd been teaching the two pooches some special tricks. Before I left, I wanted to astound Carmen and Berto. I'd taught both dogs to give a high five and kiss, which was more like a nose poke. I'd also taught Blanco to be "sad." On command, she'd put her head between her paws and look up at me with a mournful face. Her wagging tail made her look anything *but* sad—it always made me laugh.

Noche had his own way of doing things, so rather than fight him, I changed his command to "tired."

"Are you tired, Noche?" I asked him in a sympathetic voice.

Noche flopped over on his side.

"Just like a man," said a voice from the doorway. I looked up to see Carmen's cook, Rosa, watching us. "Reminds me of my husband."

I made her swear on her chile grinder she wouldn't tell anyone about the tricks.

It was late when Nick and Carmen finally returned from the doctor. Two of Carmen's fingers were in a splint and her arm rested in a sling. "Sprained two fingers," Nick said, "bad."

Carmen ordered me to tell Berto she'd slammed her fingers in the car door, and I agreed. What was one more lie?

After a light supper, everyone else retired to their rooms, leaving Nick and me to ourselves. "Come on, I'll walk you back to the guesthouse, so you don't fall asleep on the way." He opened the door and held it for me.

As soon as I stepped outside, I slapped a hand to my forehead, remembering something I'd forgotten. "Oh, no! I just remembered something. Philip hasn't had his therapy today."

Nick shut the door behind us and made sure it was locked. "Can't you skip one?"

"I want him using that leg, and each day is crucial. Just like working with Noche and Blanco. It has to be consistent."

"Then I'll help," Nick said.

I lifted an eyebrow, but he took my arm and steered me to the path. "Come on. I said I'd help you. It can't be easy, even if he does weigh...what, ten pounds? That's still heavy for a little thing like you."

I stopped. "A little thing like—? I'm not a weakling. I've lifted groceries heavier than that."

He took my arm again to put me in motion. "Now, don't get upset. I know you're strong, but I'm a man and I am stronger and I'm offering to help."

I was too tired to argue with him. Besides, he was right. He was certainly a man. No way I could forget that. As we walked to my apartment, our bodies occasionally touched, sending a spasm of longing to my very core. Around Nick, my body became a pulsating vibrator set on high heat. And that was with us both fully clothed. I got the distinct feeling from the way he looked at me, he knew it.

When we reached my apartment, I laid out some towels. Time for Nick's doggy-therapy lesson. "What we have to do is hold his front legs up, so he'll have to put weight on his back legs. Are you sure you're up for this?"

Nick bent his head to the side, and his neck popped. "Let's do it. Say when."

I retrieved Philip from the couch and carried him into the bathroom, shutting the door so he couldn't run away. I turned on the tap, and Nick and I sat watching the tub fill as if it were the Trevi Fountain in Rome. Maybe if I made a wish...

Reaching down, I shut off the faucet. Shutting off my daydreams about Nick wasn't quite so easy. "That's full enough." I looked down at Nick's jeans and hesitated. "You may want to put on a swimsuit, since you'll have to get in the tub with him. It's either that or stand and bend over, and that's not really possible with this tub. I've already tried it."

Nick's eyes twinkled and next thing I knew, he'd stripped off his jeans and his shirt. I tried to avert my eyes. I really did. I soon gave up. There he stood wearing nothing but his briefs. I counted myself among the fortunate—he was wearing men's underwear, not women's. And he filled them out in all the right places. He was what women called "hot."

So was I.

I thought back to our night in Abilene, and evidently, so did Nick. "Nothing you haven't seen before," he said. I didn't remind him he'd managed to keep his pants *on* that night. "Sure you don't want to join me?" He grinned wickedly as he lowered himself into the water.

I tried to answer but had lost my voice. I grasped Philip under his front legs and eased him into the water between Nick's legs. I thought I detected a momentary flash of panic on Nick's face, but when I looked again it was gone. Philip was already trying to scramble out. "Don't drop him!" I said.

"He's fighting me. I don't want to hurt him."

"You won't. Just bounce him up and down in the water and make him put weight on his back legs."

"Like this?" The muscles in Nick's arms bulged as he bounced Philip, making it look effortless. Bulge, bounce, bulge, bounce.

I turned my head away and spoke into my armpit. "You're doing great." I took a deep breath. "About fifteen minutes should do it. We don't want to tire him out." Nick was sweating now. I grabbed a hand towel and wiped his forehead. "I hope you know how much I appreciate this."

Nick's face grew serious with concentration. "How am I doing, coach?"

I looked at my watch. "That's five minutes. You might want to give him a little break every now and then. Just—"

Before I could get the words out, Nick relaxed his hold. Philip saw his chance and made a dive for Nick's chest, climbing onto his shoulder like a cat. I reached over and tried to help, but Philip was determined now that he'd seen an out.

"Oops, sorry about that. He's never been too fond of water."

"He's just scared."

"Uh-oh. He's scratching you." Red streaks crisscrossed Nick's chest and shoulders, but he held on.

"It's okay, little guy. I've got you." Nick used the high sing-songy voice I'd taught him. He cradled Philip to his chest, and Philip hung on to Nick as if he were a life preserver. In a sense, he was. When Nick chuckled, I heard a hint of nervousness. "I think we're bonding."

"What kind of dog did you have growing up?"

I still knew so little about Nick's background. When he didn't answer right away, I thought maybe he hadn't heard me. I was about to ask again when he spoke.

"I never had a dog. My father wouldn't allow it. Until Carmen got those two rowdies of hers, I'd never even touched one." He managed to pull Philip from his chest and resume the bouncing.

"Never touched one? You've got to be kidding!" But I could tell from his face he wasn't.

"Nope, now you know my secret. When I was a young boy, my father told me dogs would give me rabies and to stay away from them."

"Was that your adoptive father or your Mexican father?"

He let out a wry laugh. "That, my dear, was my proctologist alcoholic asshole father. He didn't like kids or dogs. Said dogs were filthy creatures and gave me a phobia I'm still trying to overcome."

He continued to bounce Philip. I would have been tired by now, but judging from the way Nick's biceps bulged, he'd been working out with weights heavier than a ten-pound poodle. "So this is kind of your rehab, too." I laughed. "Philip's biting you didn't exactly help dispel your father's teachings. Are you sure you're all right with this? You don't have to do it."

"It won't hurt me to help. Getting to know Noche and Blanco from the time they were pups and working with them has made me see dogs in a different light. To tell the truth, I've actually enjoyed it. Except for the bite. Bad timing."

My face began to burn as he continued to bounce Philip.

"Seeing how you and Carmen feel about these dogs has made me curious about the human-dog connection. Then, when this little guy bit me, I kept thinking of that movie, *Gremlins*. They looked so cute at first."

Now Nick was thinking in terms of movies. I smiled and said, "Most people have some kind of fear. Often irrational."

"Like you," he said, "flying in small planes. I understand why, because of your father's accident, but you also drive a car, and look how many people are killed and injured in automobile accidents."

And my fear of getting involved with the wrong man again. Was that irrational? Evidently not.

Suddenly, I realized Philip had been bouncing for over fifteen minutes. I leaned over the edge of the tub. "Here, let me take him from you." As I reached my arms out for Philip, my cheek brushed Nick's shoulder, and for a moment our arms intertwined. I grabbed one of the towels and wrapped it around Philip, then handed Nick another one as he rose from the tub, his underwear now molded to his body.

Three thousand volts of electricity ran from my brain out the ends of my toes, causing them to sizzle.

I looked away, turning my attention to Philip to divert my thoughts. "Good *boy*. You were a *good* boy."

Nick grinned down at me. "Thanks." He kept his eyes on mine as he reached under the towel wrapped around his waist and slipped off his briefs, tossing them into the draining tub. "I need some music. Got a dollar to stuff in my g-towel?"

"Very funny," I said. "Okay, you were a good boy too. I appreciate your help. How's your dog phobia now?"

"I'm getting better, don't you think?"

I smiled. "You've come a long way."

"Thanks," he said, filling me with a warm glow when he smiled back.

"And maybe some day I'll get over my fear of small planes."

I finished towel-drying Philip and opened the bathroom door. When I let go of him, he took off through the apartment using both back legs, running circles around the sofa and stopping every so often to shake off. I laughed and called to him. "Shake and bake!"

When I stood up, Nick caught me by the arms and pulled me to him. His partially bare body and the fresh smell of his skin made me forget for a moment his heart belonged to someone else. When he leaned down and kissed me firmly on the lips, I couldn't help myself. I molded my body to his and my arms automatically went around him, caressing his back and neck, and I'm pretty sure I moaned.

"Come with me," he said, pulling me toward the bedroom, shaking me out of my turbo-charged state.

"Wait. What? What do you think you're doing?" I stammered, pushing him away.

His eyes blazed with anger. "I *thought* I was kissing you. But I guess I was mistaken."

"You think because you've helped me with Philip I'm supposed to fall into your arms?" Though that's exactly what I'd done. "I'm sorry. You don't know me very well."

"Then you tell me, Julie Shields. What *am* I supposed to think?"

I turned my back on him without a word, scooped up Philip on my way to the kitchen, and stayed there until I heard the door to the apartment slam.

When I returned to the bathroom, the underwear he'd tossed into the tub was gone, along with the rest of his clothes. The only sign he'd been there was his towel on the side of the tub, neatly folded. The gesture had a finality to it I should have welcomed. Instead, an achy emptiness stabbed me in the pit of my stomach.

Chapter Seventeen

I have a date. I have a date. If I said it enough times, maybe I could convince myself I was excited. No jeans this time. We were going to an upscale restaurant, and I intended to look my best. I'd also told Carmen this time, so she wouldn't worry about me.

I pulled a short black dress from my closet and slipped on a pair of black espadrilles with ribbons that tied up my calves to accent my "shapely legs." Okay, so I'd heard that on *What Not to Wear*, and at the moment it was on the "what-to-wear" list, though who could keep up? I carefully applied eyeliner, concealer to hide any under-eye circles, and lip gloss guaranteed to keep my lips looking "wet and luscious for six hours." A sweep of black mascara and a tiny bit of blush, and I was ready.

Marlon could be the one. I had to learn to give guys like him a chance. My mother would probably love him because he had the same first name as my father, but she would definitely not understand why I would go out with someone who worked at Wal-Mart.

He *was* cute. I might deny it, but I did want cute or handsome or good-looking. If for no other reason, I didn't want ugly children. Marlon was a little on the short side, but cute in a Prince William sort of way, except his hair was sandier, and he didn't seem to be in danger of losing it. Too, if our children took after either of us, they wouldn't be fat.

As I waited for him in the circular drive, I decided tonight would be all about Marlon. I'd quiz him like a game show host. I thought back to the list of husband requirements I'd made before I came to Waco. My mother

238

wanted me to marry rich. I wanted someone steady and faithful who loved me for myself. At any rate, that's what I'd put on my list. But a part of me also wanted a man who'd shiver me timbers. A man like Nick. Who'd want me forever.

Then I reminded myself that men like Nick didn't make good husbands. What more proof did I need? He was in love with Babe and still putting the moves on me. Time to be realistic. I had a date with a nice young man who seemed to like me. Oh, God. *Nice young man.* Something my mother would say.

I straightened my shoulders and tried to think positively. I owed it to Marlon and to myself to make the most of this date. I would never find a husband if I kept being so picky. So what if he *was* five years younger. When Marlon was forty, I'd be forty-five. When I was fifty...little Marlon would be only forty-five. So I'd have a boy toy. Other women did it. Cher, Demi...

My thoughts were interrupted by the purr of an engine. A car was headed up the hill. Fortunately, it bore no resemblance to Butch's pickup. My eyes widened as it drew closer. Marlon sat behind the wheel of a low, sleek, black-as-sin Lamborghini.

This car, the one now pulling up beside me, driven by a *Wal-Mart* clerk, was worth at least two hundred grand. Had he rented it? Stolen it? I didn't know and didn't care. Obviously, something about Marlon didn't add up, but for now, I intended to enjoy the ride. I looked back at the house, hoping someone was looking. *Look at me, Nick!* I wanted to shout. *I can get a babe too.*

Marlon hopped out and opened the door, making a wide, sweeping gesture with his arm as if he were a knight offering his lady a ride in his carriage. I smiled and lowered myself into the low-slung seat as gracefully as I could, making sure I showed some leg. I peered through the car window toward the house while Marlon walked around to his side, but I saw no signs of life.

He wore a dark suit, crisp white shirt, tie, and shoes polished to a bright shine. Thank God I'd opted for the dress.

He eased into his seat as if he'd been born to drive such a creature. "Good evening, fair lady."

"Good evening, sir." I played along, thankful he hadn't called me *ma'am* again.

Marlon reached behind his seat, extracting two pewter wine glasses and an uncorked bottle of champagne. He poured us each half a glass, and as he handed me mine, our hands brushed, but I felt no spark. I told myself sparks were precursors to storms. Storms that didn't last long and left destruction in their wake.

Marlon offered a toast. "To Marlon and Julie. May they live long and prosper."

So it wasn't original, but it was the most romantic gesture anyone had made in some time. Except for Nick. Sleeping with me on the floor of the New Orleans airport rated five stars out of five on the romance scale. And he'd also—

My inner voice interrupted my Nick-notions. *Forget Nick! He's taken. The last thing you need is another disloyal man.*

Marlon shifted gears, and the Lamborghini sailed smoothly down the incline and out onto Lakeshore Drive. The sensation resembled flying but with the comfort of four wheels on the ground.

"And how is the lovely Lady Julie this fine summer evening?"

"Lady Julie is delighted to be here."

"I'm at your command," said my Wal-Mart clerk. He shifted smoothly into second to slow us down as we rounded a curve. "If it pleases the lady, we'll soon be partaking of a fine repast. Not only steak, but steak and lobster, should the fair Julie so desire."

"Oh, yes. The fair Julie is grateful you've slain the vicious beasts and offer her the fruit of your plunder."

With that, Marlon and I continued coasting down Lakeshore and our new life together. Wait till our future children got a load of this story.

When we reached the Prime Rib, the parking lot was already full. I looked over at Marlon as he maneuvered into an empty spot that seemed to materialize near the front door. "Are you sure we can get in?"

"Not to worry. We have reservations."

I racked up another point for Marlon. The boy...man...manchild...seemed to know his way around.

The second we entered the front door, the maître d', a solid man with short, curly hair, greeted us effusively. If he'd been a dog, he'd have been from the working group, maybe a Black Russian terrier.

"Good evening, Mr. Williams. Your table is ready. Follow me, please."

Mr. Williams?

The maître d' seated us in a dimly lit room at a cozy corner table covered in white linen. A cinnamon-scented candle flickered, creating shadows on the wall, reminding me of my night in Abilene with Nick. Was I going to need an exorcist to rid myself of thoughts of him?

A sommelier appeared with the wine list. "You like red?" Marlon asked.

"Sure, red, white, whatever you want is fine with me."

Marlon barely glanced at the list. "We'll have a bottle of the 2001 Shafer Hillside Select Stags Leap District Cabernet Sauvignon."

I looked at the description: *Outstanding. One of California's most sought-after wines and priced accordingly. It offers exotic, wild blackberry and black cherry fruit, creamy vanilla and toasty oak, plus a hint of cedar. The tannins are plush tannins, the finish long.* I reached for my throat when I saw the price. One hundred seventy-five dollars. Was it possible Marlon thought it said seventeen-fifty?

No doubt the steaks would be equally pricey. Poor Marlon. Blowing a week's—month's?—Wal-Mart salary on food and drink.

Dollar signs for his tip popped up in the sommelier's eye sockets. "Good choice, sir." Once the waiter was out of earshot, I could hold my tongue no longer. "Excuse me, but did you notice the price of the wine?"

Marlon flashed me a dimpled smile. "I know it's rather expensive, but this is a special occasion."

"It is?"

"Of course. It's our first date. It's not often I meet a woman in Wal-Mart and she says *yes* when I ask her out."

"They usually say *no*?"

He laughed. "Honestly, I've never asked a customer out before."

Quiz show time. I needed some answers. "What's with the *Mr. Williams*? Does the maître d' know you? Do you work here too?"

Marlon laughed again, then leaned over and whispered. "He knows my father."

"And your father is...?"

"I might as well confess. My father was mayor a few years ago. Most people in Waco know him or know his name. I don't advertise it because—don't take this wrong—but I've had women go out with me because my family has money."

Ha. Could I ever relate to *that*. "And the Wal-Mart job?"

"My attempt to be normal, I guess you could say. With my father's connections, I could take my pick of jobs, but I like dealing with everyday, ordinary people. And I get plenty of that at Wal-Mart. It's only part-time. I'm also working toward my law degree at Baylor. Six months to go. Soon as I pass the bar exam, I plan to leave Waco, hook up with a firm or start my own practice, somewhere no one knows me."

Unbelievable. This manchild was perfect. I could even get over my prejudice against rich people with a guy like this. Marlon could have been telling my own life story, give or take a few details.

I deliberated whether to reveal how much we had in common and decided against it. Though I liked him, I automatically recoiled when he mentioned money. I'd had my share of rich guys and found them arrogant, shallow, and selfish. So far, Marlon seemed different, but for now, I'd play my cards close to my breasts.

The sommelier brought our wine, opened it, offered Marlon the cork to smell, then poured a splash into Marlon's glass. Marlon swirled, sniffed, sipped, and nodded his acceptance.

Next, a waiter handed us a dinner menu, apprised us of the evening's specials, and said he'd be back shortly to take our orders. I took a sip of wine. Though I didn't tell Marlon, it tasted like any other cabernet sauvignon. I couldn't tell the cedar from the oak or plush tannin from…what would the opposite be? Unplush? Spartan?

One thing I had to admit. So far my date with Marlon vastly surpassed my dining experiences with Butch, Internet Joe, and all my other dates the past year. But a small voice in my head wouldn't be quieted: *What about the Coffee Pot in New Orleans with Nick? What about just being in the same room with Nick?*

I shut the voice off and perused the menu. For starters, choices included pumpkin and chickpea soup or smoked salmon and lemon risotto. Main courses were quail with figs and olives, osso bucco served with mashed potatoes and seasoned vegetables, or steak and lobster. Prices ranged from fifty to eighty dollars. Per *person.* I wondered how long the Prime Rib would stay in business in Waco, Texas. How could people spend that much money on one meal when people and dogs were going hungry all over the world?

Marlon reached over and pointed to the entrée section of my menu. "I highly recommend the steak and lobster."

"Fine with me." The thought of sweet, succulent lobster melting in my mouth did have its appeal. Just so I didn't have to pick one out of a tank.

Marlon studied his menu. "For dessert, we really need to try the little hot pots of chocolate with orange polenta biscuits."

I took another five-dollar sip of the hundred and seventy-five dollar wine, wondering what I was doing here. Meanwhile, my fresh-faced companion seemed perfectly at ease. I would have felt more comfortable at an I-Hop, but I knew how to go through the motions. I removed the origami-folded napkin and placed it in my lap. "You eat here often?"

"Not really. I save it for special occasions. When I saw you in the store yesterday, I knew if you agreed to go out with me, it would be special."

"That's sweet," I said, trying to feel something besides gratitude. What was wrong with me? Here I was in an expensive restaurant with a guy who seemed to have no flaws, and I was...well, I was bored.

And the evening was young. Time for question number two. "Tell me about your law studies."

"Well, I want to specialize in international law and hope someday to get into politics."

I did admire him for being a rich kid with ambition instead of living off his daddy's money.

"What about you?"

I took another small sip of wine. "Me? When my stint in Waco is over, I'll go back to Abilene and resume my day job as a vet tech. That's about all there is to tell." For some reason, I didn't want to talk about myself to Marlon, though he seemed sincerely interested.

"What brought you to Waco?"

"My boss went mountain climbing for a month, and a job opened up here. I'm living with a family while I train their two poodles." Could I have sounded any duller? No wonder I was bored. I was boring myself.

The steak and lobster rescued me. I managed to ask enough questions to keep Marlon talking, while I savored each delicious bite of my eighty-dollar dinner. At that price, it would be sinful not to, but my thoughts kept straying to Nick. He's the one who should be sitting across from me, not Marlon, dammit.

Marlon was Nick's polar opposite—sandy hair, fair-skinned. For some reason, I'd never been attracted to blond men. Sorry Brad, James Dean, and now Marlon. I'd always been more of a Colin Farrell-Antonio Banderas kind of gal.

I leaned against the padded back of the chair, allowing the lobster to have its way with my taste buds, closing my eyes in ecstasy. When I opened them, I was staring across the room into Nick's baby blues. I jolted upright in my seat in disbelief. In his dark, tailored suit, he could have passed for a Hollywood star. My knees began to tremble and forcing them together didn't help. My fork clattered onto my plate.

I picked up the fork and wiped it with my napkin, hoping Marlon wouldn't notice, but a look of concern crossed his face. "You okay? Your face is flushed. You aren't allergic to seafood are you?"

"It's the wine. Sometimes it makes the blood rush to my face."

Nick was walking straight toward us, his eyes locked onto mine. What was he doing at the Prime Rib? First the Cotton Patch Cafe. Now here. He must have followed me again. But why? And how? I wasn't in Carmen's Lexus this time.

Then I saw Babe. She wore an off-the-shoulder electric blue dress that was sending high-voltage currents through every male in the place. Heads swiveled like bar stools. Marlon's back was to her, so I wasn't sure what his reaction would be.

A few seconds later, they were standing beside our table. Nick smiled broadly. "Julie, what a surprise!" Okay, so Babe had him and I didn't. He didn't have to rub it in. *But the thought of him rubbing anything in...* Did Babe know he was a two-timer who'd tried to add me to his list of conquests?

When Marlon stood up and offered his hand, Nick grasped it firmly and didn't let go till Marlon looked away. Then Nick introduced himself and Babe. "Julie's been staying with us this summer," he said, as if we were a big, happy family. I glared at Nick but put on my fake smile when Marlon looked my way. He held out his hand inviting them to sit. "By all means, join us. We have plenty of room."

Babe flashed him a smile so bright I had to blink, but Marlon seemed oblivious to her charms.

Nick smiled and pointed across the room. "Thanks, but we've got a table reserved." The wine bottle caught his eye, and he lifted it from the table, examining the label. "Great choice. I have a fondness for the Shafer Hillside Selects myself. Last year when I was in California, Babe and I visited the winery in Napa. Ever been there?"

Marlon shook his head.

"You should try it sometime," Nick said. "Beautiful place, wasn't it, Babe?"

She looked up at Nick and smiled in adoration. "Fabulous," she said, turning toward Marlon. "Are you from Waco?"

"Born and raised."

Marlon was still standing, and our food was getting cold. *Why didn't they leave?*

"So how did you two meet?" Nick asked, directing the question to Marlon.

I broke in, narrowing my eyes at Nick when Marlon wasn't looking. "We met while I was shopping for a cell phone."

Nick looked surprised. "Ah, so you finally broke down and decided to enter the brave new world. About time."

I stabbed a piece of steak and held it near my mouth, hoping he'd take the hint and leave. "Just a disposable. Once I leave Waco, I doubt I'll have need of it."

Marlon smiled. "I helped her pick one out, but I forgot to deactivate the sensor device, and she set the alarm off. One thing led to another, and here we are."

Nick's smile didn't extend to his eyes. "Julie has been known to set off alarms. Where do you work?" His behavior reminded me of a male street dog, circling another dog and staring till it dropped its bone.

"Wal-Mart," said Marlon, as if proud of it.

I wanted to crawl under the table. Marlon was carrying his poor boy act too far.

Nick smiled slightly and looked down at our plates, probably thinking I was so desperate for a husband I was paying.

Marlon shifted his weight to his other foot, and I sensed he was being polite for my sake. "How about you?"

"Pilot."

"Interesting," he said, though he was sounding less interested the longer he stood there. "Sure you won't join us?"

"Thanks, but our waiter is signaling us now. Enjoy your dinner. *And* your wine." Nick glanced back over his shoulder as he and Babe headed for their table.

Steam was coming out of my ears by the time Marlon sat back down and looked at his cold food. "Seems like a nice guy."

I stuffed a piece of steak into my mouth and bit into it with a vengeance. "He's okay," I muttered.

Marlon nibbled on his lobster. "They make a handsome couple." Much as I hated to admit it, he was right. He reached over and covered my hand with his. "But they don't have anything on us."

My body went rigid, but I left my hand where it was until he pulled his away. Even the touch of another man's hand left me empty. Stranger still, I felt I was betraying Nick. It made no sense whatsoever, and I knew I had to shake this obsession. I was thirty-two years old, way too old to believe in fairy tales. No Cinderella complex here.

I looked across the table at Marlon and summoned a smile. He deserved that much for not slavering over Babe. I just hoped the rest of the evening would go faster than the first part. Was I expecting too much? My sister had found a man. My friends found them. Even my mother. What was wrong with me?

After dinner, Marlon suggested a movie. Normally, I'd have been thrilled, but instead I feigned a headache. I glanced over at Nick and Babe as we left, but neither of them looked up. Too gaga over each other, no doubt.

When we got back to Casa del Lago, Marlon insisted on seeing me to my door, but I lied and said I had business to take care of in the big house. I couldn't bear to have him walk down the same pathway where I'd walked with Nick. Where I'd kissed Nick.

Marlon gave me a quick peck on the cheek, and told me what a wonderful time he'd had. I hedged when he asked when he could see me again, telling him I'd have to check my calendar. Hell, I didn't even have a calendar.

I stood at the front door, waiting until the black steed he'd ridden up on was just a faint light at the bottom of the hill, wondering if Nick and Babe had enjoyed their dinner more than I had mine.

Chapter Eighteen

A smothering, overcast sky met me when I left my apartment. I dreamed of returning home to escape the pain of seeing Nick with Babe again. Instead, time passed by slower than an Abilene driver.

When I opened the back door to the big house, Noche and Blanco greeted me by leaping into the air and emitting high-pitched barks of joy. I hooked on their leads and led them outside to a clearing in the trees.

At first they were attentive, obeying each command, but they soon picked up on my lethargy. Each time we stopped, Noche nuzzled my hand, and Blanco leaned her body into mine. After half an hour or so, I gave up, lowering myself to the ground and hugging them to me, one on each side. "I'm okay, guys. A little down in the dumps. Not your fault."

I buried my face in Blanco's soft coat and closed my eyes. The crunch of footsteps startled me. The bushes rustled and parted. From my position on the ground, I saw a man's legs headed toward me. I let out a scream that sent both dogs into a paroxysm of barking. The man yelped, and I leaped to my feet and screamed again, ready to run.

The barks quickly shifted to yips of pleasure. Berto was leaning over, hand on his heart, chest heaving. "You scared the hell out of me!"

"Well, you scared me first!"

"I was just making sure you were safe. Waco isn't Abilene, you know. This place is like the Bermuda Triangle of news."

I feigned confidence, though my heart still beat double-time. "I'm a big girl."

We both knew better after my experience at Lovers Leap. I put the dogs in a *down-stay*, while Berto leaned against a tree and watched. I concentrated on the dogs and breathed deeply to calm my nerves, hoping he'd leave.

Instead, when I looked up, he took a step toward me, then stopped. "Can I help?"

I blinked. Was he joking? "You mean, help with the dogs?"

"Yes." He lowered his head and reached down to tighten a shoelace that needed no tightening. "I thought I could fill in for Carmen. Only if you want me to."

Was this the same Berto who'd given Carmen the ultimatum to choose between him and the dogs? What was he up to now? I'd seen no evidence he even *liked* the dogs.

I searched for a hidden motive, analyzing his face for clues. "Do you know anything about training dogs?"

"No, just what I've seen you and Carmen do. I, uh...watch sometimes. I've got to say, you've accomplished a miracle with these two. Just look at them."

Berto's words filled my heart with the most serious of the seven deadly sins—pride. Noche and Blanco *were* impressive. Neither dog had budged from the *stay*. Blanco's eyes were closed, but each time I spoke, Noche's ears twitched, as if eager to respond to my next command.

Berto watched them in amazement. "They were never this calm before. Before you came they jumped on anybody and everybody. And at night—"

I held up my hand to stop him. "Enough. Let's give it a try. First, some basics. Much of the success of training a dog is learning how to signal your expectations. Just because they obey me or Carmen doesn't mean they'll obey you, since you don't know their language. You do have one advantage though." That got Berto's attention.

He shrugged and held his palms up. "What?"

"You're a man."

"So?"

"Don't let it go to your head, but..." I switched into lecture mode. "It's not your gender they'll respond to but your voice. When a mother dog wants her pups to obey, she gives a low growl. So the lower your voice, the more they'll pay attention." I demonstrated by speaking in a lower tone.

Berto tugged his ear and nodded.

I continued my lecture. "It's imperative you be consistent. Never reward them until they've followed your command. Otherwise, they'll have no motivation to obey. Eventually, praise can become their reward, but for now, we're using these tiny pieces of fat-free wieners. The smell and the fact it's not part of their regular diet will motivate them to perform the desired behavior."

I walked over to where Noche and Blanco lay and picked up their leads. "You're free!" I said, using a high, excited voice. The dogs leaped up and looked at me. "Good dogs!" I gave each of them a small piece of wiener and a big hug.

Thus, began my training of Berto. I'd model, and he'd follow. His natural authoritarian personality translated well to the dogs, and they were eager to win his praise. No wonder. "Get out" was probably the only thing he'd ever said to them until now.

I made sure to praise Berto as much as I did the dogs.

After twenty minutes or so, we took a water break. Berto and I sat beneath a tree, while Noche and Blanco played chase with each other off lead, never straying from our sight.

Berto scratched his neck. "I've begun to see how much these dogs mean to Carmen. I decided—even before she sprained her fingers—I needed to help her more, just as I did with our children."

"In her mind, Noche and Blanco *are* her children."

"I know. And great company for her since I'm gone so much."

I slid my eyes sideways, trying to gauge the sincerity of this new, improved Berto.

He picked up a twig and poked at a fallen leaf. "Something else. Use the pool for Philip's therapy whenever you want."

Was this the same Berto who'd had the pool drained after Noche and Blanco jumped in?

He looked up at me. "After Nick told me about the tub..."

"Thanks," I said, wondering what else Nick had told him. "That would really help. He's trained. I promise he won't pee in the water."

Berto began breaking the twig into small pieces. "I'm sorry I've seemed harsh. I was skeptical at first you could pull this off. Mainly because of Carmen. You know now how headstrong she is. That's why the other trainers didn't work out. But you've gotten through to her. She's changed as much as the dogs."

A pleasant warmth suffused my face. I swallowed to clear the lump in my throat. "Thank you," I said, then directed the subject away from me. "About Carmen. I've been thinking I should keep the two dogs with me. So she can recover. And that way I can also provide added reinforcement to all they've learned. Carmen really wants them to do well at their *debut*."

"Fine with me." He stood up and tossed the pieces of broken twig on the ground. "And if you don't mind, I'd rather you not tell her I'm helping. I want this to be her success."

"I understand." At that moment I thought I understood something else. Berto had never intended to leave Carmen. He'd been bluffing all along.

He looked down at me and scuffed his shoe in the grass. "I'm not good with words, but I appreciate everything you've done for us." He hesitated. "I have another favor to ask."

I winced, knowing what was coming next. I couldn't really blame him. His family could be in danger.

"It concerns our mutual friend." He squatted, picked up a bigger stick, and jabbed it at the ground. "You know what he did to our daughter. When she quit seeing him, he also made up all kinds of stories about us. As if it was our fault. The guy's a nutcase."

I let out a deep breath. "I agree. And I'd like to help, but filing charges isn't going to do any good. For one, there are no corroborating witnesses. Two, to charge someone with aggravated assault, there has to be a knife, a gun, or a beating. Even if they arrested him—which I doubt they would—he'd bond out, and the case would get dismissed before it ever went to court. At best, it would start a paper trail, but the courts are usually too busy to deal with what they consider minor issues. Also, the fact he's a cop doesn't help our case."

Berto's shoulders drooped. "Nick said your sister's a lawyer. Did she tell you all that?"

I chuckled. "No, Judge Judy."

He looked baffled.

"Never mind. I also called my sister."

"So there's nothing we can do?" His dark brown eyes reminded me of Noche's. I lightly touched his arm.

"Don't worry. I may have something special in my doggy bag of tricks."

Berto reached up and ran a hand through his hair. "Then you better pull it out. Butch Justice was released from the hospital a few hours ago."

* * *

Back in my apartment, Noche and Blanco sniffed Philip with interest, and he sniffed back with no repercussions. Still, I feared the two males wouldn't co-exist well, and I didn't want to take any chances. Since I couldn't very well kick Philip out of his new digs and didn't want to shut them in separate rooms, I had only one other choice—I'd have to ask Nick to babysit Noche when I wasn't around to supervise.

But first, Plan B, Step Two. I picked up the phone and punched in a number. When a man answered, I identified myself. "Time to move into action," I said. He knew what to do.

When I heard Nick return to his apartment, I walked around to his side, drew a deep breath, and tapped on his door. I hated asking for favors, especially from him.

He opened the door and leaned against the jamb, barefoot and bare-chested. His jeans rode low below his navel. I forced myself to focus on his face. He stood there, silent, his lips forming a half-smile. His eyes began to caress my body, warming each part in turn. He might as well have put me on a spit over hot coals and turned me till I was done.

I should hate him. I should be disgusted with myself. But Tess, Toss, and Terone still raged inside me whenever he was near. Hormones had no pride. But it wasn't just the physical attraction. He'd helped with Philip, even though he was afraid of dogs. He'd helped with Noche and Blanco. He'd covered me with a blanket in New Orleans and stayed with me. My mind thought back to his other kindnesses.

"Coming in?" he finally asked. When I hesitated, he added, "Don't worry. I'm safe."

About as safe as a condom made from Swiss cheese.

My eyes swept over his living area, the mirror image of mine, except his had a more masculine feel, leather and rough wood with few decorative touches.

"Have a seat." He gestured to the dark leather sofa. "To what do I owe this honor?" His tone was serious now, his eyes cool, as he down sat across from me.

"I need a favor."

He raised an eyebrow. "And what could I possibly have that you want?"

Against my will, my eyes grazed his bare torso. His chest glowed with a bronzed sheen, his biceps bulged like baseballs, and his shoulders tapered down to wash-board abs that made me think of anything but laundry. He smiled, as if he might have read my mind.

"I need you to keep Noche." I held up a hand and continued before he had a chance to protest, my words tumbling out. "Though the bitch is almost always the alpha dog, two males in a pack often don't get along. It's just their nature, and I don't want Philip or Noche hurt. Philip's already at a disadvantage. It's only till Carmen's party. Once that's done, and she's proven to Berto she can control them, Philip and I will be outta here. I know you're afraid of dogs, but you've been around Noche since he was a pup, and he likes you. *Pleeese*?"

Before he could speak, I forged ahead. "You don't have to take him with you when you leave. I just need a place for him to stay when I'm not in the apartment. If you won't do it for me, then please do it for Berto and Carmen."

Nick stroked his chin and let out a deep breath. "Only if you remain on call. I'll need your phone number."

"Don't you have the number?"

"To your new *cell* phone."

"Oh, that. Deal. I'll get Noche now."

"And keep your phone turned on. You do know how to use it, don't you?"

I lifted my head and glowered at him. "I'm not a total idiot."

"You've proven that," he said with a laugh.

"And I'll need a key to your apartment so I can let Noche in and out."

Nick rubbed his bottom lip with his thumb.

"Well?"

"Sure. No problem," he said, but something about the way he said it told me he wasn't overjoyed.

Curious as to what the rest of his apartment looked like, I peered over his shoulder, but all I saw was darkness.

* * *

Plan B began to work even better than I'd anticipated. One morning as I munched on a piece of toast, the phone rang. On the other end, Carmen poured forth a mixture of Spanish and English so rapidly I couldn't even comprehend the English. "Wait a minute. Slow down. English, *por favor*."

"Some great news, Julie! Berto just woke me up to show me."

Whatever it was, it must be important for anyone to awaken Carmen so early. "It's about Butch," she said, breathlessly. "Meet us at the house."

As soon as I walked in, Carmen grabbed my arm and pulled me into the library. Berto, Nick, and Babe sat in a semicircle in front of the fireplace, and when I walked in, they all looked up.

"Here she is," Carmen said, practically pushing me into a chair. "You're responsible for this, aren't you?"

I held up my hands in protest. "I have no idea what you're talking about."

She thrust the morning paper at me and pointed to the front page. "He's been arrested. Look. There's his picture."

Sure enough, the dominant picture on Page One showed Butch in handcuffs, wearing an orange jumpsuit.

I smiled. "I did not file charges."

Babe crossed her legs and jiggled her dainty foot. "You know what we're talking about. Someone sent pictures of Butch to the police chief. It had to be you."

"Me? I don't even own a camera!" I was telling the truth about that.

Carmen was relishing her role as messenger. "Some-one sent photos of Butch wearing a red dress, makeup, and a wig to the police. So they put a stake on his car."

"They put a *steak* on his car?" I repeated.

"She means they put a stakeout on him after they got the pictures," Berto explained. "A few nights ago, a patrolman caught him speeding down Lakeshore. When the policeman attempted to stop him, Butch tried to outrun him, but his pickup stalled. So he got out and tried to run, but since he's still on crutches, he didn't get far."

Carmen pooched her lips out. "You're leaving out the best part. Tell her."

Berto looked embarrassed. "You go ahead, sweetie. You tell this part."

Carmen bounced up and down in her chair, and her hands gesturing wildly as she spoke. "He was wearing this tight tank top, a miniskirt, and earrings! And when he tried to get away from the policeman, one of his false boobies fell out. When he reached down to pick it up, the policeman grabbed him. Butch told him he was on his way home from a costume party."

"Must have been *some* party," Nick said, and everyone laughed.

I took a closer look at the newspaper. "So he's in trouble for evading arrest?"

When Nick stood up and propped a foot on the hearth, my eyes riveted on his long, lean body. "More than that," he said. "After he left the hospital, several women on his floor began reporting missing underwear. One woman said she woke up and saw a man going through her drawers—the built-in kind. When she yelled at him, he apologized and said he'd mistaken her room for his. Later, when the police showed her Butch's picture, she identified him."

Carmen leaned over my shoulder and slapped at Butch's picture. "Doesn't he make enough money to buy his own undies?"

I laughed. "Policemen don't make much money, but I think part of the thrill for him must be stealing them."

Carmen huffed. "He's one sick doggy."

"Puppy," I corrected.

Babe reached for the newspaper and examined the picture. "How could I have ever—?"

Nick put his arm around her shoulders and gave her a hug. "Don't beat yourself up over it. That was all a long time ago."

"There's more," Berto said. "The police got a warrant to search his apartment. Guess what they found? Hundreds of pairs of women's panties in baggies, labeled with the names of the women who owned them."

My jaw dropped. "You're kidding. Who would have dreamed he was that organized?"

Babe took another look at Butch's picture and grimaced. "The police also have evidence he's responsible for some unsolved break-ins."

I smiled to myself. Plan B had worked better than I'd anticipated.

Carmen began bouncing excitedly again. "He'll have to wear an ankle bracelet until he goes to court, so they'll know where he is at all times. I hope they throw the boot at him."

"She means *book*," Berto said.

"Yes," she said, "they're giving him the book. He's in big-time trouble. Tell her what else the paper said, Nick."

Nick stretched his arms and smiled with satisfaction. "His father, a former chief of police, was quoted as saying his son has shown 'disrespect for the police force and a lack of moral values and honor.'"

"Is that it?" I asked.

They all looked at me. "Isn't that enough?" Nick asked.

"It will do. It will definitely do."

Nick walked toward me, and before I could stop him, he wrapped his arms around me. "Thank you, Julie. You're our hero." I gave him a stiff hug in return, glancing toward Babe. I knew how it felt when your man touched another woman.

"I don't know what makes you think I had anything to do with this," I said.

So what if I'd hired a private detective to follow Butch and the private detective had sent me photographs that I'd sent to the police chief, anonymously. It was no big deal, and they didn't have to know I'd done it.

The way they all kept smiling at me, you'd have thought I'd caught a killer. Though I was happy for them, the whole episode merely emphasized my own unhappy state. Come Sunday, all my ties with Waco would be severed forever.

* * *

Berto helped with the dogs—with Carmen none the wiser—and Nick and Noche seemed to be batching it fine until I found a note under my door from Nick. He had to make a quick run to Mexico for Berto, but I could put Noche in his apartment whenever I needed.

Carmen, meanwhile, was caught up in planning the dogs' coming out party, her eyes lighting up whenever she talked about it. "With Butch in jail, now we can have a double celebration. I'm so glad Barbi will be here for the dogs' debut. Rosa is making turkey tamales, and I've hired a mariachi band from San Antonio." She clapped her hands in excitement. "Everyone's going to dance and have a wonderful time!"

Whenever I expressed reservations, she called me a "pooper," but I did have reservations. "Are you sure you aren't overdoing this, a party for the dogs? They've both learned a lot, but we don't know how they'll react around a crowd and a band. I'm not really sure anyone is interested in seeing them *heel* and *sit*."

Carmen stomped her small foot. "Of course they'll be interested. Who wouldn't love *mis perros*? Everyone will love them. And *mis niños* will be perfect."

I hoped she was right.

* * *

With Nick gone again, time slowed to a basset hound's pace. I told myself I'd be better off once my tempter was out of range for good. After Sunday, I'd never see him again and could resume my normal, boring existence back in Abilene.

Maybe I'd date Marlon. I might even marry Marlon. He had the pedigree. He'd said he liked dogs, and he'd asked me out again, though I'd had to tell him I was too busy for now. I *was* busy.

Or maybe I'd marry some guy my mother picked out. Actually, I'd rather live as a nun than settle for a guy my mother chose. I'd take a vow of poverty and chastity and devote my life to caring for dogs. But then, that's pretty much what I'd already done.

Toward the end of the week, I sat outside my apartment in a chaise longue, drinking an ice-cold glass of chardonnay, watching the sunset—a merging of blue, pale orange, and pink. I should have felt content. I'd done the job I'd been hired to do, and I'd helped bring harmony to a marriage.

Instead, I felt nothing but emptiness. I went inside and poured another glass of chardonnay, deciding to treat myself to one big pity party. Back outside, I moved my chair to another spot in a clump of trees near Nick's apartment for a better view of the lake.

As the sky slowly darkened, more stars appeared. I must have fallen asleep, because I dreamed of soft voices, speaking in the musical cadence of Spanish. Then, a voice deeper than the rest, speaking English, broke the mood. I awakened with a jerk.

A voice from the direction of Nick's apartment hissed. "Be quiet. We don't want to wake anyone up."

My eyes popped open. Nick! Why was he sneaking around in the dark? And who was with him? Babe? The thought brought a lump to my throat.

The darkness amplified each small sound. I didn't move. Footsteps shuffled across his porch and a key slipped into the lock. Inside, Noche gave a low growl and then began to bark.

Nick whispered a notch louder. "Dammit, I forgot about the dog. You guys wait a minute." The shuffling footsteps stopped. "Let me go in first."

The door squeaked open, and Noche bounded out with barks of welcome when he saw Nick. "Yes, I'm happy to see you, too. *Off. Quiet. Good* boy. *Good* quiet."

Peering around a tree, I saw Nick squatting and stroking Noche's thick curls while Noche whined with pleasure. Lucky dog. Then Nick stood, and behind him I made out Carmen's gardener, Ramón, and another man I didn't recognize, both holding large garbage bags.

They left the door open as they entered the apartment. Noche followed.

I crept closer.

Nick waved his flashlight toward a closet. "Put them in there." The closet door opened and closed, and the men reappeared on the porch.

My eyes were gradually growing accustomed to the dark.

"*Gracias.* Here," Nick said, pulling a wad of bills from his pocket and passing them out to the men before locking the door. Then they all began the trek back toward the big house with Nick in the lead.

I glanced at my watch. The luminous hands read two a.m. A car engine roared to life in the distance. Then all was quiet.

Was Nick coming back? I waited, unmoving, knowing what I had to do. When five minutes had passed, I sprang into action.

The key to Nick's apartment lay on an end table in my living room. I grabbed the key and a flashlight from the kitchen. If Nick came back and caught me, I could always say I heard Noche bark and thought he needed to go out.

As I slowly opened the door, Noche nuzzled my hand and yipped, still excited with all the late-night activity. "Shhh. Quiet. Good boy."

Once inside the apartment, I flipped on my small flashlight and crept to the closet, but when I tried the knob, it held firm. Locked. I tried the door key, but it didn't fit. What could be so valuable Nick needed to lock the closet? I shined the light around the edges of the door, then got down on the floor and tried to peer under the gap at the bottom, but the carpenters had done their work well. Then I spotted something.

At first I thought it was merely a few leaves and twigs one of the men had tracked in. Then my mind flashed back to our New Orleans trip and the ICE men. I thought of all the trips Nick had made to Mexico. Using my deductive reasoning, I knew what I was looking at. I'd seen it in the movies. Acapulco Gold. Mary Jane. Weed. Marijuana.

Nick was a drug smuggler.

Chapter Nineteen

I now had tangible evidence Nick wasn't the one for me. Out of all the losers I'd fallen for, none had turned out to be drug dealers. I imagined myself, baby on my hip, visiting Nick in Huntsville State Prison, surrounded by barbed wire and armed guards. My brain told me I had to quit visualizing myself with Nick at all. My heart was having a harder time letting go.

After gathering the dried stems and leaves, I returned to my apartment. About an hour later, I heard Nick's door open and close, followed by Noche's excited barking.

Should I tell the Espositos about Nick's nocturnal activities? Did Berto know? Was Nick working for Berto? I prayed it wasn't so for Carmen's sake. I finally fell into a fitful sleep and awoke early the next morning with a sleep-debt hangover.

After three cups of strong coffee, my head began to clear. Then came the knock on my door. I peeked through the window. Nick stood outside looking rested and carefree, his hair still wet from a shower. Great. I hadn't showered, my hair was a mess, and I was still in my nightgown and robe.

I opened the door a few inches. "Hello, Sunshine."

"Don't 'Sunshine' me," I said, scowling.

He drew his head back in mock affront. "Sorry. Just trying to be pleasant. I thought you might be glad to see me since we won't be housemates much longer."

"We aren't housemates now," I grumbled, avoiding his eyes.

"Aren't you going to invite me in?" I didn't answer but opened the door wider. He walked in and made himself comfortable on my couch, stretching out his long legs as if he lived there.

I sat across from him and tightened the belt on my robe. "How was Mexico?"

"Let's just say it was a productive trip."

No doubt. I couldn't begin to guess the street value of a closet full of marijuana.

"I know what's going on," I said. "I might be a little slow, but I'm not stupid."

He managed to look perplexed. With his acting skills, he should go to California. He and Babe could star together in one of her soap operas.

"You could have been truthful with me from the start. Was that too much to ask?"

He drew his legs in, sat up straight, and leaned toward me. "You have a lot of nerve talking about the truth. What about Philip? What about your house in Abilene? You call that being truthful?"

"I didn't lie."

His eyes looked sad. "No, but you led me to believe you had a boyfriend and that you were a mere vet tech."

"*Mere*? What do you mean, *mere*? There's nothing lowly or shameful about what I do. That's more than I can say for you. For your information, I *know* what's in your closet."

His face seemed to pale, and I smiled, knowing I'd finally touched a nerve.

"How could you possibly know?"

"I was outside last night when you brought it in. I saw you."

He got up and moved to where I sat, placing his hands on my shoulders, his denim eyes darkening and burning into mine. "You were spying on me?"

I shrugged. "You gave me the key. And Noche needed out."

Nick raised an eyebrow.

"You win. So I was snooping."

"But the closet was locked."

"Let's just say I saw evidence of the evidence."

He squinted at me and shook his head. "Someone must have really screwed you around for you to be so suspicious of men."

I ignored his observation, folding my arms across my chest. "What would Carmen say if she knew?"

He backed away from me. "Surely you wouldn't stoop that low. Would you? Ruin everything for her? I thought you had more integrity than that."

"You're talking to *me* about integrity?"

I turned away from him, but he grabbed my arm and made me look at him. This time his eyes pled. "Please, promise you won't say anything."

I jerked away. "I suppose Berto knows all about your 'activities'?"

"Of course he knows." Nick's words were clipped. "And he won't be happy if you tell Carmen, so don't do something you'll regret."

Before I could reply, he stormed out the door, shutting it hard behind him.

Was he threatening me? With that in mind, I decided not to tell Carmen just yet. I had no desire to sleep with the fish in Lake Waco.

* * *

That afternoon, I worked with the dogs for the last time, but my heart wasn't in it. I would miss them. They'd been the only constant this whole month. Afterward, I walked up to the big house so Carmen could brief me on her party plans. From the number of people working at the house that day, you'd have thought a marriage was in the works, not a dog party.

Carmen stood at the foot of a ladder near the main staircase, issuing instructions on where to hang colored lights. When she saw me, she smiled and wiped her hands on an old towel. "*Mi hijo* is coming from New York!" she said excitedly. "Our son, Bobby."

Bobby and Barbi. You didn't get more American than that. Bobby's arrival must be the big surprise.

"You're going to love him. He's so smart. And handsome." She eyed me suggestively, making me laugh.

"And much younger than I am." Older men, younger women—no one gave it a second thought. But older women and younger men—it happened, but the social stigma still existed.

Carmen confirmed my thinking. "You don't have a younger sister, do you?"

"Hate to disappoint you. I'm the baby."

Carmen continued chattering, mainly about Bobby's success at his Wall Street job. I tuned out, my thoughts straying back to Nick's closet and how to tell Carmen about the drugs. Berto's entire fortune had most likely been built from illegal drug trade, the imported furniture business serving as a front for laundering dirty money.

I would wait till after the party to tell Carmen. Why spoil her fun this one night? My news would keep. Nick was right about that.

Carmen hugged me excitedly, then explained her plans. To kick off the party, she and I would parade down the main staircase with Noche and Blanco, while the mariachi band played a fanfare of some sort. She swore she could handle Blanco with her uninjured hand. I could lead Noche, since he was the more spirited of the two.

She was too excited to notice my despondency. Nick's activities had dampened my spirits to the point I was no longer in the mood to show off the tricks I'd taught the dogs, but I would do it for her. If anyone deserved a night of happiness, it was Carmen. Besides, once I dropped the drug bomb on Sunday, her life would never again be the same.

After Philip's pool therapy, during which I saw no sign of Nick, I spent the rest of the afternoon in my apartment. Around five, someone knocked on the door. Hoping it wasn't Nick, I got up quietly and peered through the window. Carmen stood outside.

As soon as I opened the door, she grabbed my hand and, over my protests, began pulling me with her toward the big house. "Come with me. No questions."

I followed, sputtering protests. When we got to the house, she led me upstairs to her bedroom with its walk-in closet and adjoining dressing room the size of a small bedroom. She eyed me up and down, then ordered me to strip to my underwear and started pulling dresses from their hangers. "You're a little taller, but other than that, we're the same size. That means these will be shorter on you, but that will work. You've got great legs. I'll bet you haven't even thought about what to wear tonight, have you?"

"I do have a dress."

Carmen whipped a frothy crimson gown off its hanger and tossed it on a chair. "Let me guess—yours is plain and black."

"Well, yeah, but it's all-purpose."

"Not tonight. Tonight, you're going to wear something special. Something bright. This is a party, not a funeral."

Carmen ignored my reluctance to play dress up, and I was too depressed to fight her. I tried on at least five different dresses before she settled on a very short yellow number with sequined spaghetti straps and a little flounce at the bottom.

"That's it," she announced. "Look at yourself in the mirror and tell me that's not sexy. It goes great with your new tan."

The dress was beautiful and fit perfectly, but the face staring back at me looked tired and glum.

Next, Carmen moved to a wall full of shelves holding a collection of shoes Imelda Marcos would envy. "Slip these on," she said, handing me a pair of black sandals with three-inch heels and an ankle strap.

"Berto calls these my fuck-me shoes."

Despite my mood, I laughed. The only shoes I owned these days were the "fuck off" type. "Carmen, no way can I walk in those!"

"You'll have to learn. You want to look nice for Nick, don't you?"

"For Nick? Whatever gave you that idea?"

She crossed her arms and rolled her eyes. "I'm not blind. I see how he looks at you. Why do you play so hard to get? Nick isn't the kind of man women pass up, given the chance. And Nick doesn't give many women a chance."

"But you told me he's a ladies' man."

"No, I said women are crazy about Nick. I could count on one hand the ones he's gone out with since we've known him. Since Sandy left him."

"Sandy?"

"His fiancée. Five years ago. She suddenly decided she didn't want to live in Texas and moved back to Pennsylvania. She hated everything about Texas—the heat, the people. It was a bad match from the start. When Sandy left, he kind of gave up on women."

But what about Babe? Was it possible Carmen didn't know about them? If not, I certainly wasn't going be the one to tell her. My news of his drug dealing would be a big enough blow.

She pulled a bag from a shelf, stuffed the dress and shoes in it and thrust it at me. "You're different from most women he meets, but if you don't give him some encouragement, he's going to give up."

"Did Nick tell you that?" I felt a small glimmer of hope, but Carmen quickly extinguished it.

"No, I have a feeling about these things."

"Ha. That's where you're wrong. Nick is not interested in me. I know he's your friend, but men like him aren't the kind to get serious about. They only lead you on for the challenge, then dump you."

"*Julie.* I keep telling you, you're good with dogs, but you're terrible when it comes to judging men."

"Don't be so sure."

Poor Carmen. So naïve. I hoped she wouldn't shoot the messenger when I told her about the drugs.

* * *

That evening I hobbled up the walkway to the house in Carmen's fuck-me shoes, wearing the yellow dress with the flounce at the bottom. Strains of Mexican ballads wafted through the night air, filling me with melancholy. Despite all the craziness of Waco, I'd felt more alive here than I had in years. Life in Abilene seemed drab by comparison.

As I approached the house, I was shocked at the number of people. There must have been a hundred outside, in addition to those in the main living area. Two large doors opened out into the backyard where tables, laden with enough food to feed a small country, had been set up to accommodate the overflow. Everything I loved was on display, from Rosa's special turkey tamales to flautas, shrimp, guacamole, and countless other tempting dishes. A chocolate fountain with large straw-berries and other fruit for dipping beckoned from one of the tables.

I recognized no one. I wove through the crowd and found Carmen inside, working the room. She wore a low-cut turquoise dress with matching earrings. A tiny silver cross on a delicate chain graced her slender neck. It was all she needed. Her long dark hair hung loose, fanning out around her face in waves.

I reached her just as she turned from a couple she'd been talking with. "Carmen, you're gorgeous. But then you always are."

She smiled graciously. "Look at *you!*" She stepped back to take in my total transformation. "You're going to drive all the men wild tonight."

Only one man I wanted to drive wild, and he was off limits in more ways than one.

"Berto!" Carmen called out over the music. "Come look at Julie!" She appraised me again, her face radiant.

When Berto saw me, he drew back dramatically and bugged his eyes out. "Wow! You do clean up nice!"

"Very funny," I said, secretly pleased.

He shook his head. "I'm serious. I never realized there was a sex kitten underneath that dog nanny exterior."

I lowered my eyes, embarrassed by the attention. "I'm sure Noche and Blanco wouldn't relish the idea of being trained by a kitten," I said, then changing the conversation to a more comfortable topic. "Speaking of Noche and Blanco, where are the two guests of honor?"

Berto smiled. "We've been waiting for *you*. You ready?"

Since Carmen was dead set on the idea of showing them off, I had little choice. "Better get it over with. I'm not sure how long I can stand up in Carmen's shoes."

Berto glanced down, a look of surprise crossing his face.

Don't even think it, I wanted to say. He pressed his lips together to keep from smiling but couldn't hide the amusement in his eyes. "Forgive me for being so bold," he said, "but you need to find a good man, have children. You're too pretty to be an old maid."

"Old maid? I'm only thirty-two!"

Berto put both hands on my shoulders, the expression on his face serious. "I speak from the heart. In Mexico—"

"Enough sermon," Carmen broke in. "Julie's a modern American woman. They have different ways here."

"Like our daughter," he said with a sigh.

Carmen ignored him and pulled me upstairs, insisting we give the poodles a last-minute fluffing. When she was finally satisfied, we led them to the top of the staircase. As I looked out over the crowded room below, I spotted Nick and Babe near the bar, sharing a private laugh. My heart pounded against my ribs. The band was playing "Sin un Amor." That was me all right. Without a love.

When the band leader saw us appear with the dogs, he waved his arms and the band began a rousing version of "The Yellow Rose of Texas." Carmen and I began our slow descent to the applause of the crowd. Now I knew why Carmen had chosen the yellow dress for me. Though I felt ridiculous, she seemed to derive pleasure in showing me off.

We reached the bottom of the stairs, and Carmen led the way to a stage she had erected in the ballroom. We paraded the dogs onto the stage in *heel* position and had them *sit* and *down*. They immediately complied, and everyone applauded. Carmen glowed.

I couldn't resist sneaking looks at Nick and Babe, standing together, watching us in between giving each other long, lingering looks and smiling into each other's eyes. Carmen put the dogs through the routine we'd taught them, then curtsied. When loud applause and cheers followed, she beamed.

Time for my surprise. I held up a hand to stop the applause and took Blanco's lead from Carmen, my hands trembling. I steeled myself and concentrated on projecting my voice to the far side of the room, trying to avoid Nick's eyes, which were now keenly fixed on me.

"Thank you. It's been a pleasure working with our stars, Noche and Blanco." More applause. I held up my hand again for silence. "But none of this would have been possible without two wonderful people—Carmen and Berto Esposito. Carmen has modestly shown you only a small portion of what Noche and Blanco can do."

Carmen looked puzzled. As a hush fell over the room, I prayed the dogs wouldn't let me down.

"Noche. Blanco. *Sit.*"

They sat.

"Give me five." The dogs both raised their paws, and I slapped my palm against them. "On the other side." They raised their paws again, and I swiped the top of my hand across their uplifted paws. "Good dogs!" I said, slipping them a treat.

A small "oh" stole from Carmen's lips, and the audience laughed and applauded.

I followed with "shake hands" and "wave bye-bye," basically the same trick, but no one was the wiser.

"Kiss," I commanded. Both dogs gave me a combination nose-poke lick in the face that almost sent me sprawling backwards on my fuck-me heels. "Good dogs!" I said, patting their sides. They responded by wagging their butts in unison. That was something I had *not* taught them, but it looked impressive.

"Are you *tired*?" I asked in a sympathetic tone. Noche and Blanco immediately plopped down. Blanco rested her head on her front paws. Noche lay on his side, crossed his front legs, and lifted his head, obviously *not* tired. The crowd roared with laughter.

"Take a bow!" I told my two performers. The dogs stood, then moved into a play-bow, butts in the air, front legs on the floor. The applause was deafening. I held my arm out toward Carmen, indicating she was the one who deserved the credit. Then I smiled and told the dogs to heel, and we descended the steps and made our way through the crowd to Berto, who hugged Carmen and radiated with pride.

Carmen's eyes glowed with unshed tears. "Oh, Julie. You were wonderful. When did you teach them all that?"

I couldn't answer because Berto pulled me into a bear hug so tight I could hardly breathe. I squatted and patted the dogs, trying to calm my nerves. "Remember when I told you poodles were so intelligent they made their trainers look smart? I wasn't kidding. I taught them those tricks with about ten minutes extra practice each day. They were already in a learning curve and eager to please."

When I stood up, Carmen hugged me. "I can never thank you enough. Just having them under control is more than I ever thought possible, but this! It's too much."

"It was easy," I said modestly, though happy she was pleased.

"But you took the time to do it for *us*," she said. "That's what means so much. And now everyone will think I'm a genius, when it's really you."

"You deserve it. You came into this knowing nothing. Look how far you've come. Remember when you told me you didn't want to break their spirit."

"Oh, yes, I remember. You had to train me, too." She laughed and reached over and hugged Berto. "Thank you, Julie. You saved our marriage."

I wanted to tell her Berto had never intended to leave, but when they looked at each other, still love-struck after twenty-five years, I couldn't.

Berto plucked three glasses of champagne from the tray of a passing waiter. "Follow me." We trailed behind as he made his way onto the stage. He handed us each a glass and lifted his. "Attention, everyone! Time for a toast. To my lovely wife and our two *niños*, Noche and Blanco."

Once more, tears welled in Carmen's eyes. He'd called the dogs their children.

"And to Julie Shields, Dog Nanny 911. Our family will be eternally grateful for all she's done." He turned to me. "Julie, you're part of our family now. For always, *nuestra casa es su casa.*"

I fought back my own tears. So much had changed in a month. Now Berto was on my side. Yet tomorrow, I had to betray him.

Chapter Twenty

Though Noche and Blanco's performance was over, I still had to get through the rest of the evening. That meant letting Carmen show me off to countless relatives. In addition to the marijuana, Nick had flown Carmen's parents in from Mexico. Other relatives had driven up from San Antonio and from several small South Texas towns. Carmen insisted I meet them all. She paraded me around as if I were a prize show dog, introducing me as her "wonderful Julie."

Bobby, her son, was as handsome as she'd said. He had Berto's sturdy build and Carmen's charm. We exchanged pleasantries, and Carmen and I moved on.

After an hour of meeting and greeting, Carmen's three-inch heels had numbed my feet, and my legs were beginning to cramp. I couldn't believe women tortured themselves to this extreme just to look sexy. I looked anything *but* sexy as I hobbled from one table to the next. Finally, when I thought I'd met everyone, Carmen leaned over and whispered in my ear. "Come with me. There's someone special I want you to meet. My cousin from Mexico City."

I groaned. The woman had more cousins than she had shoes. She dragged me, limping across the room, to a man seated at a large table, surrounded solely by women, all of whom seemed enraptured by some story he was telling. When he waved his hands in a broad gesture, the women laughed. One grabbed onto his arm and stared up into his black eyes.

When he saw Carmen, he stood and straightened his tie, a wide smile spreading across his handsome face.

"Carmen!" He held out his arms in welcome, keeping his eyes on me as I tagged behind, wincing with each step. After they embraced, Carmen turned toward me. "Julie, meet my cousin, Miguel."

I took Miguel's proffered hand, but instead of the cordial handshake I was expecting, he leaned over my hand in a low bow.

Interesting. Old-World manners.

"It is a pleasure to make your acquaintance, Julie," he crooned, pronouncing my name as if it were "Hoolie." Darkly handsome, suave, and seductive, his man-of-the-world demeanor made Nick look like a down-to-earth Texas boy. The band launched into a snappy Latin beat, and danger signs flashed before my eyes when Miguel asked if I would honor him with a dance. Before I could protest, he swept me out onto the floor. Though I didn't know a samba from a black mamba, I did the best I could, stumbling a few times and blaming the shoes, knowing they were only part of the problem. I simply wasn't much of a dancer. Over Miguel's shoulder I saw Babe in Nick's arms, moving effortlessly across the floor, and a pang of jealousy shot through me like a Taser.

I felt relief when the song ended and the band switched to a slow, mournful ballad with Spanish lyrics I couldn't understand. As I was about to excuse myself from Miguel and sneak back to my apartment, Nick appeared. "This one's reserved for me," he said smoothly, whisking me away from Miguel.

"I don't remember reserving anything for you." My tone was tart, but I melted into his arms. As always with Nick, my brain said *beware*, while my body said *yes*, and for this moment, I didn't care if I stumbled or not.

Nick grinned. "I've missed you too."

"You've kept yourself entertained pretty well without me."

His expression became serious. "I understand you're leaving all this luxury tomorrow?"

I gave a wry laugh. "My work here is over. Time to get back to the real world."

"So Julie Shields leaves the Edenic splendor of Waco and returns to her job as a vet tech in dusty West Texas."

"It's not as bad as you make it sound. I love my job. I'm good at it. It's also legal. And Abilene is home."

"Ah, yes. Where the heart is. But aren't you going to miss all the excitement of Waco?"

"You mean like Lovers Leap?"

"Well, no. I was thinking more along the lines of the river, the trees, the big blue lake...and maybe a certain pilot."

"You never give up, do you?"

"Should I? What about you? Still looking for love?" He grinned. "In all the wrong places?"

"You should write a song." I gave him the evil eye, but he didn't seem to care.

"Carmen told me about the trust fund. It's none of my business, but money's not a good reason to get married."

I pulled away from him suddenly, and somehow managed to step on his foot, but I didn't apologize. "You're right. It's none of your business. I can't believe *you* are lecturing *me* about marrying for money." I glanced toward Babe, who was looking our way. "And I don't think Babe likes you flirting with other women."

"*Flirting*? What other women? Right now, all I see is you. Besides, it's none of Babe's business who I flirt with."

The song ended, and I pulled away. "See you tomorrow. I'm turning in."

"Julie!" he called, but I didn't look back as I hobbled out of the ballroom. I'd seen enough of Nick and Babe together to last a lifetime. To Nick I was just a plane he'd yet to fly.

As soon as I got to the patio, I yanked off Carmen's fuck-me shoes and limped down the path to my apartment as quickly as my crippled feet would allow.

Tomorrow, I had to tell Carmen about the drugs. No doubt Nick would have moved them by then, but I didn't care. She could do as she wished with the information, but she would know the truth.

* * *

The next morning I got up early, packed my bags, and walked down to the lake. I stood on the shore for a long time, staring out at the blue sky and the blue lake, but they only reminded me of how I'd drowned...in Nick's blue eyes. I reached down and picked up a rock and threw it as hard and far as I could, but it went only a few feet out before dropping into the water with a plunk.

Back inside, I sat at the table, watching the hands on the clock, willing them to move faster. Never an early riser, Carmen would still be sleeping off last night's gala, and I wasn't due to leave until mid-afternoon. The wait made me antsy. I needed the comforts of my own home, my own possessions around me, my real job. Waco had become too painful, and dragging out my departure wasn't helping. I turned on the TV and flipped through channels. I finally settled on watching *French Kiss* for the umpteenth time. Seeing Meg Ryan moon over Timothy Hutton—though he was a jerk and Kevin Kline was a lot sexier—made me feel better. So what if Kline's Luc was a petty thief? He loved Meg. Why couldn't she see they were meant for each other? I cried a little at the happy-ever-after ending, wondering why real life couldn't imitate art.

As soon as the clock rolled around to one, I dialed the number to the big house and asked Carmen if I could talk with her privately before I left. A short time later, we met in the library. Rosa brought in some strong coffee for Carmen, and I had a cup of tea. I dreaded having to break the news to her about Nick and Berto, but I had no choice. She needed to know.

She took a sip of her coffee, then waved her hand over the cup to cool it. "What happened to you last night? One minute you were dancing with Nick and next thing I know, you're gone. Then *Nick* disappeared." She smiled slyly. "It's about time the two of you admitted your feelings for each other."

"You've got it all wrong. I left, but not with Nick. He must have been with—"

I broke off before saying "Babe." One thing I would *not* tell Carmen was that her daughter was probably sleeping with Nick.

Carmen looked confused. "But I thought—"

I chewed on the end of my thumb and shook my head. "I went back to my apartment, alone. Sorry to disappoint you."

Carmen yawned. "Hmm. Wonder what happened to Nick? Barbi said he disappeared shortly after you did."

Nick had left the party alone? Where had he gone? I'd been unable to fall asleep until the band quit playing around three a.m., and at that point, he still hadn't come back to the guesthouse. Maybe he'd had to make a delivery.

I dunked my tea bag up and down in the cup. "It wasn't very nice of him to treat her like that."

"Oh, she didn't care. She danced with every man in the room before the night was out. She thought the same thing I did, that you two had gone off together for a twist."

"A twist? Is that Spanish for—"

Then I realized what she meant. "A tryst? No, afraid not." Now I was more confused than ever. "How could Babe not care? You know she's in love with him." There. It was out.

"In love?" Carmen closed her eyes and sighed. "Where did you get that idea? Yes, she *loves* Nick. He's always been like a big brother to her."

"Are you sure? Because, he said...I—"

I thought back to what Nick *had* said: that Babe was a beautiful person, inside and out, that any man would be glad to have her, and as long as he was around no one would ever hurt her again. He'd also said he *loved* her.

Carmen reached over and placed a hand over mine, her eyes soft with sympathy. "Oh, Julie. Is that why you've kept your distance from Nick?" She squeezed my hand.

"There are other reasons. That's what I wanted to talk to you about."

I took a deep breath, reached into my purse, and pulled out the stems and leaves I'd found on the floor of Nick's apartment. "He's bringing drugs. Marijuana. From Mexico." I left out the part about Berto's involvement. When Carmen confronted Nick, he could decide whether to tell her.

Carmen's eyes widened. "Oh, Julie. No."

* * *

Carmen and I stood in the kitchen next to Rosa looking at a dozen or so plastic zippered bags filled with stems, leaves, and seeds. Several large garbage bags sat in the corner.

"Tell her, Rosa," Carmen said.

Rosa proudly pointed to the leaves. "Oregano. And seeds for growing peppers. Other herbs and spices. A surprise from Mr. Nick when he come back from Mexico this time. You can buy in U.S. but not as good."

Carmen wagged her finger at me. "I keep telling you. As a dog nanny, you're a ten. About men, zero."

I groaned loudly. "You're right. Not a great track record. I'm so embarrassed."

Carmen smiled kindly and gave me a brief hug. "You're like Barbi. After what happened with...you-know-who. I've known Nick a long time. He's not perfect, but he's honest."

She *had* tried to tell me, but as usual, I hadn't listened.

"Come." She led me into the dining room and pointed to a chair. "Sit."

I followed, and I sat. I'd trained her well.

She took a chair across from me, tucked her feet under her, and leaned forward. "Getting hurt isn't something that happens only to women."

I lowered my head.

Carmen tapped her fingernails on the table. "Can't you see how Nick acts around you? He's different. He brightens up when you walk into the room. Even Berto has noticed. Didn't you wonder why Nick showed up at the Cotton Patch and the Prime Rib?"

I looked up. "I wasn't sure. The first time could have been coincidence. The second time..." I was too embarrassed to tell her all the crazy thoughts that had run through my mind about drugs, illegal goings-on, keeping an eye on me to make sure I wasn't acting as a snitch. "How did he know I was at the Prime Rib?"

She shrugged but smiled knowingly.

"You?"

"Sometimes little Cupid, he needs help. Playing hard-to-get can attract a man, but he needs *some* encouragement."

"But I wasn't playing. I'd declared myself a born-again virgin and was keeping myself pure for my future husband." No need to tell her how my resolve had crumbled that night with Nick in Abilene.

Carmen laughed. "If Nick isn't husband material, then no man is. Unlike some of the women he's gone out with, you're not after his money. He also admires you for working and the fact you're trying to help dogs."

"He told you that?"

"We talk."

"What do you mean, women after Nick's money? What money?"

Carmen sipped her coffee. "Nick's adoptive parents lost all their money on gambling and bad investments. Nick didn't even get to go to college. But he worked odd jobs while he got his pilot's license and eventually bought his own business—all legal. He owns several air charter companies."

"You mean he doesn't work for you?"

Carmen laughed. "Not hardly. He'd be insulted if we offered to pay. He flies for us because we're friends and because he loves to fly. Those trips to Mexico you thought were about drugs....Nick builds houses there. At his own expense. This past month, he's been building a clinic for people who can't afford medical care."

"A clinic?"

Carmen smiled, her face animated. "Shortly before he found out he was adopted, his birth mother died because she and Nick's real father were too poor to see a doctor. He's always regretted not knowing her. So, helping people like his parents became a cause for him. He does a lot of the physical work himself. Says he likes to feel he's created something. He's too modest to talk about it. Men like Nick are rare. I was really hoping you two would...well, that's water under the dam."

I didn't correct her word choice. All I could think about was how I'd really screwed the pooch. Who could blame Nick if he never wanted to see me again? Somehow, I'd have to redeem myself on the trip back to Abilene.

* * *

I said my goodbyes to Carmen and trudged back to my apartment to gather my things. An hour later, bag on one side, Philip's crate on the other, I waited in the circular driveway. But when Carmen's Lexus wheeled up, Nick wasn't driving. Ramón was. Nick must have gone to the airport early to get the plane ready.

Ramón loaded my suitcase into the trunk and placed Philip's crate in the backseat. I sank into the leather seat, rehearsing what I would say to Nick.

When we pulled up beside the hangar, Ramón helped me with my bag. The Seneca V was out, but instead of Nick, a gray-haired man old enough to be my grandfather stood beside it. "Morning." He extended his hand. "George."

I automatically took his hand but couldn't speak. Where was Nick?

George's handshake had the propulsion of a pump jack. "So we're headed to Abilene. You live there or just visiting?"

"Live there," I choked out.

George was a talker, so he didn't notice my silence. "You're probably thinking I'm too old to be flying. No need to worry. Just got my annual flight physical, and the doc says my ticker is good for another two thousand hours."

He laughed, and I managed a weak smile. A month ago, I would have been thinking "heart attack waiting to happen" and wondering if I could land the plane myself in that event, but the way I was feeling now, I wasn't sure I cared.

I looked over at Ramón. "What happened to Nick?" I asked, fighting to hold back tears.

"Mr. Nick, he fly other plane out late last night. Say he going back to Mexico."

"Did he leave a number?"

Ramón shook his head. "He say not want to be bothered."

So that's why Nick hadn't come back to his apartment. He must have left town shortly after I left the party. How could I blame him after the way I'd acted? Now I'd lost him forever.

* * *

I called my mother and sister to let them know I was back in Abilene, leaving messages when neither of them picked up, relieved I didn't have to talk with anyone. Then I unpacked, started a load of laundry, and checked my computer, but when it began to download hundreds of junk emails, forwarded jokes, pictures, and video clips sent me during the past month, I simply lost interest. My former life seemed irrelevant now.

I wandered through the house, looking at the art work and furnishings as if they belonged to someone else. The sense of comfort I usually felt at home was gone. I was going to sell it all anyway for the new animal adoption center.

Walking out onto the deck, I thought about the night Nick and I stood there. It seemed months ago instead of weeks.

Though the automatic sprinkler system had watered the lawn in my absence, there were dry patches where the spray hadn't reached and the trees looked sparse by Waco standards. Even the fish pond I loved didn't buoy my spirits.

I walked back inside, Philip at my heels, and looked down at him. "Nap?" By now he was using his leg as if he'd never been hurt. He bounded up the stairs and leaped onto the bed. When I lay down, he snuggled against me, and I hugged his warm little body, burying my face in his cottony fur. I covered us with a blanket, and when I awoke it was dark.

I let Philip out, fed him, forced down some canned chicken soup, and crawled back into bed. Tomorrow I'd return to work where I'd be too busy to think about Nick.

I kept my new cell phone turned on and in bed with me. Nick had the number. But it didn't ring.

* * *

Though it didn't rank up there with building clinics in Mexico, I threw myself into my volunteer work with

Lookin' for Love. While I was gone, an anonymous donor had made a generous contribution, so now we didn't need my trust fund. As for my biological clock running out of juice, I was too numb to care.

Marlon called several times, but in fairness to him, I told him there was someone else. Though I didn't forget Nick, the pain eventually subsided to a dull ache.

Almost three months passed.

Late one Friday after work, as I parked my car in the garage and killed the engine, I heard my kitchen phone ringing. I raced inside, and when I saw the name "Esposito, Alberto" on my caller ID, my hands began to tremble, hoping it was Nick calling from the big house.

But it wasn't Nick. It was Carmen. I tried not to let the disappointment show in my voice. She sounded strained, her breathing labored. "Julie, I need your help!"

"What is it? Are you okay?" My first thought was that Butch had come back, but last I heard he was safely locked away.

Carmen sounded close to tears. "It's Blanco and Noche. I don't know how this could have happened!"

"What happened? Have they been hurt?"

"No, no, no. Not like that. They've gone *poodle*."

Oh, no. Another one of Carmen's malapropisms. "What do you mean, 'gone *poodle*'? Are they lost? Have they run away?"

"No, I mean they've gone *poodle*! Like those mail people who go crazy."

"That's *postal*."

"I know that, but I'm saying they've gone *poodle*!" Carmen was yelling so loud I had to hold the phone away from my ear. "Blanco and Noche have forgotten everything we taught them. They've...what's the word...reverb...revert...? They've gone back to their old ways—jumping on the furniture, refusing to obey. I really need you here. Please."

Relieved no one had been maimed or killed, I let out the breath I'd been holding. "How did this happen? Once dogs are trained, they seldom forget what they've been taught so quickly, unless you start reinforcing their bad behavior."

"Just say you'll come. I can have a plane waiting for you first thing in the morning. It's Saturday. You're off, aren't you?"

"Yes, but—"

"Please say you'll come. I wouldn't ask if I didn't really need help."

"I'll have to bring Philip. My sister's out of town, and I don't want to leave him in a kennel."

Carmen didn't hesitate. "Of course."

As soon as I hung up, I began having second thoughts. Memories of Nick flooded my mind, and the dull ache once more became a stabbing pain.

* * *

At ten the next morning, I pulled into the parking lot at Abilene Regional and unloaded my small suitcase and Philip's crate. As I neared the hangar, I looked around for the old guy who'd flown me home.

Then I saw him. My heart thumped like a tennis shoe in a clothes dryer. "*Nick*," was all I could muster.

"Hello, Julie," he said, sounding detached.

We boarded the plane in silence. Even the takeoff didn't faze me.

He glanced at me and said, "I see you've gotten over your fear of flying in small planes."

I remembered that first flight when he eyed me with appreciation. Today, I couldn't read his thoughts. My chest tightened, and somehow, I managed to nod.

"Is Carmen okay?" I asked, my voice cracking. I faked a cough. "Sorry. Allergies," I lied. "She sounded frantic on the phone."

Nick's face remained impassive. "Yeah, I know. She called me last night saying the dogs had gone wild and she needed you there right away."

I wiped my damp palms on the legs of my jeans. "It was nice of you to agree to fly me."

Nick stared ahead, saying nothing until the silence became uncomfortable. I chewed on a fingernail already bitten to the quick. "I guess the other pilot wasn't available," I finally said, shooting a glance at him.

He didn't look at me. "That's what Carmen said."

So he'd come only because he was their friend and they needed him. Though the space between us was less than a foot, it felt like miles. I took a deep breath to keep my voice from quavering. "So what have you been doing the last few months? Carmen told me about your work in Mexico. I'm impressed."

"Thanks. I do it for the people, not the accolades."

"I understand."

"Same reason you love your work. Not so much a job as a calling. In fact, you were the inspiration for my current project."

Surprised, I turned to look at him, taking in the strong line of his jaw, the dark hair that seemed to ask me to reach over and run my hands through it, the lips I wanted to kiss. "Me?"

"Yep, you. Julie Shields. I also decided it was time to get over my fear of dogs. Even went to one of those therapy classes. You know, like the ones for people afraid of flying."

I couldn't help it. *My* name, emanating from *his* lips, made my blood sizzle like fajitas on a hot grill. I closed my eyes and imagined him saying it again and again.

When I opened my eyes, he was staring at me. "Are you listening?"

"Yes, every word. Go ahead."

"I was talking about my new project. An animal clinic. In Cognito, Mexico. We've almost finished the construction."

"You're kidding."

"Cross my heart." He glanced at me and smiled, his eyes crinkling at the corners. "Julie, we're alike in more ways than you realize. You aren't afraid of hard work, you like helping others, and you can be a big pain in the butt."

I grinned slightly, then swallowed hard, swallowing my pride at the same time. "I need to explain something."

"What's to explain?"

"The reason I acted...like I did."

"You made that clear. I was just slow to believe it."

"No, you don't understand. What I felt for you...that was special, but I was afraid. Gun-shy. The men I've been attracted to in the past...well, let's just say I tried to fix them when they weren't fixable. So I thought if I found someone I *wasn't* attracted to..." I couldn't bring myself to say Butch's name or Joe's or Marlon's. "I was afraid of my feelings for you, so I pushed you away. And I let my imagination run away with me. Babe, the drugs..."

"Drugs?"

Oops. Guess Carmen hadn't told him that part. "I thought you were transporting drugs from Mexico to sell in the U.S."

He winced. "You're serious?"

"Afraid so."

He surprised me by chuckling softly, causing my heart to pump faster. "You watch way too many movies."

"So I've been told. But think about it. The bags you hid in your closet."

"You mean the spices and the peppers? I didn't hide them."

"You locked the door."

"I was keeping Noche, remember. I didn't want him getting into them and getting sick. As smart as he was, I wouldn't have been surprised if he'd learned how to open a door."

When he smiled the Nick-smile I remembered, I had to squeeze my hands between my legs to keep from reaching over and touching him.

"When I got in that night," he continued, "it was too late to take the bags to Carmen and Rosa, and I wanted to surprise them."

"Carmen told me." I reached back and rubbed my stiff neck. "And Babe. When you said you loved her, I automatically thought...Carmen also explained that."

He glanced in my direction, and for a moment our eyes locked. "You accused me several times of not leveling with you, Julie, but you lied to me more than once. Did that ever cross your mind?"

"You're right. You weren't the problem. It was me. I have trust issues."

"But I never gave you reason to doubt me."

"Well, you did. Sort of. You wouldn't tell me about Babe and Butch. And the business in New Orleans was weird. Okay, so I built a lot of it up in my mind. I know it's too late, but I'm sorry. I'm really, really, really sorry."

It took a supreme effort, but I managed to hold back the tears. One thing I did know about men—they hate to see a woman cry.

"Apology accepted. I'm sorry, too, Julie. Seems we had a failure to communicate. But what's done is done. Now let's see what we can do for Carmen."

Chapter Twenty-One

Nick's hand accidentally grazed my back as he loaded Philip's crate into Berto's BMW, reminding me of the day we met, when he'd leaned over and pointed out Casa del Lago at the top of the hill. At the time I'd felt as if I were melting, and a similar sensation swept over me now, but it was tinged with regret. I tried to block out thoughts of what might have been, the *us* that might have been.

In no time we were headed up the winding drive to Casa del Lago, just as we had that afternoon months ago. Carmen was waiting for us in the circular drive, wringing her hands, while a solemn-faced Berto stood behind her. Whatever Noche and Blanco had done was serious.

"Bring Philip with you and leave the car here," Carmen said. "Someone can park it later. Come inside, quickly."

Nick and I trailed into the foyer behind her and Berto. I stole a glance at Nick. He caught my eye and shrugged.

Carmen wasted no time on greetings. She pointed to the floor. "Set Philip's crate here by the sofa. Rosa will bring him some fresh water. He'll be safer here for now."

Safer? The living area looked much the same as before. No signs of destruction I could discern.

Carmen pointed to the staircase. "They're upstairs in the bedroom. I had to fasten them in...for control."

Nick and I exchanged a worried look. At the door to their bedroom, Carmen held up her hand in the *stay* command I'd taught her. I almost smiled, but one look at the serious expression on her face stopped me.

She slowly turned the doorknob. "Quiet. So you don't stir them up."

Did she think they might attack us?

She let herself in, then left the door ajar just enough for the rest of us to squeeze through—first Berto, then Nick and me. We crept in like visitors at a funeral home viewing.

Carmen whispered. "I've been playing 'Taco Bell's Canon' to calm them down."

Nick leaned close, his breath warm on my ear. "I think she means Pachelbel's *Canon*."

I half expected Noche and Blanco to pounce on us like hellhounds, but the room was eerily quiet except for a whimper emanating from the far side of the bed. "One of them sounds hurt. Have they been fighting?"

Carmen gave me a threatening look. "Shhh. You'll upset them."

The drapes were drawn, and the large room was dark except for a tiny lamp on a corner table. No bounding dogs, no barking.

"What—?" I blurted before Carmen cut me off.

"*Quiet*," Carmen whispered again. "They're in the corner."

Nick and I tiptoed behind her, while Berto brought up the rear.

My sudden intake of breath startled Nick, who reared back and slapped a hand to his chest.

Carmen pointed. "Look."

Nick and I leaned over and stared. In the corner of the room on a blanket, Blanco lay on her side, a proud Noche standing guard beside her. Nuzzling her belly were four tiny black and white pups. *Parti-poodles.*

At first, all I could do was gape. When I finally pulled myself together long enough to look at Carmen, her face lit up in a wide smile. "*See.* I told you they'd gone poodle."

* * *

290

Later, as the four of us stood in the library, Berto popped the cork on a bottle of champagne and poured us each a glass, then held his high. "To poodles."

Nick and Carmen and I raised ours. "To poodles," we echoed. Even Nick looked happy.

"Now, everyone sit," Carmen commanded.

"Do we get a treat?" Nick asked, laughing.

"You're drinking your treat," Berto said, grinning ear to ear.

Carmen remained standing and clapped her hands to summon our full attention. "They're five weeks old today. Two boys and two girls. We've named them *Nick, Julie, Carmen,* and *Berto.*"

Berto interrupted. "Seems the little girls are already pushing the boys around. "What do you call that, Julie, *alpha* something?"

Nick laughed.

"Very funny," I said to Berto. "How long have you known?"

Carmen set her glass down, her eyes brightening. "Shortly after you left, Blanco started gaining weight. At first I thought she was depressed because everyone was gone. Even Berto was gone." She gave him one of her pouty looks, and he reached over and hugged her.

"Then I thought Blanco needed more exercise," she said, "so I walked her more often. She got even fatter. So Berto fenced in a section out back where she and Noche could exercise. But she got fatter and fatter. I got scared, thinking she must have a tumor. Finally, I took her to Dr. Julie, and he surprised us with the news."

I took a sip of champagne. "I hate to say it, but I told you this would happen if you didn't get them spayed and neutered."

Carmen gave me a smug look. "If I'd done that, we wouldn't have these wonderful puppies. I know you don't approve, but Berto insists we keep them in the bedroom with us."

Next to her on the sofa, Berto beamed like a proud father. No doubt about it—he was puppy whipped.

"We're lucky she had a small litter," Carmen said. "The vet said the average is six to twelve. But don't worry. We've already made an appointment for surgery. This litter will be the last. And no Neuticles. Noche has proven his machismo."

Everyone laughed, and Berto poured another round. "Tell them your other news," he said.

She stood up, flipped her hair back, and crossed her arms, as if defying anyone to challenge her. "Julie, do you remember when I told you I had a big surprise for Berto the night of the dogs' graduation party?"

"Your son came home. I remember."

Carmen laughed. "That was only part of the surprise. I didn't want to tell anyone but Berto until it was a— what you call it?—done deal. Now it is. I'm so excited."

She held her arms overhead, tapping her feet and snapping her fingers as if playing castanets. "I've been taking classes on how to train dogs. As soon as I'm certified, I'm opening a school. I'm calling it *Perro Bueno*, that means Good Dog in English."

Nick and I burst out laughing.

"You don't like it?" Carmen moaned.

"No, no, I love it!" I told her. "I'm just amazed at all that's happened."

Carmen eased herself onto the sofa next to Berto, set her glass on the table, and locked her arm through his. "It's all because of you, Julie. You told me I needed to do something for myself. Remember how you said lots of dogs get abandoned or can't get adopted because they aren't trained? I've already started working with dogs from the Humane Society to make them more adoptable."

She looked lovingly into Berto's dark eyes and gave his arm a squeeze. "I know it won't be as easy as with Noche and Blanco, but this is something I really want to do that *needs* to be done. Did you know they have to kill over ten *thousand* animals a year? Just here in Waco? And the excuses people give for dumping their dogs, like: *Didn't match the new furniture.*"

"Tell her the rest," Berto urged.

Carmen looked down at her lap, as if unsure how to proceed. "I-I was wondering if you'd be willing to help, Julie."

I was already experiencing sensory overload—still reeling from seeing Nick again, learning about the puppies, listening to the new Carmen, not to mention the buzz from the champagne. "What do you mean by help?"

I'd underestimated Carmen's ability to deliver a triple whammy. "I mean, move to Waco and be my partner. Help with the training. We really need someone with medical skills. This is just a start. The Humane Society has already given us the blue light!"

Berto leaned toward Carmen, "That's the green light, honey. Blue light is like a special at K-Mart."

She tossed her head. "Whatever. They gave me the okay thumbs. They said it was a great idea."

"You want me to *move* to Waco?" I was having a tough time digesting it all.

"Take some time to think about it, but I hope you'll say yes. You could stay in the apartment until you find a place of your own. Or you could stay there permanently if you want."

When Nick rose to his feet, Carmen's offer faded into the stratosphere. No way could I live in Waco where I would see him on a regular basis. Like the song said, I didn't have time for the pain.

Nick cleared his throat. "Carmen, Berto, it *is* a wonderful idea, and I have no doubts Julie would be perfect to help you with it."

I sat up straighter and glared at him. Was he trying to run my life now? This was none of his business.

He propped a foot on the hearth and leaned against the mantel. "There's a slight problem."

"Nick's right," I said. "I've got my job in Abilene, my family—"

Nick cut me off. "As usual, Julie has a problem with interpretation."

When I frowned at him, he smiled and said, "I was referring to a trip I'm taking to Paris."

"Big deal," I said. "What does your trip to some po-dunk place in North Texas have to do with *my* decision?"

His grin grew wider. "As I said, you misunderstand. Not Paris, Texas—Paris, *France*. On a *big* plane. My honeymoon."

"Honeymoon?" Carmen and Berto cried in unison. I couldn't speak. My heart sank. Nick was getting married. Tears stung my eyes.

All of us were staring at Nick. "But who?" Carmen asked.

Nick sank to one knee. "Julie. If she'll have me."

"I told you, Berto!" Carmen squealed, shaking his arm. "I told you if we could find an excuse to get them together again, they'd see they were meant for each other."

I felt like an actress in a movie. This couldn't be hap-pening to me. "You mean you deliberately told us the dogs had 'gone poodle' to get us here together?"

Carmen flashed a big smile. "It worked, didn't it? Re-member what you told me once? You said if there are angels on earth, they're in the form of dogs. Well, our four little angels have worked a miracle."

I turned to Nick. "About Paris."

"I know. Now that your animal adoption center is in the black, you don't need to get married for the trust fund money."

That's when it hit me. The anonymous donor who'd made my dream a reality. *Nick.*

Berto and Carmen moaned as they watched their matchmaking bubble burst. "Oh, nooo," Carmen cried. Their droopy faces reminded me of bloodhounds.

I raised my hand for silence. "My turn. Nick, I appreciate your offer." I paused, my face serious. "But I've been to Paris. And I'll always have Paris."

I smiled slowly, dragging it out for effect. "But I've never been in Cognito."

When I saw Nick's eyes twinkle, I continued. "You're going to need someone to help get your clinic stocked with the necessary equipment and medicine and find and train a staff—"

Carmen jumped up and grabbed both my arms and shook me. "Julie! Hurry up and tell him *yes*, would you, before you two have another interpretation problem? Then you can fight all you want about where you're going."

All eyes turned toward me. I knelt down beside Nick. I would never be submissive enough to roll over and pee on myself, but I was willing to meet him on his level. I wagged my tail and licked his cheek.

He grinned, reached over, and hugged me so tight I yelped. "I believe that means *yes* in dog language," he said.

Upstairs, one of the dogs let out a happy bark. I took it as a positive sign.

Later that night in the bed of my old apartment at Cielo por el Lago, with the light from the moon glancing off the tranquil water of the lake, Nick and I finished what we'd started that night months ago back in Abilene.

Only this time, Philip snoozed peacefully in his crate near the foot of the bed.

Turn the page to read an excerpt from Ann Whitaker's next novel, *Deadline to Desire*.

Deadline to Desire~Excerpt

by

Ann Whitaker

Chapter One

I'd had enough. I marched over to the table, tapped my order pad, and glanced at what passed for a menu. "You gentlemen ready to place your food order?" If you could call what we served food. The cuisine at Robbie's Burger's, Beer, and Bait was limited to hamburgers and sandwiches slapped together behind a small counter. Since in real life I was nightside editor at the *Desire Daily Democrat*, I tried to act professional.

At three o'clock the party of eight men had pushed two tables together and started drinking. Now, four hours later, they still hadn't ordered anything to eat. This time they would either eat or I was cutting them off. No way was I risking jail for overserving someone. Or in this case, eight someones who didn't have sense enough to drink at home.

One guy, eyes glazed, tried to leer at me. He might not be drinking doubles, but I suspected he was seeing them. "Sorry, sweetheart, we've got all the dessert we need right here in these bottles." From the gales of laughter, you'd have thought this guy was David Friggin' Letterman.

Summoning my best inner-bitch voice, I let them have it. "*No. More. Beer.*"

My proclamation prompted a chorus of groans. "No more beer? You out of beer?"

I eye-Tasered them, then turned and stalked off, glancing up at the neon Budweiser clock on the wall. Seven p.m. Robbie, my significant other, should have finished at the TV station by now. Where was he? I'd been working without a break since noon so he could cover a story.

Though he worked full time as a reporter and week-end news anchor, Robbie's second love was his beer and bait shop, which he'd named after his first love—himself. The Triple B, as I called it, was a cramped, wooden structure, desperately in need of paint, almost a mile from Lake Desire.

Since I was off Sundays and Mondays, Robbie often counted on me for backup when his regular waitress didn't show. Which was way too often.

Today was one of those days.

Just as I was about to tear off my apron and declare the place closed, Robbie sauntered in. I eyed him suspiciously. Why wasn't he wearing a dress shirt and tie? Where was his sports jacket? Instead, he wore khaki shorts and a navy T-shirt. He also sported a fresh sun-burn on his legs and arms. SPF 30 had protected his precious face. His station manager took a dim view of white circles around the eyes, and Robbie Hanson II valued his flawless skin.

He graced me with his famous wicked grin, the same one he used on TV, the one that provided simultaneous orgasms for female fans, young and old, with a small helping of the nightly news. That grin served as a con-stant reminder he could have any woman he wanted, but he'd picked me, Mahogany Marsh. The same Mahogany Marsh known throughout high school as "Mog the Hog," who thought she'd never find a man. I sighed. I might have shed the pounds, but not my inner fat girl.

"Hey, Mog. How's business, sweetie?"

"The name's Mahogany, and don't 'sweetie' me. Why aren't you dressed for work?"

He swaggered around to my side of the counter and draped an arm across my shoulder, trying to cozy up, but I stiffened like a corpse in rigor mortis.

"I changed at the station. What would my customers think if I came in here wearing a suit and tie?"

I slitted my eyes like a bad-natured cat and almost hissed. After two years, I knew when he was lying. "Did you even *go* to work today?"

"Hon, would I lie to you? Didn't you see me on the six o'clock? Nobody could have covered that murder-for-hire story but me." He bumped his hip against mine, made a rutting sound, and tried to pull me close. Of the many sins of which Robbie was guilty, a lack of self-confidence wasn't on the list.

I jerked away from him, and when I spoke, my voice registered an octave higher than normal and sounded shrill. "I'd say the *Desire Daily Democrat* did a pretty damn good job on that story in this morning's edition. I edited it myself. We even got an interview with the killer's sister, who said she overheard him bragging about it. You *know* you get most of your best stuff from the newspaper. And how could I see you on TV when I've been stuck here since noon? Look around. Do you see any big screen TV? Do you see any TV at all?"

I pointed to the group of men who were laughing loudly, slapping their thighs, and pounding the table. "You know Mama and Granny count on me to take them to Wal-Mart every Sunday. Not that you care. Instead, I've been dealing with *those* idiots over there since three o'clock!"

Sweeping my arm in a wide arc, I almost caught him on the jaw, but he ducked. "Well, baby, I'm here now. Why don't you take a break?"

"A *break*! You said you'd take over when you got back."

Robbie leaned close to the mirror behind the counter and preened, smoothing his highlighted hair and checking his porcelain-veneered teeth to make sure they were still as white as Matthew McConaughey's. "Just for tonight, hon. I've got some things I need to take care of."

"Oh, that's right. It is Sunday. Church?"

Robbie laughed again. "Funny girl." He slid his fingers under the bib of my apron, but I slapped at his hand and squirmed away.

"Don't try to charm me. I am *not* happy about spending my entire day off working."

Before I could stop him, he put his arms around me and drew me close, reaching down and gently squeezing my butt. An involuntary throb between my legs momentarily weakened me. Sex with Robbie was good. It was really, really good. And at thirty-four, good sex was something I could not afford to give up easily. Let's face it. Most guys don't know a clitoris from a thesaurus.

"I'll make it up to you later. I promise." He pulled away and shot a look at my purse, crammed into a corner under the counter. "Say, you got a twenty I can borrow? I need to get some gas, and I'm running a little short. I told the kids I'd take them out for pizza tonight."

Robbie usually pushed all my right buttons, but today he'd unthinkingly hit the one saying "STOP." The kids he referred to were three offspring from his last marriage, ranging from age four to fourteen. After working all afternoon, now I was supposed to close the place down while he took his kids for pizza? I didn't think so.

I was about to say as much when the door flew open, and Sam, one of Robbie's fishing buddies, strode in. "Man, what a perfect day for fishing! Whoo-eee! You were hot today! That last sucker you caught must have weighed eight pounds. I'm going to have to get me some of that new swimbait you were using. How many pounds did you end up reeling in?"

Sam glanced at me and waved. "Hey, Mahogany. How're you doing? You should have seen your boyfriend today. He casts a mean rod." He winked at Robbie. "Don't tell my wife about those Hooters' girls at the Bass Expo."

Robbie gave me a sideways glance.

I looked away and resisted the temptation to make a snide comment about his "rod." Instead, I contorted my face in a fake smile for Sam. "Yes, I *should* have seen my boyfriend today. He *is* amazing. Fishing and covering stories and anchoring the six o'clock news all in one afternoon."

Sam gritted his teeth and rolled his eyes toward Robbie, then back at me. "Uh, sorry. I better get home. Can't keep the little woman waiting." He scuttled out with a weak wave, his voice fading as he shut the door. "See y'all later."

Robbie reached over and tried to hug me again. "I can explain, baby. Just give me a chance."

I jerked away. "I'm sure you can. You always have an explanation. But this time you can explain it to someone who cares. I'm through."

He squatted and reached into the ice chest, pulling out a Lone Star longneck. "Now, baby, you don't mean that." He stood, twisted off the cap, and dropped it on the counter.

"My mother was right. You're a major shit-heel." I automatically picked up the bottle cap and tossed it in the trash.

Robbie took a long pull on the beer and wiped his mouth with the back of his hand. "Aw, she was kidding."

"She wasn't and I'm not."

"We're good together. You know that." He set down the bottle, leaned closer, and ran kisses up the side of my neck, which usually made me gasp for breath like a hooked fish, but not tonight.

I pushed away from him and crossed my arms over my chest. We *were* good together. In bed. And he could be really sweet at times. He always remembered me on special occasions with flowers or a box of candy, which I never ate but everyone at work appreciated. As a result, I'd let a lot of his selfish, egocentric shit-heel behavior slide off my back because he was the only man who'd ever made me feel desirable. Problem was, I'd mistaken my feelings for love. The sad truth of it hit me like an unexpected cold front. There was no light at the end of the Robbie Hanson II Tunnel of Love.

He took my chin in his hand and put his face close to mine. "Hon, I understand you're upset with me. But today was the big bass tournament, and I couldn't miss it."

I jerked my head away. "Today was *my* day off. I worked at the newspaper until eleven friggin' thirty last night editing copy. When do *I* get to fish?"

He held his hand up as if taking a solemn vow. "I'll take you tomorrow."

"Congratulations," I said. "You are now a full-fledged member of the liar's club."

"I *mean* it. I'll take you tomorrow."

I glared at him. "Forget it. I was speaking metaphorically. I hate fishing. I also hate beer and I hate bait. As far as I'm concerned, you can *sleep* with the fish from now on. I'm outta here." I whipped off the tacky brown apron with "Robbie's Burgers, Beer, and Bait" scrawled on the front in bold red letters and threw it on the counter. Then I stomped over to the front door and flung it open.

"You'll be back after your break, won't you?" Robbie called.

I whirled around and yelled at him so loud even the half-drunk yahoos' heads swiveled. "After my break? Think you can wait till Lake Desire freezes over? Maybe you can get your ex to help out in the meantime. But since you're behind on your child support, I wouldn't count on it."

Grabbing my purse, I stormed out to the parking lot, jumped in my pickup, and slammed the door. I turned the key and revved the engine. My juvenile behavior probably burned up a gallon of gas, but it made me feel powerful. Never mind cutting bait. Time to cut the *fisherman* loose.

Robbie didn't even try to stop me.

I pulled around behind the Triple B and backed up close as I could get to the door of the ratty mobile home where we'd lived in sin for almost two years. After opening the tailgate, I stormed inside and packed a suitcase with enough clothes and toiletries for the next few days. Then I filled several heavy-duty garbage bags with the rest of my belongings and a few household items and lugged them outside. I dumped the bags and my remaining clothes, still on their hangers, in the bed of the pickup. In my mind, I'd already stamped "one way" on my ticket out of this relationship.

Yanking a tarp from the toolbox, I draped it over the bed of the pickup, fastening it down tight as I could with some bungee cords. I didn't have to call Carl, my four-year-old mastiff. He'd already lumbered down the steps and waited outside, watching me. He knew something was up because he jumped into the cab before I could say "bye-bye in the truck."

Quivering with excitement, he settled on the passenger seat, and I buckled him into his doggy seatbelt. I hoisted my suitcase onto the floorboard and carefully placed my laptop behind the seats, making sure it wouldn't get jostled around. Laptops could be temperamental, and this one held valuable documents.

For several years now, I'd dreamed of becoming a Texas J.K. Rowling. Okay, so that was stretching it, even for a born and bred Texan like me. I didn't have seven installments of Harry Potter-like stories filling my brain, but I did have an idea for a romance novel. I knew how it would start, and I knew how it would end, because I'd already written the first and last sentence. I'd read somewhere there were only two plots. I would use them both.

My first line read: "A stranger came to town." My last: "A woman went on a journey." Not *War and Peace,* but it was a start.

With Robbie out of my life for good, I'd have more time to research and write. I'd just read an article about the popularity of romance novels and how many were sold each year. At present, cowboy heroes were hot commodities. I knew nothing about ranch life, but I did live in Texas. I figured that alone should give me a head start. If I didn't get that promotion soon, a writing career might be my only ticket to financial security. If I could crank out romances and snag the right publisher, I could make decent money.

As I pulled onto the road leading to town, I dug into the dark pit of my purse for my cell phone. Finding it, I glanced down long enough to speed-dial Abelena, my best friend since elementary school, now a photographer and fellow peon at the *Desire Daily*. As soon as she picked up, without preamble, I said, "I'm doing it." She needed no explanation. She'd been telling me I was wasting my time from the moment she met Robbie. Her voice was warm and reassuring. "Stay with me tonight. You don't want to be with your mama and granny at a time like this."

She was right. I was in no mood to hear "I told you so" from those two, no matter how much I loved them. Still, I hesitated. "What about Carl?"

"Carl's a good boy. Bring him. He *is* with you, isn't he?"

"Of course." I'd had Carl since he was a small pup, two full years before I met Robbie. Someone had dumped him out in the country, probably after realizing how big he would get and how much he'd eat. When I saw him limping down that caliche road near my mama's house on a hot summer day, it was love at first sight. I liked to think Carl felt the same. "No way would I leave Carl with Robbie the Handsome. I wouldn't put it past him to highlight *Carl's* hair and whiten *his* teeth."

Carl sniffed and wrinkled his forehead, the way he always did when he got excited. I reached over and patted his big head. "Don't worry, boy. Mommy's going to take care of you. We're in this together."

But a feeling of apprehension swept over me. Carl stood thirty inches at the shoulders and weighed one-hundred-ninety pounds. Who in his right mind was going to rent an apartment to someone with a dog that size?

* * *

Lena was waiting for me out front when I pulled into her driveway. As soon as I jumped out of the pickup, she gave me a big hug. "You're doing the right thing. *Finally*. What did Mr. Triple B do this time? Leave the kids with you for the day?"

I sighed, hating to admit what a sucker I'd been. "Told me he had to work, then went fishing all afternoon and left me trapped at the bait shop."

"Ouch."

"I needed the wakeup call."

"Girl, your phone's been ringing for two *years*. About time you picked up. Come on, let's unload your truck and put your stuff in the spare room."

After unloading, Lena left me to get unpacked. Instead, I flopped on the bed, suddenly exhausted. Lena was right. I'd been suffering from lust cloaked as love. Why hadn't I foreseen this moment and been prepared? I needed my own place. Soon. I required order. Control. Solitude.

I'd almost dozed off when Carl began pawing my leg, his nose twitching. I caught an enticing whiff of chili powder and cilantro. Smiling at him, I patted his head. "Come on. Let's go see what Aunt Lena's cooking."

After we ate, I returned to my room, crawled into bed with my laptop, and opened the file containing my first chapter. The dream of seeing my name in print on a published novel suddenly seemed more important than ten Robbie Hansons. Dying unpublished would be almost as bad as dying a virgin. Not that I had to worry about the latter.

Ann Whitaker

Hands resting on the keyboard, I stared at the screen with its one opening sentence, called upon my J.K. Rowling muse, and waited. She must have been at Hogwarts.

* * *

The next day when Lena got home from work, I met her at the door. "How was work today, dear?" I asked, handing her a glass of wine.

She took a sip and raised her glass to me. "I could get used to this kind of treatment. How'd the house hunting go?"

"Not so good. None of the houses had fenced yards. I tried the newspaper, the yellow pages, and the Internet. Equal opportunity housing does not apply to dogs as big as Carl."

Lena's dark eyes warmed, and she reached over and patted my hand. "You can stay here as long as you like."

"I appreciate it, but Carl is so big it's like living with another person. You don't need two homeless people sponging off you, one of whom can't hold down a job."

"You aren't sponging. And Carl's no trouble." She reached down to scratch his big head, and when she stopped, he flopped at her feet and sneezed.

I glanced down where he lay, all one-hundred-ninety pounds. "You don't pay his grocery bill."

While Lena changed clothes, I tossed a big salad. Her kitchen, a vibrant mix of primary colors, suited her personality. She'd painted the table bright yellow and added ladder-backed chairs—each in a different color— red, blue, green, and purple.

She returned wearing a pair of baggy cargo shorts and a man's T-shirt. "Need some help?"

"Thanks, got it under control. Just sit and enjoy. Fresh spinach salad, grilled salmon, and corn on the cob. All healthy. No more Mog the Hog."

"Those kids in school were just jealous. You were never fat."

I fixed an unwavering gaze on her until I got her full attention. "I was fat." I held up my fork and faked a southern accent. "I was *so* fat, when I stepped on the scale to weigh, it said 'To Be Continued.'"

Lena shook her head and snorted. "When you look in the mirror, you're not seeing what the rest of us see. You're like a taller version of Dolly Parton, with a tan. And long dark wavy hair."

"You've just described the polar opposite of Dolly Parton."

Lena took a sip of wine, observing me over the rim. "Her hair *might* be dark and wavy. She could hide a hamster under those wigs. Anyway, you've got her boobs."

"Mine are nowhere near *that* big."

"Big enough. Have you noticed the way the guys in the sports department look at you? Their eyes bug out, and they drool worse than Carl."

I rolled my eyes. "I sit next to the *vending* machine. Changing the subject, what's today's scoop from the *Daily Democrap*?"

Lena picked up an ear of corn, wrinkled her nose at the Butter Buds, and leaned over and grabbed a stick of real butter from the frig. "Got an email from Jack. A reminder to 'tidy up' our work areas. Top brass from corporate dropping in this week."

Ever since Jack Riggins, our new editor-in-chief, had come on board, we'd undergone a transformation. First, the features editor landed a job in Dallas. Then, overnight, we'd lost our city editor when his wife caught him with a female reporter in the bed of his pickup in the newspaper parking lot. The ensuing catfight, caught on a security camera, had effectively ended her husband's career at *Democrat*.

Ron, the dayside assistant editor, and I had immediately applied for the job, along with countless applicants from outside the paper. During my interview, Jack called my work impressive and said I'd be a perfect fit. I knew better than to get my hopes up, but I had. I was still hoping three weeks later. Maybe Jack had been waiting for the visit from corporate to make the announcement. If so, I should know something soon.

"By the way, Jack finally resuscitated the 'living' department. Hired a new features editor. Some blonde."

My head jerked up. "She must be the one I saw in his office last week. I'd hoped she was my replacement. Dammit!"

"You really think you're going to get the city editor job?"

"Jack all but promised me. Who else is there? Someone from outside who doesn't know the town? Ron?" I shook my head and took a sip of wine. "Ron's way too passive. City editors need serious butt-kicking skills. Ron would have to take asshole classes to qualify."

Lena thought for a moment, then nodded in agreement.

Bossing people around didn't come natural to me either, but working nights had given me plenty of on-the-job training. "I need to make more money. And I'm sick of working nights."

Lena poked at her salmon. She would have preferred Mexican, but I needed a break from the Triple B and all that grease. Besides, salmon in moderation was healthier.

She put her fork down and picked up the ear of corn saturated in butter. I averted my eyes too late. Mog the Hog's salivary glands had already gone into overdrive. "Thing is, where's Jack going to find a replacement for *you*? No one wants to move to Desire and work nights. The pay's not that great, and all the younger journalists want to live in the big city. Can't say I blame them. I'm thinking of applying in Dallas myself."

"What? And leave me? Leave Desire? You've lived here all your life."

Lena finished the corn and wiped butter from her mouth with a paper napkin. She hadn't touched the salmon. "Precisely. You'd leave, too, if you didn't feel trapped. Or are you afraid?"

"I left once," I muttered. "But Mama and Granny count on me. You know that."

Lena didn't reply.

My stomach cramped at the thought of my best friend moving away. I picked up my plate and scraped the remains into the trash. Carl looked mildly interested, but he knew not to expect table scraps. I dipped a cup into his bag of kibble and filled his bowl with his nightly portion. "Sorry, boy. It's for your own good. You can have a doggy cookie later."

As I left the room, I glanced back to see Lena setting her plate on the floor, salmon untouched. Carl inhaled it in one gulp. I could have sworn he was smiling when he looked up.

* * *

I hadn't known severing ties with Robbie would be such a relief. I caught myself humming "9 to 5" as I got ready for work the next afternoon, thinking about how great it would be to work days. If I could leave Robbie, anything was possible.

Unfortunately, I didn't have a new wardrobe to match my mood. As I flipped through the pants and tops I'd hung in Lena's closet, I saw them with new eyes. Drab colors to fit the Mahogany who'd lived with Robbie the Peacock. I finally settled on a pair of dark brown pants and a short-sleeved cream-colored top that blended with my dark hair and naturally tan complexion. A pair of sexy heels or sandals would have helped, but all I had were my scuffed brown flats. They would have to do. To compensate for my deficient wardrobe, I put on some bright red lipstick to keep me from blending in with the walls. I smiled at myself in the mirror. Not too bad. If the bigwigs from corporate showed up, I wanted to look as professional as possible.

I parked in the company lot and headed toward the back door of our three-story building, taking a deep breath and looking up at the bright blue sky one last time. For the next ten hours, I'd be trapped inside with no time to look out one of the few windows of the second-floor newsroom. I would sit inside a cubicle at a computer terminal, instead of an office with a view. Not that there was much to see in the flat landscape of West Texas, except spectacular blue skies and sunsets to die for. Desire sat smack in the middle of West Texas nowhere, mid-way between Dallas/Fort Worth and Midland/Odessa, where a daily newspaper still had a chance of surviving. Just barely.

Downtown Desire consisted of a couple of eight-story buildings in an area no one was attempting to revive. Traffic was sparse, rent was cheap compared to bigger cities, the climate was semi-arid with no overwhelmingly humid days like Houston or Corpus, but not so dry my skin shriveled like a lizard's. I liked being able to drive from one side of town to the other in ten minutes. For shopping we had one indoor mall, a Walmart, and a Target. For those with enough money to eat out, there were the usual chain restaurants and one of the best mesquite-smoked barbeque joints in the entire state of Texas. Grocery stores, two hospitals, three colleges, and a church on almost every corner provided all I needed in the way of amenities. We even had a red mud-colored lake north of town where you could fish or water-ski if you had a boat and the wind wasn't too strong.

I might knock it, but it was home. Besides all that, Mama and Granny depended on me to take them grocery shopping at Wal-Mart on Sunday afternoons.

Orville, our hefty security guard, smiled as I approached, and I waved and smiled back. Best I could tell, he'd been hired to hang around the back door to make sure some irate reader didn't hack one of us to pieces. I ran my keycard through the slot and pushed the door open, taking the stairs instead of the elevator. With a job like mine—which consisted of sitting on my butt editing copy nine or more hours a day—I had to squeeze in every bit of exercise I could. I refused to revisit the chubby cheeks of my childhood.

When I entered the newsroom, phones were ringing, reporters were typing or talking on the phone, and those editors lucky enough to have offices sat behind plate glass windows insulated from it all. The greasy smell of french fries permeated the air. A row of cubicles faced each other, separated by a low divider. The rest of the room consisted of metal filing cabinets, stacks of newspapers, and large gray trash bins labeled "newsprint" or "trash." Three TVs were mounted on the wall at the end of the room with the sound turned low. All in all, it was messy and drab, but no one had asked me for decorating advice.

I dropped my purse on the floor of my cubicle and waved across the room to Lena, who sat in the photo area. First things first. Find reporters, ask what stories were scheduled to run tomorrow, check on length, and inquire about problems. I caught a couple of reporters on their way out, found out where they were headed, and went in search of others. One part of my job was non-negotiable—making deadline by ten-thirty p.m.

The editor-in-chief's office sat in the far corner. Unlike most of the other offices, it had a window to the outside and a television. Since Jack was acting city editor until he hired a replacement, in the interim, I reported directly to him. Jack was in his mid-forties and on the thin side, except for a belly that looked as if he'd swallowed a bowling ball. But this was Texas, sixteenth fattest state in the nation. His look was almost *de rigueur* for men.

As I moved closer, I could see Jack, propped as usual, behind his large, highly-polished wooden desk, while another man sat facing him, his back to me. From the serious look on Jack's face, I figured the guy had to be one of the corporate suits Lena mentioned.

Then, as I stood there staring, the man turned toward me, and Mahogany-world switched into slow motion. My foot lifted to take a step, gray eyes met mine, my foot stayed suspended a few seconds before touching the floor. My body moved forward a few centimeters. Though my corporeal form remained in suspended animation, my mind raced at warp speed.

Oh. My. God. The man had Kennedy hair. He had Kennedy features. Not the fat Kennedys. The *young* Kennedys. John-John to be specific. I was ready to vote for him for president of Texas based on his hair alone.

He wore a gray suit, matching his eyes, so my full assessment would have to wait, but I had a feeling whatever lay beneath the suit matched the rest of the packaging. He was hot.

Jack lifted his arm and waved, as if motioning someone in. My head pivoted slowly, and I looked behind me, but no one was there. "Me?" I mouthed, pointing to my chest. He nodded.

I roused from my stupor and tentatively joined the two men in the office. I didn't usually get introduced to the corporate guys. This could mean only one thing—I'd gotten the promotion. The Kennedy-esque man stood as I entered.

Jack leaned back in his chair and smiled. "Mahogany Marsh, meet Branwell Barker. We go back a long way. Same hometown in Ohio." Jack inclined his head toward me. "Bran, this is the girl I was telling you about."

I hated being called "girl," but I wasn't going to buck the big boss. Besides, I was having a difficult time absorbing the magnificent male creature standing in front of me smiling, his eyes locked on mine. I couldn't look away.

I moved toward him as he reached out and took my hand in his. His grip was firm and warm, the kind of hand that would be soothing and comforting on a cold night. His eyes were the same dark gray as his suit. His lips looked soft...I cleared my throat.

"Nice to meet you, Mr. Barker." My voice cracked. *Damn, this man was probably used to that reaction from females. Get a grip, Marsh.*

The last thing I needed was lust in the workplace. When I'd turned thirty, my hormones kicked in overnight, cursing me with the libido of a sixteen-year-old boy. Why hadn't someone on TV warned me this would happen? Thankfully, none of the men I worked with looked like the one in front of me. Otherwise, I'd need an anti-Viagra pill to help me concentrate on work. At the moment I was having a difficult time trying to speak coherently. My legs felt wobbly, and my head buzzed.

"Please, call me Bran."

When he smiled, his eyes crinkled at the corners. Now that I was closer, everything about him switched to high definition—the dimple in his chin and the slight wave in his full head of hair. "Jack's been telling me good things about you."

I smiled, hoping the red lipstick hadn't rubbed off on my teeth. "In this business, you need to verify any information with at least three different sources."

His laugh rang out, and on the other side of the window, reporters looked up in surprise, while I grinned like the newsroom idiot.

"How's tomorrow's front page shaping up?" Jack asked.

I quickly switched to my uber-professional mode. "The follow-up on the superintendent—the one who allegedly put the hidden video camera in the women's restroom—it needs to be pared down. The news hole is only twenty inches, and he sent me forty-five." I rattled off three more stories before Jack interrupted.

He turned to Bran. "Told you. She's all business." Jack tugged his ear and began speaking to my breasts. Why did men do this? Did they think women wouldn't notice? I vowed I was going to stash a tape recorder inside my bra with a remote switch I could flip on the next time a man started talking to them. From the recorder, a deep voice would boom out: *Are you talkin' to me? These boobs weren't made for talkin'.* I stifled a laugh and began to choke on my own spit.

Jack jumped up from his desk, came around behind me, and began to pound my back.

"No, no!" I gasped. "I'm okay. You're making it worse."

Bran leaned toward me, put a hand on my shoulder, and asked if I needed some water. I nodded. His gray eyes showed real concern, and the warmth of his hand made me dizzy.

Jack, meanwhile, returned to the throne behind his desk, seemingly happy to relinquish me to someone else. Probably thought I was going to throw up on him or, more embarrassing, choke to death in his office. He pulled a bottle of water from his refrigerator and handed it off to Bran, who opened it for me. "This should help," he said, holding my hand around it to make sure I didn't drop it.

I took a sip. "Thanks. Sorry about that."

By their own volition, my eyes half closed, my body hummed, and Jack faded out. Branwell Barker was the epitome of the hero I'd imagined in my mental magnum opus—"Roving Ranch Hands." The how-to books advise to write about what you know, and I knew nothing about ranches, but I'd seen enough westerns to get my creative juices flowing. My story would take place in modern times. On a modern-day ranch.

My right brain switched on. Instead of a gray suit, the hero wore chaps and boots, a jean jacket stretched taut across his muscular shoulders. In one hand he held a branding iron; in the other, a rope. He dropped them both to the floor of the barn when the *slender*, breathless heroine appeared. Then he reached out and clutched her around the waist and pulled her to him, as she struggled to breathe.

Roving Ranch Hands
by Mahogany Marsh
Chapter 1

A stranger came to town. The stranger had traveled widely, and though he didn't know it, his heart had always longed for Desire. Though he bore the name of his Cajun forebears, Dock Dangereux was more Texan than most women could handle. But he had a feeling this one, this slip of a girl, could handle him just fine.

Her name—Jasmine—burned his brain, making him hotter than barbecued cabrito turning on a spit. From the moment she'd sashayed into the bunkhouse, he knew she'd been created for him and him alone. Jasmine. The name conjured up visions of tropical climes and delicate white blossoms with strong, sweetly scented lobes. Luscious lobes. Large lobes.

But first, he had to save her. One look at him and she'd choked. Her luscious red lips were slightly parted, her ample bosom heaved with each labored breath. Dock knew from experience her attributes were genuine. His own breath caught at the thought of smothering himself in those soft, lush pillows.

Pressing his hard-muscled body against her from behind, he grasped her tiny frame under her breasts and thrust his hips upward, hoping to dislodge whatever was caught in her throat. She would have noticed his arousal had she not quit breathing at his first thrust.

Dock whipped off his shirt and threw it to the ground, revealing a tan chest, toned by years of hard labor. "Down!" he commanded, though he doubted she could hear. Or see. Her eyes opened for one brief moment. Dark lashes, long as the fringe on his dear old granny's Victorian lampshade, framed her turquoise eyes. He took her in his arms and eased her onto the dark gray shirt that *matched his eyes. Placing his mouth over her succulent lips, he breathed life into her lungs, just as he'd practiced on Resusci Anne. He drew back, then leaned his head close to Jasmine's face, hoping to savor her sweet breath. Nothing.*

But as he started to compress her chest with his strong hands and supple fingers, her eyes fluttered open, and she clutched his arms, her voice a whisper. "Please. No more. Not now. Not here."

I blinked, took another sip of water, and nodded my thanks to Bran, relieved he couldn't read my thoughts.

Jack was speaking. Something about the city editor's job. I felt disoriented. "Excuse me?"

He tugged on his ear and told my breasts, "I'm counting on you to show Bran the ropes. Next week, he'll be manning the helm."

The hand of the large clock on the wall above Jack's desk clicked away each second, as a sixty-point headline moved toward me, growing larger and larger until the message penetrated my brain:

Democrat names Branwell Barker city editor

Now I knew why huge headlines were called "screamers."

###

About the author...

Ann Whitaker lives in the heart of Texas with her journalist husband and two dogs—Jolie Blon, a spoiled Cajun poodle, and Mardi Gras, a retired pet therapy dog.

She's been writing in one form or another all her life. A reformed high school and college English teacher, she's published poetry, non-fiction, and short fiction in newspapers, literary journals, and magazines. Her fictional characters are often larger than life and sometimes find themselves in absurd situations.

Songwriter David Allan Coe says the perfect country and western song has to have certain elements: Mama, trains, trucks, prison, and gettin' drunk. Ann's stories almost always have a dog.

She's currently working on another novel and a collection of slice-of-life essays about everything from a 350-pound roofer to a love affair with a kitchen sink. She calls it "chicken-fried Nora Ephron."

When not writing, Ann plays mah jongg, reads, sings, and plays the guitar.

Visit her at http://www.AnnWhitaker.com